I0788111

AWAY FROM KEYBOARD COLLECTION

GUARDING HIS HEART

PATRICIA D. EDDY

For those who don't ask for help because they've been burned before. When you find your safe space (and your safe people), it gets easier.
I promise.

If you love steamy romantic suspense, I'd love to send you an exclusive short story set in Dublin, Ireland. Castles & Kings is ONLY available for my newsletter subscribers. Visit my website and let me know where to send your free short story! http://patriciadeddy.com

CONTENT WARNING

Please be aware that the first chapter of this book contains a very brief mention (a single sentence) of SA perpetrated by one of the bad guys. It does **not** happen on page and no details are provided. However, please safeguard your mental health while reading.

CHAPTER ONE

Eight Years Ago

Natasha

Ripples of overheated air stretch out for miles in every direction. Along the horizon, the clear blue sky turns a hazy orange—courtesy of ultra-fine sand stirred by even the gentlest breezes.

It has a scent. Sand. Something I'd never considered before spending so many years of my life surrounded by it. Now, it oozes from my pores. A strand of hair escapes my braid, and even that reeks of the dirty, chalky, stale stench that *is* the Al Anbar province.

Our boots leave perfect impressions in the powdery substance. Chris Bowers—one of the few men I trust with my life—grabs his mic. "Lima Command, this is Foxtrot Bravo. Approaching the target location."

"Foxtrot Bravo, this is Lima Actual. Drone footage shows no heat signatures. You're good to go."

"What's Lima Actual doing on comms?" I ask, keeping my voice to a whisper.

"No fucking clue." Bowers adjusts his goggles, checks his H&K, and shrugs.

In my ear, our squad leader, Bastian, sends his own action report. He receives the identical response and a go ahead to breach the cluster of buildings four clicks from our location.

"I can't believe there's no one here. Not for a goddamn second," I mutter.

A dog trots from a burned out shell of a house across from us. He doesn't give a fuck we're here. How a part of Iraq with so few people can have so many dogs is beyond me. They're everywhere. This one isn't skin and bones, so he's clearly not hurting for food.

Bowers presses his back to the wall of the house. The high-value target was seen here less than forty-eight hours ago, with three of his cronies spotted at the location the rest of our squad is about to breach.

He signals his countdown silently. My gloved hands tighten on my weapon. With a swift kick, he decimates the flimsy door. The flash bang rolls through the main room. We wait a single second after the deafening *crack* before we race inside.

"Clear!" I call. Bowers is already in the second, smaller room to the west, and I take the one to the south. They're all empty. Not just empty. Deserted. Practically pristine other than the thin layer of dust that covers everything in this province.

I kick a rug aside. Four wood planks don't belong amid the hard packed dirt. Signaling for Bowers to cover me, I hook a finger through a metal ring attached to one of them.

He nods, giving me the go ahead.

The hidey-hole can't be more than a meter deep, and it,

too, is empty. "What the fuck?" I ask. "Something's not right here."

"Lima Command, this is Foxtrot Bravo. Target is clear. Repeat. Target is clear." Bowers doesn't wait for command to answer. He tears off his goggles, wipes the sweat from his brow, and leans against the wall opposite the busted door.

"There's no way this place was occupied forty-eight hours ago," he says with a shake of his head. "It's been weeks. Months, even."

I depress the button on my radio. "Foxtrot Alpha, this is Foxtrot Bravo. Be advised, target location Bravo is deserted. Watch your six."

Bastian doesn't answer.

"I've got a bad feeling about this."

Bowers is out the door seconds behind me, and we hoof it the mile and a half to where our Ford Ranger LTV sits behind a small rock formation. "Call it in, Chris," I say as I slide behind the wheel.

"Lima Command, this is Foxtrot Bravo. On our way to Foxtrot Alpha to provide backup."

The squelch never fails to hurt my ears, but you get used to it after so long deployed. "Negative, Foxtrot Bravo. Go to—"

The rest of his words are lost, but I slam on the brakes. "Did he just tell us *not* to provide backup?"

We stare at one another for several seconds. We can't disobey a direct order. But from the look on Chris's face, he's as conflicted as I am.

"Foxtrot Bravo to Lima Command. Say again?" he asks.

Silence.

I try. It's not unheard of for our radios to give up the ghost in the middle of a mission. The sand here is so fine, it gums up everything eventually.

But I don't get a response either. Not from Command or from Bastian. "We're exposed here. Which way do we go?"

Bowers outranks me—technically—by a single promotion. But while he's a better shot, I'm the one responsible for logistics.

"This is rotten as fuck," he says. "They're walking into an ambush. I'd bet my entire stash of Twinkies on it."

That does it. Chris is *very* serious about his Twinkies.

It takes us less than ten minutes to reach the settlement. Six houses are scattered inside an area surrounded by a low stone wall. Boot prints mixed with impressions from soft soled shoes mark the route Bastian and the others took.

"This isn't the right way," Bowers whispers. He shows me the map. The target location is on the north side of the settlement, and Bastian's size twelves are most definitely heading south. We follow in his footsteps until we clear the last building and find a set of stairs leading down a steep hill.

This isn't supposed to be here. None of the intel we reviewed this morning showed an elevation change. Or a second set of three houses in much better condition than any we've seen in months.

Goosebumps race down my arms, despite the heat in the air. A woman cries out, muffled words in Arabic I can't understand. Another scream. This one—a child's?—is immediately followed by a man's shout and a gunshot.

We take off at a run until we reach the door. It's open an inch, and as more shouts, wails, and thuds come from the interior, I angle a glance through the crack.

My stomach twists into a knot. I'm going to be sick. Bastian stands over a young girl, his pants around his ankles. She can't be more than fifteen. Her clothes are torn; she's covered in blood.

"Gun," Bastian says. Collins passes him a pistol, and I press my hand to my mouth as my squad leader shoots the girl in the head. Her mother—also half naked—pleads with Sutton for all of two seconds before he snaps her neck.

My legs won't move. Bastian pulls up his pants. He turns to face an older man kneeling in the corner. Doherty has a gun pressed to his head.

"Where's the product?" Bastian snaps.

The man shakes his head and spits. "Filthy American. Fuck you."

I urge Chris back toward the stairs as Doherty fires. More pleas in Arabic follow, along with another three shots.

Chris starts to protest, but I shove him up the last step. "Do *not* say a fucking word. To anyone."

"Natasha—"

"I mean it, Chris. You know Bastian's a piece of shit. He sent us on that wild goose chase for a reason. And now we know what it was. Trust me. *Please.* Not a word until we're back at Victory."

"We have to get to the transpo. If they find us here…"

I hold up my hand and reach for my radio. "Foxtrot Bravo to Foxtrot Alpha. Be advised, we're closing in on your location. Two minutes."

It only takes seconds before Bastian's voice echoes in my ears.

"Fall back, fall back! It's an ambush!"

At least two of our squad let loose with rapid fire rifle blasts. "That's our cue," I mutter and heft my own H&K. Bowers gives them our approach vector, and we rush toward what I already know is a massacre.

"Hostiles neutralized," Bastian says just before we burst through the door.

Blood paints every wall. The dirt floor is soaked with it. A blanket covers the young girl. The wife lies under the husband's body, and two other men are shredded with bullet holes.

"Fuck. What the hell happened?" I ask.

"First target location was a dud." Bastian shakes his head. "Totally empty. But this asshole," he kicks the husband's shoe, "was acting shifty. So we followed him."

"And shot his entire goddamn family?" I can't stop a fraction of my outrage from bleeding through. But if I weren't angry, he'd be even more suspicious. At least that's what I tell myself.

Collins grabs the dead man, rolls his body over, and pats his tunic. He comes up with a grenade and waves it in front of my face. "Fucker was willing to blow up his whole fucking family to take out a few Americans."

I glance at Bowers. He's about to lose his shit. Quickly, I step in front of him. Thank God I'm only a couple of inches shorter than he is. My helmet should hide his face.

"You gonna call it in?" I ask. "We have to get a team out here to clean this shit up."

Bastian reaches for his radio. God, I want to punch that self-satisfied smirk off his face. But I have to hold it together. Six hours, and we'll be back at Camp Victory. Until then, my life—and Chris's—depends on us saying exactly nothing.

"You and Bowers stand guard," Bastian says. "We'll take care of things in here."

<hr>

Three Months Later

"YOU'RE FUCKING *DEAD!*" A man wraps his hands around Chris's throat for all of three seconds before the MPs drag him away.

"You okay?" I ask. My dress uniform feels like it's suffocating me in the heat of the summer. The building's AC is on the fritz, and the air flowing through the vents is barely south of boiling.

Chris blinks at me, and I grab his shoulders and shake him gently.

"Hey. Focus, Staff Sergeant. Eyes on me."

The shell-shocked look fades. His hand comes up to touch his throat. "Who the hell was that?" he rasps.

"Never seen him before. But I'll give you three guesses as to who sent him."

Twenty-two hours. The first attempt on my life after we reported Bastian didn't even take forty-eight hours. Turns out, it wasn't just him and his gang of whack jobs.

We stumbled onto a drug ring that stretched across multiple regiments and at least three years. So now, we're both in protective custody—and might be for the rest of our lives if the Army Investigative Service can't find the extent of the corruption.

Four additional MPs come down the hall, putting the two of us in a protective bubble between them. I turn to the closest and get right in his face.

"Who was that and how did he get in here?" I snap.

"We're investigating, Sergeant Winters. If you'll come with us, we'll take you back to your respective safe houses now."

Chris loosens his tie—just a fraction—and blows out a breath. "Natasha, I...I can't be here for your testimony tomorrow. My wife is starting chemo. I have to be with her."

Oh, God. They haven't let us talk—not more than a quick "hello" or "see you later" as we've entered and exited the building each day. Protocol.

"Will you be back? Before...it's over?" My voice catches in my throat. Knowing Chris was on my side—*by* my side—has helped keep me from losing my shit for the past six weeks. Without him, I don't know how I'm going to get through testifying.

"I don't know. But..." He holds out his hand. I curl my fingers tightly and touch my knuckles to his. "Give 'em hell."

"Will do, sir." I stand at attention, though I haven't saluted the man in...forever. "Take care of your wife, Bowers. See you on the other side."

He follows the MPs down the hall, shoulders straight, his jacket still perfectly pressed, despite the heat. I can do this. I have to. I'm the only one who saw everything.

***

THE KNOCK COMES as I'm making my second cup of coffee.

"Sweet Jesus. I still have half an hour, Ciprian," I mutter. Stalking over to the door, I flip both locks and wrench it open. But it's not one of the morning MPs who's waiting for me.

"Logan?" My brother stands with his beret in his hands, staring down at his dress shoes. I haven't seen him in almost nine years. Not since I became a Ranger. He was there when I got my tab. But we didn't do more than share a quick, one-armed hug before he had to return to his Special Forces team.

"Can I come in?" he asks.

I throw my arms around him. Tears prick at my eyes. I didn't realize how alone I'd felt until just now.

"Natasha, we need to get inside. Now." Logan forcefully removes my arms from his waist, turns me around, and guides me back into the apartment before securing the locks.

"There's no one else here, Logan. Besides the MPs who clearly approved your entry. But whatever. Coffee?"

My brother shakes his head. "No. Sit down, Pip."

I still at the long-ago nickname. He's not here for a family reunion. This is serious.

"You haven't called me that in twenty years. I'm a fucking

Ranger, Lo." I snag my coffee from the counter and follow him to the couch.

He sits stiffly, back ramrod straight, and stares at the darkened television across the room. "Something happened, Natasha."

I've only heard that finality in his tone once before. When Dad died. "You're scaring me."

Logan turns toward me and takes my hands in his. "Chris Bowers was having dinner in his wife's hospital room last night. She was admitted because she was dangerously dehydrated."

"Is she okay?" Shit. I should really try to get a message to Chris—and his wife.

"She's fine. But an orderly entered the room, and..." Logan shakes his head. "He slit Chris's throat. Right in front of Marisol."

My mouth opens, then shuts again. No. I misheard him. "I need to call Chris. Tell him—"

My brother folds me into his embrace. "You can't, Pip. He died in seconds."

I shatter in his arms. I've never felt pain like this. The shock makes it a thousand times worse.

"Who?" I sob. "Who killed him?"

"I don't have that information. But it's being investigated at the highest levels. We'll know. Soon."

LOGAN HELD me until I had no more tears to cry. Someone convinced the judge to postpone the proceedings until Monday so they could *try* to find the guy who murdered my closest friend.

But two days later, all they have is a name. Able Parker.

Dishonorably discharged a year ago for selling drugs to locals in Afghanistan.

I'm barely speaking to Logan at this point. Every time he opens his mouth, it's to beg me to walk away. To recant my testimony, take an "Under Honorable Conditions" discharge —total bullshit—and go into Federal Witness Protection.

"Natasha, please," he says as he sweeps our takeout containers into the trash. "Don't testify tomorrow."

"Do you honestly think I'll be any safer with the Feds than I am here?" I've moved on from grief. Now, I'm fucking pissed. I grab the sketch from the table and stare daggers at the charcoal drawing. The one the artist created from what Marisol remembered of Chris's murderer.

"I know this guy, Logan. Able Parker attacked Chris outside the courtroom. Do you know how tight security is in that place? Sure, the MPs were on him in seconds. But he got in once. He can do it again. To get to me. The *only* way through this is to put them away. For good. Then...I'll disappear on my own."

"Goddammit, Natasha. I can't lose you!" he shouts.

I glare at him. "You should have thought of that a long time ago. You lost the right to tell me what to do when you went no-contact for nine-fucking-years."

"Pip—"

"*You're* the one who told me I could make a difference in this world. That Mom and Dad would be so fucking proud of me for what I've accomplished. The first woman to make it through Ranger School? Promoted to Staff Sergeant in record time? I loved my job. I was *good* at it. And these assholes took it from me! Bastian and his men killed seven people that day. And that was *one day!* They raped innocent women and *girls* for fuck's sake. He doesn't get to go free. Not if I can help it."

"Even if it kills you?" He runs a hand through his short-cropped black hair, frustration rolling off him in waves.

"Because he's so goddamn connected, he'll do it. Even from Leavenworth."

"He can't kill me if he can't find me. Go back to your hotel, Logan. Or hell. Go back to wherever the fuck you've been for the past nine years. I don't need you here if you're not going to have my back. I'll find a way to let you know I'm safe. Eventually. That's the best I can do."

The pain in his eyes should make me feel guilty. But I'm so damn tired, I can't work up the emotion.

"I love you, Pip," he says softly, then turns on his heel and walks out the door.

I'm the worst sister on the planet. And by this time tomorrow, I'll be so far gone, he'll never see me again. I wish I could cry, but instead, I'm empty. Spent. And too damn restless to sleep. A run will clear my head. It has to.

THE AIR in the hallway feels...wrong. Heavy. Still. Washington D.C. in the middle of July is a sauna—even long after the sun goes down. But this is more.

A beer and cold shower sound like heaven. If I'm lucky, they'll be enough—along with the exhaustion from my run —to let me catch a few hours. The conversation I had with Logan over breakfast plays on a loop in my head.

"Tomorrow, it'll be done. You know I have to see this through, Logan. Mom and Dad—"

"Mom and Dad are dead! You're not!" He starts to pace the small apartment. "They got to Chris. Slit his throat with his goddamned wife in the room."

Tears lend a shimmer to the room. It's almost...pretty, a stark contrast to the ugly images flashing through my head. The Army CID agents didn't want to show me the crime scene photos, but I insisted. Chris was like a second brother to me. Without him, I never would have made it through Ranger School.

"You're not going to change my mind. We've been at this for days. If that's all you came here to do, you can leave." I'm not above pleading with my brother, but when has that ever worked before? "I need you there tomorrow, Logan. I need to know you're on my side."

Anguish churns in his blue-gray eyes. He stalks to the door but pauses with his hand on the knob. "I love you, Natasha. That will never change. But I can't be on your side if you're dead."

A door slams somewhere in the building, echoing the one in my memories as Logan left in a huff. He came back an hour later with two cups of coffee and a scone. A paltry peace offering. Though we got into it again two more times before I finally kicked him out two hours ago. Will he show tomorrow? Or will I truly be alone?

My key rasps in the lock, but turns too easily. Unease prickles along my spine. A *thud* from inside the apartment is almost immediately followed by a strained groan.

I whirl around and shout for Ciprian—the MP who shadowed me on my run. "Get the fuck up here!"

All I have on me is a switchblade. What I wouldn't give for my service weapon.

Ciprian bounds up the stairs, his pale cheeks dark red from the exertion. The man *hates* running. He pulls his gun and hisses, "Get back!"

I'm already committed, so I wrench the knob and kick the door open. The harsh scent of blood clogs my throat.

The MP shoulders me aside. Parker aims over Ciprian's shoulder, but the MP shouts, "Drop it!"

A bullet hits the wall only inches from my head. Ciprian returns fire.

Glass shatters. "Oh, God," the MP says. "Get in here!"

I round the couch and freeze. My brother lies on the floor

with his hands pressed to his stomach. Blood soaks his dress uniform. Stains the drab beige carpet. Spatters the coffee table.

"Logan! No!" I kneel next to him. The red pool under my knees is still warm. "Why did you come back?"

His mouth moves, but no sound comes out. I can see it in his eyes. He's dying. He knows it.

"Hang on for me. Please." I pull off my shirt and press it to his stomach. He shudders. Pain tightens lines around his eyes. The MP barks at the 911 operator, telling them to hurry.

Warm air washes over me from the broken window. Logan fumbles for my hand. He's fading away. I've never felt so helpless. My tears hit his cheeks, mixing with his.

"I love you, Lo." I'm sobbing now.

Logan squeezes his eyes shut. His lips press together. Tendons in his neck flex, and he meets my gaze. "Run," he whispers. "Live."

One last breath, and my brother is gone.

"Montgomery Bastian, Allan Collins, Dylan Sutton, Ethan Doherty, and Rob Bowen, you have been found guilty of war crimes..."

Before the judge even finishes reading the verdict, I'm through the double doors of the courtroom.

Fleeing into the women's bathroom, I head for the furthest stall. The one with the *Out of Order* sign taped to the door. Behind the toilet, a paper bag waits for me.

Ciprian, the MP who shot and wounded Parker less than thirty-six hours ago, got me everything on my list.

Red wig. Baggy clothes. Dark sunglasses. A foldable cane. In two minutes, I emerge from the stall, lean heavily on the cane's handle, and slip out into the chaos.

Bastian will never stop hunting me. When he realized I'd been the one to turn him in, he'd told me that I'd die in the most painful way possible.

I didn't care.

Until he murdered Chris. And Logan. Now, I can only do one thing.

Honor my brother's last wish.

Run. Live.

CHAPTER TWO

Four Years Ago

Doc

I REACH for the glass of whiskey, but a massive hand snatches it away.

"What the fuck?" I'm drunk enough not to care that the guy towering over me is the size of a mountain. My punch sails past his bald, scarred head. I lose my balance, the barstool crashes to the ground, and my ass hits the sticky floor a second later.

By the time I lurch to my feet, the fucker's drained the last of my drink. A wad of bills lands on the bar top. "He's cut off. Permanently."

"Whaa...? Who you do think are—goddammit. Who *do you* think *you* are?" I slur. Trying a different tactic, I slap my hands against his chest in a futile attempt to get him the hell out of my way.

He reaches for a thermos sitting on the bar and slides it in front of me. "Coffee. Drink it, and we'll talk."

"Shove it up your ass and I'll go back to my whiskey a happy man."

In the dim lights of Slade's—one of the sleezier pubs at the edge of downtown—the hulking man is nothing but scars and shadows, dressed all in black, his long-sleeved t-shirt straining over muscles that belong in a steroid ad. Cold eyes peer down at me. I must be worse off than I thought. I can't tell what color they are. Blue? Green? Hazel?

I blink hard, waiting for him to say something. Or deck me. He's angry enough. But he merely crosses his arms over his chest and waits.

"I don't care how big you are, asshole. I was Air Force Pararescue. You want a fight, I'll give you one."

He snorts. "I did ten years in the Special Forces, Fly Boy. And any PJ worth their salt knows size doesn't mean shit in a fight. Sobriety, on the other hand..."

"I'm not that drunk."

"Bullshit." Special Forces plucks the thermos from the bar and jerks his head toward the door. "You want to test me? Come on. I'll humor you. But we're not doing it in here. Even if this place *would* look better with some...*redecorating*."

The bartender extends his middle finger at the man, who returns the gesture with an honest-to-God growl before heading for the door.

I *am* drunk enough to follow him, though the voice in my head knows it's a mistake. I'll be lucky to walk away with my life. Or the use of my legs. But my pride won't let me ignore the asshole.

Outside, purple streaks paint the sky. Summer days in Seattle last forever, but the sun's close to the horizon. Shit. I hadn't realized how late it was. I started drinking at five.

"I didn't pay my tab..."

"It's closed," the man says. With a flick of his fingers, he sends my credit card tumbling to the ground at my feet. "You're welcome."

Lunging for him, I almost manage to brush his arm before he sidesteps me with the grace of a dancer. My knees slam into the asphalt. "Goddammit."

"We can stop any time, Doc."

Doc?

"How do you know I'm a doctor?"

The guy's rough laugh grates on me. "I know everything about you. Even the name your parents gave you. The one you paid to have erased from all your government records." He offers me his hand, and I stare at it for a long moment before he shakes his head, grabs my elbow, and hauls me up.

"You were born Ga—"

"Don't say it, asshole," I snap. "No one's called me...*that*... in twenty years."

"Have it your way. Doc. You graduated from the University of Michigan Ann Arbor Medical School at twenty-four. But rather than residency, you opted for the Air Force. Probably because your grandfather was a career fly boy and he passed away in your fourth year.

"After Basic, you fought your way right into the Pipeline. Made it through on your first try. Impressive. A year into your third re-enlistment, you were shot down over the Al-Faw peninsula trying to save a frogman with altitude sickness. The docs were convinced you'd spend the rest of your life in a wheelchair, but you proved them wrong when you *walked* out of Walter Reed two months later without even a cane. How am I doing so far?"

I stare at the man who knows more about me than half the guys I served with.

"Who the fuck *are* you? Most of that is classified way above any Special Forces pay grade."

"Ryker McCabe. But if you breathe that name to anyone,

you'll regret it. I could end you in a heartbeat and not lose a wink of sleep over it."

"Lunatic," I mutter and pat my pockets, searching for my phone. "I'm done with this conversation. Thanks to you, I have to find a new bar. Don't follow me."

McCabe arches a thick, light brown brow bisected by a jagged scar. "Looking for this, Doc?"

My mobile dangles from his fingers.

"Hand it over."

I'm six-three, but this asshole has at least half a foot on me. He holds the phone aloft, and I have no hope of reaching it. "I went to a lot of trouble—and expense—to find you, Doc. Hear me out. If you tell me to fuck off when I'm done, I'll drop you at any bar in town with enough cash to pay your tab for a month. You can disappear into a bottle for the rest of your life—however long it lasts—and never see me again."

We face off with one another for a full minute before my shoulders slump. I should walk away. But when was the last time I was curious enough to care. About...anything?

Ten years? Fifteen? Not since my last mission with the PJs. This McCabe asshole knows how to get a man's attention.

"I guess I'll take that coffee now."

"You honestly expect me to agree to this?" In the distance, one of the island ferries streaks across Elliot Bay. McCabe drove us to a park overlooking the water in Sunset Hill. The houses here are worth millions. There's no one around, and I *should* be worried he's about to murder me where he can easily dispose of the body. Instead, I'm slouched against the back of the bench. Almost...relaxed.

"Yes."

He cracks his knuckles one at a time. A single pop. Then

another. And another. My gaze never leaves his fingers. Three of them aren't straight. Broken at least once in the past. Maybe more. Not set properly. Burn scars slash across his left hand. The right...those look more like cuts. Jagged ones.

"Setting up an illegal medical practice. Being on call twenty-four hours a day. Treating...anything and everything that could go wrong in the field. No one's that stupid. Or desperate."

Ryker turns his big body on the bench. I've sobered up enough to figure out his eyes aren't actually one color. Hete-rochromia. A rare, genetic trait found in less than one percent of the population.

"I am." With a sigh, he runs a hand over his bald head. More scars there. I don't know what happened to the man, but it wasn't good. Or quick. "Doc, my team goes places no one else can. We get the job done. No man left behind. No matter what. Three days ago, I had to pay a veterinarian in Bogota to give a former Navy SEAL a transfusion from my own fucking arm because it was either that or bury him."

"I'll never be field ready again, McCabe. Nerve damage in my left leg from the crash flares up—"

"I wouldn't take you on mission if the world were ending," he snaps. "I need to trust that every member of my team is the best at what they do. That they're *at* their best at all times. And you, Doc, are a drunk."

"Don't you think I know that?" I push to my feet, the coffee long gone, and stalk to the edge of the manicured expanse of grass. A flimsy wooden fence is all that stands between me and the inky darkness of the water far below. "I didn't want to retire. Even with my injuries, I fought it for two years. Until I couldn't cut it anymore. Couldn't stand watching guys I trained—guys I served with—do the very thing I was *born* to do. I tried the ER down in L.A. But that... didn't end well. Moved to Seattle and did two years up here.

But I was so fucking *bored*...so tired of feeling useless, drinking was the only thing that took the pain away."

"You need a purpose again," McCabe says quietly. I jerk back, shocked to find him standing right next to me. The man is utterly silent when he moves. "I did."

"Special Forces, you said. How long you been out?" I peer up at him, but we're far enough away from the street lights, his face is mostly hidden in shadow.

"Six years. Wasn't my choice to turn civvie. You ever hear of Hell Mountain?"

I suck in a breath. Everyone who's served in the past fifteen years has heard of Hell Mountain. And what happened to it.

"His name is classified way beyond my clearance. But the guy's a legend. Crawled through the snow for two days before he was found. Then went back and blew the place off the map," one of my patients tells me when she finds out I served in Afghanistan.

"Holy fuck. You're the one who broke out."

He doesn't confirm or deny, but he doesn't have to. The proof is all over the man's skin.

"There were two of you."

He makes a low, strangled sound. Almost pain. "I'm giving you a chance, Doc. Don't make me regret it."

A chance at what? Redemption is a pipe dream. But maybe a purpose isn't outside the realm of possibility.

It's quiet enough, I can hear my own thoughts now that the whiskey's worn off. They're too loud. The memories too vivid. One voice rings out over all the others. *Her* voice.

"I'm sorry, Doc."

Something rustles, and a second later, McCabe slaps an envelope against my chest.

"What's this?" I don't have to ask. Not much else feels like a thick wad of cash. Or smells like it.

He shrugs like I'm not holding *at least* ten grand and starts sauntering back to his truck. "Your first month's salary. And a phone number. You've got forty-eight hours. If you're in, call me."

"And if I'm not?"

The street light casts harsh shadows over his scars. "Then I was wrong about you, Doc. And I'm almost never wrong."

Before I can come up with a reply, the engine starts with a low purr. Seconds later, he's gone, and I'm alone. Holding more money than I can count and staring out over the dark water.

CHAPTER THREE

One Year Ago, July

Natasha

THE OLD FLIP phone vibrates so loudly, I jerk, and coffee soaks the front of my white t-shirt. "Son of a bitch!"

The ringer could wake the dead, but "silent" mode is even worse. Maybe I should consider that smartphone Clancy keeps offering to buy me. But those can be tracked. This ancient brick doesn't have GPS. And the battery life is amazing. I can go four days without a charge.

I don't need a smartphone. I rarely leave the island. Gladys lets me use her computer whenever I ask, and Clancy pays for a couple of movie channels.

That's enough contact with the rest of the world.

I open the text message from the resort's reservation system.

Campsite 4: D. Reynolds
Arrival time: 12:00 p.m.
Length of stay: Two days

Damn. That's the fourth guest this week—and it's only Wednesday. When I took this job, all I had to do was hand out keys for the five cabins on the property whenever someone rented one—which wasn't often. But then Clancy's daughter discovered the joys of online advertising, and since then, the cabins are booked solid every weekend, and he turned a couple of acres into campsites.

Stripping off my t-shirt, I scowl at the coffee staining my bra. Why didn't I do laundry yesterday like I'd planned?

Because the asshole in the Orca Cabin clogged the toilet. Then spent almost two hours telling me everything he thought was wrong with the place. The air conditioner makes too much noise. The sheets are scratchy. There's an odd smell in the utility closet.

Yeah. Cleaning supplies.

I snag one of my sports bras from the hamper and give it a quick sniff. Passable. As long as I don't have to get too close to anyone. Shouldn't be that hard. Campers don't need much hand holding. I'll show D. Reynolds to Site 4, make sure he— or she—knows they have to wear a life vest if they take the canoe out on the Sound, and warn them about the mosquitos this time of year. Then I can take one of the kayaks and paddle until I'm so exhausted, *maybe* I'll be able to sleep through the night.

Hauling the laundry bag down to the basement, I wonder if I should run again. Four years, six months, and eleven days on Blakely Island. It's starting to feel like...home. More than anywhere I've been since I was twenty-one and enlisted in the army.

The fresh scent of the detergent reminds me of my childhood. Of weekends spent hanging laundry in the backyard on the base. Of folding clothes with my mom. Of my brother taking me trick-or-treating wearing mom's best flat sheet—

after he'd cut eye holes in it. Mom was so angry, she grounded *both* of us.

I'd give anything to go back there now. Even just for an hour.

But I can't. Everyone I love—everyone I've ever cared for—is gone. Because of me. Because five of the men I served with were corrupt pieces of shit who thought they could get away with trafficking drugs and killing innocent civilians. Woman. Children.

"Stop it, Natasha. Don't go there."

The last time I let myself travel down memory lane, I ended up cracking the seal on the bottle of bourbon I keep behind the oatmeal. Then drinking until I couldn't see straight.

Gladys practically had to break down the front door to wake me up the next morning. Which, for an eighty-two-year-old woman who's all of four-foot-nine, is impressive.

Rather than dwell on the past, I pull on a tank top, shove the ancient flip phone into the back pocket of my shorts, and grab my ball cap before I head for the small ATV parked in the driveway. The entire island is only six miles across, and while we have a small airstrip and a marina, the main roads are more or less...suggestions.

By the time I get to the little boathouse in the center of the campground, my teeth feel like they're about to vibrate out of my skull. A drop of sweat rolls down my back. July usually brings a long stretch of warm weather, but this summer has been brutal. Maybe I'll skip the kayaking and swim instead.

I shut off the ATV, pull off the ball cap, and wipe my brow. At the bottom of the hill, Puget Sound sparkles in the sun, a million diamonds glittering all the way to the horizon.

Gladys sits on the wraparound deck, a massive insulated

cup balanced on the arm of her Adirondack chair, and a scowl twisting her lips.

"I thought you were headed to Seattle to see your niece?" I ask when she fixes her steely gaze on me. In reality, Bella is her grand-niece, but reminding Gladys about her age will only get me a lecture about how you're only as old as you feel.

"That girl is on my shit list." Her voice carries the sultry depth of more than eight decades spent *living*—as she calls it. I call it smoking, drinking, and fucking everyone she could get her hands on. I've heard so many stories I'll *never* be able to forget. Including the one time—before she married—that she made out with a certain now-disgraced movie star on the red carpet at his movie premiere.

"What did Bella do this time?" I lean against the wood pillar at the edge of the steps and stare down at the water. If Logan had lived, would I be an aunt now? He always wanted a huge family. A husband. A white picket fence. Three kids. A couple of dogs.

My eyes start to burn. Why did he have to come back that night?

Because he didn't want you to testify. Because he knew what it would cost you.

If only he'd known it would cost him even more.

Gladys snorts and takes a swig from her tumbler. I bet she's got something a hell of a lot more potent than iced tea in there.

"She had the gall to suggest I might *embarrass* her at her company picnic. Me!" Pushing to her feet, she waves her hand up and down. "There ain't nothing embarrassing here."

I stifle a laugh. Gladys has two full sleeves of tattoos, orange and purple stripes in her short-cropped white hair, and her t-shirt has "Fuck Me Sideways" emblazoned across her boobs. She's also clearly *not* wearing a bra.

Her niece is a corporate lawyer.

"Gladys, Bella loves you. Don't be too hard on her."

I've heard all about Ms. Bella Cavalli, Esquire. Top of her class at Harvard Law School. Polished and professional with shining blond hair, legs for days, and a stare that makes her opponents wither in fear. But she's only twenty-seven. She hasn't hit that "life is precious" stage yet where she'll realize Gladys won't be around forever.

The older woman snags her tumbler and takes a healthy swig. Yep. I can smell the vodka. "If my sister Maisy were still alive, she'd set that girl straight right quick. Embarrassing, my ass."

"Gladys—"

We see the man at the same time. Six-foot-something with a neatly trimmed, gray and white beard, black pants, a light blue t-shirt, and a large ruck slung over one shoulder.

"Now that's a tall drink of water if I ever saw one," Gladys says. "He taking one of the cabins? Or a campsite?"

I'm still too shocked to speak and tug my ball cap a little lower over my eyes. Greeting campers and renters is risky. But I've done as much as I can to change my appearance over the years. Chopped off most of my long black hair, had my Ranger tattoo covered with flowers and hearts, put on twenty pounds—though that wasn't intentional. Perimenopause is a bitch.

If the wrong person recognizes me and reports my location to Bastian, it won't matter that he's locked up tight in Leavenworth. He'll find a way to end my life. But this—along with taking care of Clancy's house—is the job. A job that lets me live in peace on this tiny island so far north, I can see Canada from its highest point.

Mr. Tall and Silver ambles up the boathouse steps. His gaze slides from Gladys to me.

"I'm looking for Nat."

Oh, God. Even his voice is sex-on-a-stick. Deep and smooth, with a hint of the East Coast. Boston? Or New York? I was never very good at accents.

He swats a mosquito on his bicep, and my gaze is drawn to the tattoo winding around the bulky muscle. A parachute over an angel, with four words underneath.

That others may live.

Holy shit. He's Air Force Pararescue. Or was. PJs are the most unhinged sons of bitches on the planet. And the best trained. My squad never needed them, but I've heard stories. Lots of them.

Gladys elbows me in the side. "He's talking to you, *Nat.*"

I blink hard and peer up at the man. "Sorry. That's me. You're Reynolds?"

"Doc," he says. "Doc Reynolds." He offers me his hand, and I place my fingers in his. They're warm, his grip strong.

I risk a quick glance up at his eyes. Dark blue with copper flecks. There's almost no emotion in them. Like he's shut down. Like he's *been* shut down for a long time. I know the feeling.

"You're at Campsite Four...Doc. I hope you managed to fit a tent in that ru—err, backpack. Because all we provide is a fire pit and a single electrical hookup."

His smile fades, and a muscle in his jaw ticks. "Got all I need. Just point me in the right direction and I'll be out of your way."

Well, that's a dismissal if I've ever heard one. I shouldn't be relieved. Not with the way his chest fills out that t-shirt.

Or maybe that's exactly why I *should* be relieved.

"Follow the path down to the water. Each campsite is clearly marked. You'll find a canoe propped against a huge piece of driftwood between sites three and four. Paddles and life vests are in the boathouse here. Bathrooms and showers are around the back." I jerk my thumb over my shoulder and catch sight of Gladys.

My God. She's practically drooling.

"If you find yourself in need, young man," she says, straightening to her full height, which still leaves her almost a foot shorter than me, "you call the number you got from Clancy. Nat will take care of you."

It's been forever since I've blushed—since I've had an excuse to—but two minutes with the handsome "Doc" and I might as well be a teenager again. My body's reaction pisses me off. I shove my hands into the pockets of my shorts and stare down at Doc's hiking boots.

"That number is for emergencies only," I mutter, then thrust a map at the man. "Clancy doesn't pay me enough to teach you how to build a fire or stake your tent. You don't know the basics, you're on your own."

"I can handle myself," he says, an edge to his tone. He nods at Gladys. "Ma'am." Turning, he glances back over his shoulder briefly. "Nat."

I've never called a man's voice "growly" before, but... whoa. I need a minute. Or...longer. Even if he is an ass.

Gladys sidles up to me, and we watch him head down the path in silence. He's built like a grizzly bear—barrel chest, strong biceps, a long, loping gait. Too bad his ruck is so big it mostly hides his ass. I'd bet it's a damn fine ass. With a pair of green feet tattooed on one of those tight butt cheeks. PJ tradition.

"Well, don't just stand there," Gladys says. "Go after him!"

"Wh-what?" I sputter.

"I swear, it's like you're *trying* to be alone for the rest of your life. That man is a *fox*."

With a huff, I turn away. "Fox or not, he's a camper. He'll

only be here forty-eight hours. And I'm not looking for anything. You know that."

"He's a doctor."

My brows shoot up toward my hairline. "He said his name was Doc. For all you know, his parents could have been fans of Bugs Bunny."

Gladys takes me by the arms, but I jerk back. I'm not big on human contact. Not anymore. Too many years without more than a handshake.

"Baby girl." Her use of the term of endearment drags me back to the present, and I meet her tired, hazel eyes. "That man is lonely. And so are you."

"I'm not—"

"Bullshit. You've been on this island for years. And I'm the only one you talk to."

No one fucks with Gladys when she's in full "mama bear" mode, so I stay quiet and let her say her piece.

"This is my home. Where Donald and I were supposed to live out our days together, sittin' on our porch with our morning coffee, watching the cruise ships go by." Her tone turns wistful, and her gnarled fingers run over her wedding ring—the one she's never taken off, even more than two decades after her husband's death. "But he went and had a heart attack at fifty-three. Round about the same age as that silver fox you just let walk away, I reckon."

Her gaze softens as she sinks back down into her creaky, wooden deck chair. "I don't know what brought you here, Nat. Why you stay in that big house all alone, fixing shit Clancy shoulda' taken care of a long damn time ago. He's lucky to have you. So am I. But you're too young to give up on life, and that's exactly what you're doin'."

My shoulders stiffen, annoyance prickling along my spine. "I haven't *given up* on anything. I like it here. I like my privacy. And I'm not interested in a one-night stand. Even if the guy is hotter than the surface of the sun. My Magic Bullet does me just fine."

She huffs. "Shitsicles. That toy won't keep you warm at night. Or make you chicken soup when you're sick."

"That's what I have you for." Over the years, Gladys has inserted herself into my life in so many ways I should never have allowed. More than once, I've been tempted to tell her my story. My *real* story. But she'd call her grand-niece and try to "fix" all my broken pieces. I can't let that happen. Because she's the one who would end up shattered.

"Baby girl..."

"No. I'm done with this conversation. I saw Mr. 'Doc' Reynolds to Campsite Four. Or...pointed him in the right direction. And in two days, when it's time for him to go, I'll wave him off and that'll be the last of it."

Gladys is still sputtering and cursing under her breath as I stalk away from the boathouse. She'll forgive me. Eventually. She always does. We have a variation of this conversation every few months. Whenever one of the renters looks single —and isn't a total dick. Though *Doc* scored pretty high on the dick scale.

So why am I thinking about him for so long, I almost miss the turn back up the hill to my house?

Stop it, Natasha. He's hot. Nothing more.

Except Gladys is right. My Magic Bullet can't hold a candle to Doc Reynolds.

CHAPTER FOUR

Doc

Fuck. This is a complication I didn't need. I came up here to get away from everything. Well, except the satellite phone McCabe ordered me keep close at all times.

In an emergency, I can be back in Seattle in under two hours. But I had to escape the city. Be alone. Get my head on straight.

Yet all I can think about as I set up my tent is the woman who runs this place.

Nat.

Is that short for Natalie? Natalia? Natasha?

Why do I need to know? I had my shot at happiness. Tessa's gone, and I'm not looking to start anything—with anyone. The last stake sinks into the ground, and I push to my feet, glancing out over the water.

Summer in the Pacific Northwest is beautiful. The first leaves have just started to tinge burnt orange. Days are still hot, but the temperature drops into the sixties at night. Perfect for sleeping.

I unfold the small map Nat gave me. One of the allures of this resort? It borders a large, forested area of the island. Campers are encouraged to chop their own firewood, take the canoes out on the Sound, dig Razor clams on the beaches on the other side of the island, and hike the various trails up into the hills.

Tucking my axe into my belt loop, I grab a canvas wood tote and head up the trail. After half a mile, I'm drenched. The sun warms my bare arms and the back of my neck. God, I've needed this. I've been spiraling for weeks—months even.

A handful of trees are marked with white tags as safe to cut. Most are around six feet tall, three to six inches thick. A little farther along the trail, saplings dot the hillside. They'll be ready to cut in a couple of years.

Does Nat plant them? Or does she hire one of the locals?

I shouldn't care. I'm here to reclaim some of my sanity. Not obsess about a woman who barely let me see her eyes. But that single glimpse was everything. In those gray irises, I found a whole world. Pain, loneliness, need. All the same emotions I see in the mirror every day.

Enough. You're not a good bet, and she's clearly not looking for anything.

Returning to the marked trees, I choose my target. Impact sings up my arms with each strike. The physical labor clears the cobwebs from deep in my soul.

McCabe's team has been healthy the past few months. I shouldn't wish otherwise. But damn. I'm bored. Working at the free medical clinic down in Georgetown a few days a week keeps me from diving head first into a bottle, but it's nothing like the frenetic pace of an ER. Or the constant adrenaline rush I used to get as a PJ.

But with how I left Harborview—how I was *forced* to leave —the ER is as much of a fantasy as kissing Nat.

"You're drunk!" Elias grabs my arm before I can open my locker.

I shake off his grip. "I checked my blood alcohol level before I left the house. A point-oh-four is not drunk."

He gapes at me. "You checked your blood alcohol level?"

Well, fuck. That was a mistake.

Elias shakes his head. "You knowingly drove here, while impaired, with the intention of treating patients. I knew you were struggling, Doc. Hell, I don't fucking blame you. But this is the third time you've come in hungover. How much longer until you make a mistake and someone dies?"

Sinking down onto the bench, I drop my head into my hands. I've gotten sloppy. I don't tell Elias that the reason I even have a breathalyzer is so I could figure out exactly how much I could drink—and when—without risking driving drunk. For a year, I was careful. Blew a zero point zero every time. But the anniversary of Tessa's death sent me over the edge.

"I'll get help," I say softly. The headache still thrums behind my eyes. My sour stomach gurgles. Scotch doesn't make for a proper dinner. "I need this job, Elias."

"And I need doctors I can trust." Elias crosses his arms over his chest and sighs heavily. "You're fired, Doc. I'm sorry. You were great doctor—still are most of the time. But I can't take the chance that one day, you come in with a point-oh-eight and kill someone. This is unforgivable."

Elias could have reported me to the medical board. Gotten my license revoked completely. But he didn't. I never asked why. Still, there's no way the hospital will hire me back. I don't blame them.

Camping is the latest in a long line of activities I've tried to stave off the boredom. White-water rafting, mountain biking, bungee jumping, paragliding, rock climbing, scuba... They all worked. For a time. But too soon, the excitement wears off and I start eyeing the bottle once more.

I pile the branches in the center of the tote, then spend an hour foraging for twigs and leaves to use as kindling. The hiking trails tempt me, but if I want to eat tonight, I need to get a move on.

Nat's no longer on the boathouse deck—thank God—but the older woman with the obscene t-shirt is, and she gives me the once over as I climb the steps.

"So, are you a *real* doctor? Or do you just call yourself 'Doc' to get in the ladies' pants?" she asks.

I should ignore her. I *do* ignore her until I find a set of paddles inside the immaculately clean building. When I slip back through the door, though, she's blocking my path.

"I asked you a question, young man."

She's a tiny thing. Frail, even. But there's fire in her eyes. And in the profanity emblazoned across her chest. I need to get out on the water and catch something for dinner—unless I want to go to bed hungry—but Ms. "Fuck Me Sideways" isn't going to let me pass without raising hell.

"I'm a real doctor, ma'am."

"Gladys," she snaps. "No one calls me 'ma'am.'"

With a nod, I try to bypass her, but Gladys widens her stance.

"Not so fast, Doc. I got some more questions for you."

This isn't what I signed up for. The online ad promised an escape from civilization. Or at least the pressures of everyday life.

"Each campsite has a full half-acre of land. Relax knowing you won't encounter a single soul—unless you want to."

So much for the Blakely Island Resort guarantee.

"Gladys, I didn't come here to chat. So if you don't mind..."

"I do mind, Dr. Doc Reynolds. Why are you out here all alone a few days before a holiday weekend?" She stares me down—or up, as she can't be more than five feet tall—and clucks her tongue three times. "You've got a story."

"Everyone has a story, ma'am—Gladys. Mine isn't a topic for polite conversation."

"Do I look like I engage in *polite* conversation?" She cackles, her head thrown back and her hands jammed on her hips. "You can't be a doctor. You're blind as a bat."

"I'm not. But I don't like to make assumptions about people, *Gladys*. Though, I suppose I should have taken your shirt as a warning."

Another deep, almost crazed laugh, and she slaps my back so hard, it stings. "You are a goddamned hoot. Now sit down. I'll get you a beer and we can talk."

"Thank you for the offer, ma'am, but if I don't get out on the Sound in the next hour, I'll be eating sand for dinner."

Her lips twist into a scowl, but she steps aside. "We're not done with this conversation, Doc. I don't have anything better to do but sit on this deck and wait. So one of these days... you're gonna talk to me."

Her stare follows me as I rush down the path to the campsite. Great. The last thing I need is a busybody grandmother trying to "figure me out." I'll have to stay away from the boathouse during the day. I can return the oars well after dark.

The canoe is sturdy enough, and I paddle to a beach on the other side of the island. The Razor clam season just started, and in half an hour, I have a solid pound of clams in my bucket. Enough for the night, and just in time as the sun has started dipping toward the horizon.

The trek back to the campsite is against the tide, and by the time I beach the canoe, I'm wiped.

It's another two hours before I finally sit down next to the fire pit. The grill basket with half a dozen clams and two skewers of veggies sizzles over the flames.

This is exactly what I needed. A day of intense activity. Fresh air. Remembering some of the survival skills I haven't had to use in years. I sweep my gaze around me. Puget Sound is mostly dark, a single ferry chugging along in the distance. Stars glitter in the sky—so many more than back in Seattle. There isn't much light pollution out here, and it reminds me of the first time I really *looked* up at the sky in Afghanistan. We'd been in country for three weeks. Almost died half a dozen times, but that night, I glanced up, and it was the most beautiful thing I'd ever seen.

A light winks on at the top of the hill. Is that a house? I hadn't noticed it earlier. I fish my binoculars out of my ruck and dial in the focus.

Nat steps through a pair of french doors out onto a small deck, a mug in one hand. Her fingers comb through her dark hair, and she leans an elbow on the railing.

Look away, asshole. You're not a stalker.

But I can't. She's gorgeous. Something about her calls to me in a way I don't understand.

"You don't know the basics, you're on your own."

I never considered I might have a degradation kink, but Nat's dismissal—along with her sexy as fuck voice—might be a sign I actually do.

Fucking hell. I have to stay away from her. She's probably been hit on by every single guy who's come to the resort, and I'm not looking for anything.

My dick disagrees with me. It's been six years since it last touched anything but my own hand. Six years since I felt... anything. For anyone.

The first whiff of burnt onion hits my nose. *Fuck.* This is what I get for not paying attention to the fire—and my dinner. I toss the binoculars back into the tent and ease the grill basket away from the flames. The clams are a little singed, and the onions are nothing more than soot. But the carrots and mushrooms I brought with me from Seattle are still edible.

I was going to eat under the stars, but if I stay out here, I'll be tempted to spend the entire night staring up at Nat's house, hoping for one more glimpse of her. Or worse. Wondering what I could legitimately need that would let me give her a call.

Three Weeks Later

Natasha

STREAKS of purple and red turn the sky into an impressionist painting. Curled in a chair on my deck, I try to pull my gaze from the man stacking a load of freshly chopped wood at his campsite. But it's no use.

The handsome doctor—Gladys was only too happy to tell me she'd confirmed Doc wasn't just a nickname—booked the same campsite every Monday through Wednesday for the rest of the season. I almost asked Clancy to move him somewhere else—anywhere else—but then I'd have to explain myself and what the hell would I say?

He's too good looking?

He's too quiet?

He's too distracting?

That's probably the closest to the truth.

He's built. But with just a little bit of softness that says he's not one of those guys who lives at the gym. His biceps though...I could watch him wield an axe all day long. And have for longer than I want to admit. I may have followed him into the woods last week—from a discrete distance—to see him chop wood.

He starts working on the fire. The man is precise. Old school. Small sticks and twigs arranged in a ring. Then leaves, pine needles. He strikes a piece of flint with a folding knife. The first sparks catch in seconds, and he adds a couple of larger branches. Before long, he sinks into a camp chair and starts gutting a plump salmon. He must have caught a ride on one of the trawlers out of the marina earlier today. You can't land a fish like that in the canoe.

"Nat?" Gladys calls and shuffles around the side of the house. "You here?"

I sink lower in the chair. Too late. She's already climbing the steep flight of stairs with a large, lidded casserole dish tucked under her arm. "I made too much lasagna. Don't want it to go to waste."

Gladys always makes too much lasagna. And chicken soup. And potato salad. And brownies.

"I'll get the drinks," I say with a sigh. "And plates."

"Good. Because this is my best batch in a year, and it's still hot." She nudges one of the deck chairs with her foot and slides the casserole dish onto the table. We do this dance once a week—at least—and somehow, I always end up with the leftovers. Convenient, since I hate cooking and try to do it as little as possible.

By the time I return with plates, silverware, and two bottles of beer, Gladys is leaning on the railing, staring down at the campsite below.

"He can see you," I mutter. "Sit down."

"I'm allowed to look." She accepts the bottle of Hefeweizen and downs a healthy swig. "And *you're* allowed to touch."

"Oh my God. No. We are *not* having this conversation. Did you reschedule your visit with Bella?"

Gladys shuffles back over to the table. "She's coming up this weekend."

The rich, spicy scent of tomato sauce and melted cheese waft up from the dish between us. My stomach growls, loudly. I spent the day cleaning all six cabins to prepare for the holiday weekend, and I'm wiped. Gladys slides the spoon from my hand and clucks her tongue at me.

"Sit your ass down before you fall over, baby girl. Did you eat *anything* today?"

I scowl at her. "Oatmeal. A granola bar around noon. The last renters in the Lopez cabin practically destroyed the kitchen. And don't get me started on what they left in the hot tub."

Gladys chuckles and sets a generous serving of lasagna in front of me. "Worse than the Fourth of July last year?"

"Much." I shudder. Clancy banned those folks for life. But somehow, I think this weekend will be even worse.

"I'm going to Anacortes tomorrow for supplies. You comin' with me?" Gladys asks.

I cover my flinch by shoving a bite of lasagna in my mouth. I shouldn't. Every time I go to the mainland, I run the risk of leaving a footprint. Or running into someone who'll recognize me. I have no idea if Bastian still has people looking for me. After all, he shouldn't be able to buy friendships from *inside* Leavenworth. But if his little cadre of shitheads are still out there—still alive—I'd be a fool to let myself get caught on a security camera.

If only the deep freeze in the basement weren't almost empty. I haven't been off the island in two months. And if Bella is coming to visit, Gladys probably needs to stock up on...well...everything. She can't haul all that shit herself.

I tip the bottle of beer to my lips. It's my last one, and this weekend, the temperature is supposed to hit ninety.

With a sigh, I dab my lips with a napkin. "I'll drive. But you're paying for the gas."

Her triumphant smile should piss me off. It does, on some

level. But Gladys is more than my only friend. She's two parts surrogate grandmother and one part older sister who gets off on being a bad influence. And she's fun. I don't have a lot of fun.

"Did you talk to Clancy about getting an internet connection?" she asks through a mouthful of cheesy goodness.

I shake my head. "Don't need one. Yours is good enough for me."

"Baby girl, I won't be around forever. You know that."

A sudden wave of panic twists my stomach. "Gladys? Is something—"

"No, no, no." She waves her hand—with the fork—around and gives me her biggest smile. "I'm healthy as a whole herd of horses. Went to the doctor a month ago and he confirmed it." With a wink, she glances down at the campground. "I should see if Mr. Silver Fox is taking on new patients. Or you should."

"Don't need a doctor," I mumble into my beer. In truth, it's been five years since I even had a checkup, and that was at a free clinic in Boise.

"You need something. Or...someone." Gladys reaches across the table and covers my hand with hers. Her veins stand out dramatically against her paper-thin, wrinkled skin. "I worry about you, Nat."

"I'm fine—"

"You're not. Do you know why I'm either at the boathouse or sittin' in the courtyard by the general store every single day?"

"So you won't have to be in that big house all alone?" I ask.

Gladys's eyes shimmer for a breath before she blinks her tears away. "That's part of it. There's so much of Donald there, some days, it hurts. But mostly, I make myself get up and go somewhere because no one should spend all their time alone. Have you talked to *anyone* this week who wasn't stayin' at the resort?"

She already knows the answer. So when I keep my mouth shut, she clucks her tongue and sighs. "That's what I thought. You're too young to wither away and die here, Nat. It's time you do somethin' about that."

CHAPTER FIVE

Doc

"Fuckers." Every few steps, I stoop to shovel another piece of trash into the black plastic bag. Bottle caps, cigarette butts, and burnt-out shells from too many fireworks littered the beach, but the needles sent me far over the edge. Thank God I had a small sharps container in my medical bag.

I'd contemplated spending the holiday weekend up here. But from the looks of things, I made the right choice staying home. The city was bad enough. From my house in West Seattle, I could see—and hear—the fireworks from Bainbridge Island and Lake Union. But money buys many things. Soundproofing. Anxiety medication. Noise-cancelling headphones.

By now, everyone is back at work, and the island is eerily quiet. Nat was scrubbing the boathouse deck when I arrived and barely nodded in my direction. Gladys was nowhere to be seen. Probably a good thing. That woman is a busybody of the highest order. I didn't need another one of her "interrogations."

Especially since the campsite was trashed. I hiked up to the little general store, bought a box of trash bags, and got to work. Now, I lug two of them, full to bursting, up the trail to the dumpster next to the boathouse.

As soon as I round the bend, the Heftys hits the ground with twin *thunks*. Nat balances on a stepladder, stretching to reach a broken light mounted under the eaves.

Her tank top rides up, exposing an expanse of creamy skin above her khaki shorts. With her back to me, she can't catch me staring, so I take a long moment to appreciate the curve of her ass, her legs, her toned arms.

The rickety old ladder starts to shake. Shit. I take off at a run and reach her just as she realizes she's about to go down. Her arms flail for anything to grab onto. "No, no—"

My hands mold to her hips, steadying her. But she yelps and starts to thrash. Her boot catches me under the chin. My head snaps to the side. Pain ripples down my back, and my left leg starts to tingle. But I don't let go, spinning around with her, almost hitting the deck myself before I get my bearings.

"It's...Doc!" I grit out. Once she has her legs under her, I let her go.

"Shit. Don't ever do that again." Nat presses her hand to her heart. She's spooked, and her breath saws in and out of her chest like she's just won first place in the fifty-yard dash.

"I should have let you fall?" Adrenaline is still coursing through me, but my jaw is starting to throb. I rub the ache, and come away with a smear of blood across my palm. "You've got a mean kick there."

Nat's eyes widen, and she closes the distance between us. Her fingers cup the back of my neck. This is closer than I've been to anyone but my patients in a long damn time. It feels so good to have someone touch me. Even if she's only doing it out of guilt.

"There isn't much blood," she says, relief lending a huskier tone to her voice as she angles my head slightly. "Sit down. I'll get you an ice pack. And a drink. Coke? Pepsi? Beer? I think Gladys keeps a six-pack of Pilsner in the cooler."

"Just the ice. I can't stay. Not if I expect to get my tent set up *and* dig for clams before dark."

In truth, I'd give anything to sit on the boathouse deck for a couple of hours and talk to her. Even if she's only offering out of guilt. But it wouldn't end well. I'd want what I can't have—and don't deserve—and this place wouldn't be my safe haven any longer.

"You've been here since noon and you haven't set up your tent?" she calls from inside the small structure. "You don't seem like the type to...waste time."

I chuckle, then tip my head against the back of the chair. "I wasn't wasting it. The beach was a mess. I was bringing trash up to the dumpster when I saw you about to fall. Things get a little wild over the weekend?"

"You have no idea," she says as she emerges from the boathouse with a bag of ice and a small towel. "I sat on my deck all damn night with a fire extinguisher. And fended off a group of drunk assholes at one point. You cleaned up the beach?"

"Yep." I nod toward the bags I dropped before I caught her. "This island is too beautiful to be disrespected like that."

Holding out my hand for the makeshift cold pack, I'm not prepared for her to press it to my jaw and jerk at the contact.

"Easy there, Doc." She leans over me, close enough I catch a whiff of her scent. Citrus and something soft. Flowery. God. Another inch—or three—and I could wrap my arms around her, tug her into my lap, and taste her.

One minute stretches into two. Then three. Nat pulls the bag away, and our gazes lock. I don't know what it is about this woman that calls to me. She's beautiful, sure. Especially today. No baseball cap hiding her eyes. No makeup. But it's not just her looks. Everything about her is *real*. Even the raw need written all over her face.

Until she shakes her head, and it's gone. Along with any trace of emotion. "The bleeding's stopped. You need more ice later, come on by. I won't be here, but the combo for the freezer is eight-five-two-three-eight."

"You're not afraid I'll steal Gladys's beer?"

She studies me for a beat, then cracks a smile. "If you do, it'll take more than an ice pack to make you whole again. Gladys is *very* serious about her beer."

Natasha

I flop down on the couch. It's been a day. A long, hard, confusing day. The kind of day I'd normally tell Gladys all about. Except Bella doesn't go back to Seattle until tomorrow, and I don't want to intrude on their last night together.

I spent half the weekend hiding in the basement. In there, the fireworks weren't as loud. The rest of it I camped out on my deck praying no one was careless enough to burn the whole damn island to the ground.

Until some drunk asshole started banging on my door at three in the morning. The idiot tried to feel me up. I laid him out on his ass. All while his friends attempted to goad me into partying with them.

Maybe it's time to move on. Clancy doesn't pay me much, but I've managed to save close to ten grand over the years. Enough to get myself set up somewhere else. Kansas is cheap enough. So's Georgia. Alabama.

I run a hand through my wavy hair. The humidity in the

South would do a number on it. And I hate the heat. All those years in Afghanistan, Iraq, and Kuwait? I never want to see a hundred degrees again. Ever.

My muscles protest when I get to my feet. I had to scrub every inch of the boathouse deck and half the walls today. Haul a dozen bags of trash to the dumpster at the edge of the property. I only got through *one* of the cabins.

Clancy has to start vetting his renters. Or make them pay double the deposit for holiday weekends. Then hire a whole team of cleaners.

The guy is too nice. Too trusting. Too out of touch with reality. But I brought a disposable camera with me and took photos of everything. Maybe those will convince him.

The one bright spot in this hellscape of a day? The few minutes I spent with the sexy doctor after he saved my ass— and I kicked him in the head.

God, and I never thanked him for cleaning up the beach. Just let him walk away after we shared that one moment of connection. The one that left me wanting so much more than I can ever have.

Fuck. Gladys is right. I *am* lonely. Touching him brought up so many feelings I thought I'd buried a long time ago.

Enough, Nat. He's not interested, and it's too damn dangerous.

But his hands. The way he set me on my feet like I weighed nothing at all...

He looked at me like he wanted more. Like he saw *me.*

I'm halfway to the cabinet with the bourbon when my phone rings.

"What's up, Gladys?"

"Um...this is Bella. Aunt Gladys fell. She's...she's not right. She keeps talking about Uncle Donald. Like he's still alive. I think she needs to go to the hospital. Do the ferries run this late? I can't get her into the car by myself... I don't know what to do. There's no hospital here, right? No doctors?"

Gladys is all I have. The only person in this world who actually cares about me. If anything happens to her...

"Nat? Are you there?" Bella the hotshot corporate lawyer is gone, and in her place is a terrified little girl who needs her great aunt to be okay.

"There's no hospital here, right? No doctors?"

Not officially. But I happen to know just where to find one tonight. Not that I ever bothered to find out what kind of doctor he is. But any medical training is better than none.

"I'll be there in ten minutes. Maybe less. If anything changes, call me back."

I hang up before she can say a word, shove my feet into my tennis shoes, and race out the door.

Please, God. Let her be okay.

The ATV headlights cut through the shadows between my house and the beach. I have to wind my way down the hill so the vehicle doesn't tip ass over hood with me on it, and the extra few minutes almost kill me.

Doc is tending the fire pit when I come around the bend, but jumps up, then dives into his tent.

Shit. Of course a vehicle approaching at high speed would make him nervous. "Doc?" I call as I ease the ATV to a stop. "It's Nat. I...need your help."

He emerges slowly, a slight hitch in his step and a frown twisting his lips. "What's wrong?"

I dig my fingernails into my palms until the pain helps me focus. "It's Gladys. She fell. She's...confused. Her niece is with her, but—"

"I'll get my bag." He's all business now, and in under ten seconds, he emerges from the tent with a canvas bag slung over his shoulder. "Did she lose consciousness?"

"I...I don't know." Shit. Why didn't I ask? I scoot forward on the seat so Doc can squeeze in behind me. He's warm. Solid.

"Is it okay if I hold on to you?" he asks, his lips close to my ear.

"Wha—yes. Of course." The muscles of his forearm cord as I take off. "Bella called me a few minutes ago. I didn't stop to ask. I just—"

"You did the right thing." I'm hyper aware of his presence against my back. Of the tight hold he has on me. Of how good he smells. Sweat and soap and wood smoke.

In the dark, it takes too long to make my way to the far end of the resort where Gladys lives. But Doc keeps me calm. Focused. He asks me questions. Her age. Her medical history. Her family. All things I know about her. And it strikes me that she knows *none* of those things about me.

The lights of the quaint log cabin come into view. A pair of rocking chairs sit on the wraparound porch, waiting for someone to sit in them. I almost never come here. Gladys visits *me*. I always thought it was because she liked the view from my place. But seeing those two chairs...one with a well-worn cushion, and the other brand new—yet covered with a layer of dust—it hits me. She visits me because this was supposed to be her happy ever after. Not the place she's the most alone. God, I need her to know how important she is to me.

Doc slides off the ATV—but does he give my waist a little squeeze first? Or did I imagine it? I shouldn't feel the loss of the touch, but I do.

"Bella?" I call as I climb the three steps to the front porch. "I brought a doctor!"

The young lawyer opens the door, her perfect blond hair mussed, and tears in her eyes. "She keeps saying she's going to be late to pick up Uncle Donald. I tried to tell her he was gone, but—"

"I'm Dr. Reynolds," Doc says, sidestepping me and

holding out his hand. "Can I come in and take a look at your aunt?"

She stares at him, her gaze suddenly hard. Is this what she looks like in a courtroom? If so, her opponents probably cower in fear. Doc wears a light blue t-shirt, a pair of black pants, and scuffed boots. His wardrobe doesn't exactly scream *doctor*. Or anything other than random camper Nat just *happened* to bring by.

"What kind of doctor are you? Not a Ph.D., right? You have *actual* medical training?"

Doc arches his brows, but there's a hint of respect in his gaze. "I worked in the ER for almost nine years. But before that, I spent seventeen years in the Air Force treating injuries all over the Middle East. I've seen plenty of falls. And aunts. You can trust me with yours. But if she has a head injury, the longer we wait, the more danger she's in."

I offer the young woman an encouraging nod, hoping it'll be enough.

With a sniffle, Bella steps aside. "Okay. But I'm a lawyer. Don't make me bring a malpractice suit against you."

Oh, God. That was the wrong thing to say.

Luckily, Doc doesn't react. He's already halfway to the couch, where Gladys sits, wringing her hands in front of her. She doesn't look injured or in pain. Though her white hair is mussed, and her eyes are damp.

"Ma'am," Doc says. "Gladys? Do you remember me?"

Gladys blinks up at him. She looks so small. So frail. I've always thought of her as a tornado. An unstoppable force. One that would be around forever. But she's not. And she won't be. My eyes start to burn as I realize how much I've come to care for her.

"Hot Doc," Gladys says with a weak smile. "You here to take me to the ferry? I could use a ride. My grand niece won't take me."

Doc unzips his kit and pulls out a stethoscope and blood pressure cuff. "It's late, Gladys. Almost 10:00 p.m. What's so important you need to go right now?"

"I have to pick up Donald. He takes the last ferry home on Fridays. If I don't pick him up, he'll have to walk, and he *hates* walking up the hill after he's worked all day." She tries to stand up, but Doc stops her with a hand on her shoulder.

"It's Tuesday, Gladys," he says softly, and shines a pen light into each of her eyes. "Do you know what year it is?"

My friend blinks hard, then focuses on Bella. Tears shimmer in her eyes. "Shitsicles."

"Gladys?" I take a seat next to her and drape my arm around her shoulders. "Donald—"

"I know, baby girl. He's been gone a long time now." Her tone turns sorrowful, and she leans against me, tears streaming down her cheeks. "Bella was still in pigtails when he died."

Doc tries to get the blood pressure cuff around Gladys's arm, but she waves him off. "I'm fine, Dr. Sexy Pants. Leave me alone."

He chuckles. "Dr. Sexy Pants? That's one I haven't heard before."

"Well, it's true," she retorts, then stares directly at his... package. "Though you might try wearing a pair of gray sweatpants in the future."

Oh, God. Kill me now.

"In July? I'd burst into flames." He tries once more to wrap the cuff around her upper arm, and this time, she lets him. "You're officially my patient now, Gladys, and I'm going to make sure you're okay. Can you tell me how you fell?"

"Bein' stupid," she mutters. "My foot slipped off the ladder."

"She wanted to show me one of her photo albums," Bella says. "I didn't know they were in the attic. I was packing—"

I try to pay attention as Doc examines Gladys, but my mind is racing. What if Bella hadn't been here? What if *Doc* hadn't been here? What will happen to Gladys if I run again? She talks to everyone on the island. She's lived here for close to thirty-five years. But would anyone else think to check up on her?

How many days have *I* forgotten to check on her? If I leave—when I leave—she'll be even more alone than she is now.

Doc pushes to his feet with a wince and starts methodically tucking his equipment back into his bag . "Gladys, you gave your niece quite a scare. But you're back with us now, and by some miracle, you didn't break any bones. But you *did* lose consciousness for a few minutes, so I'd feel a whole hell of a lot better if Bella and Nat could take turns keeping an eye on you tonight."

"You mean like wake her up every four hours?" I ask.

Doc chuckles. "That's old advice that we don't tend to follow anymore. All it ever did was piss people off. Gladys needs to take it easy for the next twenty-four to forty-eight hours. If she gets dizzy or nauseous, has another episode of confusion or lack of coordination, or if she has any pain, you call me." He scribbles a number down on a scrap of paper, and passes it to Bella. "It's a sat phone, so you can reach me anywhere. Nat already has my number from the campsite reservation system. Even though she's never used it." His pointed look shocks me. Like he *wants* me to use it. For what? Just to talk?

"You're sure she doesn't need to go to the hospital?" the young woman asks. "Someone on this island must have a boat we could use."

"I have a sea plane." Doc glances at Gladys, a hint of a smile curving his lips. "If I thought she needed to be admitted, I'd take her myself. But as long as she doesn't get worse, I think your girl is going to be just fine."

"I ain't anyone's girl," Gladys grumbles. "And if these two are stayin', then so are you, Dr. Sexy Pants."

Doc's cheeks tinge a dark crimson. "You don't need me here, ma'am. Nat and your niece will take good care of you."

There's a gleam in Gladys's eyes now. One I recognize. "I made a mess of potato salad before fallin' off that ladder and there's a huge slab of salmon in the fridge. You look like you can handle a grill, Doc. Since I'm supposed to 'take it easy' and all."

"I really should go," he says.

Before he can pick up his bag, I wrap my fingers around his forearm. He tenses until I give the muscles a gentle squeeze. "I took you away from your dinner. Whatever you were cooking is charcoal by now. Stay. Gladys is an amazing cook. And...I'd feel better if you were here. I'm sure Bella would too. At least for a little while."

I don't know why I care that he stays. We have his number. We could call if anything happens. Spending time with *anyone* is dangerous. Even Bella. Whenever the young woman comes to visit, I make myself scarce so she doesn't ask questions I'm not prepared to answer.

Yet now, I'm voluntarily putting myself in a position to make small talk with not one, but *two* virtual strangers.

Doc backs up a step, but doesn't make a move to pick up his bag again. "Point me to the grill, Gladys."

CHAPTER SIX

Doc

I SHOULDN'T BE HERE. Sitting around a table with Nat, Gladys, and her niece. But the desperation in Nat's voice when she asked me to stay did me in. I doubt she's used to asking for help any more than I'm used to socializing.

She stays on the fringes of the conversation. Only interacting when one of us asks her a direct question. Deflecting before anything can get too personal. She plays with a piece of sea glass under the table. I'm not even sure she knows she's running nervous fingers along the smooth edges over and over again.

Gladys leans back in her chair and pierces me with a hard stare. "So, you worked in the ER, Doc?"

"For nine years, ma'am."

She rolls her eyes at me. "If you expect me to let you sink your teeth into my famous peach pie, you'll stop with the 'ma'am' shit."

I choke on a sip of water. For the love of God, that better not be a euphemism. Across the table, Nat stifles a laugh.

"Aunt Gladys!" Bella hisses under her breath.

"What?" The older woman frowns. "I didn't say anythin' embarrassing. This time."

Bella leans over and whispers in her aunt's ear. Gladys starts to cackle.

"Dr. Sexy Pants ain't interested in my ass, sweet girl. He's only got eyes for Nat there."

"Oh, God. Gladys, we talked about this. You promised you'd stop trying to fix me up with—with anyone."

"I'm tired of watchin' you wither away here alone, baby girl," Gladys retorts.

"I'm not 'withering away.' I'm doing just fine. Except now, I need some air." Nat scoots back from the table and darts through the patio door to the deck.

No one says a word for a full minute. Then Gladys huffs. "Well, don't just sit there, Doc. Go after her. Bella can take care of the pie." Gladys crosses her arms over her chest and stares me down.

I have to put a stop to this. For Nat's sake as well as mine. "The only thing I have eyes for, Gladys, is dessert. I'm not a good bet. Nat knows it. I'd appreciate it if you'd stop trying to fix us up." Despite my words, I stride after the woman who's starred in more than one of my dreams since we met a few weeks ago.

I find her looking out over the water with her elbows resting on the railing. She's playing with the smooth, light green piece of glass, and I still her fingers. The heart-shaped bauble falls into my hand.

"The ocean is amazing, isn't it?" I ask. "To be able to take something broken with all its sharp edges and turn it into... something so soft and beautiful?"

"I found that my first day on the island." Her tone turns wistful. "Right where your campsite is now. I don't know why I keep it."

With a shrug, I press it back into her palm. "Not everything in life needs a reason."

Silence stretches the seconds, longer and longer until it's all I can hear. She hasn't relaxed even a fraction. If anything, she's more tense now than when I came out here. "You okay?"

She sighs, shifting a little further away from me before she risks darting a glance in my direction. "That woman is a menace. I love her, but she never listens."

"How long have you known Gladys?" I ask.

A small smile tugs at Nat's lips. "Four and a half years. The day after I took this job, she knocked on my door with an apple pie, a bottle of vodka, and a French press."

"A French press? Why a French press?" I'm fascinated by the old woman's thought process. And still a little worried about her mental state.

"Because Clancy—he owns the resort and the house I live in—took his fancy espresso machine with him when he moved to Florida. Gladys worries about anyone who doesn't start the day with a hit of caffeine."

"I know a few guys like that. And I probably shouldn't talk. I bring coffee with me every trip."

Nat chuckles. "I'd been drinking instant for a couple of years at that point. My first press was almost a religious experience." We're close enough for the heat of her to seep into my forearm. "After a few weeks, she started showing up with 'leftovers' that weren't *really* leftovers. She 'made too much.' She 'wasn't used to cooking for just one person.' Even though she'd been doing it for almost twenty years."

Glancing over my shoulder, I watch Bella cut slices of pie while Gladys leans back in her chair and closes her eyes. Every one of her eighty-two years is etched on her face, but there's life left in her. A lot of it. That woman isn't one to go quietly into that goodnight. She'll fight—kicking and screaming—until she murders the Grim Reaper himself. Then try to fix him up with one of the Fates.

Nat and I move at the same time—in the same direction—and our legs tangle in such a way, she loses her balance and topples into me.

"Whoa. I've got you."

Having her in my arms feels like the most natural thing in the world. She peers up at me, shock parting her lips, and need darkening her eyes. It would be so easy to dip my head and kiss her.

"I'm not a good bet."

"I'm—" Before I can apologize, she plants her hands on my hips, rises onto her toes, and seals her mouth to mine.

One taste. One touch. One moment I don't feel quite so alone.

But then she jerks back.

"Shit." Tears shimmer in her gaze. "I'm sorry. I shouldn't have—"

"Don't." I slide my hand into her hair and tighten my grip on the wavy strands. Two steps to the left, and we're hidden from view. Nat melts in my arms, letting me take control. I nip along the edge of her smart mouth, then flick my tongue gently over the seam. She opens for me with a moan.

Her nipples tighten into sharp points. Fuck. Can she feel my hard length against her stomach? God, I wish we were alone. At her house. Or my tent. Anywhere but here.

Nat's hands slide down my back. When her fingers dig into my ass, my control snaps. "We have to get out of here." I close my teeth over the shell of her ear. "Fuck the pie."

"Yes. Right. Okay. But," she extricates herself from my arms, "if Gladys figures out why, she'll start planning a damn wedding."

"Call me." I take her face in my hands so I can plant a

hard, swift kiss to her lips. "Just let it ring. I'll say it's an emergency and I have to go."

"And I'll offer you a ride?" she asks breathlessly.

Fuck. Her pupils are half blown. I push her against the railing, then give one of her nipples a hard pinch. Her yelp is lost to my mouth on hers.

"Yes. God. I have to calm down before I walk back in there." Turning away, I run through the names of all fifty states. Then all the countries I served in. My high school teachers. All the bones in the human foot. Anything to take my mind off what's about to happen.

When I get my dick under control, I swallow hard. "Call me. Now. Before..."

She nods, pulls her phone from her pocket, and dials.

"Mr. Sexy Pants!" Gladys calls. "Your bag is ringin'!"

I rush back inside and dig for the sat phone. "Dammit. Gladys, I'm sorry. I have to go. It was nice to meet you, Bella. Uh...call me—"

"Ahem." Gladys wobbles to her feet and, faster than should be possible, snatches the phone from behind Nat's back. "I'm old, Doc. Not stupid." She ends the fake call, presses the device into Nat's hand, and pats her arm. "Go on, baby girl. Get out of here. And don't you be coming back here tonight. Bella can take care of me just fine."

THE RIDE to Nat's house feels like it takes forever. My dick is so hard, it's painful, and Nat keeps shifting on the ATV's seat, which isn't helping.

She grabs my hand when we stop and practically drags me inside. The house smells like her. Along with hints of coffee. A single light next to the couch provides a gentle glow. Masculine colors, no hints of comfort. Nothing personal. But before I can wonder why, she flips the lock and reaches for me.

We don't make it to the bedroom. Nat has her legs wrapped around my hips two steps from the door. "Couch. Now," she says between desperate kisses.

I sink down with her still in my arms. She grinds her hips, and I let out a groan.

My fingers curl around the hem of her tank top, and I tug it up and over her head. A simple, black bra frames her breasts, and it's the sexiest fucking thing I've ever seen.

"Fuck, baby. I've wanted you since the first day I met you. I knew you'd feel like this."

"Like what?" Her hands snake under my t-shirt, and short nails drag along my pecs and down to my belt. She flicks the catch, then the button on my pants.

I lie her down and straddle her. Gently, I nip at the curve of her neck to her collarbone. "Home."

Her entire body stiffens. With a sharp gasp, she tries to scramble out from under me. "No. Stop. *Stop!*"

I'm on my feet in a second, hands in the air. "What happened? Did I do something wrong?"

Tears shimmer in her eyes. "N-no. It's not...you, Doc. God, it's not you." Grabbing her tank top off the floor, she backs up slowly. "But I need you to leave. I'm not good with...relationships. There's a reason my only friend is an eighty-two-year-old woman who doesn't take no for an answer. This...was a mistake."

"Nat—" Fuck. I can't argue with her. I'm too messed up to be good for *anyone*. "I told Gladys I wasn't a good bet. I haven't had a relationship in years—because I'm not good with them either. But that's not what this was. I'm sorry if I gave you that impression."

"You didn't," she says softly. "But that doesn't change

things. I'll tell Gladys it didn't work out. That we just didn't click. Please, *please* do the same?"

My heart aches to demand Nat talk to me. That she tell me the real reason she went from jumping me to kicking me out of her house. But instead, I back toward the door.

"Whatever you need, Nat. But...I wish you'd tell me why."

A single tear glistens on her cheek as I step outside and she hovers at the door. Determination and longing battle in her eyes. "Gladys wants everyone to have what she had once. True love. She doesn't realize some of us were destined to be alone."

I GRIT my teeth all the way down the hill to my campsite. I can't get Nat's last words out of my head.

Some of us were destined to be alone.

She's not wrong. I had my chance at happiness and let it slip through my fingers. I won't get another. But dammit if I didn't think I could have one night where I didn't feel so alone.

By the time I dump sand on the dying embers in the fire pit, all the lights in her house are off. I'd give almost anything to hear her voice right now. But we're strangers, and after tonight, I'm certain that's never going to change.

So I stretch out in my sleeping bag and wonder when I became such a goddamn hypocrite.

CHAPTER SEVEN

Present Day

Doc

THE PURR of the SUV's engine soothes me as I accelerate onto Interstate 5. Until flashing detour signs direct me to exit at Industrial Way. Fucking jackknifed tractor trailer is going to send me right past Hidden Agenda's warehouse.

It's been almost four months. By now, you'd think I'd be able to forget about the last time I saw Ryker McCabe. And his team. But whenever I leave my home in West Seattle, I have to pass within five minutes of the damn place.

The K&R firm rescues people from the worst of humanity all over the world. And when they're injured, they count on me to patch them up. Or...they did.

Years ago, McCabe's job offer pulled me out of a hole so dark and deep, I didn't think I'd ever see daylight again. Saving people—saving *his* people—gave me purpose. A mission. And enough money, I'm set for the rest of my life. Even if I never work another day.

"Patch up my team. Whatever. Whenever," he says, staring down at me with ice in his multi-hued eyes.

"And wherever?"

"Fuck, no. You treat my people at a neutral location. Rent an office. Buy an RV and set up a mobile clinic. I don't care. Whatever you need—equipment, money, permits—you'll have it."

For a few months, anyone he sent my way had to go to an office park in the Central District. It was damn lucky the place had a back door down an alley no one wanted to hang out in. My very illegal medical practice was sandwiched between a yarn store and a crystal shop. Someone would have noticed all the blood.

Then one of McCabe's team was targeted by a stalker. The asshole kidnapped and tortured her lover. The guy was so bad off when they rescued him, he could barely stand—let alone handle the drive from his Capitol Hill condo.

One house call earned me the trust for another. And another. I haven't needed that office since.

A cop waves me through a stoplight. Traffic is so heavy, I get a good look at the warehouse—and the single, black SUV parked out front. The same SUV McCabe was driving the last time I saw him. The night everything changed.

Seventeen years as Air Force Pararescue, saving the strongest and deadliest of the United States Armed Forces all over Iraq and Afghanistan. Eight years as an ER doc in Los Angeles. Two years at Harborview in Seattle before it all went to shit. Then all the work McCabe sent my way.

I thought I'd seen it all. Bruises so deep they were almost black. Gunshot wounds. Stabbings. Concussions. Broken bones. The most outrageous things I could ever imagine shoved up orifices they had no business being in. But nothing —not even amputating a man's leg with a glorified pair of scissors on the deck of a helo flying over the Al-Faw Peninsula—prepared me for what I saw the first, last, and only time McCabe called me to the warehouse.

Raelynn—the newest member of the team—was still recovering from a partially dislocated shoulder. But a couple of assholes broke into her home and, in less than an hour, put her in such a bad state, if McCabe hadn't been a universal blood donor, she'd probably be dead.

I've seen her and her guy—Nash—a couple of times since that night, checking on bruises, dislocated joints, and severe smoke inhalation. They're all healed up now, thank God. She's the one who told me McCabe and his wife had a baby girl. The kid is almost twelve weeks old now. I'll never meet her. Never know her name.

Why does that bother me?

I wasn't supposed to get close enough to any of his team to care. No details. No questions. Stay on the outside. Always.

But Raelynn reminds me a little of Tessa. The same smart mouth. The same attitude. The same stubborn refusal to take it easy. So when I realized how badly she was injured, I laid into McCabe. He told me to patch her up and get the fuck out.

It'd be easy enough to flip a U-turn. See if he really is there. But what the hell would I say to the man?

"Anyone need a doctor?"

"Still saving the world or are you on permanent diaper duty?"

"If you don't need me anymore, you can stop with the ridiculously large paychecks."

He'd probably kick my ass.

A horn blares. I slam on the brakes, coming to a stop only inches from the car in front of me.

Fuck. Pay attention. You got too close and you got burned.

With a quick shake of my head, I clear the cobwebs and focus on my destination. It's only been ten days since I last flew up to Blakely. But after a year of spending almost all my free time up there, the island is in my blood now.

Or maybe it's Nat who keeps drawing me back. The memory of the one night where we almost lost ourselves in one another haunts me. It was over a year ago now. The 4th of July has come and gone again, but I can't forget how she felt in my arms. How she tasted. How she wanted me as much as I wanted her.

Until she didn't.

She stopped meeting me at the boathouse after that night. But sometimes, I catch her watching me from her deck. I've waved, hoping to entice her to come down and chat. But she never has.

Gladys, on the other hand, is always waiting for me. Usually with a bag of cookies or brownies or a slice of pie for the "Dr. Sexy Pants" who came to her rescue. If it weren't for how terrified her niece was that night, I'd be convinced she faked that whole episode of confusion just to get me and Nat in the same room together.

I get the sense Gladys doesn't have many people who'll sit and listen to her—besides Nat. I try to show up half an hour before check-in every week to let her talk my ear off. Or interrogate me. Most of the time, she steers the conversation toward Nat before long. I don't have the heart to tell her Nat and I will never be more than strangers.

Once or twice, I've helped Gladys with odd jobs she can't do on her own. Like changing her lightbulbs or the batteries in her smoke detectors. I cleaned her gutters one week. Replaced a rotten board on her deck. A month ago, after several trips without a project, I offered to scrape the moss from the shady side of her house. Just to have a reason to chat with her.

I wonder if she'll have anything for me to do this time.

My phone rings, the car's in-dash display flashing: *Medical Clinic.*

"Reynolds," I say when the call connects.

"It's Angela." The young nurse clears her throat. "Um, Dr. Lambert has the flu. She can't come in today. I know you don't usually work the first part of the week, but could you cover for her?"

I should say no. I want to say no. The clear blue sky beckons. It's a perfect day for flying. An even better day for camping.

"The waiting room is almost full." Angela's voice catches. "And there's a DV case in Exam Room 2 with her eight-year-old son. She's terrified her boyfriend will find her. I called Detective Mitchell, but he can't get here for at least two hours. I know Dr. Lambert said we can't afford a security guard, but what if it happens again...?"

Fuck.

The free clinic in one of Seattle's rougher neighborhoods sees at least one domestic violence case a week. Sometimes more. A few days before Christmas, a patient's husband broke in just after closing and threatened to kill Angela if she didn't tell him where his wife was.

She was lucky. Someone at the donut shop next door heard her scream and came to investigate. The asshole fled, and the cops picked him up a few hours later. Angela was so traumatized, she almost quit.

"Dr. Reynolds?"

That others may live.

The PJ motto floats through my head on repeat. I can't leave Angela to handle this alone.

At the next light, I turn onto Airport Way and floor it. The clinic is only fifteen minutes away, but I can make it in ten if I'm lucky.

"I'm headed in. Lock the front door until I get there and keep your phone handy."

"But—"

"Do it, Angela. If anyone else shows up, use the intercom and ask them to wait outside. It's a nice day, and I'll be there before you know it."

"Okay." She lets out a slow, heavy breath. "If you're sure..."

"I'm sure. And I'm making some calls when we close for lunch. One way or another, we're hiring that security guard."

EASING the silver Lexus into a parking spot behind the building, I relax my grip on the steering wheel. In five minutes, I'll be able to assess that domestic violence case myself—and keep an eye out for the woman's boyfriend. If he tries to get to her, he'll regret the day he was born.

I'm not losing another one.

I send Angela a quick text to warn her I'm coming in the back door, then enter the six-digit code. The lock is a fucking joke, but it's light years better than the simple deadbolt we had when I started here.

Tears shimmer in her eyes when she sees me. "Dr. Reynolds, thank you. I didn't know what I was going to do if you hadn't answered the phone..."

"Dr. Lambert should have called me first thing this morning. It's not your responsibility to make sure we're fully staffed. And we need a better system for DV cases than just 'call Detective Mitchell and hope for the best.'" Shrugging into my doctor's coat, I head down the hall. "But we'll figure that out later. Let's see what our patient needs."

"You sure you want the full package?" Lucas asks. He tucks one of his shoulder-length dreads behind his ear and stares down at his tablet screen. "We could start you on the basic system. Anything else would be...well..."

"Massive overkill?" He's trying to be nice, but I know what this place looks like. The flimsy glass door. The threadbare carpet. The plywood over one of the smaller windows that's been there for six months.

"Like wearing a pair of Louboutin's to karaoke night at The Little Red Hen," he says with a grin.

"Never been. No one wants to hear me sing. But I'm assuming it's not one of Seattle's more...upscale establishments?"

Lucas snorts and shakes his head. "Not even close. We'll take your money, Doc. But even our entry-level system would be about a hundred steps up from what you have now."

I should listen to him. My bank account would be happier. Dr. Lambert can't fund this work. The clinic barely breaks even. But McCabe's given me a small fortune over the years. Enough for me to pay off my house, buy my sea plane, and live a comfortable life. Our patients don't have that luxury. They deserve to feel safe when they're here. We all do.

Scanning the list I made on my lunch break, I shake my head. "The basic plan isn't enough. I need panic buttons in every exam room. Backup power. Biometric locks at the front and back doors, and cameras covering all the public areas."

"Oversight Platinum it is, then. Cam is gonna *love* me when I get back to the office." At my confusion, he grins. "Camilla Delgado? She owns Emerald City Security. Oversight is her baby. She designed it."

Cam. I know that name.

"She wouldn't happened to be married to a former Navy SEAL, would she?"

Lucas's eyes widen. "You know West?"

Shit. I should have kept my mouth shut.

"I've met him a time or two. He asked me for a second opinion on some X-Rays before Cam had surgery last year. Acquaintance of an acquaintance. I knew his wife was in tech, but nothing beyond that."

"She took over from the founder a couple of years ago. Royce designs apps now. For us and for others."

Royce. My first house call for Hidden Agenda. This is dangerous on every level. But Emerald City is the best, and that's what I need. Even if it does put me on McCabe's radar again.

"Doc? You look like you've seen a ghost. Are you okay?" Lucas frowns and reaches out to touch my arm. He's a big guy. When he showed up, I was briefly intimidated. Until he smiled and shook my hand. If I had to guess, he's one of those people who treats everyone he meets like they're his family.

"Fine. Long day, that's all. How soon can you start? And how much is this going to cost me?"

He taps his tablet screen a few times, adding all the bells and whistles to the Platinum package, then hands me the device.

Right above the total, a single line shocks me.

Friends and Family Discount - 25%

"I barely know Sampson. You don't need—"

Lucas gives me a look that's equal parts sympathy and understanding. "I used to depend on places like this, Doc. The ones that didn't ask a lot of questions. That let me pay in cash. And anyone who knows Cam had surgery last year—let alone *saw her X-Rays*—is family."

Swallowing the lump in my throat, I nod. "Thank you."

After he checks his calendar, he tucks the tablet back under his arm. "I don't know what lucky star you were born under, but you caught us at the perfect time. Our installers finished up cabling work on another project this afternoon, and they're free for the next two days. How's 9:00 a.m. tomorrow?"

"Perfect."

BY THE TIME I get home, the sun is setting over Puget Sound. I haven't eaten all day, and my fridge is empty. I was planning on fresh clams for dinner. Days like today, I feel every one of my fifty-six years. Every scar from the crash that ended my work as a PJ. Every regret and lost patient from years in the ER.

I grab a rocks glass from the bar, add a couple of ice cubes, and cut a twist of lemon. The *hiss* from the bottle of club soda isn't what I want to hear. But it's all I allow myself.

After I accepted McCabe's job offer four years ago, I checked myself into a rapid detox program. I've been sober ever since.

But the ritual still comforts me.

I stare at the glass, but the fingers wrapped around it don't look like mine. Blood coats the knuckles. My father's voice echoes in my ears.

"See what you made me do? Why can't you listen?"

My mother sobs from the floor. I jam my hands over my ears, but it never works. I can still hear her. "I'm sorry, Gage. I'll do better."

The glass hits the counter with a solid *crack*. Club soda splashes over my hand. Fucking hell. Just a memory.

I leave the mess, suddenly desperate for air, and stumble outside to the deck. The water is only fifteen feet away, and the fresh breeze cools my cheeks. One of the evening ferries cuts through the water. I should call someone. Or go to a meeting. Anything but sink into one of my Adirondak chairs and sit here alone.

But when I pull out my phone to find the closest—and soonest—AA meeting, a text message waits on the screen.

Nat: You missed your check-in window. By a lot.

My lips twitch. I wasn't sure she'd notice my absence.

Doc: Work emergency. I won't make it this week. Sorry for any hassle.

Her reply comes in seconds.

Nat: Are you okay?

This is the most we've "spoken" since the night she kicked me out of her house. And she's worried about me?

Doc: I'm fine. Had to cover for a sick colleague. How are things there?

Nat: Same as they always are during the week. But quieter.

I'd give almost anything to hear her voice right now. To wave up at her from the campsite I've come to think of as "mine." To have a reason to keep texting her all night. But we're not friends. She made that *very* clear. Even if "quieter" makes me think she might actually miss me.

So I head back inside and flip on the TV. Baseball it is.

I haul my ruck over my shoulder and lock my SUV. I'm about ready to come out of my skin. Emerald City Security spent three days at the clinic installing their top-of-the-line system. Another full day training the staff. Then I worked the weekend with only a surly traveling nurse for company. I saw so many sunburn and dehydration cases, I wanted to scream by the end of each day.

My Cessna 172 is ready and waiting for me at the terminal in Kenmore. "Hello, gorgeous. Sorry I stood you up last week." I run my hand over the plane's nose. "You ready for some airtime?"

Less than fifteen minutes later, I'm cruising over Puget Sound on my way to Blakely. Clear, blue skies stretch out in every direction, and I take a deep breath—my first in too long.

Dr. Lambert tore me a new one when she found out about the security system.

"This isn't your clinic, Reynolds. It's mine."

"Then act like it," I snap. *"Take some goddamn responsibility for your employees' safety."*

"I could fire you for this."

"Then you'd need to find someone else willing to work every single weekend for what you think qualifies as a salary."

Some days, I wonder why I stay. With no work for McCabe's team, my days are constant repetition with little hope of anything even remotely interesting.

Mothers and kids sick with the flu, falls, and repetitive stress injuries, the occasional domestic violence case.

I should have kept my less-than-legal clinic in the Central District. Turned it legit. Done things right. But McCabe told me I had to be available whenever he needed me. So I took the job in South Park. Lambert doesn't care if I disappear in the middle of a shift. Or simply don't show up at all.

I wonder about the woman and her son from last week. Laura and Benjamin. Her boyfriend left her with a black eye and a split lip. Little Benny cried the whole time until Angela brought him a candy bar.

Detective Mitchell showed up before I was done with my examination, but Laura refused to press charges.

Maybe she'll be okay. Maybe she'll leave the asshole before he kills her. Maybe her son will grow up without any more terrifying memories. But I know how these things go—

all too well. Laura's face haunted my dreams last night. Along with so many others. Marie, Reena, Opal, Wendy...and Tessa.

"Doc, I'm sorry."

"You did nothing wrong, sweetheart. Hold on for me. Please."

But she didn't hold on. She couldn't. And I wasn't there to protect her.

The harsh scent of blood fills my nose. Thirty-seven stab wounds. Four broken ribs. A dislocated shoulder, a shattered cheekbone. Two missing teeth. All because she dared to leave him. Dared to fall in love again.

A small dot on the horizon draws me out of my memories, and I start my slow descent toward the marina.

How much longer can I go on like this? McCabe only pulled me in once or twice a month at most, but the mere *possibility* I'd get a call kept me focused. Kept me sober. Kept me alive.

Four months without those calls and yesterday, I found myself in the liquor aisle of the grocery store staring at the bottles of whiskey.

A few nights away from civilization will set me back to rights. It has to.

CHAPTER EIGHT

Natasha

For the first time in months, I park the ATV behind the boathouse at noon on a Monday, trudge up onto the deck, and drop into a chair. I didn't want to come. But I don't have much choice. Gladys is visiting Bella in Seattle, and after Doc didn't show last week, I need to know he's all right.

I shouldn't care. He said everything was fine. That it was just work. Doctors have emergencies that don't involve *them*. But I haven't slept well since he no-showed. Seeing him will settle me, though I can't figure out why.

Because he didn't text you back.

The truth slams into me so fast, my travel mug slips from my hand. It bounces down the boathouse steps, iced coffee painting the wood all the way to the gravel path. Where the insulated mug stops against a dark brown boot.

Oh, God. My cheeks catch fire. I should move, but I'm stuck to the seat like someone painted it with superglue.

"Now that's a shame." Doc slides his rucksack from his

shoulder, leans down, and rescues the mug. "Did you at least get to enjoy *some* of it?"

I can't tear my gaze from the man. A white t-shirt stretches across his barrel chest. He wears a light flannel, the sleeves rolled up to expose his corded forearms. I'm a sucker for forearms.

The memory of his hands on me is still so fresh, even though it's been more than a year since we touched—since we kissed. Since we almost did so much more...

"Nat?" Concern pinches his brows as he climbs the steps and stops in front of me. "Everything okay?"

"F-fine," I stammer and manage to unglue my ass from the seat so we're on the same level. "That was my third cup today. I guess I'm a little jittery."

Doc presses the mug against my palm. He doesn't let go for several seconds, his deep blue eyes searching mine. For what? The truth? Something more?

"It's good to see you." His voice sends a burst of warmth straight to my core. "I'm sorry about last week."

I retreat a step, needing to put some distance between us before I say—or do—something I can't take back. Like tell him how good it is to see him too. Or how sorry I am that I stayed away for so long.

"You should be. You missed out on some damn fine chocolate chip cookies. I had to take them off Gladys's hands for you. It was a major hardship to eat them all."

His smile highlights the tiny lines around his eyes, but it makes him look ten years younger. "I'll have to make it up to you somehow. Any ideas?"

Well, you could take off your shirt and kiss me again.

But I stop myself from saying the words aloud. Instead, I shrug. "I'll give it some thought."

"So where is our girl?" he asks.

"Don't let Gladys hear you call her that. You'll end up

with a batch of sauerkraut next time. Or worse. Lutefisk. She's got some Norwegian in her somewhere." It feels good to joke around with him. Even if I *am* out of practice. "She's in Seattle. Bella's boyfriend proposed, and she asked Gladys to go dress shopping with her."

"Gladys? In a dress?" Doc's laugh is like a warm hug, and I almost step closer.

"You'd be surprised," I say and shove my hands into the pockets of my shorts so I'm not tempted to reach out and touch him. "I've seen pictures. Did you know she used to work in the governor's office? She likes to say she was 'downright respectable' when she was young."

"She mentioned that. But I thought she was pulling my leg."

I drop my gaze. What I wouldn't give to see the man in a pair of shorts. Or...out of them. I bet his thighs are impressive.

Say something! Anything!

Except, I'm still stuck in my fantasy world where we're not strangers but something...more. In that world, I can let myself want all those things I'll never have again. A home. Friends. Someone who knows all my secrets—and loves me anyway.

One beat. Two. Three. Silence can kill—or at least maim—and I have to fill it before I start to bleed emotions all over the place.

If I were braver, I'd tell him about the first time I took Gladys to Anacortes. She'd booked a tattoo appointment and wanted company. Then made me sit with her while the artist spent two hours inking a hydrangea flower *on her ass.*

Instead, I take the coward's way out. "Well, you know where you're going. And you have my number. If you need anything."

The shock on his face as I brush past him cuts deep, and

all those emotions I was afraid of come pouring out of me the second I start the ATV. Dammit.

Seeing him—being close enough to touch him—and walking away was too much. I can't do this anymore. Living in a place that makes me want *more* is harder than being alone. Harder than constantly looking over my shoulder, waiting for one of Bastian's cronies to find me. Harder than watching my brother bleed out in front of me. Because here, I die a little more every single day.

At the end of the season, I'll move on. When I took this job, I thought this tiny island was so far north, maybe I could find some semblance of a home. But I should have known better.

I'll never have a home again.

MY LEGS TANGLE in the sheets as I flop over, seeking a cool part of the pillow. But it's no use. I'm wide awake, despite my exhaustion.

Damn hormones. At least that's what I'm blaming for tonight's insomnia. It's been happening more and more.

My first year on the run, I rarely slept more than a couple hours at a time. Every noise was a potential threat. But slowly, I started to relax. The first time I made it through an entire night, I wept.

And then a few months after my forty-fifth birthday, my sleep started to go to shit. Right along with my cycle. Being a woman sucks sometimes.

I flip the pillow over and draw my legs up close. Why didn't I go for a long swim this afternoon? That would have helped.

Because the best swimming takes you right by Doc's campsite.

My inner voice doesn't pull her punches.

A dull ache thrums through my nipples as they scrape against my t-shirt, and I shudder. Gladys would tell me to get my ass down the hill and strip naked outside Doc's tent. Or inside of it.

But then I'd lose another piece of myself to the handsome doctor. One night—a handful of passionate kisses and some groping—and I've fantasized about him for over a year. If we actually fucked... God.

That single missing piece has already slowed me down. A second? It could stop me completely.

I can't allow that.

"This is fucking ridiculous," I mutter and swing my legs over the side of the bed. "I don't even know him."

Except, I do. Through Gladys.

I begged her to cover for me whenever Doc was scheduled to show up. And she was only happy to do so. Now, I finally realize why.

She was vetting him. For me. And she told me everything.

He used to work in the ER. Now he spends his weekends at a low-cost clinic in Seattle. He loves thrillers and non-fiction, particularly survival stories. He flies up here on a sea plane he bought a couple of years ago. Hates the gym, but loves rock climbing. He's good with his hands. Knows his way around an electrical box. He can play the guitar.

Did she tell him anything about me?

That would require her to know anything about me. Anything real, anyway.

With a huff, I pull on a pair of loose gray pants and pad out to the kitchen for a glass of water.

But standing at the sink is a mistake. Through the trees, I catch a glimpse of Doc's tent at the bottom of the hill.

Anger and frustration start a war inside me. One so violent, I snatch a glass from the cabinet and slam the door.

No amount of self-talk can keep my gaze from the window. Not even when I reach for the faucet.

A face coalesces in the reflection. Dammit. I need sleep. I'm seeing things. But then something glints in the light from the hall. Metal.

Gun!

Whirling around, I throw the glass with everything I have, then drop to my knees behind the counter.

A *thunk* followed by a low, male curse chills the blood in my veins. I can't see the asshole, but he's too close. And armed.

There's no crime on the island. Hasn't been for a decade —according to Gladys. He's here for me. To kill me. I stayed too long, and now, I'm out of time.

Focus!

I have to get to my closet. My Glock is in my go bag. It's the only chance I have.

Glass crunches to my left. I tuck and roll to the right, then come up in a crouch. Another few inches, and I'll have a straight shot to the hallway.

I creep forward until a solid weight slams into me. My head hits the corner of the cabinet. The world goes fuzzy. Gloved fingers wrap around my throat. I can't breathe.

Lungs seizing, I drive my elbow back. His grip loosens enough for me to suck in air. My fist rams something soft. The asshole yelps.

That's right, idiot. Should have worn a cup.

Springing to my feet, I head for the hall, but only make it three steps.

An arm bands around my waist. My feet leave the ground. I'm flying. Until I hit the French doors. Glass shatters, slicing my cheek, my hands, my head.

The cuts burn. I'm dizzy. Rough decking scrapes my arm. I roll, and a shot pierces the night. Fiery pain spreads out from my hip. I can't see through the haze of blood dripping into my eyes.

A plank creaks. Too close. I blink hard. His shadow looms over me. I reach for something—anything—I can use as a weapon.

My entire body turns to ice at the metallic *click* of a hammer. Panic claws its way up my throat. My desperate fingers close around the spout of my watering can. The fancy, heavy one I bought the last time I went to Anacortes with Gladys.

I swing wildly. The metal connects with the man's kneecap. He stumbles. The next shot makes my ears ring.

Scrambling up, I grit my teeth against the pain burning my hip. The motion light winks on—finally—and cold, dark eyes meet mine.

Parker.

A thick scar stretches from his nose down to his jaw. My brother almost killed him eight years ago. If Logan had gotten another inch, the knife would have pierced Parker's carotid. And maybe...I'd still have a family.

The bastard takes a step closer. I back up the same distance. A second step, and he kicks the watering can out of the way. The gun is pointed right at my heart.

"Watch it, asshole. I *like* that can."

My back hits the railing.

"You're going to pay for what you did, Natasha."

"Eight years, and you couldn't come up with anything more original than *that*?" Baiting him probably isn't smart. But I can't help it. His line really was ridiculously cliché.

"I was going to kill you quickly. But now, I think I'll take my time." He shifts his aim lower. "I shot your brother in the stomach. It's a very painful way to die."

"Please," I whimper, cowering against the railing. Throwing him off balance is my only hope.

Confusion flashes in his eyes. It's only a second, but that's enough. The gun barrel wavers, and I vault over the railing as he pulls the trigger.

CHAPTER NINE

Doc

I sit up in the darkness, unsure what woke me. Until a loud *crack* pierces the night.

Who the hell would be shooting up here? That wasn't a hunting rifle. It sounded like a pistol.

Fuck. This island doesn't have a police force. Or any crime for that matter.

I'm out of my sleeping bag in seconds. Pants. Boots. Tactical knife. It's never far from me—even when I sleep— and I use my free hand to slowly unzip the tent flap. Call 911? It'd take them an hour to get here. Maybe more.

I scan the beach. Empty. The cabins are a mile away. But Nat's house...that's so much closer.

My watch face glows in the darkness. It's almost 2:00 a.m. I hold my breath and listen. Nothing out of place. Then again, I don't hear anything at all, and that's a problem. None of the nocturnal creatures in the underbrush. No birds. There's usually an owl or two hooting quietly in the distance.

It's like the entire island knows something's wrong.

A muffled cry carries over the breeze. Did that come from Nat's? I peer up at her house. No lights. No movement that I can see.

Maybe I imagined the whole thing. I was holding Tessa's body in my dreams. That one, terrible night has been haunting me lately. The night everything changed. The night I lost everything.

A woman screams. Nat's in trouble. Fear squeezes my heart in a vise. She's all alone up there.

I take off at a run. This isn't a dream. This is very, *very* real.

Her place is less than a quarter mile away, but the steep hillside is covered with pieces of driftwood, rocks, and shifting, sandy soil. My foot lands wrong, and I go down. Something sharp slices my knee, but I don't care. I have to get to her.

Her house is only a hundred yards away. A dull *thud* sounds from somewhere in the trees. Then another. A branch snaps. Fists land on soft flesh. Again and again and again.

"Why won't you stay down?" a man snaps.

"You...first." Nat's voice is strained. Higher pitched than it should be. Almost...thin. She gasps, then whimpers softly.

I creep closer. Years of training, and I'm still light on my feet. Utterly silent when I need to be. It's second nature, despite being a civilian for more than a decade.

A flash of light and another shot. I'm close now. Thirty yards. Twenty. I can hear Nat's ragged breathing. Uneven footsteps crash through the underbrush. They're on the move. Both of them. Their shadows are so close together. He's almost on top of her.

Gripping the knife like it's an extension of my hand, I focus on Nat's attacker. He doesn't know I'm here. Neither does she. They're too focused on each other. The crescent moon provides just enough light for me to see his outline.

He's built. Bulky, but maybe an inch shorter than I am. Dressed all in black. Nat staggers behind a tree. She's wearing a light blue t-shirt and pale gray pants. Her arms are bare. She can't hide in the darkness like he can.

Tree bark splinters with his next shot. "If I have to chase you again—"

"Fuck you—shit!" Nat yelps as the man grabs her by the hair and throws her to the ground. She tries to roll away, but he aims a swift kick to her stomach.

Retching, Nat curls in on herself.

"You were supposed to die eight years ago, bitch. Say hi to your big brother."

I don't give a shit about stealth now. Not when he jabs the pistol against her temple.

The asshole must hear me a second before I sink the blade into his shoulder. His pained cry is music to my ears. Except I missed the mark. I was going for his neck. His carotid artery to be precise.

Wrenching the knife free, I adjust my grip. He sweeps his leg back and catches me in the shins. Off balance, I only graze his arm. Nat tries to get up, but collapses before she makes it to her feet.

The gunman swings around, ready to fire. But he's losing blood. A lot of it. Maybe enough to be fatal if I can keep him focused on me. Or I'll get to slide the knife across his throat and watch him die.

I tuck and roll, coming up five feet away. "You want a fight? Bring it."

He rushes me. I'm not fast enough to sidestep his tackle. We hit the ground together. The impact drives the breath from my body. A tree branch digs into my back, into the old injury that never fully healed. Two vertebrae pop. My left leg starts to tingle, and for too long, I can't move.

Shit. Fuck. Not now. Not *now!*

"Should have stayed out of it, gramps."

A sliver of moonlight glints off the barrel of the gun as he takes aim. My diaphragm spasms. Air floods my lungs. I rear up, and the knife sinks into the soft flesh of his thigh. His eyes roll back. Dropping the pistol, he scrambles to pull the blade from his body.

Fuck. He's still not going down. My left leg is almost useless, but I aim an uppercut to his balls. A thin cry escapes his lips, and he falls to his knees.

"Respect...your elders...*son*," I grit out.

Asshole still isn't giving up. He fumbles on the ground, then slams a rock into my ribs. The *crack* of bone reverberates through me. For a few seconds, the world turns soft and fuzzy. Nat screams and leaps onto his back. Her fingernails rake down his face, leaving bloody trails on his cheeks. He lets out a roar, staggers to his feet, and slams her back into the closest tree.

She slides to the ground, wheezing.

Pine needles crunch under my fingers. The grip of the gun is sticky with blood. Getting up is harder than it should be. My knee threatens to buckle, but I draw down on the asshole. I'm in too much pain. My first shot goes wide.

I can do this.

The second two hit their mark. The man clutches his chest, turns, and runs.

The fucker just won't die. Was he wearing a vest? I stumble after him, but my leg is still half numb. He crashes through the woods to the west. I follow, but at the top of the hill, my foot lands on some loose brush and I go down. My hands find a pool of blood. So much, I don't know how the asshole isn't dead already.

A low *oof* is followed by a *thud*, and I squint down the hill in the darkness. He's rolling, sliding, falling. All the way to the main road. There's no way he'll survive this.

"Nat?" I pick my way over the uneven ground. "Say something!"

No response. My cracked rib sends sharp pain wrapping around my torso with each breath.

She hasn't moved. "Can you hear me?" I ask as I drop to my knees. Her eyes fly open, and she surges up with my knife clutched in her bloody fingers. I grab her wrist before she can strike. She's stronger than I'd expected. Strong enough I have to use both hands to pry the blade from her grasp. A low, almost feral sound rumbles in her throat a second before she collapses against me.

"I'm not him, Nat. It's Doc." I ease her back down to the ground. If she had a neck injury, she probably wouldn't have been able to attack me like that. But I can't carry her back inside. Not yet. I need to know moving her won't do more damage.

"Squeeze my hand if you can hear me."

Nothing. Shit. Why didn't I grab my ruck?

"Because even without the tent, the damn thing weighs thirty pounds, and I never would have made it up the hill in time," I mutter. Except now, I need it. I never travel without my med kit and sat phone. McCabe might never call me again, but if he does, and I don't answer, someone could die.

With the handle of the knife, I check her reflexes. Knees. Elbows. Good enough.

After shoving the knife into my pocket and the gun into my waistband, I take Nat's arm and ease her up over my shoulders. I don't know if her house is safe, but it's sure as shit better lit and with more resources than out here.

A handful of steps lead up to the back deck. My knee buckles twice, but I manage to stay upright. One of the French patio doors hangs open, shards of glass littering the wood planks. Nat hasn't made a sound, and I pick my way over the mess and through the kitchen to find more broken glass on the other side of the counter.

The house is mostly dark, but light shines from the hall. Enough to see the couch is clear. Laying her down, I weigh the risks of going for my kit. If her attacker isn't dead, I'm leaving her vulnerable. But without it...

When I find the light switch, a lamp on the side table bathes the room in a gentle glow. Fucking hell. Her left cheek is swollen and bruised, the eyelid bright red. A dozen tiny cuts mar her forehead. But she's still so beautiful. Even now.

I skim my fingers through her hair and find bits of glass embedded in her scalp.

Shit. The asshole slammed her head into that door. She's barefoot. Her feet are bleeding. But they're nothing compared to her hip. A dark, red stain blooms over the pale gray pants.

"Nat? I need you to open your eyes."

Taking her hand in both of mine, I start rubbing it vigorously. Her eyelids flutter. "There you go. Look at me." Seconds pass, each one an eternity, until she blinks up at me.

"Doc? You can't be here. Go. Run." She tries to push herself up on an elbow, but I grab her shoulders.

"You need medical attention. My kit is back at my tent. I'm going to go get it, but I want you to answer some questions for me first. Do you know what day it is?"

"Don't have time for this." She twists out of my grasp, sits up, and sways. "Shit."

"You'll make time. Unless you want to pass out on your own and possibly bleed out right here." Even if she spent the next ten minutes calling me every name in the book, I wouldn't leave her like this, but I need her to know I'm serious.

"Is he...dead?" She grabs my biceps, fingers digging into the muscles hard enough to bruise. "If he's not dead, we have to get out of here. Now."

"I shot him twice. *After* I stabbed him. He fell down the embankment behind the house. If he's still walking, he's a fucking zombie."

Nat scowls. "Not good enough." Her lips tighten with pain. "Doc, please. I...we have to leave."

"You're in no shape to get up, baby." I cringe at the term of endearment. I don't have any right, but I can't help it. Did she notice?

"Doesn't matter." She closes her eyes and swallows hard. "If we don't leave, we're dead. We have to get to the marina. You can fly us to the mainland. It's the only way we live through this."

Whoever that asshole is—or was—she's terrified of him. And she needs a hospital. We both do. At least one of my ribs is broken, and my back is seriously fucked.

I pull the pistol from my waistband and eject the magazine. Four bullets left, plus one in the chamber. "You steady enough to fire a gun?"

Nat peers up at me warily. "Yes."

"Stay here and do *not* move. I need my ruck, then we'll go. I'll get us off the island."

Her hands shake as she accepts the Glock, but she grits her teeth and they steady.

"Hurry."

THE FIVE MINUTES it takes me to double time it back to my campsite feel like forever. I don't like leaving her, but what choice did I have? She's convinced we don't have much time, and I'm slow enough as it is with a cracked rib and bum leg.

Once we're in the air, we'll be safe. At least from the shooter and any friends he might have brought with him. But I'll have to fly close to the water. The Coast Guard station in

Anacortes will be monitoring radar. If they see me without a flight plan, they could shoot me down.

I don't bother with the tent, cooler, or lantern, but roll up the sleeping bag and clip it to the bottom of the ruck. It'll be cold in the air, and Nat's lost too much blood.

The trip back up the hill is agony. Nothing can prepare you for the pain of a broken rib. How every shallow inhale sends an electric shock through your torso.

Steps from the deck, a spasm of pain steals my breath, and I go down. Hard. Another crunch comes from my rib. Not good. Nat isn't the only one in trouble here. But I force myself up, dragging the ruck behind me.

It's completely silent when I enter. Something's wrong. She's not where I left her. The house still smells like her though. Flowers and citrus amid the harshness of blood. No other scents.

Something hits the floor down the hall.

"Nat!" I drop the ruck and rush toward the sound. A large duffel bag lies on its side, and she's panting, her hand braced on the wall next to the closet. "I told you not to move."

"I don't take orders from you," she huffs and, with considerable effort, manages to straighten.

"Until we're in the air, you do. You have a car?" I heft the duffel over my shoulder and almost lose my balance. "Shit. If I find a set of dumbbells in here, we're going to have words later."

"You even *look* inside that bag, and we'll have words now." She pushes past me, her steps uneven. "I might need you right now, Doc, but the minute we land in Seattle, I'm gone. And you need to forget you ever met me."

I don't bother telling her there's no fucking way I'm forgetting her *or* letting her disappear. Not with how pale she is. With the sweat dotting her brow. With her obvious battle skills. She's got a history, and I hope she'll share it with me.

The short path to the garage feels like I'm walking through quicksand. I refused to let her carry the bags, and my strength is fading. Fast.

She doesn't have a car, but her ATV has a full tank of gas. I try to slow my breathing as Nat helps strap the bags to the back of the vehicle. That last fall didn't do me any favors. Nat, at least, doesn't appear to be getting any worse.

"Can you hold on to me?" I ask as the ATV sputters to life. "Be honest. How bad off are you?" Cupping her cheek, I make a show of checking her pupils, but I just needed to touch her. To know she's still with me.

She meets my gaze for a long moment. I've only seen that look in her eyes once before. When Gladys fell. She's scared.

"I can hold on. But floor it."

As if I wouldn't.

She settles herself behind me and wraps an arm around my waist. Pain stabs deep from under my arm all the way to my sternum. I can't take a full breath. The garage door rises too slowly. Nat keeps the Glock clutched tightly in her free hand.

"Clear," she says. "Go." I accelerate onto what passes for a road around here and get the vehicle up to speed. Nat's warm weight at my back is reassuring, even as it gets harder and harder to breathe with her arm around me.

We round the final bend. The marina stretches out below us, peaceful and still. Half the berths are empty. In a few days, boats will be tethered to one another six deep. Summer weekends see every campground, cabin, and vacation rental occupied. But for now, there's nothing stopping us from getting the hell off the island.

Easing the ATV to a stop as close to the dock as I can get, I wait for her to slide off the vehicle. I miss her body heat, but I need to be able to take a deep breath. Except, I can't. It's like someone wrapped ropes around my torso.

They're getting tighter and tighter with every passing minute.

Fuck me. The broken rib. The fall. The slight wheeze only I can hear. I could be in real trouble. Air in my chest cavity is collapsing my lung. A pneumothorax can turn fatal fast. It's only a forty-five-minute flight back to Seattle. Will I make it? God, I hope so.

The Cessna bobs gently on the water. I dig the keys out of my ruck and toss them to Nat. "Get in. Stow the bags. I'll... take care of the moorings."

She nods. In the lights dotting the dock, blood glistens along her hip. A rivulet trails down her temple. Head wounds bleed like a son of a bitch, and she has a dozen of them.

My wheezing is getting louder. I can feel my heartbeat in my ears. The thick ropes securing the plane to the dock weigh twice as much as they should.

I toss the first hank through the open door and move to the rear tie down. Before I can finish winding the second rope around my arm, a *crack* shatters the silence of the night. Followed by a metallic *plink* along the wing.

A second shot, then a third hit the fuselage. If we don't get out of here right fucking now, there won't be a plane left to fly.

"He's not...dead!" I shout as I dive through the door. "Stay down!"

Nat's glassy eyes widen. She slides lower in the copilot's seat. "He'll never stop. He'll find me. And you."

I open the throttle, flip the master switch, and turn on the fuel pump. Another shot hits the wing. "Shit." My vision tunnels for a breath. A very strained breath.

"You have a back door on this thing?" Nat asks.

"Baggage...hatch." I jerk my head toward the rear of the plane. She lurches between the seats, drops to her knees, and pulls the gun from her waistband.

I can't worry about her. Not now. Getting the plane in the air is all that matters. Fuel mixture. Beacon light. Ignition.

The propeller starts to spin. Nat gets the baggage door open. A bullet whizzes through the cabin. She takes aim and fires. The plane jerks, then starts to accelerate out of the slip. Another shot hits the opposite wing.

At this rate, we'll be lucky to get out of the marina.

I crane my neck to see out the window. The asshole should have died half an hour ago. All that blood. He staggers down the dock, a rifle aimed right at us.

"Come on. Come on," Nat chants. "A little closer."

I force as much of a breath as I can. "Last...chance."

She fires again. We're close enough, I can see the arterial spray. Kill shot. Right through the throat. The rifle clatters over the wood planks and follows him into the water.

"Close...the door... Unless you're...*sure*...he doesn't...have friends."

"Not sure of anything." Nat slams the hatch shut, locks it, and climbs back into the seat next to me.

Come on, baby. Just a little bit more.

I open the throttle, adjust the flaps, and set the rudder. I can do this. I've done it a hundred times before.

The gentle tug of the water as we lift off is the most reassuring sensation in the world. I turn us south, but as we pass over Lopez Island, the engine starts to sputter.

"Fuck...fuck!" I wheeze. The fuel gauge hovers just over *Empty*. "Asshole...shot the tanks. We're going down."

CHAPTER TEN

Natasha

"Going down? What the hell do you mean 'going down'?"

"Fuel." His voice is strained. He jabs a gauge on the instrument panel. "Seat...belt."

My hands shake as I stretch the harness across my body. Doc wheezes, easing the stick back. The plane starts to descend, and the motor whines in protest.

We're going to stall. I squint into the darkness. The moon is all but gone now, hidden behind a thick stretch of clouds. How high are we?

Doc adjusts the flaps, flips a few switches on the panel, and clenches his jaw, hard. His chest stutters with a weak cough.

"Doc? What's wrong? What...*else* is wrong?"

"Not...now." He white-knuckles the controls until the engine cuts out completely. I expect the bottom to drop out of my stomach. But instead, it feels like...nothing. Or maybe that's my panic.

It's almost completely silent other than Doc's wheezing. The plane touches down with the gentlest of skids—like a car hydroplaning on a wet road.

"Is that...it?" I ask.

"Yeah." Doc leans back in his seat. Sweat dots his brow. "But...we're...fucked. Or...I am." His fingers tremble as he tugs at the neck of his black t-shirt.

"What's wrong? Are you hit?" I smooth my hands over his chest until he grabs my wrist and hisses in pain.

"Pneumo...thorax."

I don't know what that is, but it sounds serious. Glancing around the interior of the plane, I zero in on a life raft and oars strapped to the rear wall. "We can row to shore. I'm okay. I can get us there."

"And then...what?" Doc glances at his watch. "Doubt... there will be...anyone...around this time...of night. I won't last...more than another...hour. Maybe less."

"An hour?" This man saved my life. Parker was seconds away from putting a bullet in my brain when Doc stabbed him. "There has to be something we can do."

"We're...in the middle...of the goddamn Sound. No fuel."

"Radio?" It's a stupid idea. They probably couldn't even get here in time. And when they arrive—if they arrive at all— I'm fucked. They'll demand my name—my *real* name—and I'll be in the system faster than I can give them my rank and serial number.

"Too...risky." He's getting worse. Each breath shallower. His cheeks are pale. "Need you...to put in...a chest tube."

"I can't do that! I'm not a doctor!" There's no way he should trust me with anything more than a couple of stitches. Somewhere *not* vital.

Doc reaches for my hand and gives my fingers a weak squeeze. "Trust me. If I...could do it myself...I would. But...in a few minutes...I won't be able...to breathe...at all." He tries to straighten, but his eyes crinkle with pain. "I can get...us out of here. If...I live long enough."

"How?"

He punches a button on the instrument panel, and a gentle splash sounds from outside. "The anchor," he says. "Help me...and I'll tell you."

For a brief moment, I wonder if I should take the life raft and go without him. Paddle the eight or ten miles to shore and disappear. But I can't have another death on my conscience. Especially not *his*. He's a good man. A man I *care about*.

"Tell me what to do."

With a grunt, Doc pushes himself up. He sways on his feet, then staggers over to his rucksack. "Lay out...the sleeping bag."

I shove the tie down ropes aside to make room while he unzips his bag. "Why? What's this going to do?"

"Probably...gonna pass out...after," he manages. "Floor's... cold."

Logical. God, I hope he knows what he's doing.

"You're not making me feel any better, Doc." Neither is his medical kit. It's stocked better than most clinics I've been to. Several scalpels, clamps, a bag of saline, half a dozen different vials, a suture kit, bandages, pills, an inhaler, and an epipen. And that's just the first layer.

"Doc? Or hell...that can't be your real name. What is it?"

He lands on his ass on the sleeping bag, his eyes almost closed.

"Talk to me. Please."

"Gage," he says with a grimace. "My first name...is really... Gage."

"Gage?" I almost manage a laugh. "That's one of the

sexiest names I've ever heard, and you tell everyone your name is Doc?" This isn't the time for inappropriate humor, but it's all I've got. Instead of taking the words back, I double down. "If it weren't for all this," I say, gesturing to the medical kit, "I'd have a hard time believing you were smart enough to graduate medical school."

"Have...my reasons." Doc—Gage—reaches into his rucksack and withdraws a satellite phone. "If I'm out...for more than five minutes...there's one...number saved. Tell...the guy...who answers...he owes me...for the last time."

I don't have time to dwell on his mysterious words because he strips off his t-shirt, and I get my first good look at his bare chest.

A smattering of white hair spreads across his defined pecs, but it's the bruises that send a ball of ice sinking in my stomach. Some are already dark red. Others still pink.

I knew Parker was beating the shit out of him when I came to, but they'd obviously been going at it for more than a few seconds.

Gage—or does he prefer Doc?—tears an antiseptic package open with his teeth, then swipes it over his side from his arm all the way to his waist. A second pad cleans the scalpel, one end of the tubing, and finally, his fingers.

"Take this," he says, pressing the scalpel into my palm before collapsing onto the sleeping bag and feeling along his ribs until he finds the worst of the bruising. "Make a deep cut...right here."

I swallow hard. "There has to be another way."

"Isn't." His voice is getting weaker. The pauses between his words longer. Most of the color has fled from his skin. "You'll know...when you've hit...the right spot. Tube...goes in. Tape it down."

His eyes drift closed. Fuck. No. I can't lose him too. Mom. Dad. Chris. Logan.

Doc and Gladys are the only two people left in this world I care about.

"Gage? Doc! Look at me!" His lips are blue. His chest is barely moving. Little starts and stops. "Please don't die on me," I whisper.

I press the scalpel to the spot between his ribs. It slides in easily. I expected it to be like cutting a steak. Not...a stick of butter.

Blood trickles down his side. Too much. "How will I know? You didn't tell me *how* I'd know."

The harsh, coppery scent burns my nose. Too many memories.

Logan's blood running over my hands. His eyes, staring up at me, shimmering with tears. The way his mouth moved but no sound came out. My sobs when I knew he was gone.

I take a deep breath to try to still the tremble in my fingers before I push deeper. The plane bobs gently on the water, and I have a blade an inch deep *in a man's chest.*

What if I cut something...vital? What if my hand starts to shake too much? Or the wind picks up? Is this far enough? He's barely breathing. If I kill him...

Cool fingers cover mine. Thank God. He's still alive. Still conscious. He doesn't make a sound—I'm not sure he can— but pushes down, forcing the scalpel even deeper. I feel a pop, then hear a hiss of air before his hand falls away.

"Doc? Please. Come back to me!" For the first time in years, I start to pray.

The blue tinge to his lips disappears. He's no longer struggling for each breath. I almost drop the tubing twice—my fingers are so slick with his blood—but eventually wedge one end into the gash and tape it to his side.

Wiping my hands on my light gray pants, I try to calm my racing heart. "Is that enough?" He's so still. Only the slow rise and fall of his chest give me any comfort. What if I did it wrong? What if he dies anyway?

The seconds stretch into minutes. How long until I have to call the number on that phone? Will the man on the other end even come if Doc isn't awake—or alive—to ask him? And how will he find us?

I'm about to reach for the phone when Doc groans softly. Linking our fingers, I squeeze gently. "Open your eyes. Please?"

"Working...on it," he whispers. Another sound—more of a grunt this time—and he focuses on me. "Clamp. End...of the tube. Now."

I fumble for the springy metal, then secure the clamp around the part of the tube furthest from his body. "Like that?"

"Just...like that." He lets his head fall back against the sleeping bag with a sigh.

"You'll be okay now?" I hate how pitiful I sound, then again, I did just perform some sort of demented surgery on him while we float in the middle of the Sound on a downed plane.

"Fucker...broke my rib. It caused...a pneumothorax. Collapsed my lung. The tube...will keep me breathing. For a while."

"A while? *A while?* How long is that?" Shit. He's not reassuring me. If anything, I'm more scared now than when Parker had a gun to my head.

"Long enough. If McCabe answers the phone." His voice is getting stronger, but he closes his eyes and shudders. "Hurts like...a son of a bitch."

"Do you have something in your kit I can give you?" One of those vials has to be a painkiller.

"Not yet." Doc grimaces, the muscles of his neck straining

as he tries to lift his head. "Need to stay focused. But...hand me...the phone."

Doc

The hole in my chest burns. I need supplemental oxygen, antibiotics, stitches...and morphine. But if I give myself a shot now, I might not be alert enough to keep myself alive. Or convince McCabe to come for us.

One ring. Two.

"This better be a goddamned emergency, Doc. It's the middle of the night, and the last time we spoke, I told you to go fuck yourself."

Anger prickles over my skin. If this weren't life and death —*my* life and death—I'd call someone else. *Anyone* else. I'd like to rip McCabe a new one. But I can't. Not yet.

"Some asshole...shot my fuel tanks. Plane went down. South of Lopez Island. Need medical. Soon."

A baby wails in the background, and McCabe's wife starts to sing some nonsense song about the moon and rainbows to calm the kid down.

"Define soon."

"Not...a fucking...dictionary. Look it up."

"For fuck's—fudge's—sake, Doc. Can the SEAL take a boat to your location or does he need to get a helo?"

Next to me, Nat jerks, then mouths, *"A helo?"*

If I weren't so bad off, I'd chuckle at the shock in her eyes.

"Doc? I need an answer. It'll be thirty minutes for the helo. Plus however long it takes Raelynn to get to Boeing Field and fuel up. A little under an hour for the RHIB."

A spasm of pain rolls through me, and my vision tunnels.

"Had to...walk Nat...through putting in...a chest tube. My lung could...collapse again any minute. Send...the helo."

"Roger that," Ryker says, all business, like I didn't just wake him up from a sound sleep and demand he save a dying man he hates. Hell, he didn't even ask who Nat was. "Keep your phone on. I'll call you back when they're close."

He hangs up before I get a chance to say thank you. Or anything at all.

CHAPTER ELEVEN

Natasha

"Who *was* that?" For five full minutes, I've been trying to work up the courage to ask, though I'm not sure I truly want to know.

Doc tries to roll onto his uninjured side, but hisses out a breath and stops. "Fuck, that hurts. I'll take...a little of that morphine...now."

"How much?" I check each one of the clear vials until I find the one he needs.

"Four milligrams. In my upper arm." He's shivering, so once I give him the shot, I stretch out next to him. Gently, I ease his arm around my shoulders and rest my head on his shoulder.

"Is this okay?" The last thing I want to do is cause him more pain. It's getting colder out here. He's not wearing a shirt, and I'm only in short sleeves and thin pajama pants. The blood soaking the material from my hip is no longer warm, and pretty soon, we'll both be in trouble. The lights are still on, but the heater cut out with the engine.

He nods, and I reach up to link our fingers.

"So...about the guy you called...?" He never answered my question, and I need to know before these men come and take me to the nearest police station.

"McCabe was Special Forces. He runs a K&R firm...in Seattle. I used to...help them out sometimes. Enough they won't leave me out here."

Shit. Special Forces. If this McCabe gets a whiff of who I am, my life could be over. Hell, even if doesn't, I'm compromised. Parker found me. That means Bastian knows where I am. I have to get the fuck away from Doc. And everyone I've ever known.

"Nat?" Doc coughs weakly. "What's wrong?"

"Nothing." I force myself to relax, hoping he won't press me.

"I'm depending on you, baby," he whispers. "You're the only one who...can keep me alive. Tell me the truth."

Shit. This man is much more perceptive than I gave him credit for. Even hopped up on morphine.

"Someone just tried to kill me. We're in the middle of Puget Sound, and I just cut a hole in your side. That's not enough to be upset about?"

I didn't lie. Not technically. All of that *is* true.

"Do you have a record?" he asks.

"No! Why the hell would you think that?" I start to pull away, but Doc is holding my hand tightly. Gripping it. Like he's desperate for the contact. I get the sense he doesn't *need* much. From anyone. But right now, he needs me. So I relax—or try to—and return my cheek to his chest.

"Because you tensed...when I said Special Forces."

Of course, he'd pick up on that. In eight years, my poker face hasn't gotten any better.

"They're going to deliver me straight to the nearest police station. I killed a man. And I almost killed *you*."

"McCabe and his team...they're the good guys. They won't..." His voice fades away, his eyes closing once more. I don't try to keep him talking. I can't. Those four words shattered my control.

I killed a man.

It doesn't matter that I killed hundreds in my almost twenty years in the army—directly and indirectly. Dozens of firefights. RPGs. Drone strikes executed on intel from my team.

Parker is the only man I've killed out of uniform. It doesn't matter that it was him or me. Him or *both* of us. That doesn't make it right.

Nothing about this situation is *right*. Bastian was supposed to be one of "the good guys" too. Same with Collins. Sutton. Doherty. Bowen. I trusted them, and they took everything from me.

Will Doc's "good guys" do the same?

I almost get up half a dozen times. My gaze keeps drifting to the bright red life raft strapped to the rear of the plane with the blue and white paddles.

If I leave now, I can make it to shore in an hour. But then what? My feet are bloody inside my boots, and my hip is on fire. There's a whole drum section playing against the inside of my skull. A concussion? Probably.

Pressed to my side, Doc still shivers. He needs me. And right now, I need him too.

My eyelids are so heavy. I'm almost floating. But not. My limbs don't want to move. Even my fingers feel sluggish. You're not supposed to sleep with a concussion though. Right?

Doc coughs weakly.

"You're okay," I say softly. "Just breathe."

"How long...has it been?"

I tighten my fingers on his and angle his hand to see his

wrist. "Twenty minutes. I'll get you some water." Carefully, I extricate myself from his hold and dig in his rucksack until I find a canteen.

He takes a couple of sips, but he's so pale. There's less blood than I expect when I check his side, but what if he's bleeding internally?

"Your friends will be here soon," I say, hoping I'm right.

"McCabe isn't a friend. It's...complicated."

"Sounds like a story I need to hear. And we're stuck for now. So..."

Doc shakes his head, then grimaces. "Not mine to tell. McCabe would kill me."

I'm not sure I want to meet this McCabe. I hope the others with him are less inclined toward murder.

Doc is restless, shifting his legs on the sleeping bag, flexing his fingers like he needs something to grab onto. But when he tries to push up on an elbow, I plant my hand on his chest and hold him in place. His heart thumps steadily under my palm. "Stay down, Doc."

"Can't just...lie here."

"Yes. You can. You're just proving that the clichés are true. Doctors make terrible patients." He's not the only one who's shivering now, and I slide back down to share my body heat. "Well, here's a different question. Why don't you go by Gage?"

He grimaces and turns his head away. "Ask me anything else."

"Nope. This is what I want to know. You made me cut a hole in your chest. I'm bruised from head to toe, and I probably have a concussion. Humor me."

With a sigh, Doc reaches for my hand. His tight grip reassures me. "Gage Reynolds was my father."

"So you're Gage Junior?" The smile tugs at my swollen lip, and I wince.

"No." He practically snarls the word. "I legally changed my name thirty years ago. I'm Doc now."

"I'm sorry...Doc. I shouldn't have—" The satellite phone buzzes, the sound muffled against the dark gray carpet, but it's so quiet out here with no engine noise, that it startles us both.

"You close?" Doc asks when I flip the switch and put the call on speaker.

"West, Raelynn, and Graham are five miles out. Be ready to move," the rough voice says.

"Gonna need some help with that." After a pause, he adds, "McCabe?"

I check the phone. "He hung up on you."

"Fucker." He squeezes his eyes shut. "Open the door. They'll...need to get in." Once again, he tries to push himself up, but the tube, tape, and pain conspire against him. His boots scrape over the sleeping bag but fail to find purchase.

"Stay still. That's an order," I snap and climb into the front seat to unlatch the door. The steady *thump, thump, thump* of the helicopter blades gets closer, but they must be running dark, because I can't see a damn thing.

After another minute, the smooth surface of Puget Sound turns choppy, and the wind picks up so dramatically, it whips my hair into my eyes.

It's too rough. I lunge for the seatbelt and wind it around my hand three times so I don't tumble into the water. I glance back at Doc. The motion can't be doing him any good. His eyes are closed again. Shit.

A dark shadow streaks across the sky, slows, and hovers directly above us. I squint. Is that a person balancing on the helicopter's skids? The end of a rope splashes into the water next to the plane. I blink, and there's a man hanging just in front of me.

"Shit!" I scramble back, my heart in my throat.

"Who the hell are you, and where's the Doc?" the man asks as he raises his night-vision goggles.

"He's inside. I'm Nat. I...uh...run the campground on Blakely." It's the truth. Well, part of it, anyway.

"Well, Nat...I'm Graham. Permission to come aboard?" From the look in his eyes, it's not a question, but I nod and rush back to Doc's side.

Graham clips a carabineer around the rope, then climbs in after me. "Hey, Doc. Got yourself in some trouble?"

"Nah. This is...my idea...of a vacation," he manages. "Can't you see...my tan?" He's starting to wheeze again. Tears prick at my eyes. If he doesn't make it back to Seattle, I'll never forgive myself.

Graham takes a knee next to Doc and examines the tube and my terrible scalpel skills. "Next time, get yourself some higher SPF. Maybe you won't burn a hole in your side."

"Fuck you," Doc says. "Get us out of here."

Us.

"Well, your bedside manner seems to be intact," Graham says with a grim smile. "Is it safe to move you?" The young man presses two fingers to Doc's carotid artery.

"You don't," Doc grits out, "I'm gonna die out here. Just... watch the tube.""

Graham touches his ear. "West? I need the litter. You're going to want to take a look at Doc before we move him."

"West?" I ask.

"He calls the shots," Graham says as he climbs back over the front seats and peers out the door. "And he's our field medic."

I stay out of the way as West—he's older and leaner than Graham—maneuvers a bright orange backboard with half a dozen straps into the small cabin.

He's as shocked to see me as Graham was. Steely blue

eyes unnerve me, and I shrink back against the cold metal wall.

"West, that's Nat. Nat, that's West. Former Navy SEAL and all around badass," Graham says.

West gives me the once-over. "You injured?"

Before I can tell him no, Doc clears his throat. "Probable concussion. Shot to her thigh. Cranial lacerations—"

"I'm *fine*. You're the one with the hole in his chest." My voice cracks, and I stare down at my hands. They're still stained with Doc's blood.

The SEAL pulls a harness from a small pack at his waist. "Put this on while I secure the Doc. Unless you've never used one of these before?"

"I got it." Dammit. From the look on his face, I probably should have played dumb. How many civilians know how to put on a full hoist harness?

West rummages through his pack until he finds a thick roll of stretchy tape. "Sit him up," he tells Graham. "We need to make sure that tube doesn't come out in transport."

The two work together, winding the bright blue gauze around Doc's chest half a dozen times. With each pass they make over the tube, Doc looks worse, until I'm about to yell at them to stop.

"You doin' okay, Doc?" West asks when they finish.

"Hell...no. Hurts like a motherfucker." The words are too weak. Too slow.

West cracks a wry smile. "Just be grateful we didn't come by boat. The ride back would be miserable." He moves to Doc's feet. "On three. Roll him onto his right side."

The SEAL slides the litter under Doc's body. He and Graham work in tandem, covering Doc with a blanket, then securing one strap after another over his shins, thighs, waist, and chest. By the time they're done, I don't think Doc can move at all.

"Got an anchor on this thing?" Graham asks as West climbs back out of the plane and the two position the litter across the two front seats.

"Already dropped." Pain roughens Doc's tone. "Not gonna matter. I'm...in the middle of a shipping lane. Someone'll have her...towed by morning. Or...sink her."

Graham chuckles. "Doc, we're a full-service rescue operation." He winks at me. God, the ladies must love him. He's got that wholesome, boy-next-door look about him, with the muscles of a fighter. "Kidnap and ransom, rescue, retrieval, pet sitting, housecleaning, window repair...and towing."

The rope jerks twice, and Graham pats Doc's shoulder. "Up you go."

The litter slides out of the plane, leaving me with a sense of loss I'm wholly unprepared for. Suddenly, everything hurts. I'm a little dizzy and sink down onto the floor next to a pool of Doc's blood.

"You're next," Graham says. "Nat?" The young man offers me his hand. I stare at it for so long, worry furrows his brow. "You're worse off than you let us believe. What hurts the most?"

My heart.

"I'll live. Doc needs us to go. Right now."

I let Graham pull me to my feet, blinking hard to force away the darkness creeping along the edges of my vision.

He eyes me, his gaze lingering on my hip. And the strap digging into the wound. Much longer, and I won't be able to hide the pain. I focus on the goosebumps covering my arms and the cold air tousling my hair.

After what feels like forever, the young man nods. "Okay, then. Got to get you clipped in." He snags my duffel bag. "This yours?"

Lunging, I snatch it from his hands and clutch it to my chest. "I need that."

"Wasn't suggesting we leave it behind. But I can take it up for you. Along with Doc's ruck."

"No." I can't let that bag out of my sight. If anyone gets a look at the passports, the wads of cash, and the pistol inside, they'll know I'm not who I say I am.

Plus, my favorite sweater's in there. My *only* sweater now. I'll never see the house on Blakely with the rest of my clothes again.

"I mean, I can get it. You have enough to deal with," I say. "Thank you."

He stares me down for a long moment, but then cups his ear. "Roger that. Sending Nat up in sixty." Helping me over the seats, he reaches for the rope with one hand, and the carabiner on my harness with the other. "Fair warning...it's going to be bumpy. And loud."

I almost tell him I've jumped out of a perfectly good helicopter before. Dozens of times, actually. But that would raise more questions, and once we get to Seattle, I need them to let me go. Or at least not care that I disappear.

CHAPTER TWELVE

Natasha

THE WIND WHIPS my hair into my eyes and stings my cheeks. Or maybe that's the fear prickling along my skin. West hangs out of the helo, ready to grab the harness as soon as my head is level with the skids.

I land on the deck of the Black Hawk. My legs won't quite hold me, and I'm on my ass the second he unclips the carabiner from the D-ring.

Crawling over to Doc, I catch the gaze of the pilot. Blond. Beautiful. And pissed. At me.

The helicopter wobbles in the air, and West shouts, "Keep her steady!"

The woman turns her focus back to the controls. "I'm tryin'. Someone needs to light a fire under Graham's ass. The wind's pickin' up!"

"He's packing up Doc's kit and securing the plane. Ry would tear us a new one if he left the sat phone behind." West levels his stare at me. "You. Get in the jump seat and strap in. Now."

I want to stay with Doc. To dig his hand out from under the emergency blanket and hold on tight. But the former SEAL has a look that warns me he's ready for a fight and he never loses. It's only a little after 3:00 a.m. These people got up in the middle of the night, commandeered a helicopter, and few all the way from Seattle to save our asses. I'm not going to argue with them.

Doc gives me a nod. *"It's okay,"* he mouths. He's too weak to shout over the roar of the blades cutting through the air.

God, I hope so. It's another five minutes before West helps Graham back onto the deck, and the pilot turns us around.

"Take these," Graham shouts and hands me a heavy pair of headphones with a built-in mic as well as a thin, gray blanket. Now that the adrenaline has worn off, I'm a solid block of ice. "We'll be back in Seattle in twenty minutes. Raelynn knows how to get the most out of this bird."

Raelynn. That's the pilot. She keeps stealing glances at Doc, and the look in her eyes...she's worried.

"Doc, you hang on. If you die on us, I'm gonna be pissed," she calls back to him.

He's struggling to breathe again, but the look in his eyes is almost...nostalgic. He has a history with these people. He cares about them. And I think they care for him too.

My eyes burn. How far are we from a hospital? *Any* hospital? If he doesn't make it, will our three rescuers have any reason not to murder me? Or turn me in?

I huddle under the blanket, watching West and Graham do their best for Doc. The younger man fits him with a mask hooked up to a small canister of oxygen, and West keeps an eye on the pulse-ox monitor clipped to his thumb.

"What happened?" West asks, staring me down like he can see right through me. "Besides someone beating the shit out of both of you."

"Break-in," I offer. "The guy had a gun. I fought him, but

he got a shot off. Well, a couple of them. Doc heard it and came to help."

On the deck between me and the SEAL, Doc shakes his head and calls West's name.

"You're in no condition to talk. Not this far from the hospital," West says and rests his hand on Doc's shoulder.

His eyes crinkle with pain. "Dead body...at the marina. Went...into the water. Need you...to take...care of it."

"Fuck." West glances at Graham, then turns back to me. "Who killed the guy?"

Before I can admit the truth, Doc wheezes, "I did."

The look on West's face...he doesn't believe it. But he's not going to call Doc on it. Not now. "I'll wake Inara and Wyatt. Landing this bird on the island would be difficult. And loud. They can take a boat and be there before sunrise."

He pulls a cell phone from the pocket of his tactical vest. His fingers fly over the screen, and I wish I knew what he was saying to these other people I've never met.

"We're seven minutes out," Raelynn calls.

West fiddles with his mobile again, and after a minute, whoever he dialed must pick up.

"Wright? This is West Sampson. I need that favor we talked about." There's a pause, and he shakes his head. "No. You listen. Get a trauma team to the helipad in the next five minutes and make sure they don't ask any questions. We're about to drop off a patient with a field-treated pneumothorax."

Holy shit. He has a contact at the hospital who can do that?

His expression hardens. "Your medical assistant *drugged* a pregnant woman so she could be kidnapped from your office. You're lucky you're still practicing medicine at all. Do it, or my next call is to the hospital administrator. How happy do you think he's going to be if I wake him up this early and tell him all about it?"

He swears under his breath as he shoves the phone back into his pocket. "We're going to need a better *in* at the hospital after this." His cold gaze lands on me. Shit. This man could probably kill me in under ten seconds and not break a sweat. "You stay in the helo," he says. "I have more questions that need answers."

Sweat dampens my palms, and I hug my duffel to my chest. "I—"

"She comes with me," Doc says weakly. "Non... negotiable."

"Doc, we just airlifted you from the middle of the fucking Sound at 3:00 a.m. You have a hole in your chest, and you've both been beaten to shit. Not to mention the dead body. The favors we called in for this...the ones we'll *keep* calling in..."

"Non-negotiable," he repeats. "You want to talk...about favors?" His gaze flicks to Raelynn. "She's alive. So is Cara. Hope. Quinton."

Graham sucks in a breath and turns to the SEAL. "I'll stay with them until you're back."

"You have to take care of Doc's plane."

The younger man shakes his head. "I can do that from here. I've got a contact at the Coast Guard station in Anacortes. He'd love a little action."

"A little action?" Raelynn chuckles as the helicopter sinks smoothly toward the helipad on the roof of the hospital. "Did *you* get a little action with him before you met Q?"

Graham's cheeks turn bright red. "No! He's not gay. Even if he were, he's not my type. Too over-the-top gym bro."

"Focus," West snaps. "Not a fucking word to the trauma team." He arches his brows and stares me down. "You stick to Graham like glue. He gives you an order, you take it."

I nod. Can he see it in my eyes? That I'm going to run the first chance I get?

The skids touch down, and within seconds, Doc's on a gurney, the trauma team rushing him through the automatic doors and into an elevator.

Graham keeps his hand at the small of my back as we wait for the car to return to the roof. "They'll take care of him," he says, as much to himself as to me. "When we get to triage, let me do the talking."

"I don't need a doctor."

He narrows his eyes at me. "And I work with the Tooth Fairy, the Easter Bunny, and Santa Claus. Try again."

"Okay, fine. I can get by with a couple of aspirin and a clean pair of pants."

"Be honest, and I'll get you both of those things. *After* you see a doctor."

I sag against the back wall of the elevator as Graham punches the button for the main floor. "A guy broke into my house and shot me. Then slammed my head through a glass door and beat the crap out of me."

Graham whistles, takes my right hand, and examines my knuckles. "You fought pretty hard."

"Didn't plan on dying tonight. Err. This morning." I wrap my arms around myself tightly, hoping Graham won't press me any further. He's too perceptive. And though there's kindness in his green eyes, I don't know him at all.

The doors slide open with a *ding*. The ER waiting room is quiet, only a handful of people slouching in chairs. Graham curls his hand around my elbow and pulls me with him to the triage desk.

"Excuse me. My sister was mugged. She needs to be seen." He leans in and lowers his voice. "Dr. Wright is my neighbor. She said you could get us back ASAP. Without all the usual...fuss."

The nurse pauses for a beat, then sighs. "I'll buzz you through. Bring your sister back and we'll get you in a room."

A LITTLE AFTER 6:00 a.m., I pull on a clean pair of scrubs. Nat Templeton—that's apparently Graham's last name—has seven fresh stitches in her hip and another half dozen in her scalp. The doctor wanted to admit me and give me a CT scan, but I refused, and thank God, Graham didn't force the issue. I have a prescription for antibiotics, but the pharmacy doesn't open for another two hours.

Graham knocks as I reach for my boots. "Nat, if you're decent, we can head upstairs to wait for word on Doc."

I peer out from behind the privacy drape. "You don't need to wait for me. I'm...not moving all that well."

"West would kick my ass. And Doc would never forgive me if I let anything *happen* to you."

Shit. He knows I'm going to run.

"I promise I'll be up in a few minutes."

The kindness fades from his eyes. "We don't say those words unless we mean them."

"Well, maybe it'll take me ten or fifteen. Everything hurts—"

"'I promise.'"

Oh.

"You do what we do," he says, "you learn to read people. I don't know what your story is. And until West gets back, I won't press you for it. Doc wants you with him, and that's all that matters right now."

I nod, then regret the motion as the room spins around me. Graham wraps an arm around my waist and helps me into a chair.

"Who is he to you?" I ask when I no longer feel like I'm about to pass out.

"He patches us up when we need it. Most of what we do isn't as simple as pulling people out of a downed sea plane."

"Rescuing us was simple?" I choke back a laugh.

Graham cracks a smile. "Relatively. We didn't have to sneak past border security, pay off a foreign government to look the other way, or find electrical power in the middle of the jungle."

"Who were the other names Doc mentioned?" Gingerly, I reach for one of my hiking boots. "Besides the pilot. Q? Cara?"

"Family. Q—Quinton—is my partner." Graham pulls out his phone and taps the screen. A man with light brown hair grins back at us, an orange cat in his lap. "Don't tell West—or Ryker—I showed you that photo."

"Why did you?" I take my time with the laces. My fingers ache, and it lets me steal glances at Graham.

He pushes to his feet, standing between me and the door. "Like I said, I read people. Beyond treating us off the books, Doc doesn't lie. The man is about as straight and narrow as they come. Yet he trusts you enough he's willing to do it for you. That raises a lot of questions we need answered. But it also means I can probably trust you too."

I scramble for something—anything—to say. But after a breath, he holds out his hand.

"You don't have to talk to me now. Hell, you don't have to talk to me at all. But since we both know your attacker wasn't a random burglar, consider me your bodyguard until West gets back. Surgery is on the fifth floor. I'm sure they'll be done with Doc soon, and he's going to want to see you when he wakes up."

It only takes another half an hour before a doctor in light green scrubs pushes through the double doors that hide the surgical wing. "Mr. Templeton?" the woman calls.

"That's me." Graham rises. *This could be my chance. I only need a few seconds of distraction to bolt. I hope.* But he doesn't leave my side, waiting instead for the doctor to cross to us.

"Dr. Reynolds is in recovery. He'll have a chest tube for the next twelve to twenty-four hours, but assuming no complications, he can be discharged sometime tomorrow. He was lucky. Whoever treated him saved his life." She gives Graham a pointed stare, but he doesn't react. With an exasperated sigh, the doctor shakes her head. "Fine. Don't tell me. I only risked my entire medical license when I treated the very obvious *bullet wound* to his upper arm. One of the nurses will come get you in a few minutes."

She stalks back through the doors with a huff. All the tension I've held since the second Parker showed up in my kitchen melts away.

I collapse back into the chair, and my tears finally start to fall.

CHAPTER THIRTEEN

Doc

I'M LOST in the dark. Can't fight my way back to where I need to be. Voices pierce the silence, but they're too muffled. I can't understand the words. There's something I need. *Someone* I need. Where is she?

Where am I?

"Doc."

The single, breathy word is my anchor in the storm. I'm floating. Light and shadow, soft sounds that linger in a sea of confusion.

But that word cuts through the fog.

"I'm sorry." Lips brush mine. A light caress flits over my cheek. Something presses to my palm, and then there's a tug over my heart.

Alarms start to blare. People shout. I'm jostled, rough hands moving over me. My chest. My arms. The clamor fades, replaced by the steady beat of a heart rate monitor. And a single voice I recognize. Not hers.

"Nat! Get back here! Dammit!"

I force my eyes open in time to catch a glimpse of Graham racing down the hall.

Nat's citrus and floral scent still lingers in the room. But when I feel the smooth ridges of the sea glass heart under my fingers, I know. She's gone.

THE CLICK of the door drags me from the hazy cloud I'm floating on. I refused the last dose of pain meds, but there's still enough coursing through my system to keep me from staying awake for more than an hour at a time.

"You look like shit, Doc."

I blink hard until Ryker McCabe's scarred face comes into focus. I almost don't recognize him. The bags under his eyes could hold a week's worth of clothes. I've never seen the man in anything but all black, and today is no exception. It's almost laughable. He could walk right onto the set of any action movie and fit right in. If it weren't for the bright yellow baby sling with his three-month-old strapped to his chest. And the diaper bag slung over his shoulder.

It's the change to his demeanor that's truly jarring, though. He's at peace, and I don't think I've ever seen that before.

Wren, his wife, slips through the door behind him. "Is she still sleeping?"

"Of course. She likes it in here." He pats the baby's back gently, and Wren scowls.

"Well, then you're wearing her for the rest of the day. I need some sleep once we get home." She offers me a wan smile. "Hey, Doc. Harlow's teething. It's been a rough couple of weeks."

Harlow. So that's what they named her. Wisps of red hair

peek out from under Ryker's massive hand where he cups the back of the little girl's head.

"So," he says once Wren sinks into the visitor's chair and pulls out her tablet. "Want to tell me why I had to finance a rescue operation in the middle of the fu—fudging—night for you and a woman who rabbited the first chance she got?"

In a word? No. I don't want to tell the man a thing. But he saved my ass. I owe him my life.

"I don't know." At his snort, I sit up a little straighter. The chest tube catches on the hospital gown, and I hiss out a breath. "It's...the truth."

"Breathe, Doc." Wren touches my arm, concern in her green eyes. "Do you need me to get a nurse?"

"Fuck, no."

"Language," Ryker snaps. "If I can watch mine, you can sure as shipping lanes watch yours."

"Sure as shipping lanes?" Chuckling is a mistake. Then again, my entire life feels like a mistake right about now.

"I'm working on variations." One corner of his mouth twitches into what might be his version of a smile. "Wren vetoed shifter though. Said it sounded too much like—"

"I get the idea. Fine. Shipping lanes. Fudge. Gosh darn it."

"Goldilocks." Wren grins. "Though if we ever read her that story, she's going to be really confused."

Ryker scoffs. "I have better stories."

I can't imagine the man's stories involve anything other than murder and mayhem, but then again, I never expected to see him with a baby in his arms either.

"Back to the matter at hand," he says, his voice taking on the grave tone I'm used to. The one that warns he won't accept bullshit from anyone—especially not me.

With a sigh, I turn my gaze out the window. The sun shines brightly, and a stand of pine trees sways gently in the breeze. It's barely noon. Nat's been gone for five hours. She could be on a plane by now. Hell, she could be in Canada. I reach under the blanket for the piece of sea glass and rub my fingers over the ridges.

"I camp up on Blakely every few weeks. Been going up there for a year or so. Last night, I was asleep in my tent when I heard gunshots. I investigated."

"And almost got yourself killed." Ryker shakes his head. "You've been out of the game too long to play the action hero, Doc."

"I was holding my own, assho—jerk. Until the guy slammed a rock into my ribs. And I still managed to get the gun and shoot him. He must have been wearing body armor to survive two shots, center mass. There was so much blood, I was sure he was dead, so I got Nat up to her house and made sure she was okay." I don't tell McCabe about my leg going numb. Or how if I'd been two inches higher with my first knife strike, we wouldn't be having this conversation. He'd probably snap at me some more, and I'm kicking my own ass hard enough as it is.

"Fine. You're a godda—gosh-darned knight in shining armor. Who the fudge is Nat and why was this guy after her?"

"She manages the resort on Blakely."

"Does Nat have a last name?" Wren asks.

"Not one I know."

Ryker's brows shoot up. One lifts a little higher than the other. Half of his face looks like a jigsaw puzzle. The other half...he was a handsome man once. "Doc—"

My chest constricts, the tube and the broken rib lending a rasp to my voice. "Do *you* know the name of the guy who bags your groceries? What about the hotel clerk at the last place you stayed? Your house cleaner?"

The big man levels me with a frosty glare. "Yeah. I do. All of them."

Wren reaches for his hand and gives his gnarled fingers a quick squeeze. "You're not exactly *normal*, Ry. You know all of their names because you're obsessive about our safety. Doc's a civilian."

The term hurts. Even if it is true.

A muscle in his jaw ticks Once. Twice. Three times before he releases a long, slow breath. The baby picks that moment to wake up and let out a wail worthy of a banshee.

Ryker cringes and starts bouncing on the balls of his feet, making desperate *shhhing* noises and...*cooing* at her.

How can the man go from lethal as fuck to doting papa so quickly?

Wren glances down at her watch, then digs in the diaper bag. "She's hungry. Can you feed her so I can keep looking for Nat?"

Ryker plucks the bottle from her hand. The only other chair is across the room, and his massive frame barely fits in the damn thing. I watch, mesmerized, as he unbuckles the harness and has Harlow cradled in the crook of his elbow, bottle in her mouth, in under thirty seconds.

"We have her leaving the hospital," Wren says. "Caught her on the camera outside the ER. But after that, she disappears."

"West better be ripping Graham a new one," Ryker grumbles. "How hard is it to keep an eye on *one* woman in a hospital room? He's not allowed to babysit Harlow once she starts walking. She'll slip right out the door under his damn nose."

Wren rolls her eyes. "Our daughter isn't going to yank the leads off an unconscious man's chest to summon a trauma team and slip out in all the confusion. And Harlow loves her uncles."

The ache in my chest grows the longer I watch the two of them together. Their love is a physical presence in the room, filling every look, every touch, every good-natured barb.

I thought I was happy alone. I'd accepted my solitary existence. It was better than risking the pain of loss again. But seeing this hard-as-nails man with love in his gaze makes me want what I can never have.

It makes me want *Nat*.

"Back to business," Wren says. "I pulled Nat's number off your phone, Doc. But it's registered to the owner of the resort. Clancy McNamera. Also, it's a freakin' flip phone. No GPS. I'm working on getting the text messages and call log from the carrier, though."

"You hacked my phone?" I glare at McCabe—as best I can since exhaustion is threatening to pull me under again. "What the fu—"

"I'd stop right now if I were you," he says quietly. "I've never punched anyone in a hospital bed before, but there's always a first time."

"You had...no right." Breathing—simply existing at this point—hurts. If he weren't holding his kid, I'd tell him to go fuck himself.

"I had *every* right." He sets the bottle down, puts Harlow over his shoulder, and starts patting her back gently. "Wyatt spent two hours in the water this morning scouring the bottom of the harbor. The guy you claim *you* killed? We disposed of his body. And his rifle. You were right about the body armor, by the way. He and Inara wiped Nat's house clean. They even found some plywood to nail over the broken door. But do you know what they *didn't* find?"

I don't bother trying to come up with an answer. He's going to tell me anyway.

"Anything that would tell us who the *fudge* she is. There wasn't a goddamn thing in that house with her name on it. No paperwork. No driver's license. No passport. No bills in her name. Not even a single photograph. So yes. We hacked your fucking phone. Because whoever this woman is, she's either *in* a mess of trouble or she *is* a mess of trouble."

The very idea of taking a breath deep enough to speak exhausts me. But as I close my eyes, I manage seven words. "*In* trouble. Bet...my life on it."

CHAPTER FOURTEEN

Natasha

"Clancy, the man is a doctor. He clearly needs his phone. Just give me his damn address so I can return it to him."

"Well, I don't know." The old man's voice isn't as strong as it used to be. It probably doesn't help that I woke him up from his afternoon nap. "I should call him and ask him if it's okay."

"And how do you expect to do that when *I have his phone?*"

Shit. I guess Doc could have a landline. Or Clancy could realize that I'm lying. I have no idea where Doc's phone is. But this was the only excuse I could think of that Clancy would buy.

"Oh..." Clancy chuckles—more to himself than anything else. "I suppose you're right. Well, give me just one minute. I'll get you that address."

I blow out a breath and sink down onto the narrow bed. The hostel on the edge of downtown isn't much. But the closet-sized private room was only a hundred bucks, and they let me pay in cash.

Clancy rattles off the address. I write it on the little notepad next to the bed, then squeeze my eyes shut. How do I tell him I'm leaving? That I'm already gone? This job gave me a home. A *life*. My only friend. Shit. Gladys goes back to Blakely on Friday. If she gets anywhere near my house—Clancy's house—she could be putting herself in danger.

"Um, Clancy? There's one more thing I wanted to talk to you about. Once I drop Doc's phone off at the Post Office, I need a few days off. Can you have this week's renters pick up their keys from Milt at the General Store?"

"Well, I guess so. Is everything all right, Nat?"

The concern in his voice shouldn't affect me this much. But I'm exhausted. My hip is on fire, and the headache currently trying to split my skull in two laughed in the face of the four ibuprofen I took an hour ago.

"It's fine. Just some family shit—stuff—I need to take care of, and Gladys is visiting her grand-niece in Seattle this week. Otherwise, I'd ask her to help out. You know how much she loves to talk to the guests."

He chuckles. "That I do. I'll give Milt a call. You take care now, Nat. Let me know if you need anything."

"I will. I'll...talk to you soon. Thanks." I hang up and burst into tears. In a few days, I'll have to send him a text and tell him I'm never coming back. But until then, I can pretend I still have a home.

It's been eight hours since I left Doc in the hospital. Thirteen since I last saw my house. Thirty-two since I've slept. And in that time, I've been to Goodwill for clothes and a backpack, grabbed a burger and fries from one of the cheaper local chains, and found the hostel. I've got nothing left. Bleeding all over the damn place with a concussion hasn't helped, I'm sure.

I lock the door and limp out to the front desk. The bored clerk is all too happy to give me directions to the address in West Seattle. It's three buses and a half-mile walk to the residential neighborhood. There's no way I can make it without sleep. And the cover of darkness will let me surveil the place without arousing suspicion. I hope.

Back in my tiny room, I set the alarm on the old clock and remove my jeans. A small bit of blood stains the gauze over my hip. I peel the tape back an inch to peer at the wound. Shit. The skin is hot to the touch. Why didn't I get a first aid kit at the drugstore? I'll have to pick up some antibiotic cream on my way to Doc's. And more ibuprofen.

I *should* hoof it to the bus station and get on the first Greyhound out of here. I could be in Mexico by tomorrow night. The ten thousand dollars sewn into the lining of my duffel bag should last me long enough to disappear.

As I start to drift, I wonder why I'm still fighting. Why I even care if Bastian kills me. Because without Gladys—*without Doc*—what do I even have to live for?

FIVE HOURS of sleep wasn't enough. Not even close. I think I have a fever. My body aches. Then again, I got the shit beat out of me less than twenty-four hours ago. I pop a handful of ibuprofen and wash them down with half a bottle of water I bought on the way to the bus stop.

I have to know Doc will be okay. Parker was too much of an idiot to have found me on his own. Bastian must know he's dead by now. He'll send the others to Blakely. They'll talk to the couple who own the marina. Threaten them if need be. Find out that a sea plane disappeared overnight. It won't be hard for them to track down a name. Or an address.

The oversized sunglasses cover the deep purple bruise on

my cheek and my black eye. A brand new baseball cap from the hospital gift shop hides my hair and the butterfly bandages on my forehead.

My hip screams at me with every step. I scored a pair of designer jeans at Goodwill for ten bucks, but the seam presses against the bullet wound. The very swollen bullet wound.

One hour, three buses, and a painful mile of walking later, I peer out of an alleyway between two houses. Doc's home is right across the street. The porch light is on, but all the windows are dark. He should still be in the hospital. But Bastian won't know that. Does he have men inside right now? Waiting?

I sink down behind a cluster of trash cans and watch. One hour. Two. My ass is numb, and though it's summer, the heat wave broke, and the temperature starts to drop rapidly.

Shivering, with a headache that leaves me nauseous, I brace my hand on one of the big, black bins and pull myself to my feet. I can't stay out here all night. For all I know, Doc has an expensive security system. This is a ritzy neighborhood and he's clearly not hurting for money. Not with a house right on the water. But infil was always my specialty. Exfil...not so much.

When the pins and needles fade away, I sweep my gaze up and down the street. All clear. I don't rush. Don't try to hide. I look like I belong here. Or, I hope I do. Until I reach the sidewalk and catch sight of his doorbell camera.

Pivoting quickly, I pass one neighbor's house, then another. The third house is undergoing renovations. Major ones. Perfect. Even if there *is* a camera, the likelihood anyone's paying attention to it is low. I scramble over their fence and land in a crouch in their backyard. Something in my hip pops. Fuck. Was that a stitch? Two?

The water laps at a short retaining wall at the edge of the

property. I take off the new-to-me sneakers, tie the laces together, and drape them around my neck. The water soaks the denim up to my knees, but cutting through backyards is too risky. This...I'm far enough away from the houses no cameras should catch me.

The back of Doc's place doesn't sport a camera—at least not one I can see. My teeth are chattering when I haul myself up onto his deck. I squeeze the water from my jeans, shove my feet back into my sneakers, and peer through the floor-to-ceiling windows into his living room.

Still dark. No telltale blinking red lights, though expensive systems are usually completely silent.

I shine a flashlight around the patio door. There. A small, rectangular box sits at the top of the frame. From the outside, there's no way to get around it. Unless I can overload the circuit.

There's an outlet only a few feet from the door. Spreading my tool kit out in front of me, I make quick work of the switch plate and the screws holding the frame in place.

This is dangerous as fuck with my jeans still wet, but what choice do I have?

You could walk away. Right now.

No. Doc saved my life. I owe it to him to safeguard his. At least until I can explain.

He looked so pale in that hospital bed. I couldn't even stay long enough to look him in the eyes. But Graham was on the phone with West. Distracted. It was my only chance.

So I kissed him. Pressed the piece of sea glass into his palm. And disconnected the lead over his heart. Did he know what I was doing?

Even if he didn't then, he does now.

I cross the wires in front of me. Sparks dance over the deck. But it's not enough. They're still hot. I can *feel* the electricity buzzing through the shielding. On my second try, there's a loud *pop*. I took too much of a shock, and for a few moments, I'm frozen, praying my heart stops racing.

When it does, I seal everything back up again, then move to the glass door. My lock picking skills have languished the past few years, but five minutes later, I'm in.

I drop my bag next to a leather couch and fish out my Glock to clear the house. His scent fills the large bedroom. I almost whimper when I see the ensuite bath with a jacuzzi tub. My body is on fire, but I'm wracked with chills at the same time. The idea of a bath...

Focus.

Tall bookshelves line the walls in his office. A second bathroom, several closets, and a third room with nothing but a dozen boxes, a ladder, and three cans of paint are all clear. So is the garage.

I find the fuse box and reset the breaker. No one came for him. At least...not yet.

But that could change any minute. I'll stay until dawn. Make sure no one breaches his home under cover of darkness. And then I'll run.

Until then, I can explore. The living space is simple. Almost sparse. A large TV over a brick fireplace faces a dark leather couch. I kick off my shoes and sink my toes into the thick area rug over the hardwood floor.

On the mantle, Doc has a small collection of photos in silver frames. Three are obviously from his days as a PJ. God, he was so young then. Black hair. No beard. He was almost thin. Wiry. With a smile that lit up his entire being.

In the last one, he has his arm around a woman with blond hair. They look happy, but there's a hint of sadness in her eyes. I pick up the frame, and a small card flutters to the floor.

In Loving Memory
Tessa Cole

From the dates on the card, she died a little over six years ago. Fuck. She was only thirty-four.

"I don't do relationships."

Is this why? Because of her? Was he in love with Tessa? God, why did I ignore him for *a year?* I could have known this man. Now, I never will.

Running a hand through my hair, I wince as I catch one of the bandages. The chills haven't let up since I came inside, and I'm starting to worry I'm in real trouble here. Physically.

I down another four ibuprofen and head for his office. On his desk, I find a pad of paper and a fountain pen. I'll never know more about him than I do right now. But maybe, I can give him a small bit of me before I go.

Dear Doc,

I'm sorry. For so many things. You almost died because of me. Because you were in the wrong place at the wrong time. Or...the right one. You came to my rescue, despite the danger.

I wish I could tell you everything. But if I did, you'd try to help. Don't deny it. We may not have spent much time together, but I still know what kind of man you are.

A good one.

The night we kissed, I wanted more. Did you ever wonder why I spooked? I wanted to tell you, but I was too scared.

You said I felt like home. One word, and I knew we had to stop. But it wasn't because I felt like home to you. It was because you felt like home to me.

I panicked and took the coward's way out. Then I made it worse by having Gladys greet you every time you came to the island. I thought if I did that, I wouldn't fall for you. I wouldn't want what I couldn't have.

But my plan backfired in the worst way. Because Gladys told me everything. How you always remembered her aches and pains. How you cleaned the gutters for her one week. Changed her smoke detector batteries another. How you started to smile after a few months. How much you liked her chocolate chip cookies.

I fell for you through her stories.

You're in danger now. Because of me. Parker has friends. It won't be hard for them to figure out who owns the sea plane that left Blakely in the middle of the night. Or track down your address.

They're not stupid. You'll be fine during the day. But as soon as you see this letter, I need you to call those "not friends" of yours and tell them you need protection.

I'm leaving town in the morning. Right after I call Gladys and tell her to stay with Bella for a while. I have a few things to do—affairs to put in order—and then I'll let them find me. In a week, I'll be gone, and they'll have no reason to come after you again. You'll be safe.

I wish we'd had more time. I wish I could have told you all of this in person. But I'm afraid if I tried, I wouldn't be able to walk away.

Yours,

Natasha

My tears soak the fancy leather blotter. When did I start crying? I can't tear the paper from the pad. My hands shake too much. I'm starting to get dizzy. Stress, exhaustion, and my injuries are all threatening to pull me under.

I can sleep for a few hours. Then I'll be steady. Then...I'll be able to walk away.

Stretching out on the couch, I cover myself in a blanket from the foot of Doc's bed. It smells like him. Woodsy. Fresh. Like...home.

My tears have stopped. But now, the regrets are a thousand tiny daggers piercing my heart.

"I'm sorry, Doc. For everything."

CHAPTER FIFTEEN

Doc

"You decent?" Raelynn pokes her head in the door with her hand over her eyes.

Of course McCabe would send her. He knows I have a soft spot for the woman. Or maybe this is his way of washing his hands of me. After all, she *was* the last member of Hidden Agenda I treated.

I try one more time to get my left arm through the sleeve of the button down shirt but give up when darkness creeps along the edges of my vision. The only other option in my ruck—a black t-shirt—was a no-go from the start.

"A little help?" I ask.

Raelynn drops her hand and her eyes go wide. "Shee-it, Doc. Is there any part of you that ain't bruised?"

"Bottom...of my right foot? Maybe."

Before I can pass her the shirt, Raelynn's at my side with her hand on my shoulder. "Tell me the truth. Should you be leavin' the hospital?"

"Probably not." It's still hard to take a deep breath. The

chest tube only came out a few hours ago. The attending physician wanted to keep me another day, but I signed myself out "against medical advice." Lying in a hospital bed while Nat's out there alone? Fuck that. I have to find her. "But I'm going...with or without your help. Or a shirt."

"Well, you're lucky I have some experience bein' down an arm," she says with a smile and a wink. "Drop your left shoulder."

I do, and she works the shirt up my arm. It's easier to maneuver my right hand into the sleeve with her help. The sight tremble in my fingers pisses me off, but I manage to fasten the buttons before Raelynn offers to do them for me.

"If you even *try* to pick up that bag," she warns, "you'll be sorrier than a one-legged man at an ass-kicking contest."

I'm not about to fight her. Standing is hard enough. If I make it to Raelynn's car without losing consciousness, it'll be a fucking miracle.

"Got you a stylish ride down to the garage," she says, opening the door to snag a wheelchair waiting in the hall.

I don't object.

Once we're in her car, Raelynn turns and pins me with a hard stare. "Ry gave me your address. But we ain't movin' until you tell me who Nat is and why you're riskin' your life for her."

"You try...talking with a broken rib and...a hole in your chest."

"Been there. Done that. Try again, sugar," she says with a sweet smile.

"Sugar?"

Her blue eyes sparkle. "In Texas, that means '*idjit*.'"

"What did McCabe...tell you?" I let my head fall back against the seat and close my eyes.

Raelynn puts the car in reverse. "Everythin'. We don't keep secrets in this family. Wren tracked down the phone number for the resort's owner. But I convinced her not to call it. Yet."

I force my heavy lids open and squint in the bright mid-morning sun. "Why?"

"Nash."

I've treated her enough to recognize the way her voice changes when she talks about the man she loves.

"Those pig fuckers who cut off my ear found Nash by accident. One of them was out in Seattle makin' a deal to supply the DeLuca crime family with oxy. He ran right into us outside a coffee shop." She shakes her head with a little huff. "If he'd come out here a month earlier...I'd still need two earrings every day. But Nash—and his father—would be dead."

"Still doesn't explain..."

Raelynn shoots me a look I can't quite read. "I reckon you have some idea where Nat is. Or where she's goin'. Ry agrees. We ain't about to spook her until you tell us to."

"McCabe—" A spasm of pain steals my next words. I refused a breathing treatment this morning, knowing it would keep me at the hospital at least another hour—if not two. I didn't tell the attending I had plenty of oxygen at home. But if I don't give myself one soon, my lung could collapse again.

"Doc? Goddammit. I'm takin' you back to—"

"No," I grit out. "How long...did you have to stay...in the hospital with Nash? In Chicago?"

She eyes me warily. "'Bout fifteen hours. Which was twelve hours too long. But you can't string more than five words together in a row without wheezin'."

"Which one of us has a medical degree?" I glare back at her. "And that was more than five words."

"Stubborn idjit," she mutters and veers off onto the West

Seattle Bridge. "We can handle this, Doc. Findin' people...it's what we do. Just say the word."

I choke out a laugh. "McCabe wouldn't risk...his team... for me. Not after what I...said to him. And I'd never ask him to."

Raelynn's quiet until she pulls into my driveway. Before I can open the car door, she wraps her fingers around my wrist. "Ryker ain't an easy man to know. I've been with Hidden Agenda for almost a year and I still can't read him half the time. But somethin' inside him broke that night." Her free hand brushes the remains of her ear. "West and Inara got there first. To my place? Ry was on comms. You know how they saved me?"

"No. I never ask for details."

"Well, tough shit. You're gettin' them now." Her shoulders curl inward, and her eyes unfocus. "They had me tied to a chair. Diego Ruiz—he worked for the DeLuca family—was about to put a bullet in my knee. Inara took out Diego's partner from the roof of the house next door. I tipped the chair over. Damn near cracked my head open. Diego shot me in the arm. The next bullet would have killed me. But West threw a goddamn knife and caught the asshole in the throat."

"Shit."

A shiver runs through her slim frame. "Ry had to listen to the whole thing on comms, knowin' he couldn't do a goddamn thing. And on the way to the warehouse, he about lost his shit on me for scarin' the ever-lovin' fuck out of him. He ain't good at givin' up control."

"That's a massive understatement."

Raelynn throws her head back and laughs. "Damn straight. Yet, a week before Harlow was born, he turned Hidden Agenda over to West. We've taken on four jobs since, and he's been hands off with all of them."

I don't know why she's telling me all of this. Or what she expects me to say to her.

"So imagine my shock when six hours after we save your life, he moseys on into the warehouse, baby girl strapped to his chest, and tells us to make sure our go bags are packed, because the minute you pull your head out of your ass, we're doin' whatever it takes to find this woman you went and caught feelings for."

If she'd revealed that McCabe was secretly an opera singer, I'd be less shocked.

"All I'm sayin', Doc, is you don't need to *ask* us for help. We're here. We've always *been* here. You've saved all of us at one time or another. Ain't a single member of this family who'd think twice about returnin' the favor."

Dipping my hand into my pocket, I find the heart-shaped piece of sea glass. "I don't need saving." The absurdity of that statement slaps me in the face. My chuckle turns into a pained cough. "Again."

"Doc..."

I grit my teeth, shove the car door open, and stand. Thank God the world only tilts on its axis for a few seconds. Once I'm alone, I'll call Gladys. She'll be able to help me find Nat. After a couple hours of real sleep—not the broken, restless sleep one gets in a hospital—I'll be strong enough to go after her. I just need to know she's okay.

Raelynn's phone rings as she grabs my ruck, and she pulls the device from her pocket. The soft smile gracing her lips tells me all I need to know about who's on the other end of that call.

"Take it," I say and ease the bag onto my shoulder. "I can manage from here."

"That ain't a good idea—"

"I mean it, Raelynn. Leave me...alone."

Before the hurt in her eyes can change my mind, I rush into the house and shut the door.

What the hell did I just do?

Over the months I treated Raelynn—first for the shoulder, then for so many other injuries—we've talked here and there. About life. About what matters. I think of her like...my favorite niece—if I'd had any brothers or sisters. Almost family. And I just slammed the door in her face.

I let the rucksack slide to the ground and limp into the kitchen. I didn't say a word to the doctors about my back. It's still fucked, but that's nothing new. A week—maybe two—and it'll heal up enough for me to ignore it again.

Snagging a bottle of water from the fridge, I head for the bathroom—and the industrial-size bottle of ibuprofen in the medicine cabinet.

"Fucking hell."

My heart shoots into my throat. The water bottle hits the tile, rolls, and comes to a stop against Nat's bare foot.

She's collapsed on the floor next to the shower, wrapped in one of my towels. I can't tell if she's breathing.

"Nat? Baby, can you hear me?" I crouch down and check for a pulse. It's weak, but steady. Thank fuck. She's burning up. A soft moan escapes her lips as I cup her cheek. "Open your eyes for me."

She tries, and I get a glimpse of the gray depths before she loses the battle. "Doc..."

"I'm here. Need to get you...off this floor." Slowly, fighting against the agony tearing a hole through my chest, I ease her up to sitting. Her head rests on my shoulder.

"Have to go," she whispers.

"You're in no condition to go anywhere. Except bed. But I need you to help me. I can't carry you this time."

Nat draws her knees up to her chest. The motion shifts the towel off her hip and reveals the bullet wound. No bandage. Fuck. It's so much more than a graze. She's lucky that Parker asshole didn't hit bone. Two of the stitches have popped, and I can smell the infection over the scent of my shampoo clinging to her hair.

"Up on three, okay?" I count it out and pray I have enough left in me to get her all the way to the bed. It's touch and go for a few steps until she gets her legs under her.

"Can't stay..." Nat clutches my shirt as I ease her down to the mattress. "Isn't safe."

"Shhh. This is the safest place for you right now." I brush a hand over her hair, hoping like hell I'm telling the truth. "I promise."

CHAPTER SIXTEEN

Natasha

A GENTLE HAND cups my cheek. My skin feels like it's about to crack into a thousand pieces, but that touch...I lean into it, desperate for more. This is a dream. It has to be. I'm alone. I'm always alone.

"Open your eyes, baby. I need you to drink some water for me."

Doc.

It takes more effort than it should to lift my heavy lids. I lock onto the blue depths of his gaze. This is real. *He's* real.

The furrow between his brows eases, and he smiles. "There you are. I'm going to help you sit up. Take it slow."

He slides his arm behind my back. The pale beige walls start to pulse with my heartbeat. As the blankets fall away, I catch sight of the plain, black t-shirt covering my body. It's not mine.

I'm so confused. I shouldn't be here. I was supposed to leave at sunrise. But...I woke up shivering—and sweating—at 4:00 a.m. I got in the shower. Or...did I? I remember taking off my clothes. The thick bandage over my hip was bloody. And oozing.

Doc puts his back to the headboard and settles me against his chest. I should complain about the position. About him holding the bottle of water like I'm helpless. But my arms don't want to work and this just feels so...nice. Real.

Then I get a sip. Ice cold. A weak moan escapes between swallows. This might be the best thing I've ever tasted.

"You were damn lucky," he says when I've had my fill. His voice rumbles through me, rich and comforting. "If I hadn't come home when I did..." He tightens an arm around my waist and buries his face in my hair. "You had a fever of a hundred and two, Nat. I couldn't get you to wake up."

Pain bleeds from his every word. I want to tell him I'm fine. That he doesn't need to worry about me. And something else. There's something else I should say. But I can't figure out what it is.

"I gave you IV fluids. A shot of antibiotics. The infection hasn't spread—that I can tell. But sepsis was—still is—a possibility. If your fever doesn't break in the next few hours, I'm taking you to the hospital."

"No." I can't manage more than a hoarse whisper. I know what I need to say now. "Have to leave..."

"You're in no condition to get out of this bed. Let alone leave town." He's not as gentle now. Almost...angry. With me? "You popped two stitches. And you didn't stick around the hospital long enough to get the antibiotics they prescribed for you. What the hell were you thinking?"

He wants to snap at me? I'll snap back. Or try to. "You almost died. Because of me. Can't let that happen again." My words would be so much more effective if there were any strength behind them. Or if three sentences didn't completely exhaust me.

For several minutes, Doc holds me. His breathing is

uneven, almost jerky against my back. I wish I could see his face. Or apologize. But I don't know what to say. Instead, I focus on a handful of dust particles illuminated by a ray of sunlight coming through the window. It's late afternoon from the angle. God. How long was I out?

"I need to clean your wound," he says softly, his lips close to my ear. "Make sure the infection isn't getting worse. I'll be right back."

Doc eases me down onto my side, and I watch him leave the room. He moves slowly. Carefully. I cut a hole in his chest not more than thirty-six hours ago. And now, he's taking care of me.

He returns with a steaming bowl of water and sets it on the nightstand among bandages, antibiotic cream, and several precisely folded white cloths. Carefully, he arranges the blankets to expose my hip, but nothing...indecent, then sits next to me.

I stare down at my bare legs. I vaguely remember standing in the shower. Wrapping myself in a towel. But now, I'm wearing one of *his* shirts. And nothing else. "Did you...? Was I...naked?" Flames lick up my cheeks. I shouldn't have asked. I'm not sure I want to know the answer.

"All I found in your bag was a cashmere sweater and two pairs of socks. That's the softest shirt I own. I wasn't sure you'd want to wake up in a pair of my boxers." Doc shrugs, dips one of the white cloths into the water, and wrings it out before removing a thick, white bandage from my hip. "This is going to hurt. I'm sorry."

When the compress hits my skin, I whimper and turn my face into the pillow.

"Breathe. I promise it'll be over soon." With his free hand, Doc rubs slow circles up and down my back. The steady, rhythmic motion calms my racing heart. "Want to tell me how you broke in? And why?"

"Not while you're trying to parboil me," I mumble.

Anger stiffens my shoulders at his laugh, but before I can snap at him, he starts to wheeze. The compress falls away a second later.

"Fucking...hell." He reaches down and comes up with a portable oxygen tank. One twist of his fingers, and the thing hisses as he holds the mask over his nose and mouth.

"Oh, God. Doc? What—"

He shakes his head, then takes my hand and holds on tight. After another minute—maybe two—he drops the mask and shuts off the airflow. "I'm okay," he says, though the strain in his voice doesn't reassure me. "Oxygen is standard...after a pneumothorax. But maybe...don't make me laugh again...for a while. My ribs hurt like hell."

Tears prick at my eyes. He's in terrible pain, but he half carried me to his bed, got me into one of his shirts, and God knows what else. I have a vague memory of screaming in pain at one point. But nothing more than snatches as I faded in and out.

Doc spreads a thin layer of antibiotic cream over the new stitches, then tapes a fresh bandage in place. "Are you hungry? I don't have much in the house. Broth. Ice cream. Club soda. I was supposed to be on the island until tomorrow. But I can get something delivered."

I grab his forearm, digging my fingers into the corded muscles. "No. You're not safe here. *We're* not safe here."

He stares at me for a beat. "I was Air Force Pararescue for seventeen years, Nat. I can handle myself. Even now. There's no way I'm letting anyone get to you again."

The fever is making it hard to think. If I'm not careful, I'll tell him too much. Or not enough. But I have to make him understand. If Bastian has any idea who Doc is, it's only a matter of time before he shows up here.

My stomach rumbles before I can figure out what to say.

Doc pulls the blankets up to my chest and tucks them around me. "Broth to start. And after that, you can tell me who's after you."

Doc

Six hours. I spent six hours stretched out on the bed next to her. Sleeping in fits and starts between cool compresses on her forehead. Hot ones on her thigh to draw out the infection. Fresh stitches. Fluids. Antibiotics.

I've had enough ibuprofen to eat a hole in my stomach lining. Plus three oxygen treatments. My entire body aches, and more than once, I've contemplated taking something stronger. But I have to stay alert. If for no other reason than to reassure Nat that she's safe here. And stop her from running again. I have no doubt that as soon as she can stand, she'll try to leave.

The last rays of the setting sun streak the sky. Red and orange so vibrant, the sight would take my breath away—if I had any to spare.

Bone broth bubbles on the stove, the rich scent comforting. I add a handful of spices, then find a package of noodles in the cabinet to dump in at the last minute. She needs calories. Hell, we both do. I haven't eaten since that godawful hospital breakfast they forced on me early this morning.

I have half a mind to order pizza right now. But someone coming to the door might send her over the edge. She was spooked enough to run without even waiting for me to wake up yesterday.

So why the hell did she break in to my house less than twenty-four hours later?

The answer comes as I'm ladling the soup into bowls.

I'm not a threat to her. But she thinks Hidden Agenda is. She's not wanted. She said as much on the plane, and I believe her. So why would she be afraid of them?

"Doc?" She limps into the kitchen like a drunken sailor, almost hitting the wall more than once. A pair of my navy blue boxers peeks out from the hem of the t-shirt. "Please. We have to go. I need...my clothes."

"Wasn't up to doing laundry today." I stalk over to her, take her arm, and lead her to the small dining table. "Sit. The soup is almost done."

"No."

"Dammit, Nat. You're shaking. You can't do anything *but* sit. You're lucky I can't carry you right now or you'd be back in bed already."

With the back of my hand, I check her forehead. The fever hasn't broken. If she doesn't respond to the antibiotics soon, I'll have to decide if I call an ambulance or swallow my pride and reach out to Hidden Agenda. My SUV is still at the marina in Kenmore.

"Fine," she says on a sigh. "But it's almost dark—"

"What the fuck does the time of day have to do with anything?" Back at the stove, I shut off the burner and ladle the soup into bowls.

"If anyone knows I'm here, they'll come for me." Her voice trembles, and she sweeps her gaze out the floor-to-ceiling windows. "Someone could be watching the house. Even now. They could see me."

After setting the bowls on the table, I move to the windows and punch a button on the wall. It takes a full minute for the shades to hide the rest of the world from view. As they hit the halfway point, her words finally register.

"We have to go."

Not her. Both of us. She's worried about me. When we're hidden from view, I ask, "Better?"

She nods, though she doesn't look convinced. Her gaze follows me as I head for the fridge.

"I have water, coffee, and club soda."

"No beer?" she asks with a weak smile.

I force a deep breath—as deep as I can. "I'm sober. Four years."

"Shit. Sorry. I...Gladys told me that." Her hand trembles as she reaches for her napkin. Each knuckle bears a sickly yellow bruise. I almost lost her on Blakely. Then again to the fucking infection. Does she have any idea how close she came to dying?

"Gladys kept trying to get me to have a beer with her." I shake my head, wishing the old girl were here now to talk some sense into Nat. "Once I told her, she started offering me lemonade instead. So? What can I get you?"

"Water is fine. I really am sorry..."

Needing the ritual, I pull out the rocks glasses, add ice, and fill them from the tap before joining her at the table.

"You don't have to apologize." Shame has me picking up my spoon and digging into the soup rather than meeting Nat's gaze. "Six years ago, I lost someone. Drinking made being alone a hell of a lot easier. Or at least, I thought it did. Turns out, scotch is a fucking liar. Along with its sisters, whiskey, tequila, and vodka."

"Tessa?"

I snap my head up. "How—?"

"The picture." Nat points to the mantle over the fireplace. Her cheeks turn bright red, and she drops her gaze to her bowl. "I didn't mean to pry. I just...I knew I'd never get a chance to see you again and I..."

A single tear glistens on her cheek. We're close enough for me to reach out and dash it away. "I met her when I was working in the ER in Los Angeles. She came in with a spiral fracture to her radius—it's a bone in the forearm. Her boyfriend had twisted it so hard..."

I can still see her sitting on the narrow bed, eyes downcast, shoulders hunched.

"She'd driven all the way from San Diego to get away from him. I treated her and gave her a card for one of the local women's shelters. I didn't think I'd ever see her again. But three months later, I ran into her at a coffee shop near the hospital. I almost didn't recognize her. She'd found a job, made a few friends—even signed a lease on an apartment. We talked for over an hour. Before I left to start my shift, she gave me her number."

"What happened to her?" Nat asks. From the hesitation in her voice, I wonder if she already knows.

"Her piece-of-shit ex tracked her down. He saw us together, and three days later, he broke into her apartment and..."

"I'm sorry, Doc."

Nat's hand covers mine. "You don't have to tell me."

"Yes. I do." Forcing a slow breath, I link our fingers. "He stabbed her thirty-seven times. Beat the shit out of her first. By the time I got there, she'd lost too much blood. I tried to save her, but...she died in my arms."

For several minutes, we sit in silence. I'm about to tell Nat to eat more when she clears her throat.

"Parker killed my brother."

Her eyes turn glassy as she disappears into her own memories. "Logan wasn't supposed to be there. *I* was. Parker came for me. But I'd gone for a run to clear my head before —" She reaches for her water and downs half the glass. "If I'd never left the apartment that night, my brother would be alive."

I wish I could change the subject. Ask about her favorite movies or books or whether she likes deep dish or thin crust.

But this might be my only chance to get her to open up to me. I need to know why this asshole was hunting her. And who the fuck he was working for.

"Tell me why he was after you. Or hell. Tell me anything, Nat. I've been trying to *know* you for a year now."

Her flinch is the last straw. I'm tired of waiting for her to decide I'm a halfway decent guy. She knows enough about who I am now.

"*You* kissed *me* that night, remember? *You* took *me* back to your place. You had your hands under my shirt."

"I know." She won't meet my gaze, and her voice drops to a whisper. "I'll never forget it."

"The second you said 'stop,' I stopped. I backed off. I wanted you. Fuck. I *still* want you. But I would have been happy just being your friend. Am I that much of an asshole, you couldn't even give me that?"

The pain in my chest is too much. I push away from the table. If I don't get some air, I'll say something I can't take back.

As I slip out the sliding glass door, Nat calls my name, and fuck if I don't want to run right back to her.

CHAPTER SEVENTEEN

Natasha

I can't bring myself to step outside. But Doc left the door open a crack, and a light breeze cools my overheated skin. Too bad it can't touch the shame coursing through me.

Standing isn't working out so well, so I put my back against the wall and let myself sink down to the floor. "You're not an asshole," I say softly.

No response. He's only a foot away, so I know he heard me. "Gladys would tell me to strip off my clothes—well, the clothes I'm wearing—and throw myself at you right now."

Doc's laugh is a gentle balm to my battered heart. "She may have suggested I take up naked sunrise yoga a time or two. Apparently, the best place for it is exactly halfway between your house and my campsite. I didn't ask her how she figured that out."

"Oh, God. Do you think she and Donald...or... Shit. She and Clancy..."

"That's not a visual I needed. Ever." Doc glances back at me. When he sees me on the floor, my head tipped back against the wall, he swears under his breath. "Fucking hell, Nat. You're going back to bed."

"No."

"That wasn't a question." Doc loops my arm over his shoulder, grits his teeth, and helps me to my feet. His groan tears at my soul.

"Stop. You're hurting yourself." I try to pull away, but he doesn't let go until he deposits me back onto his bed. "Stay there. You need another dose of antibiotics."

His breathing is too shallow. Too rapid. And under his arm, a small spot of blood seeps into his pale green shirt. He limps out of the room before I can beg him to stay. To listen.

All of this is my fault. Chris. Logan. Doc. I've hurt so many people by not being honest with any of them. By not realizing I can't handle this on my own.

He comes back with a small black pouch. Without even glancing in my direction, he fills a syringe from a clear vial.

I've had enough of this. "Doc? Sit down."

"Not yet. This goes in your thigh or your ass. You pick."

"Thigh," I snap. If he wants surly, I'll show him surly. Two can play at this game.

It burns going in. Enough to bring tears to my eyes. But after he caps the needle and tosses it back into the pouch, I reach for his hand. "Your turn. Sit down."

"Nat—"

"No. You're bleeding. Sit down. Now."

He's wary. I can't blame him. I made him feel like I didn't care—like I didn't *want* to care—when nothing could be further from the truth.

He sinks down onto the mattress. My fingers aren't entirely steady, but I manage to undo the buttons and ease the shirt off his shoulders. All his bruises are so much darker today. Tracing one of the worst of them with my fingers, I fight the tidal wave of emotion about to pull me under. "Doc...God. I'm so sorry."

The warmth of his skin seeps into my palm. Even with the ache from the fever, my body reacts to his closeness. His scent. The way he covers my hand with his and squeezes gently. "For what? You didn't break into your own house and throw *yourself* off the balcony."

"About that second part," I say quietly as I guide his arm up so he can rest his hand on my shoulder. The hospital bandage comes away easily. There isn't a lot of blood, but it still worries me. "I might have...well..."

"You mean Parker didn't—?"

I huff out a laugh. "I hit him with my watering can, then jumped."

His eyes widen. "You could have broken your neck."

"I know how to fall." Plucking the antibiotic spray from the nightstand, I rest my free hand just above his waist. "It's only bleeding a little. But you have to stop this. You're putting your own life at risk...for me."

Doc nods to the tattoo covering his bicep.

That others may life.

"This is who I am, Nat. It doesn't matter that I've been out for almost fifteen years. I can't...*not* take care of you. I don't know how." With a shallow sigh, he closes his eyes. "Do what you need to do. But distract me. Tell me how you learned to fall."

"In Ranger School."

He's not prepared for that answer. Fair enough, since I wasn't prepared to give it. The spray hits his wound, and he hisses out a breath. "Fuck, that burns."

"You really are a terrible patient." It feels good to smile. Even better to sit so close to this man I've wanted to know for so long and joke around with him. "What did you expect?"

"To come home and sleep for a few hours. To call Gladys

and hope she could help me track you down." He reaches up and traces the edge of the swelling under my eye. "I should call her anyway. Or you should. She'll be worried about you once she gets back to Blakely and discovers you're not there."

"Shit. She can't..." My heart pounds so hard, I'm afraid Doc will *hear* it. "She has to stay away from my house. All the blood... If she calls the police, they'll find out. They'll use her to get to me. I need my phone. Where's my phone—?"

I'm suddenly dizzy. The walls are closing in. Trapping me. Squeezing the life out of me.

"Nat. Look at me." His sharp words slice through the panic, but fighting my way free is too hard. My eyes burn. I'm on fire, but freezing at the same time. Shaking. Until my cheek presses to his chest, and it's *his* heart beat I hear, *his* voice rumbling through me.

"We'll call Gladys. And McCabe. And anyone else you need. I'll keep you safe, baby."

"You can't." I draw back. Tears cool on my cheeks. "Don't you understand—"

"I don't understand a fucking thing. You're talking in circles. You won't answer *any* of my questions. We can't stay here, yet you're the one who broke in. Why? If you were only going to run again?"

Shit. He didn't find my note. There's my answer. He can read it, and I won't have to explain.

"Your office. On your desk. I wrote you a letter," I whisper. I'm too weak to hide it from him. But it's not just my body betraying me. My mind—and my heart—they're in on it too.

His expression hardens. "No."

"No? What the hell does that mean?"

"It means you're not going to take the coward's way out here, Nat. If that's even your real name. You're going to talk to me. Tell me all of it. Right now."

"Or...? Ultimatums like that usually come with an 'or

else.'" I shouldn't push him. This is what I wanted. Isn't it? For him to know me? This is my chance. But I'm so scared he'll decide I'm not worth the effort and walk away. Or worse. Kick me out of his house before I can warn him of the danger he's in.

He stares at me, his blue eyes churning like the sea before a storm.

Here goes nothing.

"Nat is my real name. Sort of. Natasha Janelle Winters. Sergeant First Class, United States Army. Second Battalion, Seventy-Fifth Ranger Regiment."

"Natasha." He's still wary. But he relaxes enough to rummage among the medical supplies for a fresh bandage, hand it to me, and turn so I can smooth it over his side. "I only knew of one woman who made it through Ranger school. A sniper. She works for McCabe now."

"They don't talk about me. Because of...what happened." God, why is this so hard? I want to tell him. I *need* to tell him. But I can't get the words to come. So instead, I roll up the sleeve of the t-shirt and show him the flowery tattoo on my left arm. "Can you see it? I still can. Barely. But..."

He traces a finger over one of the roses. Down the stem to the next bud where the letter *S* forms the edge of the flower. "*Sua Sponte*. Why did you cover it up?"

"Because I knew if anyone found out who I was, my life would be over."

Doc

Natasha's gaze darts to the window—and the encroaching darkness outside. "Blinds. Please? And...my gun. If we're staying here tonight, I need it."

I pull the shade, then move to the walk-in closet. I'm not sure she can even *hold* a gun at this point. But I can manage. The biometric lock on my safe beeps, and the door pops open. When I searched her bag for something she could wear, I found her Glock, and it sits next to mine on the top shelf.

I grab both of them, check the magazines, and secure the door.

"You're in no condition to shoot. But if it makes you feel better to have it close by, so be it." I set her pistol on the nightstand, clip my holster to my jeans, and sit on the bed, facing her. She's tense, her gaze fixed on the gun with her fingers clenching and unclenching around the blankets. "Natasha, look at me."

Fucking hell. The fear in her eyes twists at my heart. I want to find out who put it there and end them. Painfully.

I'm a healer. Hurting people goes against everything I am. But I'm falling for this woman. Keeping her safe is the only thing that matters.

I cup her cheek and relish the way she leans into my hand. "The doorbell camera will capture anyone who approaches the house from the front. I have a spare camera in the kitchen I can set in the back window. They're both motion-activated. My alarm system isn't the best—clearly, since you managed to break in without setting it off—but I can probably get someone out here in the morning to install a better one. If I haven't used up *all* my favors with McCabe and his team."

She still doesn't look convinced.

"It's been almost forty-eight hours since that fucker broke into your house. You were here last night. No one came for you then. No one's coming for you now."

She shakes her head. "You can't know that. There was blood all over the dock. Someone would have called the police. And when Parker didn't check in... How long do you think it would take for the owners of the marina to give up your name? Your address?"

"You ran out of the hospital before McCabe showed up, baby. His team found the body. Took care of your house—as best they could. There's no evidence Parker was ever there. Whoever sent him won't have any reason to talk to the harbor master. And that's assuming McCabe didn't pay the woman off to stay quiet. I wouldn't put it past him. You're safe here. *We're* safe here."

A single tear tumbles down her cheek. The tension leaves her shoulders and her eyelids start to droop. "I'm not safe anywhere. Not for long."

"You are for tonight. I'm going to set up the other camera. Then you can tell me the rest." I pull back the blankets, and it's a testament to how exhausted she is that she lies down almost immediately.

"Doc?" she asks after I tuck her in and reach for my shirt. "You're coming right back? I don't want to be alone."

The shirt slips from my fingers. This woman is so fucking strong. She had to be to make it into one of the most elite units in the armed forces. But the desperation in her tone threatens to break me.

I lean down and brush my lips to hers. "I'll be back in ten minutes. Maybe less. You're not alone." The words I want to say stick in my throat.

You'll never be alone again.

CHAPTER EIGHTEEN

Doc

Natasha's eyes are closed when I slip back into the bedroom. If anyone gets within ten feet of the cameras, my phone's alert is loud enough to wake the dead. But I still sent a message to Lucas with Emerald City Security to find out how quickly I can get one of their systems installed.

I still don't know who's after her—or why—but waking her is the last thing I want to do. So I tuck the gun between the mattress and the headboard, then stretch out on top of the duvet.

My jeans have been strangling my dick all day. I can't help how I feel around her, even if it is inappropriate as fuck. She was half dead when I found her this morning, and I still wanted her. Getting her into my t-shirt almost killed me.

"When I asked you to come back, it wasn't as a babysitter," Natasha says. The sleep-roughened edge to her voice rockets my arousal up to eleven—or eleven hundred. With a groan, I try to adjust myself before I do permanent damage.

Her skin is almost cool when I touch my lips to her forehead. Thank God. Relief floods every muscle in my body. Before I can pull away, she cups the back of my neck and pulls me closer. The kiss is swift and hard, full of promises I'm aching to keep.

"We can't, baby. Soon. But not yet." I'd give anything to be able to take her. But we both need sleep, and I won't rush this. I want hours with her. Days, even. Time to learn what she likes. To memorize her taste. To discover the parts of her body I can kiss to send her flying.

"Then get under the covers."

"Natasha—"

Tears shimmer in her eyes. "Please, Doc. I'll tell you what you want to know. But I'm terrified it's going to break me. I...I need your arms around me."

Fuck. I almost fall over trying to get my jeans off. Putting up the camera did a number on my back, and my left leg is half numb again. But I'll give her whatever she needs. As long as she stays with me.

I tuck her against me, her head on my shoulder, and our legs intertwined. I can't see her eyes in this position, but I hope that'll make it easier for her.

"I didn't want to be a Ranger." Her fingers slide down my chest to trace the ridges of my abs. "I was happy where I was. I'd been in the army for seven years. I thought maybe I'd make it all the way to Sergeant First Class. Maybe Master Sergeant if I was lucky. Never gave a single thought to being an officer. I was good at taking orders. Hell, I spent as long as I could as a Specialist. That's where the real fun was."

I cover her hand with mine and chuckle. "The mafia was good to me too. A couple of us had desk plaques that said 'United States *Chair* Force.' We used to see how long we could leave them out before our Staff Sergeant noticed."

"I once spent three whole days taking inventory of a supply closet." Natasha sighs, some of the tension returning to her muscles. "But right before I was promoted to Sergeant, the congressman from my district got a shit-ton of bad press. He'd sexually harassed some young aide and was desperate to find a way to redeem himself before the next election. He decided parading around the Army's first female Ranger—from his hometown—was the way to do it."

"What's this idiot's name? He's not still in Congress, is he?"

She laughs, but there's no joy in the sound. "Last I checked, he was still there. But I've had very limited access to the internet for the last eight years."

I make a mental note to add this fucker to whatever list I end up giving McCabe. He's toppled governments before. He can disgrace one measly congressman.

Her lips skim one of the healing bruises on my chest, and she squeezes my hand. "I failed out twice. Both times, I told the bastard to find someone else. But he refused. I was perfect for the job."

"Perfect?" I ask. "How?"

Her sigh overflows with sadness—and sarcasm. "I was pretty. Not too hard or too jaded. Nice hair. A nice ass."

I tighten my arm around her, but that only aggravates my bruised ribs, and I force myself to relax.

"The third time, I glued myself to another candidate's side. Chris Bowers. We'd gone through Basic together. He was a friendly face, and God. I needed that. Most of the guys hated having a woman around. Especially one who'd washed out twice. Chris got me through. Talked me out of quitting when I got low, helped me figure out how to silence some of the assholes who kept making my life a living hell. And that last time, I passed."

"How long were you a Ranger?"

"Nine years. We spent most of our time in Iraq. The last few deployments were in the Al Anbar province. I *hated* my squad leader. He was a lecherous piece of shit who fucked every woman he could get his hands on—then bragged about his conquests whenever he could. But Chris and I were in the same squad, and as long as we stuck together, Bastian never tried to touch me."

"Natasha, he never—?" I don't want to ask, but I have to know.

She shudders in my arms. "No. Never...that. He'd slap my ass every chance he could, but that was pretty standard behavior. I got used to it. Mostly."

A gentle kiss flutters over my collarbone. She hasn't stopped touching me in little ways. Her fingers skimming my waistband. Her lips grazing my neck. My pecs. Her toes brushing my ankle.

"A little over eight years ago, we were searching for a high-value target. But we had mixed intel. Two locations, four clicks apart. Command ordered us to split up. Chris and I went to one cluster of two houses. Bastian took the rest to the primary location. It wasn't standard operating procedure. The entire squad should have stuck together. But those were the orders. We followed them."

The longer Natasha talks, the more I want her to stop. She hasn't gotten to the truly terrible part yet, and when she does, I'm afraid I won't be able to give her what she needs. Or keep her from running away.

"Our location was deserted. There hadn't been a soul there for months. Chris and I *knew* something was wrong. We radioed command, told them we were going to rendezvous with the others. Comms cut out." Her words are coming faster now, the memories stealing her away from me. "Bastian, Collins, Sutton, Doherty, and Bowen were in a house that wasn't on any of our scans. We heard a woman screaming, so we approached. The door was cracked open. I saw...everything. Bastian's pants were down. The daughter couldn't have been more than fifteen. He shot her first," she says. "Then the mother. I watched him pull the trigger with his dick still covered in that poor girl's blood."

Sobs wrack her body. I'd give anything to lift this burden from her shoulders. But I can't. All I can do is hold her.

"Tell me the rest of it, baby. Get it out. I'm here. And I'm not going anywhere."

Natasha

Doc knows everything now. How many times Bastian tried to kill me. How Parker found the safe house the night before I testified. How I escaped. How I came to Blakely. And how many times I thought about leaving.

I don't have any tears left to cry. My eyes are hollow, the lids nothing but sandpaper.

"You have to sleep," Doc says, his deep voice my only anchor in this storm. "He won't find you here. Not tonight."

"You can't promise me that." I wish I could believe him. I *want* to believe him. But he doesn't know Bastian like I do.

"Maybe I can." Doc reaches for his phone. The movement costs him. His ruddy cheeks pale, and his chest stutters until he gets his breathing under control.

"I can't believe they let you out of the hospital," I mutter as I rub slow circles over his bicep.

"Terrible patients, remember?" He types out a text message, then shows it to me before he sends it to Raelynn.

Doc: Did Wyatt and Inara leave any cameras at Natasha's house? Or the marina?

It only takes the woman two minutes to respond.

Raelynn: This ain't our first rodeo. The marina's a busy place. But no one's touched Nat's house. And the harbor master has all the records she needs to send these idjits all over hell's half acre searching for a man who don't exist.

I rub my gritty eyes and stifle my yawn. I'm so tired, I could sleep for a week straight. If only I thought I'd be safe that long. "What in the world is hell's half acre?"

Doc chuckles and returns his phone to the nightstand. "Raelynn's from Texas. They speak a whole other language there. I'm pretty sure she means anything that might have tied me to Blakely has been thoroughly and completely erased."

I scoff. "Not Clancy's reservation system."

"Yep. Even that. McCabe's wife is a hacker. One of the best in the world, from what Raelynn's said."

Snatching my phone from the nightstand, I scroll through the text messages the computer sends me every week. All the ones that used to say D. Reynolds now show C. Jacks. "Who is C. Jacks? And how the hell did she hack my phone?"

"Now do you believe me?" he asks as he eases the device from my hand. "There's still a lot we have to talk about. Including how McCabe and his team can help put an end to this. For good. But for tonight, you're safe. *We're* safe. Sleep with me, baby. In the morning, we'll figure out what to do next."

CHAPTER NINETEEN

Doc

My head and my heart battle for control. But this is a war neither can win. For an hour, I've watched Natasha sleep. I shouldn't have been so reluctant to involve Hidden Agenda. That one text message from Raelynn was all it took to reassure the woman I'm falling for. She's been asleep for almost ten hours now—a testament to how serious the infection was when I found her.

I know I'm not a good bet. I'm a fifty-six-year-old alcoholic who once showed up to my shift at the ER so intoxicated, the attending physician could smell the scotch on my breath.

I've lost everyone I've ever loved. My mother. Half my crew. Tessa. I couldn't protect them. What makes me think I can protect the woman in my arms?

You can't. You'll lose her too. And then what will you have? Nothing.

It's always his voice in my head. His words that come back to haunt me when I get low.

Why can't I silence him? He's been dead for more than

thirty years. Killed in a bar fight that should have been the first sign for me to stay the fuck away from alcohol.

Instead, I followed him down that path. But where he took his rage out on the world around him, at least I only hurt one person. Myself.

Was that because I'm a better man? Or because my self-imposed exile left me no other choice?

Natasha stirs in my arms, and her ass brushes my aching dick. Only my boxers and her thin t-shirt separate us. My dick goes from half-hard to aching in a heartbeat.

I press a kiss to the curve of her neck. She smells like my shampoo, and I'm unprepared for the possessive growl rumbling through my chest.

"You stayed," she whispers.

I risk a deep breath, happy when my ribs only send a dull thrum of pain through my torso. "You seem surprised."

Natasha turns in my arms and blinks up at me. Fuck. There's a lifetime of sadness in her gray eyes.

"I haven't made any of this easy on either of us." She reaches up to stroke my cheek. "He'll find me eventually, Doc. I can't stay. But I hope you know how much I want to."

"I'm not letting you go that easily." My fingers cup the back of her neck, squeezing gently. "It's been years since I've felt *anything* but alone. When I met you, my heart started beating again. It didn't matter that you wouldn't give me the time of day. I still wanted you. With you, I'm alive again."

Tears shimmer in her eyes. "That's exactly why I have to go."

Arguing with Natasha won't get us anywhere. Yet. So I shuffle out to the kitchen to make us some coffee. My left leg is back to normal—thank fuck—and while I won't be chopping wood or carrying anything heavy for a while, I'm feeling pretty damn good for someone who had a tube in his chest only thirty-six hours ago.

I add the beans, jab the button to start the grind, and check my phone. Shit. When did that text message come in?

Raelynn: I gave you last night for free, Doc. But it's time to pay the bill. Check in or I'm coming over. With Ry.

It's barely 8:00 a.m. I thought I'd have more time.

Doc: I'm fine. Tell McCabe to go back to diaper duty.

The chocolatey scent of the Guatemalan blend curls around me as the first drops sputter into the pot. She'll give me a few hours. Maybe half a day if I'm lucky.

I've earned a little luck in my life, haven't I? Apparently not, since another message comes in too quickly.

Raelynn: Any word on Nat?

I should come clean. After all, that's what I require from my patients. Every time I saw Raelynn after her shoulder injury, I asked her if she was in any pain. If she was taking it easy. If she was doing her physical therapy exercises. And every time she tried to hedge—or outright lied to me—I called her on it.

But while Natasha might trust *me* at this point, she doesn't trust Hidden Agenda. Knowing her history, I can't blame her. She—and her brother—should have been safe with two MPs guarding them twenty-four-seven. Yet Parker still got in. And found her on Blakely.

Doc: Working on it.

Setting the phone down, I say a little prayer she'll accept that—for now. Before I can pour the coffee, however, the phone vibrates again.

Raelynn: You slipped up last night, Doc. Natasha? Not Nat? I know you've been in contact with her. I reckon I've got two hours before West asks me for an update, and I won't lie to him.

Fucking hell.

Doc: She's here. But if you show up now, she'll run. I need time. Please. Give me today?

The phone rings, Raelynn's name flashing across the screen. I send the call directly to voicemail.

Filling the mugs, I return to the bedroom and hope Raelynn doesn't break down my door in the next few hours. It's a real possibility.

Natasha's gaze latches onto me. Her tongue darts out to wet her lips. Fuck. I rush to get back in bed before she notices the bulge tenting my boxers. Or the phone in my hand.

But she's so focused on the cup in her hands—and her plans to run—I don't have to worry.

"I have to call Gladys before I go," she says, staring into the coffee like it holds the answers to life itself. "I don't know what to say to her."

Draping my arm around her shoulders, I wait for her to settle against my chest. Having her here—in my bed—feels right. We belong together. If only I could convince her to give us a chance.

"What about the truth?"

The quiet sniffle shatters my heart into dust. She's protected herself for so long, I'm not sure she realizes how much she cares for the older woman. Or how much Gladys cares for her.

"I can't. Anyone who knows who I really am...it's too dangerous. It's bad enough I told you." She lets her hand trail down my stomach, tracing the edge of one of the darker bruises. "You know how to take care of yourself. Gladys is eighty-three years old, and she's all alone up there. Or will be, now that I'm gone."

With each word, Natasha makes herself smaller and smaller. The coffee is half gone, and she clutches the mug like a shield.

"There is no world where he doesn't find me, Doc. It

doesn't matter that he's still in Leavenworth—or was the last time I checked—he's connected. He has to be. The first attempt on my life was less than forty-eight hours after I reported him."

She won't meet my gaze, and it takes me a beat to understand why.

"Someone way above his pay grade was in on it."

Natasha's shoulders slump, and she nods. "That's why I have to keep running."

"You don't." I nudge her chin up so I can look her in the eyes. "Let me call McCabe. Or...West. Apparently, he's running things now."

She jerks away. "No. They're all former military, right? They could be part of this. God, I was so stupid coming here. *Staying* here. I should have gone directly to the bus station from the hospital. I could have *mailed* you that goddamn letter."

"Then why didn't you?" Anger sharpens my tone—or is that pain? I can't tell anymore. I thought we'd moved past this last night, but if she's still determined to shut me out, I was wrong.

"I didn't have a choice!" Natasha throws the covers back, jerks up, and starts pacing the room in short, choppy steps. "The first day we met, I saw your tattoo. My dad used to talk about PJs like they walked on water. When I left for my first deployment, he said, 'You ever get in trouble over there, you find yourself a PJ and they'll get you out of it.'"

Pride stirs in my chest. It doesn't matter that I'm a civilian now. That I've *been* one for more than a decade. I'll always be a PJ.

"I thought if I stayed away from you, it would be easier." Natasha runs her fingers through her hair, wincing as her thumb catches on one of the butterfly bandages along her forehead. "But once Gladys sets her mind to something, there isn't a force on this earth that can stop her. And after that night—when we fooled around?—she made it her personal mission to get us together."

I'd suspected as much. "Gladys isn't exactly...subtle."

Natasha's laugh surprises me, but I think it shocks her even more. "God, no. She's the polar opposite of subtle."

Holding out my hand, I meet her gaze. Does she care enough—trust me enough—to come back to bed? "Please, baby. Let me hold you."

For a moment, I think she does. But she stops right in front of me, her arms wrapped tightly around her torso. "Why couldn't you just read the damn letter?"

"Because I want to hear you say it. Whatever *it* is. Tell me why you trusted me."

With a sigh, she climbs onto the bed, straddling me. I cup her ass, digging my fingers into the soft globes.

Soft kisses feather along my collarbone. "What do I feel like, Doc?"

Her teeth score the shell of my ear. I reach up and pinch a nipple between my fingers. Her little whimper shoots straight to my dick. If I'm not inside of her soon, I'll be in a world of hurt.

"What did you tell me I felt like that night?" she asks.

"Home."

The single word hangs between us. It's in her eyes. In the part of her lips. In the breath catching in her throat.

In her tears.

Fuck.

"I felt it too. It terrified me. That's why I kicked you out. Why I stayed away for so long. Why I couldn't let myself *talk* to you, let alone...touch you. Because I'll never have a home again."

"You have one here, Natasha. With me. If you want it." I

slide my fingers into her hair, twisting the silky strands so I can seal my lips to hers.

Grinding her hips against me, she lets out a desperate moan. I'll feel every one of my fifty-six years later, but I don't care. I need her naked. I need to taste her. I need to watch her come apart in my arms.

The t-shirt bunches in my frantic grip, sliding over her head and baring her to me. I toss it aside, then flip our positions so she's on her back under me. "These too," I grit out before I slide the boxers down her legs.

She's laid out like a banquet, and I'm a starving man. I palm one breast and roll a nipple between my fingers. The other bud tightens under my lips.

Her fingers claw at the sheets. "Doc. Please..."

"You like this?" Scoring my teeth over her dusky skin, I reach down and press the heel of my hand to her mound. "Are you wet for me, baby?"

"God, yes," she whimpers.

"Show me." I sit back, watching her for any signs of pain.

Her lips curve into a smile. "Demanding, much?"

I'm about to apologize when she spreads her legs. Trimmed curls glisten with her need. The scent of her wraps around me, pulling me closer until I'm helpless to resist.

My first taste teases her clit. Her tiny gasp is quickly followed by a keening cry. I slide a finger into her channel, and her inner walls tremble.

"I'm going to make you come, Natasha. I want to hear you scream. If that's not okay, tell me right fucking now."

"Do it," she manages.

I add a second finger. She's so damn tight. Burying my nose in her curls, I let my tongue explore. It's been a long time, but after a few strokes, I find my rhythm.

Every few seconds, I flick my gaze to hers. I need to see

the moment she shatters. Her mewls turn more desperate, and I pick up the pace.

"Oh God...I'm..."

Her body tenses, and then she lets go. There is no sweeter sound than her scream. Except, maybe the way she says my name.

I drink her in, slowing my strokes until her tremors start to fade. The pain in my side should warn me away from the next round, but this might be all we have. If I can't convince her she's safe, she'll run, and I'll have no choice but to let her go.

Natasha

Oh. My. God. I can't move. He told me I'd scream. Did I scream? I think I screamed.

"Come here, baby." His deep voice soothes my raw edges. Strong arms gather me close. I could snuggle with him for days. Weeks. Maybe even a lifetime. He's...solid. In this room —in this bed—nothing can touch me. Nothing but him.

"You've seen me naked twice now." I curl my fingers around the waistband of his boxers and lick my lips. "That's not fair."

"I tried not to look the first time," he says with a smile.

"Even so..." He's hard enough I can see the outline of his crown. And the precum soaking the silk. "Don't make me beg."

"You were begging earlier."

The amused glint in his eyes is sexy as sin. This is the real Doc. The man I started falling for the first day we met. He's funny, protective, and demanding. And I'm dangerously close to being completely in love with him.

"I'll beg again. Later. Off with these." I hold my breath. The glint fades into what I think might be pain. What is he waiting for? Does he not...want this?

"I haven't been with anyone in almost six years, Natasha. I...shit. I don't have protection."

Oh. Relief floods my muscles and loosens my tongue. "It's been just me and my Magic Bullet since I ran. And I was clean before that."

I'm suddenly ready to give him my entire sexual history—what little there is of it—in under ten seconds flat.

"I'm not on birth control, but I haven't had a cycle in two years, so I don't think I even could get—"

"I had a vasectomy after I retired from the Air Force." He's already on his feet. A grimace darkens his expression for a brief moment as he shoves the boxers to the floor. "I want this. I want *you*. But only if you're sure."

I can't tear my gaze away from his body. He's fit. Strong. But with a softness that makes him *real*. His abs angle gently into a *v*; his erection juts proudly from his patch of neatly trimmed white curls.

"Natasha?" He curls his arms over his torso, like he's afraid I don't like the view. "If you've changed your mind—"

"Get over here." I scoot to the edge of the bed, spreading my thighs so he can step between them. "I'm sure. I haven't been this sure of *anything* since I ran. And I might not be sure of anything else ever again. I want you inside me, Doc. Now."

He wraps his hands under my knees and gives me a quick tug. I fall back onto the mattress with a yelp. "Next time, I'll be on top of you."

His tip nudges my channel. I stare into his deep blue eyes, finding another piece of home in the gold flecks of his irises. "Or I'll be on top of you."

The low rumble in his chest is almost feral. Doc's thick

enough to stretch me to the point of pain. But I crave it. I *need* it.

Hooking my leg around him, I dig my heel into his ass and pull him closer. Doc sinks deep in one swift move. I swallow my gasp. "Again."

With the second thrust, pain gives way to pleasure.

"Again."

I don't have to ask a third time. Doc wraps his hands around my hips to hold me still while he pounds into me like a man possessed. "Touch yourself, Natasha. I need you to come with me."

My hands move to my breasts, twisting my nipples, skating my nails over the tips until sparks of electricity race all the way to my clit.

I'm close. Doc is too. He's harder now. Thicker. His eyes darken. The veins in his neck cord. I slide my hands lower. I'm so wet. My index finger glides over my clit. Again and again, until I'm panting.

"Won't last long," Doc manages. He wraps his arm around me, pulls me up, and climbs onto the mattress.

I cup the back of his neck. We're eye to eye now. Lines of pain crinkle around his lips, but he's a man possessed. With a low growl, he quickens his pace. The new angle lets his cock rasp over my clit.

"Let go, Doc. Let go with me."

He does, and we fly together, higher and higher until I'm not sure we'll ever come down.

CHAPTER TWENTY

Doc

My ribs ache, but I ignore the pain to hold Natasha close. She runs her hand down my back to my ass, then wriggles out from under me.

"Where do you think you're going?" I ask and snag her around the waist.

"Nowhere. But I have to know if it's true. And what side it's on." Natasha's laugh cuts through the darkest clouds. She's my sun, the center of my world.

She traces her finger along the outline of the green feet inked on my ass. "Fucking hell. *That's* all you wanted?" I grab her hand, then roll onto my back to stare up at her. "You know the story?"

"The PJs flew Jolly Green Giant helicopters in Vietnam. Some batshit crazy PJ decided he'd use the symbol from General Mills instead of an outline of a helo?"

She served. Of course she knows the story. I shouldn't be surprised. Still, I tell her the rest of it—at least as much as I know. "Those particular birds would leave an impression in the brush that looked a lot like feet. So he wasn't quite as crazy as everyone made him out to be. Though he was apparently drunk when he got to the tattoo parlor."

Natasha's other hand skims up and down my arm, constantly moving, constantly touching me. I draw the blankets over us, needing more time with her before reality intrudes and I call Hidden Agenda. We could have had this for a year. If only we'd trusted one another.

"Gladys is going to have something to say about this." I twine our fingers and hold her hand against my chest. "Like, 'I told you so,' 'about damn time,' or 'what the hell took you so long?'"

In a heartbeat, Natasha shuts down. Her body stiffens, and she tries to pull away, but I won't let her.

"Doc—"

"No. Not this time. I know what you're going to say. 'Gladys will never see us together. You can't stay. This can't last.' But you're wrong." I flatten her palm over my heart. "Feel that?"

"Yes," she whispers.

"It's yours, Natasha. My heart. It belongs to you. If you want it."

Tears shimmer in her eyes. "I...I'm falling for you. Or...I've already fallen. But—"

"Then trust me, baby. Talk to McCabe and his team. Listen to what they have to say. If you're not convinced after that...we'll leave together."

With a gasp, she sits up, shock parting her lips and blowing her pupils wide. "You have a life here."

"No. I don't." The realization should come with an ocean of sadness. But instead, a sense of peace settles over me. "The only thing here for me is *you*."

"You're willing to give up all this," she gestures around the bedroom, "because we spent one night together?"

I stifle my grunt as I reach up to touch her cheek. "I've been alone for a long time, Natasha. I know what love is. I lost it once. I won't lose it again. And if you think there's a damn thing in this house that I'd miss—other than you—you're wrong."

She's not convinced. It's too soon, and she's still too raw. But it's the truth. I realized it the moment I found her unconscious on my bathroom floor. I'm in love with her. It's not logical. We've talked more in the past twenty-four hours than we have in a year. But thanks to Gladys, I *know* Natasha. Maybe not her favorite color or the types of movies she likes or whether she's a morning person or a night owl. But I know her heart. And she knows mine.

Her stomach growls, loudly. Shit. "Let's take a shower. After that, we'll call McCabe. If he's going to swagger in here like he owns the place—and he will—the least he can do is bring us lunch."

***

Natasha

"If I had a shower like this," I adjust one of the four heads to rinse the shampoo from my hair, "I wouldn't want to leave it behind. And that tub...I'd give anything for a long soak in a tub that deep."

"Not until those stitches dissolve." Doc reaches for the soap, and I forget all about the tub—and the sharp edge to his voice.

"Oh my God. What happened?" A thick scar runs half the length of his spine, with a handful of smaller, round patches dotting his lower back.

I run my hands down his shoulders, needing the feel of

his skin under my fingers. This close, I can tell his hips aren't completely even.

"Helicopter crash. You don't find many PJs who retire voluntarily." He doesn't elaborate, so I wrap my arms around him from behind and press my cheek to his back.

"Go on..." If he thinks he's the only one who can demand answers, he's wrong. I don't know what's going to happen this afternoon. Or tonight. Or tomorrow. Or...for the rest of our lives. But I'm going to steal as much closeness as I can for now. If he'll let me.

He sighs, and I pluck the bar of soap from his hands. His lats tense under my gentle touch, and I'm careful to avoid the wound from the chest tube as I wash him.

"I don't remember much about the crash. We were on our way to rescue a SEAL team that had been ambushed. We were trying to refuel mid-flight. Something went wrong, and I only remember snatches after that. Half my crew didn't make it. I shattered three vertebrae and bruised my spinal cord. I was in the hospital for weeks. Then rehab. I'll never be a hundred percent again, but I manage. Most of the time."

"And these?" I touch one of the round scars. They're not surgical. Burns, if I had to guess. He flinches, and I drop my hand.

"I had those before I enlisted." He backs me up against the wall, caging me with his arms. "If we weren't beaten half to shit, I'd take you right here."

He's avoiding the question. But unlike earlier, there's something darker in his tone. These are personal. And I have to wonder—will he ever tell me everything? Or for all his talk of trust, will this be a part of him I never truly know?

"I don't have any clothes." Wrapped in one of Doc's fluffy towels, I stare at my duffel bag. I got sloppy. My gun, cash, and passports were always ready to go at a moment's notice. But a change of clothes? I raided the bag for those years ago —probably on a day I was avoiding laundry—and never put them back.

Doc grunts as he pulls a dark gray Henley over his head. The color turns his eyes a brighter blue. "I washed everything last night while I was installing the camera. Once we talk to Ryker and West, it might be safe enough to go out and shop for some essentials. You probably don't want to keep using my shampoo."

There's an odd note infusing his tone. Almost...disappointment.

"Oh, I don't know about that. I like your scent on me."

He hauls me into his arms before I finish speaking. "Fuck, baby," he growls in my ear. "Do you have any idea how much I want you right now?"

Palming the bulge in his jeans, I shudder. "This much?"

"More. So much more."

His phone rings from somewhere over his shoulder.

"Goddamn fucking timing." He releases me, stalks over to the nightstand, and puts the call on speaker. "Couldn't even give me until noon?"

Raelynn's Texas drawl carries through the room. "I would've. But someone's workin' damn hard at trackin' down C. Jacks. You're outta time, Doc. Either you make the call, or I will."

Oh, God. I sink down onto the bed. If Bastian can't find who he *thinks* he's looking for, he'll call Clancy. Or worse. He'll hurt the old man until he talks.

Doc runs a hand through his hair with a sigh. "I'll call. They're your family, Raelynn. I won't let you do anything to break their trust."

I CAN'T SIT STILL. The conversation Doc had after hanging up with Raelynn lasted all of sixty seconds.

"McCabe. Since I expect you're planning on showing up at my house in the next hour, do me a favor."

The man's raspy laugh carries an ominous tone. "Another one? I already saved your life. Twice. What do you need now? The game-winning ball from the 2004 World Series?"

"Pizza. Breadsticks. Throw in a salad for good measure. Natasha needs to eat."

"Done."

He didn't say a word about me being here. Like he *knew*. That was almost an hour ago. I tug at my tank top. It's not *mine*. Neither are the jeans, the underwear, the bra, the tennis shoes... Not really. For years, I lived in whatever I could get from Goodwill . But once I found Blakely, I felt safe enough to order clothes *I* wanted. Courtesy of Gladys and her credit card. She was only too happy to help once I told her an ex had ruined my credit score.

She's never going to forgive me for lying to her.

"Natasha, breathe." Doc comes up behind me and wraps his arm around my waist. "McCabe is an asshole of epic proportions. But he's been through some shit. He'll understand."

"When I asked if he was a friend, you said no. Then said he'd kill you if you explained that statement. And I'm just supposed to trust him?" I turn in his embrace. "How?"

"Do you trust me?" His fingers skim along my jaw with the lightest touch.

"Yes." The answer comes so easily. It shouldn't. The last time I trusted anyone, Parker killed my brother. But whether out of desperation or some connection I'm only starting to understand, I trust Doc with my life.

"Raelynn got hurt a few months ago," he says. "It was... bad. She lost enough blood, I wasn't sure I could save her. McCabe and I got into it that night, and I told him if he didn't back the fuck off, I was done."

He's still touching me, but now he's tracing circles over the back of my neck.

"I hadn't heard from him since that night. The money kept coming, but the calls stopped. I lived for those calls." He drops his hand, limps over to what once was obviously a bar just off the kitchen, and flattens his palms against the marble. "He pulled me out of the bottle when he gave me this job. Last week, I was dangerously close to falling back in."

"Doc—"

"I fucking loved being a PJ. When I had to retire, I didn't know what to do with myself. Working in the ER was enough for a while. But after I lost Tessa, I...gave up. Some-how, McCabe knew. I never asked how he found me. Or why he thought hiring a drunk to patch up his team was a good idea. But he saved my life. You can trust him to save yours, too."

There's so much I want to say. To know. But before I can go to him, someone pounds on the front door.

"Trust them, Natasha. Not just for you. But for me."

Doc rests his hand on the butt of his gun. He clipped the holster to his belt minutes after getting dressed, and I regret putting my weapon back in his safe.

The man standing on the porch must be close to seven feet tall. Dressed head-to-toe in black, bald, and covered in scars, he's lethal in every way. Except for the five pizza boxes he holds in his massive hands.

"Doc." He nods, then beelines for the kitchen like he

knows right where to go. West strides in after him with two large takeout bags.

Raelynn is next, followed by a man with a German Shepherd pressed to his side, and a gorgeous woman with a dark, angled bob.

Once he's locked the door again, Doc holds out his hand to me. I let him draw me against him. "Natasha, that's Ripper and his service dog, Charlie. This is Inara. She's—"

"The Ranger."

"The *other* Ranger, you mean." Inara stares me down for a long moment, and her words sink in. She knows who I am. Fuck. This was a bad idea. If she told anyone, we could all be in danger. "Relax, Natasha. We ID'd you from the security camera outside the hospital. But no one outside of Hidden Agenda has access to that information. Ripper and Wren made sure of it."

"How long have you known?" Doc asks.

From the kitchen, Ryker snorts. "We knew who she was before you checked yourself out against medical advice, Doc. And I had a pretty good idea *where* she was after Raelynn borrowed one of the SUVs last night."

"Well, shee-it." Raelynn rummages around in Doc's cabinets while West sets out containers of salads, breadsticks, marinara sauce, and ranch dressing. "I knew I shoulda' taken my own car."

"Your car doesn't have tinted windows. Someone would have noticed you staking out Doc's house in a red Mustang," West says and snags a slice of pepperoni pizza.

Doc gapes at the SEAL, then turns to Raelynn. "You were outside all night?"

"Wasn't about to let some idjit get to you and Natasha just because you decided to dig in like some Alabama tic. You've got a hole in your side and at least one busted rib. What did you expect?"

Doc's fingers tighten on mine. No one speaks for several minutes as everyone fills their plates and Raelynn passes around bottles of water. Fear keeps me rooted in place, despite the scent of the food twisting my stomach into a knot.

Ryker leans against the wall with his arms crossed over his massive chest. His face is a mask. No emotion. But his eyes regard me with what I think might be curiosity.

Screw this. I'm tired of being scared. Dropping Doc's hand, I walk right up to the man. Well, as close as I can get without having to crane my neck to meet his gaze. "How long until someone finds us here?"

One light-brown brow arches slightly. The other is split by a thick scar. "Four days if we're lucky. Two if we're not."

"My luck ran out eight years ago. My former squad leader, Montgomery Bastian, wants me dead, and he'll kill anyone who gets in his way." I have to force the words out over the lump in my throat. "Doc *can't* be in his way."

"Natasha, fucking hell. I will absolutely be in that asshole's way. I told you I'd keep you safe."

"Enough!" Ryker doesn't have to yell. He commands attention simply by being in the room. Everyone turns to him. Even West. "We're all *in the way*. And we'll stay there until that fucking piece of shit is nothing but dust I can wipe off my boot. That's how this works."

"This?" I ask.

West clears his throat. "Family."

CHAPTER TWENTY-ONE

Doc

"Sit down before you fall down," West says with a nod in my direction. "You too, *Natasha*."

He's pissed I lied to him. That we both lied to him. But to his credit, he hands us plates and then snags a breadstick for himself.

My small dining table only seats four. Inara and Raelynn join us. Ripper takes the couch and Charlie stretches out across his feet.

From his spot next to West at the kitchen counter, Ryker commands the entire room. "Wren wanted to come. But until this is over, she and Harlow aren't going anywhere but the warehouse and the condo. Wyatt and Graham are with them now."

Fuck. This is more than him being a normal, overprotective asshole. He's legitimately worried.

I drop my slice of pizza back on the plate and stare the big man down. "Tell us what you know."

"I just came here to look pretty," Ryker scoffs. "I'm out. Mostly. This is Sampson's team now. Ask him."

Ripper chuckles, reaches down, and rubs Charlie behind the ears. "You have a very warped definition of 'out,' Ry."

"I don't know," West says. "It fits with his definition of 'pretty.'"

My anger burns so hot, I'm ready to burn down the world. They're joking around? Now? I slam my fist down on the table, rattling the silverware.

"Fucking hell. Will *someone* tell me what we're going to do about the men after Natasha?"

No one speaks for a full five seconds. "You've been out a long time, Doc." West's voice is deathly calm. "But you know what we do. And how we do it. Trust me when I say *this* is why we're the best at what we do. We listen. We understand each other. We're a family."

"A very large, *very* dysfunctional one," Inara adds.

I sink against the back of the chair and reach for Natasha's hand. "Noted. But you do have a plan, right?"

West's dry laugh isn't reassuring. "Fuck, no. I heard about this shitstorm when it went down. Some of it, anyway. We need Natasha to fill in a lot of the holes before we get anything that even *resembles* a plan. That's why we're here."

Ripper pulls a tablet from his bag and taps the screen a few times. "Wren tracked down the guys she testified against. Montgomery Bastian, Dylan Sutton, and Ethan Doherty were released from Leavenworth a month ago. Allan Collins and Rob Bowen got out last year."

At my side, Natasha shudders. "They killed seven people —while they were running drugs all over Iraq and Afghanistan. The prosecutor asked for multiple life sentences to be served consecutively. How did they get out?"

"I can't answer that," Ripper says. "Yet. Dax suggested we let Trevor handle that thread."

"Who the hell are Dax and Trevor?" I ask. This was a mistake. If they've told anyone else, I won't even try to convince Natasha to stay. I'll run right along with her.

"Dax is our brother." Ryker sets his plate down and straightens his shoulders. "You remember the day we met, Doc?" At my nod, he continues. "When you figured out who I was, you said 'there were two of you.' Dax was the second. Rip was the third. Though we only got him back two years ago. We thought he'd died months before we escaped."

"I had," Ripper says under his breath. Charlie whines, then puts his front paws on the man's thigh and licks his hand. "I'm okay, buddy. Down."

I never heard Ripper's story. I treated his wife after she was kidnapped. Though they weren't married at the time. But hell, I don't know most of their stories. Only their injuries.

"And Trevor?" I ask.

"CIA." West snags another breadstick. "He and Dax are out of Boston. Figured if anyone he asked was dirty, it wouldn't come back to us in Seattle."

"None of this is making me feel any better." My appetite gone, I push my plate away and turn to McCabe. "I've never asked you for a fucking thing. You gave the orders, and I showed up. But I'm asking now. Get us out of the country. Help me access my accounts in a way that can't be traced, and we'll disappear."

His stare turns cold. A vein in his temple throbs. "Not how this works, Doc. You're one of us. Natasha is too. No man —or woman—left behind."

"Bullshit." I shove the chair back and lurch to my feet. My ribs send lightning bolts of pain wrapping around my torso, but I don't care. I'm so fucking done with the man, I'm ready to snap. "If I were *one of you*, I wouldn't have gone *four fucking months* without a single goddamn call!"

West gets between me and McCabe. "Easy there, Doc.

We've been lucky. Five jobs and we haven't had anything more serious than bumps and bruises. One knife wound, but I took care of that. We weren't going to bother you for a handful of stitches."

"Well, we *did* almost die the day Harlow was born," Ripper mutters. "*That* was pretty fucking serious."

"What?" I look from Raelynn to West. The pieces fall into place slowly, and when the last one clicks, the phone call he made from the helo finally makes sense. "It was *Wren* who was kidnapped from the hospital? While she was in labor?"

"Bait," Ryker grits out. "Fuckers wanted me and Dax. Then they discovered Rip was alive and took him too. Beat the shit out of them. By the time we got to them, Wren was ready to push. West delivered Harlow."

"And you didn't call me." The realization shouldn't hurt this much. My shoulders slump. I sidestep West so I can look Ryker in the eye. "I've treated every member of this team and half the people you all love. I've kept your secrets. Not because of the obscene sum of money you pay me every month. Because I believe in what you do. Because I can't save people anymore. Not the way I want to. But you can. I would have been there."

The big man looks beaten. "If you want to run, I'll make it happen."

"For fuck's sake," West says. "Enough of this shit." He stalks over to Natasha and braces his hands on the table. "Do you want to run? Or do you want to put an end to these assholes?"

"You—" Her voice cracks, and she swallows hard. "You can't stop them."

"That's not what I asked. Do. You. Want. To. Run?" The SEAL stares her down, waiting. No one makes a sound. I hold my breath, not sure what answer I should hope for.

The one that lets us stay together.

"No." She shakes her head. A single tear glistens on her cheek. "No," she says again. Louder this time.

"All right. That, we can work with."

Natasha

The pizza sits like a lead weight in my stomach. Doc slides another cup of coffee in front of me—my fourth of the day—and sinks down with a small wince of pain.

Telling my story the second time was easier. And not, since West, Inara, and Ryker asked me dozens of questions. The name of every Ranger I ever served with. All the places we were sent. Any time Chris and I were separated from the rest of the squad. Everything I could remember about the general courts-martial proceedings. The location of the safe house in Washington D.C.

"Even the smallest detail could be important," West says.

I drop my head into my hands. "You're asking me to relive the most traumatic month of my life. I'm doing the best I can!"

"I found something," Ripper says from the couch in Doc's living room. He's been hunched over his laptop for the past hour, occasionally talking to someone through his Bluetooth earbud.

West stops his pacing. "What is it?"

"This." With a few clicks to his keyboard, he sends an image to the various tablets littered around the room. Every member of Hidden Agenda brought one, and Inara's sits on the table in front of me.

"Oh, God. That's...me."

On screen, a drunk college kid lunges for me, his hands

going straight for my breasts. One of his friends shouts, "Come party with us, Nat. You know you want to!"

I grab the groper's wrist, give it a hard turn, and have him on his ass in under two seconds. "Get the fuck out of here," I snap and slam the door in their faces.

"That was posted to SnazzClip a month ago," Ripper says, "with the caption, 'Remember when Sammy got his ass kicked?' The hashtags are BlakelyIsland, Nat, HotChick, and WouldTapThat." The man's ruddy cheeks turn several shades darker. "They...uh...put a still shot up too."

Now I'm the one who's embarrassed. It was the middle of the damn night, and I'm only wearing a pair of skimpy shorts and a tank top. Without a bra.

"Fucking social media," West says under his breath.

"I'm running a search for anything geo-tagged from Blakely Island in the past four years." Ripper's fingers fly over the keyboard. "But your house number is clearly visible in the video."

"How would Bastian even find it, though?" This is the problem with staying off the grid for so long. My tech skills were passable eight years ago. But the world has changed so much since then. "I highly doubt he's spending time on Snaz-zClip watching drunk college kids get their asses handed to them."

"The United States government has one of the most advanced facial recognition algorithms in the world," Ryker says. He pushes off the wall by the back door and rubs his hand over his very bald, very scarred head. "It's obvious Bastian had friends on the outside. Powerful friends if they're able to get him out of consecutive life sentences in Leavenworth without raising too many eyebrows. Those kinds of friends wouldn't have any problem accessing facial rec."

"Or hiring a hacker to do it for them," Ripper adds. He

pushes up the long sleeves of his Henley, exposing thick scars around his wrists and a tattoo on his forearm.

Special Forces.

Like Ryker.

Like Logan.

"We fight for those who can't fight for themselves, Pip."

He was so proud the first time he came home wearing that green beret. I'd only been in the army for two years at that point, but I'd wanted to follow in his footsteps. I'd even asked my CO if women could go through Special Forces Assessment and Selection. But he'd none-too-gently told me a woman would never be accepted and kicked me out of his office.

"Natasha?" Doc rubs small circles over my lower back. "Ryker asked if you'd ever seen those guys before—or after that video was taken."

I grind the heels of my hands against my eyes. "I have no idea." God, I'm so fucking tired. Tired of running. Tired of being afraid. Tired of protecting myself from *everyone.* "I never paid attention to the renters Clancy sent to the resort."

At my side, Doc stiffens.

"Until you." I cup his cheek, skating my thumb under his eye. "I paid attention to you, fly boy."

"Fly boy?" he asks. His smile makes me think everything could be okay—if we live through the next four days. Or however long it takes Bastian and his crew to find me.

"Yes. Unless you'd prefer I start calling you the Jolly Green Giant."

"I did not need that visual," Ryker says. "Fucking PJs." He pulls out his phone, and his lips twitch into what might almost be a smile.

Inara stares at the man, then jabs West in the arm. "There's something wrong with Ry's face."

The SEAL chuckles. "Nah. I'd say Wren just sent him a picture of the baby."

He rubs his palm over his head again, but there's much less stress in the movement now. "Sampson, let me know when and where you need me. Until then, I'll be working from home. Harlow just rolled over for the first time."

Before he reaches the door, he turns back and pins Doc with his stare. His eyes are a strange mix of hazel, green, and blue. Almost mesmerizing in a terrifying sort of way. "Pack up what you need for at least three or four days. Raelynn will take the two of you to Graham's old place in Capitol Hill."

"What for?" Doc stands—with some difficulty—and I wrap my arm around his waist to steady him.

"To keep you safe, asshole. Wren's C. Jacks trick isn't going to stop them for much longer. When they figure out he's a figment of my wife's imagination, they'll dig deeper. And you're sure as shit not going to be here if they manage to turn up your name."

"Well, shee-it," Raelynn says and slaps her thigh so hard, I jump. "C. Jacks. I just got it. Cracker Jacks."

"What's so funny?" I ask, looking around the room. Everyone's laughing now. Including Ryker.

"Wren doesn't really swear," he says. "Cracker Jacks is her version of 'shit.' Sometimes 'fuck.' I've got a whole dictionary of them. Up here." He taps his temple. "'Sure as shipping lanes' is our newest one."

I wish I could meet this woman. Hell, I wish I could meet anyone and know that it wouldn't put them in danger.

"Doc, please." I stand in front of him, my hands on his hips. "Do it. I'd feel a lot better if we were staying somewhere that wasn't tied to you in any way."

He sighs, then leans down to press a kiss to my forehead. "Fine. But Graham's old place better have a working coffee maker."

West just stares at him. "Doc, don't take this the wrong way, but your coffee is shit. The safe house not only has a better machine, but beans that won't tear a hole in your stomach lining after two cups. Tomorrow morning, I expect you to call and say, 'You're welcome.'"

CHAPTER TWENTY-TWO

Natasha

"The freezer is fully stocked," Inara says as she sets two of Doc's duffel bags next to the overstuffed couch in the main room. "Fresh stuff...anything you need, you can order through the tablet on the counter. It'll be delivered to the lockers downstairs. Combination is next to the tablet, along with the wi-fi password."

I pull off the sunglasses and oversized floppy hat she gave me before we left Doc's house. She was confident the vague "disguise" would protect me if we happened to be caught on any traffic cameras.

"Facial recognition is both smart and incredibly stupid at the same time. The sunglasses and hat make you unrecognizable. If the camera can't see the shape of your eyes, the curve of your forehead, and the angle of your chin, it can't make a positive ID."

I wish my life didn't depend on her being right.

"Stay inside unless one of us is with you. But there's privacy film on all the windows, so even at night, no one will be able to see in. We have all the movie channels and an encrypted high-speed internet connection." With a musical chuckle, Inara gestures to the flat screen TV on the wall. "We hope you'll leave us a five-star review at the end of your stay."

"Keep us alive, and we'll sing your praises...well...nowhere," Doc says.

"I'm headed back to your house." Inara glances at her phone, then shoves it into her back pocket. "Wyatt and I will stay there for the next few nights. If anyone comes looking for you, they'll get a hell of a lot more than they bargained for. Natasha, you can call Gladys from that new phone West gave you. It's perfectly safe as long as you don't tell her where you are."

"She's going to hate me. I've been lying to her for years." I have to call Gladys soon. She's supposed to go back to Blakely tomorrow. But how am I supposed to tell her I couldn't trust her?

Doc cups the back of my neck and touches his forehead to mine. "She'll understand, baby. She loves you like a daughter."

"She won't when this is all over. If this is ever all over." For a time, surrounded by obviously lethal men and women at Doc's home, I held on to a spark of hope. But now, I can't seem to find it again.

"Natasha, this is what we do." Inara touches a pink stone pendant hanging at the hollow of her throat. "I've worked with Ryker for more than six years. West joined us almost five years ago. Graham, a few months after that. Wyatt's the new guy, but he and West went through BUD/s together. Raelynn...well, I suspect Doc told you a little about her. She almost died in April. The asshole cut off part of her ear. And less than forty-eight hours later, she dragged her unconscious boyfriend out of a burning warehouse with a bum knee, two broken toes, and a concussion."

My God.

"We're the best at what we do. That's not a brag. It's a fact. Why do you think Ry chose a former PJ as our on-call doc?"

At my side, Doc straightens. "He never told me why he picked me. Or how he found me."

"You'll have to ask him for that story." Inara offers him a small smile. "I need to go to the warehouse before I head back to West Seattle. I'll pick up a wig that'll match Natasha's hair and change into something a little more...flexible." She smooths her hands down her slim pencil skirt. Apparently, she works as a translator when she's not saving people all over the world, and she came to Doc's house right from work. "You need anything, call Ry. He's handling comms for this one."

With a wave, she slips through the door, and we're alone.

FOR A SHORT WHILE, I manage to pretend everything's okay. We order groceries, and I learn that Doc actually taught himself to cook after he left the Air Force.

He promises me chicken piccata for dinner, along with garlic bread and fresh green beans. My mouth waters, but by the time everything arrives, I'll have called Gladys. Will I have any appetite left after that?

"What's wrong, baby?" Doc asks, pressing a kiss to my neck and sliding his arm around my waist.

"I'm fine." The overwhelming sadness in those two simple words fills the room, expanding into every corner until I can taste my own helplessness.

"Don't lie to me, Natasha. You're *not* fine." His words hold such pain. I remember what Graham said to me in the hospital.

"Doc doesn't lie. The man is about as straight and narrow as they come. Yet he trusts you enough he's willing to do it for you."

I haven't trusted anyone that much since Logan died. But maybe...I could try.

"Even if West and his team *can* do everything they claim, Bastian could still find me. Maybe not today or this month or even this year. But he will *never* stop looking for me. And when he finds me, he *will* kill me."

"Fucking hell. No. He'll never touch you again. Not while you're with me."

Doc is a protector to his very core. It's all he knows. All he is. Every cell in my body wants to believe him. But he doesn't know Bastian. I do.

"I can't lose you." I take his hand, holding on with all my strength. "Somewhere in the middle of all of this...I started falling in love with you, Doc. If Bastian finds me—*when* he finds me—you have to let me go."

"No fucking way. How can you ask me that, Natasha? If you really *are* falling in love with me, how can you be okay with letting me go?"

"Because it's the only way to keep you alive."

We face off for almost a minute before Doc tries to pick up one of the heavy duffel bags he brought from his home. With a grunt, his grip fails, and the bag hits the floor.

"Let me get that." I can't stand to see him hurting. He won't take anything stronger than ibuprofen, which he's been popping like candy since the moment he got up this morning.

As if he needs to eprove—to himself *and* to me—that he *can* protect me, he tries again. This time, he manages to haul it onto his shoulder.

"Dammit! Stop!" I stalk down the hall after him. He doesn't get to walk away from me. Not like this. I'm so tired of feeling invisible. Of *being* invisible.

No friends. No family. No home. No future. Always pretending I'm okay.

"Put the bag down, Doc. I don't know what the hell you think you're doing, but it stops right now."

"I'm trying...to take care...of you." He's wheezing again. Fuck.

He won't look at me, instead staring out the bedroom window down at the street below.

I snuggle up to him, wrapping my arms around his waist and breathing in the scent of him. "I can't lose you, Doc."

He doesn't react. His voice, when he finally speaks, holds no emotion at all. "Then how can you expect me to be okay with losing you?"

I LEAVE him in the bedroom, stretched out on the king-sized bed with an oxygen mask over his nose and mouth. These bouts of wheezing could continue for days, but he brought three portable tanks with him and claims he'll be fine in half an hour.

So I curl up on the couch and stare at the new smartphone West gave me. I don't understand how it can possibly be safe to use it. Ripper tried to explain how he'd installed some sort of encryption program that would stop anyone from tracking me, but by that point, I was so tired, nothing made any sense.

Gladys picks up on the second ring. "Nat! Did you miss me?"

I'm frozen, a hundred different replies racing through my mind.

I'm sorry. I've been lying to you for years.

You have to stay in Seattle.

I'm not who you think I am.

"Baby girl, what's wrong?" In the background, I hear Bella say something before Gladys lowers her voice. "It's Nat. But she's not saying anything."

"I'm here," I manage. "Did you—did Bella find a dress?" I'm stalling. I don't know why. It won't change anything. But I need my friend more than anything right now. Even if I'm going to lose her before the end of this call.

The snort is so very Gladys. "That girl has tried on forty-seven dresses in the past five days, and none of them were 'right.' But half the stores serve you drinks! I've been buzzed the whole time."

Warmth prickles over my skin. Gladys is so damn happy. Not about being buzzed—though she does love her vodka and beer—but about spending time with Bella.

"Why don't you stay a little longer, then? Bella shouldn't have to pick a dress on her own." I shouldn't be avoiding the truth. But I'm desperate.

"Well, I would, but she has a trial starting Monday. I'll come back next month. Besides, I don't like you being all alone for too long."

"You have to stay, Gladys. If you go back to Blakely, you'll be in danger." The words tumble from my lips so quickly, my chest tightens, and I have to suck in a sharp breath. "I'm so sorry. But I lied to you. For years. If I could take it back, I would, but I've made a mess of everything, and I can't fix it."

"Baby girl, what are you talking about? Our little island is about the safest place in the world. Unless you're talkin' about the sushi Milt tried to stock at the General Store. Last I heard, at least six of the tourists from 4th of July weekend got food poisoning."

This isn't going well.

"There are people after me, Gladys. Bad people who won't hesitate to hurt anyone and everyone I care about. You have to stay in Seattle!"

"Nat..." She sounds so lost. Confused. "Where are you right now? That sexy doctor is back in Seattle by now. I'm gonna call Clancy and get his number. He can fly me back to Blakely on his plane. He'll know what to do."

My frustration escapes in a high-pitched growl. "I'm *with* Doc. And you're not listening!"

Gladys huffs. "Well, it's about damn time the two of you did the horizontal tango."

"Oh, my God. That is *not* the conversation we're having right now. Did you hear me? If you go back to Blakely, you'll be in danger." Tears burn hot trails down my cheeks. Why did I think I could do this over the phone. I should have gone to Bella's apartment. Except I don't know where she lives.

"I heard you, baby girl. But what I ain't heard is why. Or if you and Dr. Sexy Pants are safe." In the background, Bella shouts for her aunt to put the call on speaker, but Gladys shushes her. "I'm handling it."

Handling it? She thinks she's *handling it?* I swipe my tears away and sit up a little straighter.

"We're safe. Doc..." How can I explain everything that's happened over the past few days?

You can't.

"Doc saved my life on Monday night. The people after me...someone broke into my house and tried to kill me. Doc heard the shot. If he hadn't been there, I'd be dead. We left Blakely and we won't be coming back. I can't tell you more, Gladys. I wish I could. But I can't."

"You mean you won't." Her harumph breaks my heart into pieces. "I thought we were friends."

"We are. Gladys, I love you. You're my *only* friend. But that's why I need you to listen to me. If you get hurt..." I'm barely holding myself together. "One day, I might be able to tell you why. Or..."

"Or what?" she snaps.

"Or Doc will. Please. If you care about me at all, don't go back to the island. At least not for a week or two. Stay with Bella. Go to a hotel. Anywhere but back home." I hold my breath. She has to agree. If she doesn't, I don't know what I'll do. Beg Hidden Agenda to protect her too?

Gladys sighs. "All right. I'll stay here until next week. But I expect you to call me every single day to let me know you're safe. If you don't, I'll track you and Dr. Sexy Pants down, and you'll find out why three members of JuneBug took out restraining orders against me."

She hangs up before I can sputter out a reply—or ask her why the most popular band from my youth could possibly need even *one* restraining order against her, let alone *three*.

I rub my hands up and down my thighs. I'd give anything to go for a long swim. Or kayak around the island until my arms are about ready to fall off. But trapped in this small apartment, all I can do is pace.

Until I turn around to see Doc watching me.

"You won't explain, but Doc will?" His frustration spills over, and he clenches his fists at his sides. "You still think you'll be dead—or gone—and I'll be the only one left to explain things to Gladys?"

I can't lie to him. I won't.

"Yes.

"No!" he snaps. "I'm not explaining a damn thing to Gladys. You are. I called McCabe because there's no fucking way I'm losing you."

"You won't have a choice!" I drop the phone onto the couch and stalk over to the window. People pass by on the sidewalks, couples arm-in-arm, groups of teenagers, families... Restaurants put out their sandwich boards and turn on signs.

Life is happening just below us. Beautiful, messy, sometimes even ugly. But it's *life* all the same. A life I'll never have.

"You have to let me go, Doc," I say softly when I turn back to face him again. "It's the only way this works."

The betrayal etched on his face crushes what's left of my heart. We stare at one another for several beats.

"Fuck it." Doc strides over to me, hauls me into his arms, and crashes his mouth into mine.

The kiss isn't gentle. Or sweet. He kisses like a man possessed. His hands rove over my body. My breasts, my back, my hips. Strong fingers dig into my ass. "You are mine, Natasha. Until you tell me you don't want me. You. Are. Mine."

CHAPTER TWENTY-THREE

Doc

I HAVE Natasha up against the wall in four steps. I haven't stopped kissing her, and the little moans coming from her throat are the stuff of dreams—or fantasies.

Her fingers dig into my ass. "Doc." She trails kisses along the curve of my neck, and her warm breath fans over my ear. "This...isn't a good idea."

"Why not?" I hitch one of her legs up so I can grind my hips against her. "Can't you feel how much I need you, Natasha?"

She answers with a whimper. How can one sound be so damn sexy? Her hands sink into my hair, pulling me closer for another desperate kiss. My tongue teases hers. We're at war—one I'm determined to win. She thinks she has to leave. I'm going to prove her wrong.

"Bedroom. Now," Natasha says when I break off the kiss so we can breathe.

Fuck, yes. I need to be inside her. She's woken something

in me I thought died years ago. My need to keep her safe is almost feral, and it scares me.

The sway of her ass makes my dick throb with each step. I'm going to do serious damage if I don't get these jeans off soon.

"On the bed, baby."

"No." Natasha turns, the backs of her thighs pressed to the mattress. "This time, *I* get to be on top."

Fuuuuuck. I'm not one to give up control—never have been—but Natasha can do whatever she wants with me. To me. I'm hers every bit as much as she is mine.

Carefully, I work the zipper lower. My dick is so hard, even the slightest pressure is agonizing. As the denim hits the floor, Natasha sinks to her knees.

Her lips press to the bulge in my black silk boxers.

"Fucking hell."

"I never used to like this." She nuzzles my dick, inhaling deeply. "But I think with you..."

My shirt is in the way, so I strip it off while Natasha slides my boxers down my hips. Her tongue swirls over my crown. White spots float in my vision. I won't last if she keeps this up.

"No." The word escapes on a low growl. "I want to be inside you when I come. And you don't belong on your knees, baby."

I only take my eyes off her long enough to pull back the blankets. But in that time, she's shed her tank and jeans. The black cotton bra and panties shouldn't be the sexiest fucking things I've ever seen. But I'll be picturing her like this in my dreams for the rest of my life.

She starts to reach for the catch on her bra, but I wrap my arm around her waist and pull her against me. "The first night I spent on Blakely, I dreamed about you."

Releasing the catch, I take a step back and drink in the

sight of her. Her breasts are perfect handfuls, the nipples hard against my palms. "But dreams are nothing compared to reality. You're so fucking perfect, baby."

Natasha's head falls back. Goosebumps cover her skin. I kiss my way from her jaw down the curve of her neck until I close my teeth over the soft flesh above her collarbone.

The sound she makes is something between a scream and a whimper. Her hand wraps around my dick. Slowly, she circles the crown with her thumb. "Lie down, Doc. I need you inside me."

I stretch out on the mattress as she sheds her panties. The bed dips, and she climbs on top of me. Wet heat coats the head of my dick. Her scent is intoxicating. It's the sea after a storm, something as sweet as candy, and so very *her*.

I grab Natasha's hips and guide her onto my length. She's my home—so tight and wet, I can feel my shaft pulse with each beat of my heart.

Her first thrust threatens to undo me. "Fast and hard, baby."

"No." Natasha braces her hands on the mattress and lowers herself down to press her lips to one of my nipples. Her tongue laves over the hard nub. I'm on fire for her, every kiss stoking the flames.

Natasha's hips move so slowly, it's pure torture. I try to reach for her, but she pins my wrists to the bed. "Not this time, Doc. This is for me."

I'll give her anything she wants. Everything. Including my heart.

Her lips skim the edge of each bruise. Each scrape. Each part of me that thought I'd never be happy again.

She guides one of my hands to her mound. "Touch me, Doc."

I rub my thumb over her clit. The little button rises to meet my touch. Her weeping channel starts to tense around me. She quickens her pace until she's slamming into me. I match her thrust for thrust.

I'm so close. My balls draw up tight. My release rockets from the base of my spine. With one last pinch to Natasha's clit, I take her over the edge with me.

I'M NOT sure I can move. Nor do I want to. Natasha is pressed to my side, her head resting on my shoulder. She plays with my chest hair, a soft smile curving her lips. But there's a sadness to her entire being.

"Talk to me, baby."

"I've never felt like this before." She peers up at me, her gray eyes shimmering.

"Like what?" I ask.

"Safe. And..." she drops her voice to a whisper, "loved." She's so gentle as she seals her lips to mine. Tender. And it hits me. She's saying goodbye.

It doesn't matter that it won't happen today. Or even tomorrow. A part of her heart is already shuttered. She's leaving me bit by bit and there's nothing I can do to stop it.

Fuck. I wish I could bring her back to me. But I can see it in her eyes. She's made up her mind. All I can do now is make sure those assholes never touch her and hope that one day, she'll come back to me.

Natasha

I said it. Well, almost.

"I love you" was too hard. I can't even be sure I *do* love him. But I do know he makes me feel loved. He makes me feel so many things I thought I'd never feel again.

Protected. Cared for. Safe.

Now, we sit on the couch, his arm around my shoulders, with a movie on the flat screen TV.

Doc made chicken piccata, and as he cooked, we talked. Favorite books and movies, stories from various deployments, funny stories from childhood. We sat across from one another at the table, shared a bottle of sparkling soda, had ice cream sandwiches for dessert. It was so damn normal. And I loved every minute of it.

On the quick shopping trip with Inara, I was able to pick clothes *I* wanted—including these purple yoga pants and a soft, pink tank—and I almost feel like *me* again for the first time in years.

Except for the overwhelming sadness at knowing I'll have to leave Doc soon. Not tonight, though. Tonight, I want—no, I need—to soak up as much of his presence as I can.

On screen, two of the characters battle against an invading horde of robots trying to kill all of humanity. "Clancy had a couple of movie channels, but I've never heard of this franchise. Clearly, I've missed a lot."

Doc chuckles. "I watch a lot of baseball in the summer. But in the winter, it's all action movies and documentaries. We'll catch up."

We. God. I want there to be a "we." And a future where we can "catch up" on all the *life* I've missed over the years.

"I like sci-fi. And Gladys got me hooked on true crime."

"Why am I not surprised?" Doc presses a kiss to the top of my head. "I can do true crime and sci-fi. I'll do anything as long as you're with me."

From the slight edge to his voice, he knows. But he's not calling me on it. Whatever it is I feel for him...it just took another step toward love.

"Baseball, huh? You better not be a Mets fan."

Doc clutches his heart. "God, no. Red Sox and Mariners all the way. I've never understood why the National League won't adopt the designated hitter."

My laugh lifts a little of the weight threatening to crush my heart. No amount of wishing can make my dreams come true. But for tonight, I can pretend I have a future with this amazing man at my side.

THE POUNDING on the door wakes us moments before a woman's shout. "Doc, it's Raelynn! In thirty seconds, you better be decent!"

We scramble for our clothes. Doc pulls on a pair of sleep pants seconds before Raelynn bursts into the room.

"What is it?" he asks.

My heart pounds so hard, I'm surprised no one else can hear it. It's not quite 3:00 a.m. according to the clock on the nightstand. Something is *very* wrong.

Raelynn is dressed all in black, her hair pulled into a high ponytail. Oh, God. Her left ear is...half gone.

"Get your gear, Doc. Inara and Wyatt got hit at your place an hour ago. They killed one of the assholes, but Wyatt took a bullet to his bad leg. Through and through. Inara stopped the bleedin', but he's havin' trouble walkin'."

It wasn't supposed to be this soon. We should have had more time. How did they find his house so quickly?

"I need five minutes." Doc beelines for the bathroom, while I sink down onto the mattress.

"Natasha," Raelynn says, sitting next to me and resting a hand on my shoulder, "Graham's gonna stay here with you while Doc takes care of Wyatt. You okay with that?"

I don't want to let Doc out of my sight. But I'm not sure I

can face this man—Wyatt—who almost died for me. Then something Raelynn said clicks into place.

"You said…they killed *one* of the men. How many were there?"

"Two." She reaches up and brushes her fingers over the remains of her left ear. "West has the other one. He'll get what he can out of the pig fucker."

I choke back a sob. "He's going to kill him?"

Raelynn's eyes harden, and she purses her lips for a beat. "Darlin', the idjits after you ain't gonna stop until they're no longer breathin'. We've been at this for a long time." She shakes her head with a little huff. "Well, Ry has. I've only been with Hidden Agenda for a couple of years. But my first job? Graham's guy was kidnapped. The asshole didn't ask for ransom. His plan was to drug Q until the man was so messed up, he'd sign over his whole company. Then Alec was gonna kill him. That psychopath had destroyed half a dozen lives—and murdered at least two people—and he wasn't even forty."

My eyes start to burn with the threat of tears. I've cried more in the past week than I have since my brother was murdered. I can't seem to stop.

"He's…dead now?" I ask.

"In about a million tiny pieces spread out over the Utah desert. Ry put a bullet in his head and West set off a whole mess of explosives. Couldn't leave any evidence behind." She pats my knee once more as Doc emerges from the bathroom. "What I'm tryin' to tell you, darlin', is that we don't kill for the sake of killin'. But sometimes, it's the only way. This is one of those times."

Doc, now dressed in a pair of black pants and a gray t-shirt, reaches for one of the duffel bags, but Raelynn beats him to it. "Now I *know* you ain't in fightin' shape, sugar. I got this."

I snap my gaze to Doc's. Jealousy rears up, unfamiliar and unwelcome.

Doc pulls me to my feet, slides one hand into my hair, and kisses me until all I can think about is how quickly I'm falling in love with him. "Don't worry, baby. She speaks Texan, remember? Sugar doesn't mean what you think it does."

Raelynn laughs. "Damn straight. Anyone from Texas ever calls you 'sugar,' what they're really sayin' is, 'you're an idjit.' Like Doc here, who thinks a broken rib and a hole in his chest are *minor* injuries."

Her phone beeps, and she checks the screen. "Graham's on his way up. Wyatt's hoppin' mad. Ry and Rip are at the warehouse tryin' to stop him from joinin' West and Inara for the interrogation. Time to go."

Doc frames my face with his warm hands. "I'll be back soon. Try to get some rest."

He leaves me with one last kiss, and as I watch him go, I wonder how long it'll be until *I'm* the one who's leaving.

CHAPTER TWENTY-FOUR

Doc

"How bad is it? Really?" I ask Raelynn. Her hands grip the steering wheel hard enough, her knuckles are white.

"He done got his ass into a sling. But he's talkin'. And cursin' Ry for benchin' him. Damn fool has a hole clean through his thigh and he still thinks he should be with West for the interrogation."

I've met Wyatt a few times while treating his girlfriend, Hope. Nothing Raelynn says surprises me. "He's about as stubborn as McCabe."

"Damn straight." She offers me a tight-lipped smile. "But he's only been with us a few months. He ain't figured it out yet."

"Figured what out?"

Raelynn accelerates onto I-5, quickly gunning the Mustang up to eighty miles an hour. Thank God it's so early in the morning.

"There ain't nothin' more important than comin' home." She shakes her head softly. "Hope is his everythin'. *Shee-it.* He wouldn't even commit to joinin' us until Ry announced he was steppin' away. But Wyatt hasn't been with us long enough to know we *always* have each other's backs. He don't have to go on every mission to be a part of things."

We don't speak again until she turns onto Industrial Way. "Uh, Doc, there's one more thing you should know."

I tighten my hands on my thighs, digging into my quads hard enough to leave bruises. This isn't going to be good. Not with the way her shoulders hunch.

"Spit it out."

"Your couch, television, and fridge are about as useless as teats on a bull. You're gonna want to replace the carpet too."

"Is that all?" My grip relaxes, and I let out a chuckle. "I always hated that carpet. Those assholes did me a favor."

"STAY THE FUCK DOWN." McCabe's booming voice ricochets off the high ceiling as I follow Raelynn into the warehouse. It's not my first time here, but I still gape at the sheer enormity of the space.

The climbing wall rises more than thirty feet, and I spare it more than a passing glance. The one at the little gym by my place can't compare. A boxing ring sits in the center of the building with large mats on either side of it. But what's most impressive is the quarter mile track that runs around the perimeter.

Close to the kitchenette, Wyatt lies on a table with McCabe standing over him and Murphy, Wyatt's Belgian Malinois, whining softly from the floor close to the man's head.

Not far away, Ripper is hunched over his computer with Charlie lying at his feet.

"About damn time," McCabe mutters. "If you won't listen to me, maybe you'll listen to the doc."

I drop my bag on the chair. Wyatt's black pants are ripped open up to his briefs. Around his thigh, two of *my* t-shirts are held in place with a tight length of cord.

"Fucking hell. If the bullet caught your femoral artery—"

"It didn't," Wyatt grits out. "Know what that feels like."

That wasn't the answer I was expecting. "All right, then. Let's take a look." I point to a spot close to Wyatt's balls. "McCabe, put pressure right there." I half expect one—or both—of them to refuse, but Ryker moves into position as I don a head lamp and shine the light directly on my patient's leg.

"Do. Not. Move." I glare at Wyatt until I'm sure he understands how serious this is. "And you owe me two new t-shirts."

"Put them on my tab," Ryker says. "Along with...uh, never mind."

"Raelynn already told me I'd need to redecorate." I cut the cord and pull the first soaked shirt off the top of Wyatt's thigh. "Jesus Fucking Christ. This wasn't a 9mm."

"Nope. Sombitch had a .45." Wyatt's words are starting to slur. I don't dare delay long enough to give him a shot of morphine if he's this close to passing out.

It takes me an hour before I add the final stitch and wrap his leg in several layers of gauze and surgical tape. He's conscious, but mostly quiet now. Worn out from the pain, I'd guess.

"He's benched for at least two weeks." I wash my hands at the sink in the kitchenette while Ryker starts a pot of coffee.

"I'll tell West." The big man runs his palm over his bald head. His fingers trace several of the deeper scars the Taliban left him with after fifteen months of what I suspect was constant torture.

"You really are out, aren't you?" I lean against the counter, watching some sort of struggle play over his features.

"Advisory capacity only," he says. "West has run every op since the day he joined Hidden Agenda. He's more than capable."

"McCabe, we're not friends. I don't know much more about you now than I did when you hired me four years ago. But I *do* know that you're not the type of guy who just... retires."

His raspy chuckle sounds like someone's strangling a chicken. "You never know. I could take up bird watching."

"Fuck no. You'd be out of your mind in less than twenty-four hours. The birds would turn on you." The idea of the man doing *anything* but this is too ridiculous to contemplate.

"Every time we take on a job, there's a chance we don't come home." He stares over at Wyatt, who hasn't moved off the table. "Wren and Harlow are my whole world. I can't leave them."

"You're my whole world, Gage. Don't go."

I haven't heard my mother's voice in more than thirty years. But now, it's like she's right next to me.

"Doc?" McCabe stares down at me, a coffee mug in his hand. "I said, 'do you want a cup?'"

I shake off the long-ago memory. "Wyatt's stable. I should go."

He sets the mug in front of me anyway. "West and Inara will be back soon. Natasha's safe with Graham. Have a fucking cup of coffee."

This isn't the same man who told me to get the fuck out after I treated Raelynn. I stare at him for so long, he shakes his head.

"Last time you were here, I fucked up, Doc. Wren was eight months pregnant. Ripper had just gone on his first mission since Hell. And when Raelynn got hurt—and I couldn't get there in time—I lost my shit. You were a convenient target." Ryker stares into his coffee, his multi-color eyes unfocused. "Too convenient."

"And after?" I ask.

"After…" He hangs his head. "I'm not used to being wrong. And I'm not good at apologies."

"Clearly. Since you haven't managed to actually say the words yet." I lift my own mug to hide my smile.

"Asshole."

I turn, setting the cup on the counter, and shove my hands into my pockets. I don't think the man shakes hands. Ever. "Apology accepted, McCabe."

"Ryker." A muscle in his jaw ticks for a moment before he adds, "Or Ry. My…uh…friends and family call me Ry."

TWO CUPS OF COFFEE LATER, the door to the warehouse opens. West and Inara look like I feel. Exhausted. Beat to hell. Haunted.

"Ry, you get to clean up the mess we made," West says and beelines for the coffee pot. "Because we've got a problem."

"What is it?" I jerk to my feet from my spot on the couch across from Ripper. "Is Natasha—"

"She's safe," Rip says. "Graham checked in five minutes ago."

West downs half his coffee in two swallows, then fills the mug up to the brim again. "The fuckers who attacked Wyatt and Inara got Doc's address from the resort owner—Clancy McNamera. They claim they didn't hurt him, but I called a friend of mine who lives in Georgia. He's on his way to St. Augustine now to check on McNamera."

"Fuck. Natasha…she won't handle this well." I've never

met Clancy in person, but he's always been kind over the phone. "He's got to be close to eighty. If not older."

Inara huffs. "He's seventy-nine. But that's not our biggest problem. West needs to mainline a gallon of caffeine before he tries to give a sit-rep. He's burying the lead."

"I had my thumb in a man's eye less than twenty minutes ago. Cut me some goddamn slack." The former SEAL braces his elbows on the counter, then jerks up and curses at the smear of blood he left on the granite.

Ryker turns to Inara. "If we take ten minutes, is anything going to blow up in our faces?"

"No. But we should see if Pritchard's available. We're going to need him." She grabs a bottle of water from the fridge, cracks the seal, and downs half of it before she comes up for air.

"Sampson, hit the showers," Ryker orders.

The former SEAL draws up straighter, staring his former boss down like he's about to knock him on his ass. But Inara makes a comment about needing to talk to her husband, and West blows out a breath.

"Ten minutes. Not a second longer." He trudges toward the lockers, taking his very large coffee mug with him.

Ryker turns around and stares out the little window over the sink. Inara heads for the far corner of the building with her phone in her hand. Wyatt passed out on one of the cots a while ago and hasn't woken yet, and Ripper is still heads down at his laptop.

Great. Whatever pep talk McCabe needs now is apparently up to me.

"What was that all about?" I ask.

"Sampson has the most interrogation training." Ryker keeps his voice low and casts a quick glance back at Ripper. "Most of what we—they—do is retrieval. Hell, half of the time it's non-lethals only. Tranq darts, rubber bullets, flash bangs. Get in, get the target, get out. But when it's one of our own..."

He grips the edge of the counter hard enough, his knuckles crack.

"I thought I'd seen it all. Didn't think there was anything worse than all the shit they did to us in Hell. And then, I found Rip at the bottom of a goddamned well in Afghanistan six *years* after we blew Hell Mountain off the map."

"Fuck."

"He barely knew his own name, Doc. Thought I was a hallucination. I didn't understand how he could lose himself like that. Until West and Trevor explained it to me. How to break a man. They both know. They've both done it. And every time West has to extract information like he did tonight...it costs him a little more. One day, he's not going to be able to do it anymore."

"You're worried that day isn't too far off."

Ryker shakes his head. "He's got a few more years. Maybe even a decade. The man fucking loves running this team. But that's partly why I...'retired.' Once Harlow's a little older, Dax and I are going to start recruiting. Not for the team here. That's West's job now. But for new Hidden Agenda locations around the world."

I stare at the man, not quite sure what I'm hearing. "You're...*franchising?*"

His laugh isn't as forced this time. One corner of his mouth tips up, and some of the tension leaves his shoulders. "I guess we are."

***

"Huddle up," West says. His hair is still damp, but he's changed into a pair of jeans and a blue t-shirt. He has that look so many elite operators get after years in the field. Cold.

Hard. Detached. McCabe—Ryker—is right. In five or ten years, the former SEAL might not have anything else to give. I hope to God this team has some sort of therapist on speed dial.

We all take seats, filling the couches, loveseats, and recliners surrounding several large monitors on the north wall. West taps his tablet a few times, and a man's face appears on the center screen.

"This asshole is Michael Lyden. He and his brother, Parrish Lyden, broke into Doc's house a little after 2:00 a.m. this morning. They were both wearing body armor, which is the only reason they lived long enough to shoot Wyatt in the leg. Inara slit Parrish's throat and put a bullet in Michael's knee cap before he could finish Wyatt off."

I sit up a little straighter. "The guy on Blakely—Parker—was wearing body armor. Either that or I've forgotten how to shoot a gun in the past fifteen years." It suddenly occurs to me that's a real possibility. I can't remember the last time I went to the range.

"He was," Wyatt says. His eyes are half closed, and from the odd thickness to his words, the morphine is still doing its job. But he's with us enough to pay attention.

"Michael," West continues, "cracked after less than an hour. He gave us eleven names. Six, we already knew. Rip?"

With a few keystrokes, Ripper sends half a dozen photos to the center screen. "Bastian and the rest of the Ranger squad Natasha testified against. Wren and I have been hoping they'd pop up on facial rec, but they're doing a damn good job hiding. Or they have help."

"Like your kind of help?" I ask.

"Yup." He scowls, the annoyance on his face obvious. "If there's someone better than us out there, I don't want to be around when Wren finds out."

"No one's better than the two of you," Ryker says, pride lending a tone to his voice I've never heard before.

Five more faces appear on screen. "These are the new players," West says. "Two Army captains, the Ambassador to East Timor, and a Marine Corps Lieutenant Colonel. This is the kind of power we're dealing with. And why, if we have any hope of keeping Natasha and Doc safe, we need Pritchard's help."

"Who's Pritchard?" I ask.

West arches a brow, then quickly shakes his head. "Sorry, Doc. You've been around so long, I forget you always stayed on the outside. Major General Austin J. Pritchard. Former head of the Joint Special Operations Command. He was shit-canned a few years ago for going rogue to save Trevor and Dani down in Venezuela. So he started his own black ops team."

"With the world's worst name," Ryker mutters. "Rescue Operations Group? The man has no creativity. At the very least, he could have called it Rescue Operations Group and Underground Experts."

Everyone turns to stare at him. "The hell?" West asks.

"R.O.G.U.E.?" Ryker shakes his head. "No one here appreciates my sense of humor."

"Because until recently, you didn't have one," Inara says and elbows the man in the side.

I'm losing patience. "So, where is this guy? Will he help you? Me? Us?" My words trip over one another. I'm too tired. Drained of all my energy and running on pure adrenaline and caffeine. But I don't get the sense anyone at Hidden Agenda has a problem with dragging someone they need out of bed at all hours of the night.

West rubs the back of his neck, something I can't quite read in his eyes. "Oh, he'll help. But he scheduled a fucking colonoscopy for this morning. So until he comes out of sedation in an hour, we wait."

A HAND on my shoulder startles me awake. "Natasha's on her way with Graham," West says.

I don't remember lying down on one of the couches. I definitely don't remember someone covering me with a thin, gray blanket. But I sit up and blink the sleep from my eyes. "Isn't she safer if she stays at the apartment with Graham?" I'd give anything to have her in my arms right now, but she's in enough danger already.

"You're in the safest place in the goddamn world." This, from Ryker, who ambles over with a cup of coffee in his hand. "All the traffic cameras in a four-block radius loop whenever one of our vehicles is in range. If anyone *did* get wind of us, this entire place can lock down tight. The walls, ceiling, and doors are reinforced. No one's getting through without a fuck-ton of firepower, and even then...it'd be a goddamn miracle if they managed it. Should a lockdown be triggered, every member of our family around the world gets notified. They can be here in anywhere from three to twelve hours. Not to mention the fucking arsenal we have locked behind some of the best biometric security money can buy."

"She'll be safe, Doc." West unwraps a protein bar and sinks down across from me. "And this is *her* fight. You're just along for the ride."

CHAPTER TWENTY-FIVE

Natasha

I DIDN'T THINK I'd be able to sleep after Doc left, but Graham arrived armed with chamomile tea and, twenty minutes later, I could barely keep my eyes open. His knock startles me awake, and I check the clock. Shit. It's almost 8:00 a.m.

"Natasha? We need to get to the warehouse in the next half an hour. Are you decent?"

I'm on my feet in under a minute and yank the door open. "What's wrong? Is Doc okay?"

"He's fine," the young man says. His smile is so easy, like he's never come up against a problem he couldn't solve. But there's also a lifetime of pain and worry in his eyes. "He patched Wyatt up. But West got some intel out of the guys who broke into Doc's house, and we're calling in some of the big guns for help."

"The big guns? There's someone out there bigger than Ryker?"

Graham's laugh lights up his entire face. Any exhaustion

he carried from the long night fades away—or maybe that's the coffee he obviously made. My mouth waters at the scent.

"Impossible. The man's almost seven feet tall. His daughter's in the one hundred and twenty-fifth percentile for length. That kid is going to tower over Wren by the time she's a teenager. The big gun I'm talking about is the former head of the Joint Special Operations Command. He retired a few years ago. He's part of the family in a weird way. Grew up best friends with Trevor, but no one knew it until we had to rescue Ripper from Afghanistan." Graham shrugs. "It's a whole *thing*. Once this whole mess is over, you and Doc should come to one of West's BBQs. That's where the newbies get to hear all our stories." Graham turns and heads back down the hall. "Do you take anything in your coffee? I'll fix you a cup while you change. We're out of here in ten minutes."

"Black, please. I'll hurry." I grab a pair of tailored pants and a flowing blue tank top. At the last second, I dart back to the shopping bags and fish out a black lace bra, and high-cut panties. I don't know why, but I want to feel *pretty* today.

Because this might be the last day I have with Doc before I run?

I want to memorize everything about him. The way he touches me. The sounds he makes as I wrap my fingers around his dick. His taste. But also, his smile. His laugh. The crinkling around his eyes. The feel of his hand on mine.

The hot water stings when it runs over the stitches at my hip. But the wound is healing. No trace of the infection that could have killed me.

Carefully, I smooth body wash over my skin. Why didn't I ask Doc to bring his soap from home? When he smells it on me, he gets this possessive look in his eyes. It shouldn't be so arousing. He's not some over-the-top romance novel hero and I'm not a damsel in distress. But I can't help the way I react to him.

When I emerge from the bedroom, Graham has two travel mugs sitting on the counter next to the floppy hat and oversized sunglasses I wore on the way here.

"We control all the cameras in the building." He shows me his phone screen with a long list of devices. "The internet connection is encrypted to hell and back, but I'll loop them all until we're in the SUV for good measure." He dons a light jacket to hide the gun strapped to his hip.

"How long have you worked...uh...here?" I ask when we're in the elevator.

"Almost four years." A grin curves his lips. "Best job in the world."

"Wyatt almost *died* tonight. How can you say that?" I might need to change my mind about Graham. I'd thought him smart and capable, if a bit young. Now, I wonder if he's just naive.

He sobers, and as the elevator reaches the garage, takes my arm and leads me to the black SUV in silence. He doesn't speak again until we're on the road. "When someone calls us, they're out of options. Did you know the average ransom demand these days is over four hundred thousand? That's *average*. One of the cases we took on last month had a three-million-dollar price on his head. He was an executive for a tech company out of Malaysia. The company itself was worth a fortune, but they refused to pay. His family didn't have that kind of cash. We got him back for two-hundred-and-fifty thousand. Safe. Nothing more than a broken arm, a handful of bruises, and some really awful memories. But when we breached the old factory where he was being held, we found six other victims. Including a husband and wife who'd been taken while doing volunteer work in the Philippines. Their entire net worth was only a little over a hundred-and-fifty thousand. The terrorists were asking for over a million. That couple had been there for a month. No one was ever going to come looking for them." He meets my gaze as he stops at a traffic light. "Sam and Debra are back in Spain with their three children now. A boy and two girls, all under the age of twelve."

"Shit."

The SUV accelerates smoothly onto the freeway. "Kidnapping is a global business, Natasha. I get to save people for a living. All over the world. Yes, it's dangerous. Yes, every single time we go out on a job, there's a chance one of us—or all of us—could die. Q worries—a lot. But he's alive because of what we do. And how good we are at doing it."

"What do you do when you're *not* saving people? You don't go on jobs every day, right?"

He chuckles. "No. We only take on two to four jobs a month at most. We train three nights a week. I work as a bartender on the weekends. West owns a Krav Maga studio. Raelynn works there part time. Inara's a translator. Wyatt's retired—for now. Hope does some book keeping work, and they go up to his cabin in the mountains every few weeks. Rip is on staff at one of the local animal shelters. Wren works for Second Sight—that's Dax's firm in Boston—on more mainstream jobs when she's not helping us."

I hunch a little lower in the seat. These men and women are saving lives. And for the past eight years, I've done...nothing. Before I found my way to Blakely, I worked a bunch of odd jobs—anything I could get that would pay me under the table. Washing dishes, cleaning motel rooms at a place I *know* rented by the hour, even being a line cook at a truck stop diner.

What would my life have been like if I'd been able to choose? If I'd been able to use my college degree in political science? Or get a master's degree in...anything?

"Natasha? We're here." Graham touches my arm lightly, concern in his eyes. "Are you okay?"

I sweep my gaze over a large parking lot with half a dozen vehicles. Three identical SUVs, a white coupe, and a vintage blue pickup truck.

"Sorry." I grab my new purse—an impulse buy from yesterday's shopping trip—with my passports and a thousand dollars tucked away in various pockets. "It's been a long few days."

He doesn't look convinced. But I'm out of the SUV before he can say another word.

The warehouse isn't much to look at from the outside. Gray. Industrial. Like every other warehouse in every other major city. Some of the windows close to the roof are cracked. Others have clearly been replaced at one time or another. The walls haven't been cleaned in years. But as soon as we step through the door, we're in another world.

Everything is so clean, it's practically sparkling. A climbing wall with multi-colored handholds rises all the way to the ceiling. I stop short, staring at the boxing ring and full set of free weights. I've seen gyms that aren't this nice. On the opposite side of the space, Ryker and West stand next to a coffee pot, watching me. A few feet away, Raelynn and Inara face off at a foosball table, and in the far corner, there's a living space, complete with couches and a thick carpet. Ripper sits on one, and another man—almost as big as Ryker —sprawls on another.

Doc strides across the warehouse, his sole focus on me. The power of his stare almost knocks me off my feet. We've been apart less than four hours, but it feels like a lifetime. He wraps me in his embrace, and I press my nose to his neck.

"Graham said...there was news?" I ask.

"Names." Doc smooths his hand over my hair. It's such a tender gesture, my eyes burn for a moment until I blink the sensation away. "West interrogated one of the men who broke into my place. Bastian and his crew—the ones you testified against—weren't working alone."

My stomach flips, threatening the coffee I managed on the drive here. "How many more?"

Doc's expression shutters. "We don't know yet, baby. But Ryker's—West's team won't give up until they figure it out."

"Pritchard's calling," West shouts across the massive space.

"Who's Pritchard?" I ask. "Is he the guy from JSOC?"

Doc nods, tucks me against his side, and leads me over to the couches. He doesn't let go as we take our seats. West taps his phone, and the center monitor lights up.

"Austin," he says. "About damn time, old man."

"For fuck's sake." Austin's East Coast accent is more pronounced than Doc's. "Colonoscopies aren't just for the elderly, frogman."

"Yeah, well, which one of us still has all his hair? That widow's peak of yours is looking a little sharp."

"Uh...West?" Austin's brows arch, confusion in his tone. "Speaking of AARP... Did you do some recruiting without telling me? From the local senior center?"

"Fucking hell. I'm only fifty-six," Doc mutters. "Seventeen years as a PJ gave me all this gray."

West chuckles. "This is our doc. Doc Reynolds, meet Austin Pritchard."

"Got a first name, Doc?"

"Yeah. Doc." His shoulders are so stiff, they might as well be granite. "I changed it more than thirty years ago. This is—"

"Natasha Winters," Austin says with a hint of a smile. "Your disappearance made waves in my world. Well, when it was still my world."

"Austin was the head of JSOC until eighteen months ago,"

West explains. "Now he runs a group a lot like ours. But they tend to go after some of the dregs of humanity."

"As opposed to the unicorns and rainbows and Nobel Peace Prize winners we—you—take down?" Ryker snorts into his coffee.

"It's still 'we.' You and Wren are just...backup now," Ripper says and nods at the screens. "Can we get to it? Cara's shift at the restaurant will be over in a couple of hours, and I want to be home when she gets there."

I look at the five photos on the monitor next to Austin's face. "Oh, my God. That's...Ambassador Norton. He's the one who *insisted* I go through Ranger school."

"Louis Francis Norton," Austin says. "Formerly Senator Louis Norton of the great state of Louisiana. All around garbage pile of a human being. He's been accused of sexual harassment six times. Rumor has it, that's why the President sent him to East Timor."

"Is he going to be a problem for us?" West asks.

Austin shakes his head. "I know people who can put pressure on him. He's a coward. The other fucks on this list, however... They've got a good thing going—they've *had* a good thing going for fifteen years. Kuwait, Iraq, Afghanistan, Syria..."

I look from Doc to West to Austin. "They've been running drugs for *fifteen years*?" I ask.

"Maybe more. A few of us in senior command suspected, but we never had any proof. Not when we could do something about it. But now..." Austin grins. "I have resources I never dreamed of when I was at JSOC. What say we make a case against them and wrap it up in a pretty little bow? We do that, and the Uniform Code of Military Justice will put an end to all of them."

RYKER HELPS WYATT out to his SUV. Ripper is talking to Austin's tech genius, Zephyr. Something about following the money. The two Army Captains and the Marine Corps Lieutenant Colonel all have offshore bank accounts, and at least one of them—Captain Bishop's—has more than ten million in it.

I lean against Doc, my head on his shoulder. Raelynn said she'd take us back to the apartment in a few minutes, but she and West are in the middle of an intense discussion about purchasing an old helicopter she found online.

"How did they find your house so quickly? Ryker said it would be at least two days. Maybe four."

He links our fingers and brushes a kiss to my knuckles. "Bastian sent someone to see Clancy."

"Oh, God. Did they hurt him?" I can't believe no one thought to tell me. Panic claws its way up my throat. I start to shake, but Doc takes me by the shoulders.

"West had someone check on him. Apparently, the guy Bastian sent chatted him up for an hour or so, trying to rent Campsite Four. He's fine, baby."

I press my hand to my chest, trying to calm my racing heart. "I lied to him—told him I needed a week off for a family emergency. I knew I'd never be able to go back, but... he's going to hate me when he figures it out. Just like Gladys."

"Who's Gladys?" West asks.

I jerk around, shocked he's suddenly right behind me. The man moves with a lethal silence I haven't encountered since my days in the army.

"She's a friend. My...only friend. She lives on the other side of the resort."

Doc clears his throat. "She's also eighty-three years old, swears more than McCa—Ryker, and decided the first day she met me that Natasha and I were supposed to be together."

"We need to get someone on her. If you're close, chances are Bastian's gonna figure that out." West looks around the warehouse and frowns. "I don't have enough goddamn people to cover Seattle *and* Blakely. Not with Wyatt out of commission for the next two weeks. Need to make some calls."

"Gladys is in Seattle," I say. "I convinced her to stay here with her niece for at least another few days."

West blows out a breath. "Well, that's something. Do you know the niece's address?"

"No. But I can get it. Can I see her? Gladys?" I don't want to face my friend. But I need to say goodbye before I run. To give her one last hug and tell her I love her.

"Don't see why not. Call her. If we can leave in a few minutes, Graham and I will follow you and Raelynn. The kid can keep an eye on her until I get some private security in place."

I pull out the new cell phone and dial. But four rings later, the call goes to voicemail. Bella doesn't answer either. "Maybe they're dress shopping?" I check my watch. "Are department stores even open at 10:00 a.m.?"

"You know her niece's last name?" West is on full alert now, and I shift closer to Doc, needing his steady strength to ground me.

"Cavalli. Annabella Glory Cavalli."

"Rip? Annabella Glory Cavalli. Need an address!" he calls before turning his attention back to me. "Does Clancy know about Gladys? Would he have any reason to talk about her? And her niece?"

The panic returns with a vengeance. I grip Doc's arm, my fingers digging into the corded muscle. "He knows who she is. They're close."

"Got it," Ripper says. "Sending to your phones now. Ry's going to be closest. He could be there in fifteen, tops. Think he'd give the woman a heart attack if he knocked on her door?"

"Bella isn't easily intimidated. She's a lawyer." Doc gives my hand a squeeze. "Take a breath, baby. I'm sure she's fine. You'll see it for yourself soon enough."

I wish I could believe him.

"Send him," West says. "We're out of here in five minutes. Graham? Gear up for surveillance. I'm not taking any chances."

As Raelynn pulls up to the small apartment building off Pike Street, her car's display flashes with Ryker's name.

"How close are you?" he asks before she can even say hello.

"I'm fixin' to park. Why?" She glances over at me, and something's very, *very* wrong.

Ryker's gravelly voice is rougher than it was only half an hour ago. "I need Doc up here right now. We've got a problem."

CHAPTER TWENTY-SIX

Doc

THE SIXTH FLOOR is utterly silent as the elevator doors slide open. Raelynn sweeps her gaze up and down the hall. "Clear. Stay on my six." Tapping her ear, she adds, "Ry, we're comin' in."

"Oh my God." Natasha swallows a sob. A vase of flowers lies shattered on the kitchen floor. One of the end tables is upended, and blood stains the carpet in long streaks.

"Doc, over here." Ryker is on one knee in front of the couch, and it only takes me another two steps to understand why. Bella lies on the pretty floral cushions, a large lump swelling on her forehead and a bloody towel pressed to her shoulder.

"Gladys?" Natasha asks, her voice so shaky, I'd give anything to sweep her into my arms and carry her out of there. But I can't. I have a patient who needs me.

"They...took her." Those three words seem to take everything Bella has left, because her head lolls to the side and all the tension leaves her body.

Fuck. "Out of my way," I snap. Ryker moves with a speed a man his size shouldn't have, and I take his place. "She's breathing. Rapid heart rate. Clammy. Someone get me a blanket."

I'm vaguely aware of Raelynn trying to comfort Natasha. Of Ryker, West, and Graham talking about security cameras. Of someone draping a soft, gray blanket over Bella's legs.

Normal pupil dilation. Normal breathing sounds. I remove the towel and cut her green blouse down the center. The moment I get my first good look at the wound, she opens her eyes and screams.

"Bella! It's Doc!" Taking her arms, I try to hold her down, but she fights like a hellion and catches me just below my bruised ribs.

Ryker catches her, steps from the door. "Stop. We're here to help."

Bella tries to claw at his face, probably too panicked to hear a word. Ryker grabs her wrists and pins them over her head. "Calm the *fuck* down, Bella!"

"Let me go! I don't know *anything*! I just want my aunt back, please!" She starts to sob, and Natasha ducks between her and Ryker.

"Bella, look at me, sweetheart. It's Nat. You're safe."

From her tone, Natasha doesn't believe that any more than I do. But the familiar voice seems to do the trick. Bella sags in Ryker's hold. He releases her, and Natasha wraps her arm around Bella's waist to keep her upright.

"No. Get away from me!" The young woman shoves at Natasha. "This is *your* fault. They took Aunt Gladys because of *you.*"

Tears brim in Natasha's eyes. Her entire body starts to tremble. She's about five seconds away from losing it completely, but she's trying to be strong for Bella.

"Come on now, sugar. Let's get you back to the couch."

Raelynn takes Bella's arm. "Doc needs to take a look at your shoulder." She nods at Graham, who wraps his hand around Natasha's arm and leads her into the kitchen.

Fucking hell. I need to comfort her. I told her everything would be fine. That no one would go after Gladys. She'll never trust me again after this. Gladys could already be dead. Or...worse.

Raelynn helps Bella sit back down, and I tear my gaze from the kitchen. Assess the patient. Keep her alive. Everything else...I have to put away.

With half of Hidden Agenda in the room—and armed— we're safe for at least a short time. Graham is one of the most understanding men I've ever met. If anyone can keep Natasha calm until I'm done, it's him.

Lowering myself down onto the coffee table, I meet Bella's red-rimmed eyes. "I need you to take off your shirt. West and Ryker will turn their backs, okay?"

Bella tightens her fingers on the two halves of her blouse and looks around slowly. Shit. I don't think she had any idea how many people were in her apartment until just now. But after a moment, she drops her hand.

I ease the bloody material from her shoulders. The stab wound is deep, but based on its location, the knife didn't hit anything vital. She was lucky. I dig in my bag for the vial of morphine. As I lift my gaze, I suck in a sharp breath.

Her torso is covered in bruises. They beat her up before they stabbed her.

"Doc, please..."

A long-ago memory steals my breath. Then another. This one so much worse. My mother's broken body lying on the living room floor. Not a single inch of her unmarked. My father standing over her with a bottle in his hand.

"Doc?" Raelynn touches my shoulder, jerking me back to the present. "You okay?"

Focus on the patient. You can do this.

I shove my feelings down so deep, they can't possibly escape—for now—and measure out four milligrams of morphine. "This is for the pain. I'll also give you a local anesthetic and a shot of antibiotics before I stitch you up. Okay?"

She nods, tears staining her cheeks. I work quickly. Three injections, saline to irrigate the wound, antiseptic, four stitches, and a thick bandage. Raelynn brings Bella a fresh shirt and helps her put it on.

Natasha doesn't look at me when I move to the kitchen sink to wash the blood from my hands. "I thought Gladys would be safe here," she says quietly. "Bella has a different last name. How did they even find her?"

I pull Natasha against me, rubbing small circles over her lower back. "I don't know, baby. But Gladys is a force of nature. Those bastards don't know what they're in for."

In the living room, West clears his throat. "Bella, can you tell us what happened?"

"Who are you people?" she asks. "And why are you even here? They said if I called the police, they'd *kill* Aunt Gladys. If she dies—"

"We're not the police. My name is West. I'm a retired Navy SEAL. That wall of muscle over there is former Special Forces. Graham was in the Coast Guard. Raelynn, Air Force. The men who took your aunt have been selling drugs in the Middle East for more than a decade, and they're after Natasha because she tried to stop them."

I keep my arm around Natasha's waist and urge her into the living room. Bella glares up at us. "Aunt Gladys loves you. She talks about you all the time. How could you do this to her?"

"Natasha didn't *do* anything." I can't imagine what Bella is feeling right now, but there's no way I'm going to stand by and let her blame Natasha for what Bastian and his piece-of-shit *associates* did. "You want to blame someone, blame Clancy. He's probably the one who gave those assholes your aunt's name."

"Doc." Ryker shoots me a look that clearly says "shut up."

West lowers himself down next to the young woman. "I know you're scared, Bella. But I need you to tell me everything you can remember."

"Take her to the Five Points," West says. "I sent the remote key to your phone."

"Gotcha." Raelynn slings Bella's bag over her shoulder and takes the young woman's arm. "Come on, darlin'. I've got you."

"She'll be safe at a hotel?" I ask.

West pins me with his icy stare. "The Five Points uses Emerald City Security. That's Cam's firm. She doesn't like it, but we have access to their camera network. Rip and Wren can monitor Bella's door twenty-four-seven."

Natasha hasn't said a word since Bella started telling us what happened.

"We were having coffee," Bella says with a sniffle. "I was supposed to go to work today, and Aunt Gladys was going to watch her murder shows and cook us dinner.

"Someone knocked. I thought it was the grocery delivery. But when I opened the door, three men forced their way in. I broke the first guy's nose." Bella almost smiles, even as she swipes a fresh trail of tears from her cheek. "Aunt Gladys insisted I take some self-defense classes when I went to college. But I couldn't fight all three of them. Aunt Gladys was so brave. She just told me she loved me and she'd see me again soon. I thought...they'd all leave, but one of them stayed. He..."

She wraps her arms around herself with a wince. "He told me if I called anyone, he'd make Aunt Gladys's last few hours..." More tears, and she shakes her head, unable to continue.

West passes me a small, plastic case. "Keep this on you, Doc."

I open the lid to find two small earbuds.

"Multi-channel comms units. They can piggyback off the app Rip installed on your phones. I don't know what Bastian's end game is yet, but I'd lay odds he'll call Natasha in the next three or four hours with his demands. Make sure you put those in the second her phone rings."

"Why does it matter?" Natasha asks. "Whatever he wants, I'll do it. I can't let him hurt Gladys."

"Hell, no." I frame her face with my hands and brush the tears from her cheeks. "You are not giving up."

"He's already won. He took the only home I've had in eight years. My only friend. He almost killed you on the island. I won't give him another chance. I can't." She twists out of my hold, then turns to West. "You have to keep Doc safe. Please."

"We'll keep you both safe. This is what we do, Natasha. Doc's family, which means you are too. We don't give up on family." West taps his ear. "Inara just pulled up. She and Graham will take you to the warehouse. We'll meet back there in two hours. Ry's picking up Wren and Harlow. After what I did this morning, I need to see Cam for a few minutes. Once I do, I'll be clear."

The haunted look in his eyes reminds me just how much West has done for us in the space of four days.

I tuck Natasha tighter against me and meet the former SEAL's gaze over the top of her head. "I can't pay you back for—"

"We owe you twenty times over, Doc. This? Raelynn would say it 'ain't nothin' but nothin'.' And she'd be right."

Natasha

Inara ushers us back into the warehouse, and I tear the floppy hat from my head, crumple it in my hands, and barely stop myself from flinging it as far as I can.

These men and women have sacrificed for me. They've given me three days with Doc. Three wonderful days I'll hold close until Bastian kills me. How much more can I ask of them?

"Graham's stopping for burgers, fries, and shakes," Inara says. "He'll be here soon. Doc, clean off the table, will you? Pretty sure there's still some of Wyatt's blood on it. Bleach is under the kitchen sink."

I start to follow him, but Inara snags my wrist. "We're going to have a little talk, Ranger. Come with me."

My stomach flips, but I follow the only other woman who knows how hard I worked to prove myself.

In the far corner of the lounge area, Inara points to one of the love seats. I sink down, waiting for her to tell me I shouldn't give up. Or that I'm being an idiot. But instead, she takes a seat next to me and leans forward, her elbows on her knees.

"We're a lot alike," she says. "Not only because we're the only two women in history to get our tabs, but because a few years ago, I ran away from the man I was falling in love with."

I don't stifle my flinch quickly enough.

"You should work on your poker face. It's not very good." She chuckles, the sound almost delicate. Everything about Inara is delicate. Refined. Gorgeous. I can't picture her in the middle of the Afghan desert drawing down on an enemy target. Except, there's a calm about her I can imagine a sniper needs.

"Before West joined us, it was me, Ry, Coop, and Landow for a little over a year. Coop was an ass. He didn't like following orders, but he was decent under pressure. But then Landow was killed by a drunk driver. We were down a man, so Ry brought West in. Our first mission, Coop went off book. Got himself killed. At least that's what we thought.

"A couple of months later, shit started going sideways for me. Someone slashed my tires, almost plowed into me while I was on my morning run, and...when I let one of my coworkers borrow my car a few days later, he ran her off the road and almost killed her."

"Oh, my God." Goosebumps race over my arms, the shock making my skin tingle.

Inara doesn't look at me. She's still staring down at her hands. "I couldn't believe those things were related. It made no sense. And we thought Coop was dead. Hell, I'd *watched him die.* So I didn't think twice about bringing Royce home with me one night. Until we woke up and my bedroom was filled with smoke. The fucker burned my house down."

She fiddles with the pendant at her throat, and a soft smile curves her lips. "Royce saved my life. We were new, but that night, I realized I loved him. I was terrified that whoever was after me—I didn't know it was Coop at the time—would kill him too. That scared the shit out of me. So...I ran."

Why is she telling me all this?

Finally, Inara lifts her head. "A few hours after I left, Coop came to Royce's door, pretending to be Graham. He took Royce to one of the rail yards, tortured him, and wired the train car with explosives. I almost lost him. Because I was so stubborn, I thought I'd be better off alone."

"But...you're married. He survived."

Inara's cheeks take on a dusky red tint. "Royce lived because Ryker and West wouldn't let me handle shit on my own. They came for me. They kept me sane. They risked their lives for me—and for Royce.”

“It's not the same thing—”

“It *is*.” Inara scoots forward and takes my hands, holding on tight. “Do you love Doc?”

The strange sensation strangling my heart gives me the answer. “I...think so. I want to.”

She nods. “He loves you. That's obvious to all of us. Hell, Dax—he's in Boston—could probably tell too and he's blind.”

“Love isn't going to stop Bastian.”

Inara's gray eyes lock onto mine. “No. It won't. But if you trust us, we will.”

CHAPTER TWENTY-SEVEN

Natasha

THE WAREHOUSE IS ALMOST silent save for the clicking of
Ripper's keyboard and the beating of Doc's heart under my
ear. He's exhausted, and every time he moves, lines of pain
tighten around his eyes.

We sit on the love seat together, his arm around my shoulders and my head on his chest. I wish I knew what to say to
him. How to make all of this okay—or at least make sense.

"I wasted so much time." I slide my hand under his shirt,
needing to feel the warmth of his skin. "If I'd listened to
Gladys a year ago, we would have gotten together, and...I
know you, Doc. You would have pushed and demanded and
made me open up. If Bastian hadn't gotten out, if those drunk
assholes hadn't come to my door...maybe we could have had
a chance."

Doc presses his lips to the top of my head. His entire body
tenses, until he releases a heavy sigh. "Tessa called me the
night she died. I was working a double shift, and I didn't
answer right away. I was tired, and when the phone rang, I'd

just stretched out on one of the beds in the lounge to catch an hour of sleep."

Sorrow and regret ooze from his every word.

"She'd seen her ex outside her apartment building. I was going to ask her to move in with me that weekend. I'd made her a key—even put it in this little velvet bag I was carrying around in my pocket. As soon as I got her message, I found another doctor to cover for me and I left. But...I was too late."

I hold him tighter. Nothing I say will take his pain away. And I get the sense he's not done.

"I moved to Seattle a month later. I'd started drinking—a lot. But what did it matter? I was alone, and I was going to stay that way. If I didn't let myself get close to anyone, I couldn't lose them. If I didn't care, I couldn't be hurt. If I didn't try, I couldn't fail. Life is full of 'ifs,' baby. And wasted time. We can't go back and change the past. All we can do is hold on to what we have now."

I squeeze my eyes shut, fighting against another wave of tears. For days, I've been bouncing between the highest highs and the lowest lows. Between despair and joy. Sadness and peace. Anger and passion.

I'm alive again for the first time in forever. But for how long?

Doc shifts so his tired blue eyes meet mine. "I'm holding on, Natasha. Please promise me you'll hold on too."

If I could, I'd promise him forever. But I'm not that naive. Neither is he.

Before I can find the right words—or any words—the warehouse door opens with a loud whine. A tiny woman with fiery red hair stops after three steps, looks around, and grins. "Good gravy, I've missed this place."

Ryker ambles in behind her, a diaper bag over his shoulder and a baby carrier in his hand. "You were here last month, little bird."

"For all of five minutes. Installing a new hard drive in one of our servers doesn't count as 'work.'" She shakes her head and stares up at him like he hangs the moon. With his height, he probably could. "You can't tell me you haven't missed it."

"No, I can't." Ryker stares down at the sleeping baby. "But I can't leave the two of you either. Not now. Maybe not ever again."

She reaches up to touch his cheek. "We'll talk about that later. When we don't have an audience."

Ryker nods, and the two of them move almost as one toward the couches. He sets the baby carrier down in the center of the rug. "I'll get the Pack 'n Play."

The redhead drops a cross-body bag next to one of the fancy, overstuffed recliners. "Hey, Doc. Natasha? I'm Wren." Her firm handshake comes with a smile. "That's Harlow."

The baby stares up at her mother, cooing and balling her tiny fingers into fists.

Doc leans closer, a look of wonder on his face. "She has Ryker's eyes. Heterochromia isn't always passed down."

I scoot to the edge of the cushion to get a better look at the little one. Her irises are mostly green. The left has a bright blue streak, while the right also has flecks of hazel.

"They just started to change color a few weeks ago," Wren says. "Ry almost gave me a panic attack when he noticed it. He was just staring at her, frozen. Like she was some sort of alien." She laughs, then drops to her knees to unbuckle all the straps holding the baby in place.

"She is," Ryker mutters, almost under his breath. "At least she was until those two teeth came in. Now, she's an angel again." Ryker unfolds the bright blue Pack 'n Play next to the recliner and glances around the warehouse. "Where's Graham? I thought he'd beat us here with the food."

Inara calls from the kitchen, "It took him almost half an

hour to get through the line at Northwest SmashBurgers. He'll be here in a few minutes."

"Doc? Want to hold Harlow?" Wren asks.

My heart squeezes at the look on his face when he cradles the little girl in his arms. She squirms, stretching out her tiny hand. Her fingers brush his trimmed beard, and she smiles up at him.

"She's beautiful, Wren," he says, smoothing one hand over her wispy curls.

Ryker drapes his arm around his wife's shoulders. "She's perfect."

With a delicate snort, Wren tips her head up. "You might be a little biased, Ry."

"I'm *a lot* biased." He drops a kiss to her lips. "You have a problem with that?"

"Never."

Watching the two of them interact is almost mesmerizing. They're so in sync. The moment Ryker came into view with the Pack 'n Play, Wren shifted slightly, a hint of a smile curving her lips. Now, he lets his hand drift up and down her arm, the motion so casual I'm not sure he realizes he's doing it.

"Food's here!" Graham calls, and the warehouse door bangs shut behind him. He's laden down with three huge takeout bags and two drink trays. "West got caught at the light. He'll be here in a minute."

Doc passes Harlow to Ryker, who lifts her high in the air, then presses a kiss to her belly. "Nap time, baby girl. Go down easy, okay?"

Wren is already halfway to the long table where Graham is unpacking the food. "There better be a strawberry shake in there."

"Two of them," the young man says as he slides one of the drink carriers toward her. "And I got you extra pickles."

"Oh, thank God. I thought the cravings would go away after I gave birth, but now, I think I just really love pickles."

I don't think I can eat, but Doc's stomach has been growling for half an hour, so I follow him to the table. Wren and Ripper carry their food back to the sitting area, and the petite redhead pulls out a laptop. In minutes, the two of them are so buried in geek-speak, I don't understand a single word.

Ryker, Inara, and Graham join us at the table, everyone but me digging in to their meals in companionable silence. I can't pull my gaze away from the phone in front of me. Why hasn't Bastian called? What is he doing to Gladys? Where is he taking her?

Doc nudges a bag of fries closer to me. "Eat something, Natasha. Please."

"They took Gladys three hours ago. What if they've already killed her?" I press my hand to my mouth. If I don't hear something soon, I'm going to be sick.

"Sergeant, you will eat those french fries. That's a goddamn order," Ryker says in a tone I know all too well. The response is automatic, even after eight years. I grab a handful and start to chew.

"That was a low blow," I mumble through a mouthful of potato.

Ryker nods. "Damn straight. But it worked, didn't it?" He unwraps a second double cheeseburger. The first one disappeared in under two minutes. "I've been where you are, Natasha." He drops his voice to a whisper. "I almost lost Wren a few years ago. She was taken in Russia, and..."

"Ry, don't go back there." West sinks down across from me and snags a chicken sandwich from the pile of food. "When Inara and I got to the safe house outside of St. Petersburg, I don't think he could have told you our names, he was so wrapped up in how he'd 'failed' Wren. Like one man going up against a Russian drug czar with more than thirty goons on his payroll was *ever* going to be a fair fight."

"Well," Inara adds, "the three of us, plus Wren, going up against Kolya and his men wasn't a fair fight either. For Kolya anyway."

The three share a look—like they can reach each other's thoughts. It's scary, but also reassuring.

"The two things you have to do—above all else—are eat and sleep." West pins me with his steely gaze. "You'll think it's impossible. But if you don't try, when the call comes in and we have to make a plan to get Gladys back, you'll be compromised. We need you at your best. You're the most valuable asset in this room."

I choke on another fry. "I've been out for eight years. You're wrong."

West sets his sandwich down slowly, picks up a napkin, and wipes his hands. Every movement is deliberate. No energy wasted. And he does it all while staring right at me.

No one else says a word. Even Ryker holds his breath.

"This is what I do, Natasha. It's what we *all* do. You served with Bastian and the others for years. You know how they think. And you might not believe me now, but you know how to get in their heads. So you'll eat—at least a little—and you'll sleep when you can. Because soon, Gladys is going to need you. And so will we."

Doc

After West's "pep talk," Natasha managed half a cheeseburger, and we shared a chocolate milkshake. Now, she's stretched out on one of the sofas with her head in my lap. Her fingers trace patterns on my thigh, though her eyes are closed.

"Got 'em." Ripper's shout wakes the dog napping at his feet. Charlie leaps up in front of his human, paws braced for a fight with a low growl. "Whoa, buddy. Calm down. I'm good."

The dog plops back down, and Ripper scratches him behind the ears. "A car left the underground garage in Bella's building at 8:23 a.m. I have the same car entering Boeing Field parking at 9:08. Can't see who's in it, but a Gulfstream C-37A took off at 9:53 a.m. bound for Davison Airfield in Fairfax, Virginia. If that's not them…"

"Shit." Inara gracefully rises from her cross-legged position on a yoga mat next to the boxing ring. "At average speed, they'd land around…"

"Now," Rip says. "But there's no fucking way I can get into the traffic camera network around Davison in time to confirm."

"Have a little faith." Wren threads her fingers together, flips her hands palms out, and stretches her arms in front of her. Her knuckles crack one by one. "Let mama work her magic."

"Magic?" Natasha asks, her voice rough with exhaustion. She pushes up to sitting and rubs her eyes.

Ryker sets a bottle of water on the table next to his wife with a smile. "Rip can track a dollar, ruble, afghani, or yuan through a hundred transactions without breaking a sweat. And he's a damn good hacker in his own right, but Wren's the best in the world."

"Well, I used to be." Wren stifles a yawn. "Until I spent thirteen weeks so exhausted, I could barely remember my own name. But Harlow cut two teeth yesterday, and I slept five hours last night. I feel like a whole new woman. So let's see where these wing nuts are going."

Natasha rubs her eyes again. "Wing nuts? God. Now I know I'm tired. I'm hearing things."

Ryker chuckles. "Sweetheart, I think we need to get you a t-shirt with all of your swear words on them. Otherwise, we're going to keep having this conversation again and again and again..."

Wren's fingers fly over the keys as she lets out a delicate snort. "Anyone who spends time with me learns pretty darn quick. Raelynn figured out C. Jacks." She gets a gleam in her eye and peers over at me. "Cracker Jacks. And you and Natasha are staying in an apartment leased to H. Pucky Barnes."

I shake my head. "H... Pucky Barnes? I don't get it."

"Horse Pucky," Ryker supplies.

Wren is still typing away, so I glance up at the man. "And Barnes?"

"Bucky Barnes." Ripper pushes up, but sways on his feet. His fingers flex, a slight tremble to them until he balls his hands into fists. Charlie steadies him by pressing his big body to Rip's thighs. "The Winter Soldier? From Marvel Comics. It's one of Graham's favorite movies. And since that used to be *his* apartment, we went with it."

The man shuffles off to the kitchen for a cup of coffee, and I squeeze Natasha's hand. "I'll be right back, baby."

She nods and draws the blanket up to her shoulders. We should have gone back to the apartment. At least there, we'd have a bed. And some privacy. Having her head in my lap for the past hour was pure torture. I'm sporting a near constant hard-on, despite the worry beating like a drum against my skull.

"Ripper?" I stop a good ten feet from him. The man spooks at the slightest unexpected sound—probably why Charlie never leaves his side.

"I take it you noticed?" He doesn't look at me as he refills his mug and adds a single spoonful of sugar.

"The tremors? The dizziness when you stand? Yes." Now that he knows I'm here, I put my back to the counter only a foot away. He still won't meet my gaze. Charlie wriggles his sleek body between the two of us, his focus locked on Ripper.

"Not worth talking about, Doc. We got so many TBIs in Hell, I lost count. In the six years after..." He shrugs. "I'm fucked in the head. In a lot of ways. When I remember to stand up slowly, I'm all right. Usually."

"Did you have any serious infections...where you were?" I ask. "Especially ones that caused nerve pain? Or neurological symptoms? Hallucinations, seizures, numbness..."

Ripper turns to me slowly, the fingers of his right hand brushing over a single spot on his chest. Charlie tenses, whines, and starts licking Rip's other hand until the man shakes off whatever memory he was momentarily trapped in. "More than one, yeah. Why?"

"Because this might not be related to all those TBIs. It could be POTS."

His brows knit together. "What the hell is POTS?"

"Postural orthostatic tachycardia syndrome. Basically, it's a circulation issue. When you stand, your heart rate shoots up and your blood pressure bottoms out. POTS also causes tremors, sweating, chest pain..."

"Is it...terminal?" he asks, his voice barely a whisper.

"Fuck, no." I almost reach for the man before I stop myself. "It's not curable, but it's absolutely treatable."

The spark of hope in his eyes is heartbreaking. "*You* can treat it?"

"You'd have better results if you went to a neurologist—"

"No." Ripper almost snarls the word, then curses under his breath. "I don't... Doctors... No. I trust *you*, Doc. It has to be you."

I nod. "Okay. When Natasha's safe, we'll talk about it. For now...drink a little more water with all that coffee. It'll help."

He almost smiles. "I'll try."

CHAPTER TWENTY-EIGHT

Natasha

THE CLOCK at the bottom of the center monitor mocks me. Every minute that passes ratchets my anxiety even more. So much so that when my phone *does* ring, I yelp loud enough to wake Charlie.

Every member of Hidden Agenda leaps into motion. Wren passes the baby to Ryker and picks up her laptop. West and Graham duck out of the boxing ring where they were sparring, and Inara taps her ear twice.

"Raelynn, switch to channel bravo and make sure Bella stays quiet. The call's coming in."

They're all on comms. Even me. The tiny earbud is barely noticeable, but works with both my phone and the encrypted system the team uses whenever they're on mission.

Doc links our fingers. "You can do this, baby."

Across from me, Wren gives me the signal. She's ready to work her magic tracing the call, though she's not sure she'll be successful. Not with the tech power Bastian so obviously has on his side. I always thought tracing was easy, but apparently, that's only in the movies.

"Where is Gladys?" I ask without even saying hello. He doesn't deserve the courtesy.

"Natasha, is that any way to greet an old friend?" His nasally voice grates along my last nerve. I'm squeezing Doc's hand so tightly, I'm afraid I'll hurt him.

"Fuck you. I'm not playing your games, Bastian. Let me talk to Gladys or this conversation is over."

"Turn on your video."

I swallow hard. We were prepared for this. But God, I don't want to see his face. Or let him see mine. I scoot as far from Doc as I can without letting go of his hand. Wren nods, and I tap the screen.

Holy shit. She actually did it. Instead of the warehouse kitchen behind me, it looks like I'm in a cheap hotel room. Alone. Down to the garish patterned carpet and the 1970's-era bedspread.

Bastian isn't anywhere recognizable. Plain, cinderblock walls. Bright lights. No furniture I can see. West moves closer to the flat screen monitor on the wall that mirrors my screen.

The years haven't been kind to my former squad leader. His black hair has started to thin. His nose looks like it's been broken at least once, and his skin has a sallow texture that would be worrisome if I gave two shits about his health.

"I admit," Bastian says with a sneer, "I expected Parker to have done more damage than that." He gestures to me, and I reach up to touch the dark bruise under my left eye. "Your hand-to-hand skills always were decent...for a woman."

"Parker talked too much. So do you. Where. Is. Gladys?"

His gaze flicks up, behind the camera, and a second later, the view switches.

Another cinder block wall, this one with part of a steel door visible at the edge of the frame. Gladys sits in a rolling desk chair, her hands clasped in her lap, wearing a pair of bright pink sweat pants, house slippers, and a shirt that says, "I sleep naked. Join me?"

She squints at the screen, frowns, then pushes to her feet. But Doherty steps into the frame and shoves her back down again, grabbing the arm of the chair to stop it from rolling halfway across the room. She narrows her gaze at him. "Your mother didn't teach you a lick of manners, did she?"

The look Doherty gives her chills me to my core. But Gladys doesn't seem to care, simply *harrumphs* and turns back to the camera. "Baby girl, did they hurt my Bella?"

"She's okay. She says she loves you." My eyes start to burn, but I can't let her—or Bastian—see me cry. "I'm so sorry, this is all my fault—"

"Hush now. *You* didn't kidnap an old woman before she finished her first cup of coffee. The only thing you gotta be sorry for is not tellin' me your real name. Natasha suits you a hell of a lot better than *Nat*."

I choke out a laugh. "You're my best friend, Gladys. My only friend. I love you, and I'm going to get you back home. Back to Bella."

"That girl is going to make the most beautiful bride," she says, her scratchy voice taking on a wistful tone. But then her expression turns fierce, and she grabs the arms of the chair and sits up straight. "Don't you listen to these assholes for one minute!"

Doherty slaps her across the face.

"You fucking bastard!" I scream. Only Doc's hold on my hand stops me from jumping up to pace. The tech Wren is using to mask my location won't work if I move around too much.

The video switches back to Bastian. I can hear Gladys moaning in the background. "If you hurt her—"

"You'll do what? Kill me? Send me back to prison?" He

scoffs. "I have too many powerful friends, Natasha. Even if you and that doctor of yours have killed three of them. I'm willing to let the old woman go, but you and the good doctor are going to do exactly what I say."

"Leave Doc out of this."

With a chuckle, Bastian shakes his head. "You should have let Parker kill you days ago. Then, this would all be over. But as I checked in with my parole officer the other day, I realized I was thinking too small."

I'd roll my eyes if I didn't think he'd hurt Gladys again to spite me. "Get to the point, will you? Those two idiots you sent after Doc showed up in the middle of the goddamn night. I'm tired."

"I've fantasized about killing you every day for the past eight years," he says. "We all have. We had a good thing going in Iraq. I was clearing a quarter million a year. Tax free."

In my ear, West mutters, "Is this a fucking shakedown?"

Bastian continues, oblivious to the former Navy SEAL—and everyone else—listening in. "Doherty, Collins, and I had eleven months left to hit our twenty years. Eleven months till we'd be able to draw our pensions. Senator Norton had jobs lined up for us that would let us keep the operation going without risking our lives every fucking day. All that's gone now. We're war criminals. Unless you recant your testimony."

"You have got to be kidding me. No one is going to believe I *made the whole thing up*. You're fucking delusional."

"They will. Not only that, you'll take responsibility for the entire operation. It was so much bigger than anyone ever knew."

I scoff, but Bastian's grinning like he just won the lottery. My stomach twists into a knot, and I squeeze Doc's hand harder.

"The doctor will surrender himself to a location of my choosing, while you will report to CID. You'll give them details I kept secret for years. Verifiable information you could only have if you were the mastermind of the entire operation. You'll cop to everything. The murders of the family outside of Albaghdadi *and* so many more. Once you're arrested, we'll let the old lady go."

"I'm *a lady*," Gladys snaps. "I'm not *old.*"

"Shut *up!*" someone—Collins, I think—says. "Can I gag her?"

Bastian nods once, and the sounds of soft scuffling come from just out of camera range. I squeeze my eyes shut to stop my tears from falling.

"You have twenty-four hours, Natasha. But don't worry. I've made all your travel plans for you."

My phone dings with a notification from Air Northwest. Two tickets on a red-eye flight out of Sea-Tac for 9:00 p.m. A second later, another message arrives with the subject line, *"For your reading pleasure."*

Bastian stares daggers at me through the screen. "If you don't get on that plane, your friend dies. If anyone besides the doctor boards with you, she dies. If you try to contact the authorities—"

"She dies. I get the idea." I wish I could see West. Or Ryker. Or even Raelynn or Inara. I need to know there's a plan. But I can't. I have to keep my focus on the man who wants to take the only good things left in my life. "I want to talk to Gladys as soon as I get off the plane. And again before I walk into CID. Non-negotiable."

"Fair enough. Make sure you memorize everything in that file I sent you. See you soon, Sergeant."

The screen goes dark. West grabs my phone and shoves it into a shiny gray pouch. The loss of it sends my heart into overdrive.

"I need that! Gladys..."

"That fucker found a villain handbook in his box of

Cracker Jacks this morning." West shakes his head and tosses the bag to Ripper. "Until we know the file he sent you isn't infected with malware, the phone stays in there. Wren's monitoring your number. If he calls again, it'll ring through to Doc's phone."

"Take it, baby." Doc presses his phone into my hand. Holding the device makes me feel marginally better. Until I realize we only have six hours until we have to be on a plane to D.C. And none of Hidden Agenda can go with us.

"I have the plane's manifest," Wren says. "It'll take me an hour—maybe two—before I know which tickets were sold in the last few days. He put all this together after he sent Parker to kill you. We need to know how many hostiles we're dealing with."

A long list of names appears on the biggest flatscreen monitor. It takes me only seconds to zero in on one name in particular. "Ben Kerr."

"Who?" West asks.

A single tear tumbles down my cheek. "The night my brother was killed, he was one of the MPs assigned to protect me. I'd gone out for a run. Ciprian—I think his first name was Thom—went with me. Kerr stayed behind." I turn to Ryker. "Logan was Special Forces. I could never understand how Parker got the drop on him. He was too good. But now I get it. Kerr let him in."

Doc

Someone—Raelynn, I think—went to the apartment and returned with...everything. My medical kit. Passports. Clothes for both of us. Natasha refused to look at any of it. She's spent the past three hours memorizing all the dates, times, and places in Bastian's file. Ryker taught her some of his memory tricks, and he's currently quizzing her. I can't listen any longer. The sick fuck killed dozens over the years. Assaulted even more.

I shower, letting the hot water ease my sore muscles. We have a plan—of sorts. But so much of it depends on luck. Or on Bastian not counting on Hidden Agenda.

I wish Natasha and I had a few hours together somewhere private. I'd make sure she slept. Even if I had to wring multiple climaxes from her body to exhaust her. Instead, I dry myself off alone, wrap a towel around my waist, and shuffle out to the lockers.

"Doc, I'll check those stitches for you." West sits on one of the long benches, his field kit spread out in front of him.

"They're fine."

The former SEAL's brows shoot up. "That wasn't a question. Sit your ass down."

I don't work for the man, but more than once, Raelynn's told me that "no one fucks with the SEAL," and I can see why. When he's on mission—and though we haven't left the warehouse, we are very much "on mission"—his icy blue eyes hold almost no emotion. He's so clearly in control, it's scary.

So I do as he says.

"Can you lift your left arm over your head?" he asks.

"Not easily." I grimace, but can almost salute the man—though I think I might technically outrank him.

West aims a pen light at my side, then gently palpates the swelling around the wound. "Natasha's a Ranger. She knows her shit. But she's too close to this."

"She'll never forgive herself for what Gladys is going through." I'm not sure the woman I fell in love with will come back from D.C. Even if West's plan works and Gladys escapes unharmed.

"You land at 6:00 a.m. That gives you two hours until the

Army CID office opens." West swabs an antiseptic pad over the stitches, waits for the skin to dry, and pulls out a roll of medical tape. "Inara and I will be at Dulles when you land. Clive and Tank from Second Sight will be close, but Tank was a Ranger and Clive was Army, so we can't have them anywhere visible. Just in case. But they'll be in short term parking.

"Trevor, Vasquez, and Ella will be watching CID. They'll swap cars on the regular"

"What about comms?" Talking through the plan helps to keep me focused, though my gaze hasn't left Natasha's face since I sat down.

"If Bastian's not a complete idiot, he'll have a scanner or a signal jammer. But Inara's currently modifying one of your hiking boots to hold a spare unit in the heel. If we can't take him down before he and his band of village idiots get their hands on you, use it. It'll work with your phone or—since I can't imagine you'll be allowed to keep *that*—any unsecured wi-fi network. Though it'll default to broadcast only."

West secures half a dozen strips of tape over the stitches. "Scale of one to ten. How bad is the rib pain?"

"Three." At his stare, I sigh. "Five."

"Any way to get that lower? Say...to a one?" he asks.

I scowl. "Doubtful. Not for more than a few hours. Morphine would be out of my system in four. Same for Dilaudid. Ibuprofen will have to do me."

"Not good enough. With Raelynn—"

I swear under my breath. "Fucking hell. That wasn't my idea. You know that. And I doubt it lasted very long."

"Long enough. But...no." West repacks his field kit. "We could be fucked here, Doc. We don't know who we can trust in CID. If we can't find Gladys before 8:00 a.m., you and Natasha won't have a choice. Bastian will take you, and she'll have to turn herself in.

"Fuck no!" Halfway across the warehouse, Ryker stares at us, holding the baby to his chest and patting her back gently. I lower my voice to a harsh whisper. "There's no scenario where that asshole just lets Gladys—or me—live. No matter what Natasha does. You know it as well as I do."

"That's why we need you as...agile as possible. To protect Gladys and do everything you can to get her the fuck out of there." He rubs the back of his neck, stress lines bracketing his lips. "This is what we do, Doc. And we're really fucking good at it. But no one—not even me—can anticipate every outcome. We have to be prepared. For anything."

"Even a shot of lidocaine—or two—directly to the nerves might not last long enough. But it'll give me the best chance. I don't have what I need here. We'll have to stop at the clinic before we go to the airport. And you'll need to be the one to handle the injections."

West nods, checks his watch, and pushes to his feet. "Be ready to go in an hour. I need another gallon of coffee."

He hasn't slept since this morning's interrogation. None of us have. Not really. And in less than twenty-four hours, we need to be at our best. Or I could lose Natasha forever.

CHAPTER TWENTY-NINE

Natasha

"We're here." Nash turns in the front seat of the SUV. "Doc? You okay?"

"Been better. Been worse." Doc holds the younger man's stare for a long moment. "Thanks...for doing this."

When Nash showed up at the warehouse, Raelynn held onto him for a full five minutes. He's not a part of Hidden Agenda, but he was the only one available to drive us to the airport. Everyone else left on a private plane out of Boeing Field thirty minutes ago.

They'll beat us to D.C. by at least two hours. Maybe more.

Nash doesn't say another word as Doc and I get out of the car. The fake Lyft decal on the side of the vehicle *should* fool anyone Bastian might have watching the drop-off area. But we have to act like we don't know him.

Wren and Ripper were able to identify almost a dozen passengers on our flight who bought their tickets in the past twenty-four hours. Including the two seated directly behind us, and Kerr in the last row. There isn't a single empty seat, even if West *had* been willing to take the chance and send Graham with us.

A muscle in Doc's jaw ticks as he slings a backpack over his shoulder. We don't have luggage. Only a rudimentary medical kit, our wallets, and two extra sweatshirts. By tomorrow afternoon, we'll either be on our way back to Seattle with Hidden Agenda, or I'll be in lockup and Doc...

Stop. We have a plan. It's going to work.

Except, the plan is based on West and his team being able to track Bastian down, and all Wren was able to get from tracing the call to my phone was the general area. Fairfax, Virginia.

It takes us half an hour to make it through security, and Doc gets tenser by the minute.

I'm numb. Four hours spent memorizing all the sick details of Bastian's crimes. Another thirty minutes learning codes and phone numbers in case we're cut off from the team. Then the GPS trackers. I rub my right ass cheek as we approach the gate. It still stings. The tiny devices might only be the size of two grains of rice, but they hurt like hell going in.

The gate agent scans our boarding passes. The long walk down the jetway feels like the end. Of everything. I haven't been on a plane in eight years. Too risky. And now, I'm about to be trapped on one. With at least three men who want me dead. And the man responsible for killing Logan. I don't care that Kerr is eight rows behind us. It's enough to know he's there.

The worst part of all of this? Doc and I haven't *talked* in hours. He doesn't want me anywhere near the CID office. With what I know—what I'll have to confess to—there's no doubt I'll be arrested immediately. There's so much I want to say to him. A week's worth of tenderness. A year of apologies. A lifetime of stories and questions and plans.

But I can't find the words. So when the plane lifts into the air, I rest my head on his shoulder and cry.

———

"Natasha."

A warm hand cups my cheek, and I lean into the touch. It's the best dream. Doc holding me, in bed, the sunrise shimmering over the waters of Puget Sound...

"Wake up, baby. We're going to land soon."

I jerk upright, my gaze pinging wildly around the cabin. No. No, no, no. We were supposed to have five hours together. Instead I passed out within minutes of takeoff.

"How could you let me sleep the whole time?" I wriggle out of Doc's arms as the flight attendants make their final pass through the aisle.

"You were exhausted." His voice is rougher than usual. Dark circles brace his eyes. I doubt he slept at all. No. He kept watch. All night.

"You're the one who needed rest." Anxiety sinks in my stomach. The plane races toward sunrise, lower and lower until lines become roads, specs of color coalesce into cars, and my hope for a future together fades away. Doc leans closer and brushes his lips to my ear. "West and Inara are in the terminal. Trevor, Ella, and Vasquez are watching the CID office. We're not alone. We'll get through this."

The plane touches down with a jolt. I turn my face into Doc's shoulder to stifle my sob. "I wasted so much time."

He nudges my chin up, and his eyes hold so much emotion. Fear, determination, and maybe...love. "Don't go there. We're going to get through this. I want a life with you, Natasha. I'm not giving up. Promise me you won't either."

Before Bastian's call came in yesterday, Wren told us how

sacred she—and all of Hidden Agenda—consider those words. *I promise.*

I can't say them. But maybe...I can show him how I feel. Sealing my mouth to his, I pour everything into one passionate kiss. Doc's hand slides down my back, all the way to my ass. If it weren't for the seatbelt, I'd be in his lap, damn all the people around us. His tongue sweeps over mine. He takes as good as he gets, pulling a moan from my throat, nipping at my lower lip, and reaching between us to cup my breast and skate his thumb over the hard nub of my nipple.

I have to tell him. Now. Before I lose the chance forever.

"I'm falling in lo—" My phone beeps in my pocket. I drop the damn thing and almost lose it between the seats. But Doc rescues it and presses the device into my hand. "Gladys?"

"Baby girl, tell me you didn't come..."

She doesn't sound right. Weak. Sad. Distracted.

"Of course, I came. What's wrong? Did they hurt you?"

Someone jostles Doc's seat, and he hisses out a breath. A tall man in a three piece suit moves into the aisle next to him. "Give me the phone, Natasha."

I blink up at Kerr, and he snatches the device from me, ends the call, then claps his hand on Doc's shoulder. "That pinch you felt was a dose of fast-acting insulin. In five to ten minutes, you'll be unconscious. In thirty—unless Natasha does exactly what she's told—you'll be dead."

Doc grabs Kerr's wrist, but the man shakes off his hold easily. "I haven't...eaten anything in twelve hours...asshole. I won't have...ten minutes." Sweat dots his brow, and he tugs at the neck of his Henley.

"Doc? God. What do I do?" I surge up and jab the call button, but all around us, the other passengers are getting their luggage. The flight attendants can't get to me even if they want to. Doc's breathing is too rapid, and he's starting to shiver. His pupils are blown.

One of the men from the row behind us joins Kerr. He unzips a small, black pouch and shows us a syringe. "This is glucagon. It'll counteract the insulin. Eventually. Once you're off the plane, Natasha, I'll give it to him."

Doc fumbles for my arm. "No choice... Do what they say. But don't turn yourself in...unless you know...it worked and Gladys...is safe." He's shaking harder now. His words are starting to slur. Kerr grabs my elbow and lifts me to my feet.

"Time to go, bitch." He muscles me around Doc, but at the last moment, I throw my arms around the man I *know* I've fallen in love with. Quickly, I slide the folded letter into Doc's pocket. He said he didn't want to read it, but...it's all I'll ever be able to say to him.

"Now!" Kerr growls.

I let him propel me down the aisle, stealing glances back at Doc until I can't see him any longer. "If you say a word to anyone in the airport, he and the old woman are both dead."

I can only nod at his side. As we reach the terminal, a pair of EMTs shout for everyone to get out of their way. Please, God. Let one of the other passengers have called 911. But as they pass us by, I think Collins is one of them.

Kerr steers me toward baggage claim, but before we can pass through the security gates, he removes a badge from his pocket, veers to the left, and swipes the piece of plastic against a card reader.

"Where are you taking me?" I demand. The doors slam shut behind us. I drive my arm down, breaking his iron grip on my elbow. "I need to know Doc's going to be okay."

"That depends on you. Right now, he's on his way to join the old woman. If he doesn't make trouble—and you do as you're told—they'll live."

I take two steps back. "I'm here, aren't I? But I'm not going anywhere with you until I know the insulin didn't kill him."

Kerr shoves me against the wall, his arm across my throat.

"This isn't 'doing as you're told'." The punch to my stomach steals my breath. I double-over, barely managing to twist away before he can grab me again.

Panic drives every thought from my head but one. *Get to Doc.*

I stumble for the door, but as my fingers close over the handle, my entire body seizes. The pain is like nothing I've ever felt before. My vision tunnels into twin points of gray. Kerr's fingers dig into my shoulder even harder, and his other hand finds the pressure point between the bones of my right arm.

In seconds, I'm on the floor, Kerr looming over me. "If you want more, by all means, keep fighting me."

I can barely breathe, but manage to shake my head.

Kerr drops to one knee, grabs my wrists, and pulls out a zip tie. The plastic tightens almost to the point of pain.

My thoughts ping wildly, the pain scrambling what little focus I had left. If he's tying me up, he's not worried about anyone seeing us. We're not going back into the terminal. We won't pass West and Inara.

Kerr grabs the plastic and tries to drag me to my feet, but my legs won't support me. So he throws me over his shoulder and starts walking down a long hallway. I want to tell him he's a piece of shit, but I can't form the words.

He badges us through another security door—I hear the beep, though I can't see shit with my face pressed against his back—and sensation starts to return to my muscles. "Put... me...down...fucker."

Setting me on my feet, he wraps his fingers around my throat and squeezes. "Try anything else and I'll shove you into a suitcase from lost-and-found."

"Won't," I manage. My gait is more of a stumble than anything else, but I stay upright until we emerge into the bright, morning sun. A car pulls up to the curb and Kerr drags me around to the passenger side, opens the door, and shoves me into the seat.

"Hello, Natasha." From behind the wheel, Bastian offers me a gleeful smile. "I thought I'd drive you to CID personally. After all, I wouldn't want you to get lost." He leans over and snaps my seatbelt into place, trapping my arms against my body.

"I told you I wasn't walking through that door until you showed me proof Gladys was safe."

"You'll see her—on video—before you get out of the car." He checks his mirrors, then pulls into the street with a squeal of tires.

"And Doc?" My voice cracks. Every time I close my eyes, I see his face. Pale, his eyes unfocused, his mouth slack. He knew he was in trouble. The panic in his voice...

Tears lend a shimmer to the traffic all around us. *Stop. Don't let him see you cry.*

Bastian taps the car's in-dash controls, and Collins's name appears on the display. After a few rings, he picks up. "Yeah, Sarge?"

"Sit-rep on the doctor."

I take a deep breath, gritting my teeth so I don't lose my shit completely.

"His blood sugar is back up to fifty. He's still out, but he'll wake up in an hour or two. Taking him—"

Bastian hangs up and glances over at me. "By the time we reach CID, he'll be with the old woman. I'll even let you talk to them—for a minute. But now, you're going to prove that you took my orders seriously. Start from the beginning and explain exactly how you're planning on convincing the CID officers that *you* were responsible for everything."

CHAPTER THIRTY

Doc

A BONE-JARRING impact yanks me back to awareness. The headache threatens to crush my skull, and my muscles feel like limp noodles. Something's very wrong, but I can't figure out what. Metal bangs from behind me. Then silence.

I was with Natasha. A sharp pinch to my arm. Fuck. Insulin shock. I try to rub my eyes, but my arms won't move. I can't feel my legs. Can't feel anything, really.

"Doc? You alive?" The weak, familiar voice sounds like it's underwater. Or I am.

I blink hard, desperate to focus, but all I can see is a single, dim light above me.

Roll over, dumbass.

Easier said than done, but with a groan, I turn onto my side. A hazy form sits against the wall. White, orange, and purple hair.

"Gladys."

"You were supposed to protect her," she says. "Nat's all alone with that man now."

Slowly, I pull my knees to my chest. "Didn't have a choice." I'd tell Gladys that we didn't come to D.C. alone, but I don't know if anyone's listening.

She crawls over to me, moving too carefully. They hurt her. Anger gives me the strength to struggle up to sitting, though the room spins around me. At least the nerve block is keeping the pain from my broken rib at bay.

Gladys's cheek is several shades of purple. Fingertip bruises darken around her arms. She's not bound, thank God, but she's favoring her right side. Her wrist is swollen. Tears shimmer in her eyes. "They're going to kill her."

"No. They want her to go to prison for the rest of her life." That single hope is all I can hold onto. All I have. Hidden Agenda won't stop until they get her out. Even if it takes days. Or weeks. With their contacts, they'll get it done. Though we won't be here to see it.

With a slow shake of her head, Gladys sniffles. "The asshole in charge is gonna kill her after she signs her confession. He said she'll be arrested, and they'll be able to get to her. That the Colonel wants to be the one to do it."

Fuck. I have to warn West. Ryker. Someone. "Wait. Who's the Colonel?"

She shrugs. "Some big muckety-muck. They were talkin' to him on the plane."

My vision has adjusted somewhat to the dim light in the room. Cinderblock walls, a metal door, and nothing else. It's cold—despite being the middle of August. "Are we in a basement?"

"Yep. Those fuckers made me walk down a whole mess of stairs," she says. "With my knees! And the only bathroom is on the first floor. 'Course, they only let me use it once. Not that they've given me anything to eat or drink either."

Shit.The GPS tracker won't work through thick cement walls. Assuming it's even still under the tape on my side. I can't tell. But if it was transmitting up until they threw me in here, West and the team should be able to figure out where I am.

I don't know how long I was out. I vaguely remember being rushed through the airport on a gurney. Sirens blaring. An intense pain in my chest. Oh, fuck. "Gladys, lift up my shirt."

"Huh?" She frowns. "Are you tryin' to come on to me? *Here?*"

"No. Please. Just do it."

Her hands shake, but she raises the Henley all the way to my armpits. Fucking hell. Two burn marks. One on the right side of my chest, the other just below the bandages under my left arm. My heart stopped. And the electric shock...it'll be a miracle if the GPS chip was transmitting after that.

"Enough," I manage. Everything's fucked. Up, down, and sideways.

"What did those punks do to you?" She smooths the shirt back down, and suddenly, she looks more like a frail, doting grandmother than her usual zero-fucks-to-give badass self.

"Too much." I close my eyes, but an intense wave of dizziness almost sends me pitching over.

Gladys rubs her hands together, then blows on them as she shivers. Her thin t-shirt, pink pants, and house slippers aren't enough to keep her warm down here.

"Come closer. Put your arms around me. You're freezing."

"Don't be flirtin' with me, Dr. Sexy Pants," she says, a deep sadness to her tone. "You're Nat's man, remember?"

Despite her words, she scoots until we're hip to hip, then winds her spindly arms around my waist.

"She won't mind. She knows I love...fuck. I never told her. I didn't get the chance." The realization is too much. She almost said the words to me on the plane. And I would have said them right back. Now...will we ever have a chance?

The minutes stretch from one to another. Exhaustion tugs at my heavy lids. I'm so fucking compromised, physically and mentally, there's no way I'll be able to fight my way out of here.

I must nod off, because I jerk awake when the door bangs open. Collins and Doherty enter, with Sutton hanging back in the hall, a pistol in his hand.

Gladys's arms tighten around me, though she glares at the men with fire in her brown eyes.

Doherty holds up his phone so we can see the screen. Natasha sits in a car, her cheeks glistening with tears. "Doc? Gladys?"

"Don't do this, baby. Please. Walk away. Right now." I can't let her confess to all Bastian's crimes. She doesn't know what they're planning. She thinks she'll be safe—that Hidden Agenda will get her out, even if it takes them a few days. She doesn't have that long.

Collins bites back an oath. Sutton beelines for me, then jams his pistol to my temple. "Shut up, old man."

Bastian's voice comes through the speaker. "Natasha won't dare disobey me. If she does, the two of you serve no purpose."

I sit up a little straighter. "Get it over with, fucker. We all know Gladys and I aren't walking out of here alive."

Sutton slams the butt of the pistol against my skull. Stars burst in front of my eyes, and Collins drags Gladys away from me. Her fist connects with his nuts, but there's no power behind the punch, and it only serves to piss him off. He shoves her to the floor, and she whimpers softly.

"Stop! Don't hurt her!" Natasha cries. "I'm here! I'll walk in there right now and confess to everything. But let Gladys and Doc go!"

"I'm not a complete monster," Bastian says. "The old woman knows I can get to her and her pretty niece any time

I want. I'll return her to Seattle—alive—once your signed confession is part of the public record and you've been arrested. As for the doctor...he's dead either way. But if you try anything—or if you fail to confess to even one of the crimes on my list, I'll torture him for *weeks* before I kill him."

Natasha swipes at her tears. Her gaze pings from Bastian behind the phone to someone obviously in the back seat.

Even if she *were* willing to walk away, the asshole won't let her. I can hear it in his voice. He'd kill her right now if she tried to run.

With a nod, she clears her throat. "Just...let me say goodbye. Please. Give me this one thing."

The video shakes, and he must hand her the phone, because her face fills the screen. "Gladys?"

Doherty turns so she can see the older woman huddled on the floor.

"You're the grandmother every woman wishes she had. But you're also my best friend. I should have told you everything from the beginning. I hated keeping so much of myself from you, and I'll regret it every day for the rest of my life. I'm so sorry."

Gladys pushes up on an elbow. "Ain't nothin' to forgive. Love you, baby girl."

Doherty pans back to me. "Doc, on the plane, I tried...I wanted to tell you—"

"No. Not like this." I straighten as much as my body will allow. I thought I had to tell her—and I do—but I won't give that fucker the satisfaction of listening in. "He's taken too much from you—from us—already. I'll always be with you. No matter what. Get a good lawyer. Stay out of prison as long as you can. It's...dangerous inside. Everyone has a *hidden agenda*. Make sure you find yours. Watch your back. *Live*, Natasha. Live for me."

Sutton cocks the pistol. He's not going to wait. He'll kill me in front of her. Fuck. I can't let her watch this.

"Hang up, baby. Right now!"

"Enough!" Bastian snarls. "He stays alive until I know Natasha has done her part. Sutton, back off. I'll let you know when you can have your fun."

The call drops. Sutton punches me in the face, and I taste blood, before the three men stalk out of the room and lock the door behind them.

Was it enough? Telling her to find Hidden Agenda? Will she understand I was trying to warn her? Or is this the end for all of us?

Natasha

I cast one last look over my shoulder. Bastian leans against the hood of the car, a crazed smile on his face. Kerr takes his place behind the wheel, glaring at me.

My former squad leader sends a pointed look at the door to the Army CID office, a not-so-subtle warning to get my ass inside.

My fingers find the sea glass in my pocket. It's the only piece of freedom I have left, and in minutes, I'll lose this too.

Does he have people on the inside? Probably. He's had them everywhere else. The plane. The airport. From Doc's cryptic warning about staying out of prison, he probably has someone there too.

Swallowing my sob, I push through the door.

Nothing's changed in eight years except the photo of the Special Agent-in-Charge. The same beige walls, the same polished floors, the same armored door separating the reception area from the offices and interrogation rooms.

"Can I help you?" A man in his mid-forties dressed in a rumpled suit steps up behind the counter to peer at me. CID employees all wear civilian clothes, though they're far from civilians. Warrant officers, mostly.

Help? I'm beyond help now.

I clear my throat and place my hands, palms down, on the tall desk between us. "My name is Sergeant First Class Natasha Winters. Second Battalion, Seventy-Fifth Ranger Regiment. Retired. Eight years ago, I accused five members of my squad of killing a civilian family in the Al Anbar Province of Iraq. I testified against them and was instrumental in their conviction and prison sentences. I'm here to recant my testimony and confess to those killings, as well as numerous war crimes over the course of almost fifteen years."

The man's eyes widened with every word. He reaches for his service weapon. "Don't move."

"I won't. I'm unarmed." Can he see my terror? How badly I want to run?

A buzzer sounds. I flinch as two other men—also in suits—rush into the lobby, weapons drawn.

"Turn around," one of them snaps. "Hands behind your head. Interlace your fingers."

I obey, then shiver as the cuffs tighten around my wrists. I pray West and his team know where Doc and Gladys are. My fate is sealed, but they still have a chance.

The full body search is humiliating, but it's the loss of that single piece of heart-shaped glass that hits me the hardest.

One of the officers brings me into a windowless room with a single table and three chairs. "Wait here. Someone will be with you. Eventually."

"No! I need to give you my confession now. Please!" His stare warns me that my time to make demands is over. Whatever happens now, the Army controls.

Doc

Gladys cried for ten minutes after Natasha said her goodbyes, then fell asleep against me. My hands and arms are almost completely numb, and my heart rate has been ticking up steadily.

The shot of glucagon they gave me to counteract the blood sugar crash is wearing off, but the insulin will stay in my system for another few hours. If I don't get some sugar in my system, I won't last long enough for them to kill me.

"Gladys?" I elbow her gently.

"Wha...?" She flinches, then shoves at me. I'm so dizzy, I go down. "Oh, shit. Hot Doc."

I don't bother trying to sit up again. It won't go well.

"What's wrong?" Narrowing her eyes at me, she leans closer. "You don't look so good."

"I need sugar. Or juice." My strength is fading, fast. "Will they hear you if you bang on the door?"

Worry and fear deepen the lines across her forehead. "You want those assholes to come back in here?"

"Not much choice...if they don't, I'll slip into a coma. Please, Gladys. Try."

"All those muscles and you can't do it yourself?" She huffs, but wobbles to her feet. Her steps aren't even, and her path to the door is anything but a straight line. Shit. She's in bad shape too. Have they fed her? Given her any water?

Her fists don't make much impact on the metal, but she's got a set of lungs on her. "Get your asses down here right this minute! Your mothers would be ashamed of you! Treating an old lady like this!"

"Thought you weren't old?" I ask with a wink.

"I can be old when I want to be." After a beat, she backs up quickly. "They're comin'."

The door bangs open, and Doherty glares at us. "Make that much noise again, bitch, and you'll regret it."

"Hey, asshole." I roll onto my side. "If you don't want to tell your Sergeant...that I died on your watch, get me...some fucking sugar."

"Huh?"

"You shot me up with insulin, idiot." A tremor wracks my body. The single bulb overhead takes on a halo. Shit. I'm losing focus. "Glucagon doesn't last...long enough. Sugar. Now."

For a moment, he actually looks scared. But he turns on his heel and races up the stairs. "Allan! Get me a can of pop! And a candy bar! The doctor's crashing again!"

They didn't shut the door. Gladys looks at me, questions in her eyes.

"Don't risk it. Not...yet."

After almost a minute, two sets of heavy footsteps come back down. Doherty has a can of Coke in one hand and a Snickers bar in the other. Collins is right behind him. No Sutton this time. Is he still in the building?

"Stop," Collins barks, stopping Doherty in his tracks. "Give the shit to granny. He could be fucking with us."

"Do I look...like I'm fucking with you?" It's getting harder to force my tongue to work, but I add a little extra slur to the words for good measure. If they underestimate me, I might find an opening. Later. When I'm not minutes away from hypoglycemic shock.

Gladys takes the soda and eases herself down next to me with a symphony of pops and groans. "Next time you kidnap a senior citizen, take their arthritis medicine with you," she mutters.

The first sip of the sugary drink makes me want to gag,

but I force half of it down before I close my eyes. "Gonna need more in a couple of hours, assholes."

Collins whispers, "Is he serious?"

"Do your fucking research next time. Insulin...is serious shit."

The two men leave, slamming the door hard enough to make Gladys flinch. She scoots closer, and the candy bar wrapper rustles. "Eat some of this, Doc."

With my hands still bound, she has to feed it to me, and the longing look she gives the chocolate is too much after a couple of bites. "You need to eat too."

"I won't die without sugar. You will." Her voice cracks, and she licks her dry lips.

"Gladys, finish the damn candy bar. I'll be okay."

More than okay, I hope. Because now, I know these guys don't want me to die before their boss is good and ready. And I can use that.

CHAPTER THIRTY-ONE

Natasha

THE CLOCK on the wall ticks loudly. They've let me stew here for more than two hours. No water, no coffee, nothing but four beige walls, a dark wood table, and hard metal chairs.

At least they took the cuffs off. But my butt aches from sitting for so long. I'm not willing to risk pacing. Someone might decide I need to be restrained.

The door lock buzzes, and I stifle my yelp. Shit.

I'm not ready. I'll never be ready.

"Natasha Winters. I'm Warrant Officer Hastings."

"Sir." I know better than to stand and salute, though the urge is still there.

Hastings sets a laptop down on the table, pulls out his chair, and unbuttons his suit jacket. "I've been reviewing your testimony from eight years ago. Sergeant First Class Chris Bowers corroborated your story back then. Some reason he would do that?"

"He...he was in on the whole thing. His wife had cancer.

He needed the money." My eyes burn. Marisol made a full recovery. If the Army wanted to, they could cut off his death benefits now. She needs them. But no one would believe I did everything alone. Bastian is going to ruin Chris's memory along with my life.

"You disappeared after the verdict against Montgomery Bastian, Allan Collins, Dylan Sutton, Ethan Doherty, and Robert Bowen. You haven't renewed your driver's license or passport since. You haven't collected a single pension check. No parking tickets, credit cards, or student loans. So...why come in at all? Why not stay gone?"

I fiddle with the hem of my tank top. Bastian's *instructions* didn't cover this.

"I couldn't live with myself any longer. The nightmares. What I did to Sarge and the others. They didn't deserve any of it." A single tear slips down my cheek.

No, they deserved all of it. And more.

Hastings leans back in his chair. "Start from the beginning."

Doc

There's a sip or two of soda left. But the candy is gone. So are the heart palpitations. The pounding headache. I'm still weak, but we're running out of time.

Across from me, Gladys sits against the wall with her knees drawn up to her chest. Her lips took on more color after she had some of the soda. Her hands don't shake so badly.

I manage to get to my knees, and when the room only spins for a moment, try standing. So far, so good. But that was the easy part.

This is going to hurt. I bend over partway, ball my hands into fists, and raise my arms as high as I can before slamming them down against my ass. The plastic bites into my skin.

It takes me three tries before the zip tie snaps in half and my hands are free.

"Fuck, that stings." My fingers are nothing but pins and needles.

"You could have done that the *whole time?*" Gladys asks. "You've been holding out on me, Dr. Sexy Pants."

"My blood sugar still isn't stable. I'll crash again before the insulin's out of my system. But those assholes upstairs know it. They'll be back. And we can use that. Did you see anything when they brought you in here? Is this a business? A house?"

"I saw a whole room full of computers behind some thick glass doors. Must've been hundreds of them. People too."

Shit. Are there people upstairs right now? If so, could we make enough noise for them to hear us?

"What time was it? Do you remember?"

"It was still light outside. Hot enough sweat was pourin' off my tits. The big one—the one in charge—told me if I made trouble, I'd regret it. That's when he gave me this." She points to her cheek.

I was already planning on killing Bastian for what he did to Natasha—if I ever get out of here. But hitting Gladys too? I hope I get the chance to make him suffer.

"They're taking a serious chance keeping us somewhere with people. Why?" I press my ear to the door, but I can't hear shit.

"The guy with the soda? What's his name?"

"Doherty."

"His brother owns this place. He said no one would hear me 'cause of the big air conditioners they needed to cool down all those computers. But the big one wasn't so sure."

"Well, we are now. You can yell with the best of them, Gladys."

Her chest puffs up, which only serves to highlight the fact that she's not wearing a bra.

"Donald always said he could hear me halfway across the island."

"Your husband was a wise man. But if there were so many people up there, how did they get me in without someone noticing?"

Gladys snorts. "Shitcicles, Doc. They had you stuffed in a damn suitcase."

No wonder my back hurts like hell.

Some of the sensation has started to return to my fingers. I drop to one knee and reach in to my boot. The comms unit won't work if it can't get a signal from my phone. But West said it could also connect to any unsecured wi-fi network. Though it would default to broadcast only mode. Would it work all the way down here?

I shove the tiny device into my ear and tap it. Nothing. No reassuring beep. Only the dull hiss of static. I'm not surprised. Either we're too far underground, or there's a signal dampener somewhere.

"What are you doing?" Gladys shuffles closer. The soda and candy bar did her some good. She's steadier on her feet than she was.

I drape my arm around her shoulders and lead her over to the wall next to the door. "Sometime in the next hour, at least one of those assholes is going to come down here to check on me. Hopefully with another soda."

I pop the earbud free and show it to her.

"You got some music on that thing?" she asks. "Might help pass the time."

I chuckle. "Nope. But on the other end of this little device, there are a whole bunch of people trying to find us. And save Natasha. If you can get out of here, you can contact them."

"And how do you think I'm gonna do that?" She snorts. "In case you haven't noticed, Dr. Sexy Pants, that door is locked up tight. And I got bad knees. I ain't runnin' nowhere."

"If we're lucky, all you'll need is a fast shuffle. Do you remember how to get out of here? Once you're up the stairs, can you find the door?"

"Well, duh. It's only one hallway, then out to the parking lot. I'm old, Doc. Not stupid."

"Gladys, you're not old *or* stupid. If you do this, you're a super hero."

"You know what to say?" With every passing minute, I'm afraid we'll run out of time. Thank fuck my blood sugar seems to be stable, but that could still change, and after this stunt, there's no way I'll get another soda or candy bar before the end.

"Tell them where I am, that they're gonna kill Natasha once she's arrested, and the word 'firefly.'"

"Good. Make sure you stay in public. Stand in the middle of the goddamn street if you have to. Flash your tits. Stop traffic. And if those fuckers come near you, tell anyone who will listen that they kidnapped you and you want to call your nephew. What's his name?"

Another snort, and she shakes her head. "My memory is sharp as a tack. Two tacks even. Dax Holloway with Second Sight in Boston."

I frame her face with my hands so I can press a kiss to her forehead. "Good girl."

"Bet you say that to all the ladies." Her brown eyes shimmer. "I don't like leavin' you down here. They're gonna beat the shit out of you and I don't think you can take much more."

I gather her against me, holding her tightly. I'm not sure I can either. But this is our only option.

After a few seconds, she sighs. "Knew you'd be a good hugger. Nat is damn lucky you didn't give up on her."

I chuckle, then ease her back. "Okay. Stand right here. As soon as they go for me, you get up those stairs as fast as you can. Put the earbud in once you're clear of the building. It'll beep when it finds a signal. You hear that, you start talking and don't stop until someone talks back or comes for you with that codeword."

"I got it, Hot Doc. Don't die."

I offer her a weak smile. "Yes, ma'am. I'll do my best."

THOSE ASSHOLES ARE LATE. I could be dead down here for all they know. Gladys has been sitting for at least half an hour—she needed to conserve her strength—and I can feel my blood sugar dropping again.

"This is taking too long," I mutter. There's still a little soda left, so I drain the warm, flat liquid in a single swallow. "It's now or never, Gladys. Want to try out your acting skills again?"

She lifts her hand, and I help her to her feet. "If it'll get me warm, I'll strip naked and do a hand stand."

"Fucking hell. I did *not* need that visual." Moving all the way across the room, I sink down onto my side and tuck my hands behind my back. "Make them believe I just had a seizure. If they think I'm dying, they'll try to resuscitate me, and we might have a better chance at this."

With a nod, Gladys shuffles over to the door. "Help! Oh,

God! Doc's dyin'! Get your asses down here!" She keeps up her cries until the lock *thunks*. Doherty and Collins burst into the room. I keep my eyes mostly closed. Just enough so I can see her grab onto Doherty's arm.

"You have to help him! He started floppin' around and moanin' just a minute ago, and now he won't wake up!"

He shakes off her hold, and the two of them rush over to me. Gladys slips out of the room. Thank fuck.

Collins crouches next to me. As soon as he reaches down to check my pulse, I slam my fist into his jaw. His ass hits the ground, and I'm on top of him in a heartbeat. My knee lands on his dick. He yowls, and I hit him again, then kick my leg out to catch Doherty in the ankle.

"Shit!" Doherty growls. His phone skids across the concrete floor. My fingers tighten around Collins's throat. His eyes bulge. Lifting him halfway up, I grin, then slam him back down.

Before I can spin around, pain explodes across the back of my head. My grip loosens. Desperate, I throw myself toward where I *think* Doherty is, but find nothing but air.

A boot slams down on my lower back. With a pop, my left leg goes numb. Fuck.

I'm not out of this fight yet. I can't be. Straining, I reach back, find denim, and pull with all I have in me.

Doherty stumbles. The intense pressure lifts. But I can't get to my feet. Rolling, I grab for the soda can one of them dropped and lob it at Doherty's head.

He ducks easily. The gun slams into the side of my skull. An arm bands around my throat from behind.

Everything turns soft and fuzzy. My body bucks, muscles straining for the smallest bit of air.

"Where's the old woman?" Doherty's voice sounds so far away.

They're not letting go. This...this is it. I'm going to die. A warm, quiet peace settles over me.

Gladys got out. She'll be okay.

Gladys

"Holy shitsicles!" The bright sunlight blinds me. A wall of heat makes it hard to breathe. Or that could be my heart pounding.

Those two jackwagons didn't pay me a single mind after Doc started wailing on them. I had to pull myself up those damn stairs by the handrail, but I made it out the back door.

"Make sure you stay in public."

This parking lot ain't public. But that big street at the far end sure is. Ignoring the pops and cracks from my knees, hips, and ankles, I stumble around the half a dozen cars until I reach the sidewalk.

The earbud is too damn small, and my fingers ain't working right. But I get it into my ear and tap it like Doc said to do—all while shuffling toward the corner.

The stoplight turns green as I get there. Where should I go? Nothing much to the left. A couple of folks coming out of a restaurant with a doggie bag. Damn. I'm starving.

Up ahead, a big neon sign announces the grand opening of the "Fairfax Shopping MegaPlex." A whole mess of balloons sways in the breeze, and the bright lights promise hourly giveaways, big sales, and "more." There have to be people there.

The beep in my ear is so loud, I almost trip over my own damn feet as I start to cross. Halle-fucking-lujah!

"Hello? This is Gladys Henshaw. Those fuckers are gonna kill Natasha tonight. You lot better come get me before they find me too. I'm on Center Parkway headin' toward the Fairfax Shopping MegaPlex. Oh, and Doc said to say 'firefly.'"

I'm out of breath by the time I get all that out. The light at the next corner is red, and I check behind me. Shitsicles. The dark-haired one—Doherty—runs out of the parking lot and scans the street. When he sees me, I wave and smile.

A group of handsome men in suits come out of a restaurant between us and hide him from view. They're walking toward me. Maybe I should flash my tits like the Doc said. But then the light chirps, and it's the second best sound I've heard all day. Right behind those damn beeps in my ear.

"Did you hear me, firefly people? Doc said you were the cavalry, and that mall won't keep me safe very long if you don't find me. The Colonel's gonna kill Nat tonight at the prison."

"Holy fuck. Gladys?" The rough, deep voice in my ear scares the shit out of me. I yelp, and a mom pushing a stroller looks at me like I'm two sandwiches short of a picnic. But I shuffle through the big automatic doors. A blast of cold air hits me square in the face.

"Yep. Who the hell are you and how long do I need to wait for you to get here? Doc's in a building two blocks away with a whole mess of computers. In the basement. If they didn't kill him for what he did to get me out of there, he needs savin'."

I wonder if any of Dr. Sexy Pants's friends are as hot as he is? And single. It's been a long time since I had anything nice to look at.

"We're on our way," the voice says, interrupting my fantasy. "Ten minutes. Are you safe?"

"As safe as I can be. But you ain't said the code word."

"Goddam—goldilocks."

"That ain't it, sonny." I look around for the best place to wait. The food court is packed, so I shuffle over and sink down at one of the few available tables. My stomach rumbles. I wonder if any of these people would take pity on an old woman and buy her some french fries?

"Firefly, Gladys. The code is firefly." He lowers his voice and adds, "She called me 'sonny.'"

"Well, *now* I'm satisfied. I'm sittin' in the food court. You get to Doc first, young man. Then come find me. I'll be waitin'."

CHAPTER THIRTY-TWO

Gladys

I KEEP EXPECTING Doherty or the other one—the mean one—to come and drag me out of the food court, but after ten minutes, I start to relax. Until a tall drink of water with some gray in his brown hair and an easy smile strides my way. Then I sit up straight.

"Ma'am, I heard you might like fireflies." He sweeps his gaze around the mall, then leans closer—which ain't easy since he has to be at least six-and-a-half feet tall. "Gladys, my name's Ford. I'd like to get you out of here if that's okay with you."

"Hey, you in my ear? This your man?" He had the code word—sort of—but that raspy voice has been quiet since I sat down, and I don't like it. Not one bit.

"For fuck's sake," the voice mutters. "Yes. Give him the damn earbud, will you?"

"No. I want to know what's goin' on, and I doubt any of you are gonna tell me. So I'm gonna listen in." With a huff, I take Ford's hand and let him help me to my feet. "You find Doc?" I ask.

"No. By the time we went in, the basement was empty." Ford drapes his arm around my shoulders. "No more questions until we're in the van. Got it?"

I huff. "One more. You got any cash on you? All I've had to eat in the past two days is a bag of chips and part of a Snickers bar. I'd kill for some french fries."

Ford pivots so quickly, I almost topple over, and heads straight for a burger chain at the end of the food court. "Foxtrot to Delta team. We're...stopping for food. SmashMelt D.C. You want anything?"

When we reach the counter, he waits for me to order a double-smash meal deal with a lemonade, then pulls out his phone. "Add four additional meal deals, two with Coke, two with lemonade, and three extra orders of fries."

"Shitsicles. How many folks you got in that van with you?" I whisper after he's paid and we're waiting off to the side for the food. "And are they all as hot as you? Because my heart might not be able to take much more sexiness."

He lets out a rich laugh. "Everyone 'in the van' is spoken for. Except Vasquez, but he's way too young for you, Gladys."

"Well, fuck me sideways. Can't blame a girl for asking."

"Is that even possible?" Ford shakes his head. "Never mind. I don't want to know. Sierra, get up here. Need an assist with all the food."

Five minutes later, "Sierra" hasn't shown, and laden down with two large bags, a drink carrier, and a boatload of napkins, we head for the elevator.

The doors slide open, and a blonde dressed all in black pushes off the wall. "Damn, darlin'. That's some shiner."

"Who the hell are you?" I look to Ford, then back to the pretty young thing in front of me.

"Raelynn. Also known as Sierra when we're on comms. I

was comin' to help y'all with the food, but looks like you got it handled." She jabs the button for P3, and the doors close with a whisper. "Sierra to Delta team. Come and get us."

"Someone want to tell me why I can't hear anyone you're talkin' to?" I stare up at Ford, but the position makes my neck ache before the elevator dings. He's just too damn tall.

"Because the asshole you were talking to earlier is a control freak," Ford says with a grin.

"You want to repeat that?" the raspy voice in my ear asks.

"Nope."

A black van pulls up as soon as we step into the garage. The side door slides open. My jaw drops. Shitsicles. Two men and a woman are in the back, with a young guy behind the wheel. Ford hands off the food, while Raelynn takes my arm.

"Come on, darlin'. We can't stay here." She helps me into a seat, and the young whippersnapper behind the wheel turns.

Dark hair, even darker eyes. Wowza. Is he the single one? He ain't too young.

"Where to?" he asks.

"That park we passed on the way from the airport. It's between CID and the Correctional Treatment Facility," a man with a pistol strapped to his hip says.

Raelynn pats my arm. "Gladys, that's West. Vasquez is drivin'. Then you've got Ripper, and Inara."

"Where are Doc and Nat?" I demand.

"Natasha is still at CID—the Army Criminal Investigation Division," Ripper says. "Her GPS tracker hasn't moved since a little after 9:00 a.m."

"We have two people watching the office," Ford adds. "They won't be able to move her without us knowing."

"And Doc?" I'm scared to ask. "I told you all where he was. Why didn't you storm in there and rescue him?"

"We tried." West pops the top off a Thermos, and the

scent of coffee fills the van. "By the time we got there, the basement was empty. Nothing but a busted zip tie, an empty can of Coke, and a small pool of blood on the floor."

I drop the fry back into the bag. "Shitsicles. He was too sick to fight them."

"Sick?" West straightens, his eyes narrowing on me. "Sick, how?"

"They injected him with insulin. On the plane. He said that's how they separated him and Nat."

"Fuck. They could have killed him. Ford? Call Joey. We need to know how long Doc's going to be compromised. And what we might need to do for him when we get him back." West pulls a tablet out of the bag at his feet and fixes his hard stare on me. "We need to know every single thing those fuckers said from the moment they took you."

Natasha

Hastings stopped trying to hide his contempt hours ago—when I told him that *Chris and I* killed an entire family outside of Albaghdadi because the husband wouldn't hand over a shipment of opium. Every time I have to implicate Chris, I want to throw up. Killing him wasn't enough. Bastian is determined to ruin him, even in death.

Hastings hasn't given me a break. Or any water. I'm dehydrated, exhausted, and terrified. For all I know, he's working with Bastian. My testimony has to be perfect. But I only had five hours to memorize four pages of information. Ryker taught me some memory tricks that helped, but I'm sure I'm forgetting *something*.

He folds his hands on the desk and stares at me. "Let's go over it all again."

I sink my fingers into my hair, tugging at the strands until the pain helps me focus. "We've been over everything twice already. What else do you expect me to say? Nothing's changed. If you give me that computer, I'll access my bank account in the Maldives. There's five hundred thousand dollars in it. All I have left. You can see the deposits I made when I was in Iraq."

I want to scream at him. *It's Bastain's account. Bastian's blood money.* But I can't. It—like all his other crimes—officially belongs to me now.

Hastings arches his brows. "I'm not letting you *touch* a computer."

"Well, then we're about to spend two more very boring hours going over the same exact information we've already covered. Twice."

"If you have somewhere to be," he says, "you won't make it. At six, the D.C. police will arrive to take you to booking. From there, you'll be processed and sent to the Correctional Treatment Facility until your arraignment on multiple counts of felony murder and war crimes. As those are capitol offenses, you won't breathe free air for the rest of your *very* short life. You don't have a choice here, Winters. If I want you to go over it all again, that's exactly what you're going to do."

Tears prick at my eyes. "Can I at least have some water?"

"No. Start from the beginning."

I lick my lips. Or try to. This is my life now. Doing what I'm told. No freedom. Nothing of my own. Of *me*. Someone will tell me when to eat, when to sleep, when to shower, when to take a piss. And when to die.

Before I can manage enough strength—mental or physical—to say a word, someone raps solidly on the door.

Hastings locks his laptop and stands as the door opens behind me. "Mr. Hastings, you're needed in the Chief's office."

If I weren't so exhausted, I'd weep at the man's voice. As it is, when Hastings stalks out and Graham takes the seat across from me, I can barely stop myself from reaching for his hand. He passes me a bottle of water, and I down half of it before I lift my gaze to his.

"Winters, you're in some serious shit." He taps his tablet, turns it around, and slides it across the table to me. "This is the list of crimes you're about to be charged with. Read it."

"Wh-what?"

"Read. It." Though his voice doesn't soften, his eyes do, and I glance at the document on the screen. I have to squint; the text is fuzzy.

"This is Ripper. We don't have a lot of time and we can't hack the cameras here. But this font is unreadable at any distance greater than three feet. Each message will last twenty seconds."

The words fade away, and another paragraph appears.

"Gladys is safe. Doc got her out. But he couldn't escape with her. His GPS tracker died early this morning, so we have no idea where he is."

Tears spill onto my cheeks. He could be anywhere by now. Or...nowhere.

The second message disappears. I glance up at Graham to find his gaze pinned on the door. Oh, shit. Hastings could come back at any time.

"We can get you out of there right now. Tell Graham you want a lawyer and refuse to sign the affidavit. But that'll make it harder for us to find and get to Doc. If you stay, you'll be arrested, processed, and sent to the CTV for violent offenders. We think that's where they're planning on getting to you."

Shit. He doesn't need me convicted. He just needs my confession.

"Bastian has a full-bird colonel behind him. We don't know who it is, but Gladys says he wants to be the one to kill you. Bastian just wants you to suffer. There's no better way to do that

than killing Doc in front of you. We have a plan to get into the CTF. And we can track your location inside. But it's a big place, and we don't know how many hostiles we'll encounter. We might not get there in time. Or be able to save you both. You need to decide, Natasha. Right now."

The text fades away, and I slide the tablet back to Graham.

"Are you asking me for a lawyer?"

The hope in his voice breaks me. I wish I could. But there's one thing I want—no, that I need—more than my freedom. I need to know Doc is safe. Staying here is his only chance. Rubbing my hands over my face to hide my lips, I lower my voice to a whisper. "No. If I do, Doc dies."

Graham taps the screen a few times and turns it toward me. *"We won't give up on him. I promise."*

I lower my gaze to the table and blink back tears. "If I'm inside, there's a better chance Doc lives. Yes or no?"

He pauses for so long, I raise my head. His green eyes are full of sorrow. "Yes."

The door opens, and Hastings stalks back into the room. "Some asshole rammed my car in the parking lot. Now I'm going to have to fill out a fuck-ton of paperwork with my insurance company. You can go, Mr. Tempelton. I'll take it from here."

"Winters?" Graham stands, tucks his tablet under his arm, and meets my gaze. "I need an answer."

Under the table, I dig my fingers into my thighs as hard as I can. "I don't need a lawyer, Mr. Tempelton. I'm guilty of my crimes, and I intend to pay for them."

CHAPTER THIRTY-THREE

Doc

THREE TIMES SINCE GLADYS ESCAPED, I've passed out. Three times, I've been jolted awake in the most painful ways possible. The first was when Collins and Doherty dumped me into the trunk of a car. The bright sun blinded me for all of a five seconds before they slammed the lid. I couldn't move. They'd hogtied me and slapped a strip of duct tape over my mouth. I don't think I'd been unconscious for long. Minutes, maybe. I could still feel the arm around my throat.

Exhaust fumes, combined with the intense heat, made it hard to focus. I thought I could turn over—maybe pull the trunk release level, but I'm a big guy, and it *wasn't* a big car. Eventually, I gave up, and the motion, noise, and my own exhaustion pulled me under.

Later, someone ripped the tape from my lips and poured juice down my throat. I choked, aspirating enough of the sweet drink I can still feel it burning my lungs. After gagging me again, they turned out the light and shut the door. I wheezed around the tape, and my head hit hard porcelain.

Fucking hell. They'd dumped me in a bathtub.

I tried to get free, but all I managed to do was bang my forehead against the spout and get blood in my eyes. Eventually, I fell asleep—or passed out.

It's the light that does it this time. And the door banging open. And Montgomery Bastian tearing the gag away so violently, my lower lip splits.

Rage twists his expression, and he grabs my arms and shakes me hard enough, whiplash is a distinct possibility.

"You had better hope the old woman knows what's good for her," he snarls. "I'd kill you right now if I could."

"Do it," I manage. "What are you waiting for?"

Bastian's eyes darken. "Natasha. Of course. She'll be on her way to lockup in a few hours. After lights out, *her* lights will go out. Forever."

"Really? *That's* the line you're going with? I thought criminal masterminds only used bad puns on television." I groan, then lose my breath when he punches me in the stomach. The coughing fit sends pain snaking around my torso. Fuck. The nerve block is wearing off. But Gladys got away. Even if the earbud didn't work, she would have gone to the police. Or called Bella. Hidden Agenda will protect her.

Bastian turns to Doherty. "He better last until tonight. The Colonel wants to be the one to put an end to Natasha. But *I'll* make her suffer. She'll watch me carve her lover into pieces before the end."

Fuck. He's going to torture me in front of her. I don't know why I'm surprised. Everything about this asshole is over the top. Pretty sure he could step right into one of those murder shows Gladys likes to watch and fit right in.

"Get him ready." Bastian pushes his way past the other men in the small bathroom. "We leave in two hours."

Collins and Bowen each grab one of my arms to haul me

out of the bathtub. After so long in one position, my muscles scream at me. My vision blurs.

They drop me face first onto old, disgusting carpet. Cigarette smoke lingers in the air.

"Make a sound," Bowen says, his knee pressed into my lower back, "and I'll cut out your tongue so you can't even say goodbye to her."

I'll do anything to see Natasha again. To have the chance to hold her. To tell her she saved me from my own crushing loneliness—even if it was only for a short while. And for that, I need my tongue. So I keep my mouth shut.

The four of them work quickly, cutting the zip ties around my ankles, stripping off my boots and jeans, then replacing them with gray uniform pants and scuffed black shoes.

My arms are so stiff, when they free my wrists, I can only watch as they cut off my Henley and force me into a gray, button down shirt. Fucking hell. It's a prison guard uniform.

So that's the play. Get me into the prison and...what? Make it look like Natasha killed me? Then this Colonel can kill her and no one will think twice about it.

The zip ties are replaced by thick, heavy flexi-cuffs. They're not taking any chances. These, I'm not sure even McCabe could break.

But this time, when they shove me back into the tub, I have a purpose. I don't need to get free. With four of them in the next room, even if I could, there's nowhere to go. They'd just tie me up again. All I have to do is keep my muscles loose. When they get me to the prison—when I see Natasha again—I need to be able to fight.

Natasha

The constant *tick, tick, tick* of the clock is now my least favorite sound. It counts down the minutes until Bastian and some nameless, faceless Colonel try to kill me and the man I love. It's almost six. The police will be here any minute.

Hastings moves to the door and presses the intercom button. "We're done here. Bring in the affidavit."

I fiddle with the hem of my tank top. My life is over. Everything that was *mine* is gone. Soon, I'll have to give up these clothes too.

Someone bangs twice. Hastings opens the door, accepts a thick, brown envelope, and shuts it again.

He makes a big show of pulling out the stack of paper. "Your crimes. Sign and initial where indicated."

My hand shakes as I pick up the pen. "What happens next?"

I know...most of it. But I need to hear him say it. If only to give my panicked mind something to focus on as I sign my name to so many of Bastian's heinous acts.

"The D.C. police are waiting to take you into custody. Given the time of day, you won't be arraigned until tomorrow —at the earliest." Hastings jabs his finger at the first little yellow flag where I'm supposed to sign. "Hurry up. They won't be happy if they have to work overtime, and their shift ends in an hour."

My tears spill over, dotting the paper. Will I even be alive by this time tomorrow? And what about Doc? If Hidden Agenda can't get into the correctional facility, is there any way we survive this?

Ten minutes later, I've signed and initialed every page of that damn document. All of Bastian's crimes...they're mine now.

Hastings calls another warrant officer to join him, and

they escort me back through the secured metal door to the reception area.

"Natasha Winters." A uniformed D.C. police officer approaches with a set of cuffs in his hand. "We have a warrant for your arrest. Turn around."

The metal snaps around my wrists. I'm unprepared for how helpless I suddenly feel.

"You have the right to remain silent. Anything you say can and will be used against you in a court of law. You have the right to an attorney to be present during questioning. If you can't afford an attorney, one will be appointed for you. Do you understand these rights?"

A tear trails down my cheek. I can't even wipe it away. "Y-yes. I do."

A dull roar fills my ears. The officers exchange a few words with Hastings, then the younger one—his name tag says Hill—takes my arm.

The squad car smells like stale coffee and sweat. I can't brace myself when I sit down. Can't put on my own seatbelt. Can't rub my eyes. I'm so hungry. The last thing I ate was a protein bar while Doc and I were waiting to board the plane.

Outside the dirty window, the city passes by in a blur. People stroll along the sidewalks, oblivious to how precious their freedom should be. I squeeze my eyes shut.

There's a plan. Graham got into CID. He wasn't even in the Army. They'll find a way.

At the station, another officer enters my passport and the heart-shaped piece of sea glass into inventory before I'm fingerprinted, photographed, and placed in a holding cell with four other women. Two are obviously here for solicitation. The other is high as a kite. My hands are cuffed—in front of me this time—and I sit on a well-worn bench, not making eye contact with anyone. Five minutes turns into ten. Then twenty. I'm starting to wonder if they plan on keeping me here all night. But they can't get to me here. It's too public.

Finally, two officers amble up to the cell.

"Winters! Your ride is here. Stand and approach the door."

I do as I'm told, but flinch when they snap a pair of leg irons around my ankles, then add a belly chain and lock the handcuffs to my waist. I wasn't planning on running. Being *unable* to...it's enough to send me into a full-blown panic.

"I won't make any trouble," I say quietly, keeping my head down.

"You murdered more than a dozen people," the older one snaps. "Shut your fucking mouth."

The back of the van is empty. A heavy metal grill separates the two front seats from a pair of metal benches—one on each side of the vehicle. There's nothing to hold onto, so when the driver accelerates, I slide three feet before I can stop myself.

Thank God it's not a long ride. Twenty minutes later, a woman in a dark gray uniform leads me into a sterile room with polished tile floors, a row of showers in one corner, and an exam table in the other.

The strip search is humiliating, but after that, she tells me to shower and put on the bright orange prison "uniform."

Washing away the scent of Doc's shampoo breaks me. Sobs wrack my body until a guard comes in and tells me to hurry the fuck up.

Then comes the doctor. Questions about my medical history. Allergies. Surgeries. I don't bother telling her that I'll be dead soon. I don't tell her much of anything.

I'm so tired. The clock on the wall must be lying. It's only 8:37? Will they come for me right away? Doubtful. After lights out will be easier. They'll have to get me somewhere...private. Somewhere no one will hear me—or Doc—scream.

Another guard shows up to take me to my cell. I don't look at her, keeping my head down, trudging along beside her until she stops. "This is you, sugar."

Sugar?

My head snaps up, and Raelynn passes me a small, resealable bag. She doesn't smile and barely makes eye contact. "Toothbrush, toothpaste, comb, washcloth, soap, deodorant, feminine hygiene products, and ear plugs. No one sleeps well the first night. Once you're alone, make sure you have everythin' you need."

"Wh-what happens now?"

Raelynn glances up and down the cell block. All the doors are still open, but only half the cells are occupied. "This here is our intake wing. It's a little quiet at the moment. Lights out is in ninety minutes. I reckon you're gonna want to brush your teeth, comb your hair, and use those ear plugs. Maybe wash up a bit too. Go on. I'll radio up for them to lock you in. After that...try and get some rest."

I back up three steps, and Raelynn reaches for the mic clipped to her shoulder. "Close 21-B."

The loud metallic *clang* sends a shiver down my spine. I can't help but wrap my fingers around the bars. "Please. Tell me something," I whisper.

"Nothin' to tell, darlin'," she says under her breath. "We're wingin' this one. Don't know nothin' from nothin' yet. But we're here with you until the end. That's a promise."

I wait until I can't see her anymore, then sink down onto the thin mattress. A fresh sob tears from my throat, and I let go, helpless to stop the terror from ripping my heart into shreds.

CHAPTER THIRTY-FOUR

Doc

IN THE BACK of the SUV, I flex my legs under a thick blanket hiding me from view. Sutton and Doherty dragged me from that tiny motel tub half an hour ago. I couldn't see much in the minute or so I was outside, but it's dark. The kind of dark you only get at least an hour or two after sunset.

I don't have much time. The women's prison is in D.C., but the city isn't that big. They had me in Virginia somewhere. I don't know why it's so important that I figure out where. I should be concentrating on what I'm going to do once we arrive.

Every time I shift my focus, though, it's Natasha's face I see. The fear in her eyes as they took her from me on the plane. The way her voice cracked when she said goodbye.

How she *almost* told me she loved me. Twice. Why didn't I say it back? I didn't want Bastian to take that moment from us. But what if it was the last one we'll have?

I lose track of time. The SUV stops, starts, and stops again. The hatch opens, the blanket is ripped away, and I'm muscled up a set of steps and through a loading door at the back of the prison.

"Where the fuck are you taking me?"

No one answers. Or cares if I make noise. My legs are free, but I let them think I'm too weak to walk. They don't need to know I've been working my muscles for hours to be ready for anything.

Plastic-wrapped pallets are stacked three high in long rows. Instant potatoes, rice, oatmeal, flour, detergent. I don't see a single person around. Even late at night, there should be patrols.

"This way," Bastian calls. "Hurry. We only have half an hour before lights out. I want some time with the doctor before Natasha joins us."

"I didn't know you cared, asshole," I mutter as Collins and Sutton carry me past him, through another door and into the prison's laundry facilities.

The fluorescent lights are dimmed, lending too many shadows to the large room. A dozen washing machines line one wall. The dryers, another. Water pipes stretch across the ceiling. They ping from time to time, but it's otherwise quiet.

Doherty pulls out a piece of thick rope and tosses it over one of the pipes. There's no point fighting as he loops it around the middle of the flexi-cuffs, then pulls my arms high over my head. The position tugs at the stitches in my side. One of them rips, and I hiss out a breath.

The door across from me shuts with a solid *thud*, and Bowen takes up position next to it, holding a silenced pistol.

A second door at the far end of the dryers is partially hidden by a line of carts and several long tables holding stacks of folded orange shirts and pants.

Spinning a stun gun in his hand, Bastian circles me. Electricity arcs between the twin points. "Natasha's confession has been entered into the system. There's enough evidence against her that the Colonel can easily get our convictions overturned now."

"Is this the part where you gloat, asshole? Because I'm really fucking tired. Just skip to the torture already. Or better yet, go fuck yourself."

The prongs dig into my side. I barely manage to go limp before pure agony ripples through my muscles. My scream goes on forever like I'm some demented Wookie. I twitch helplessly, hanging by my wrists as my thoughts scramble.

I lose all track of time, though somewhere in the back of my mind, I know it's only a five-second hit.

"Happy now?" Bastian asks. He examines the stun gun, a small smile curving his lips. "This particular model can be used ten, twelve times before recharging. Doherty, how many others do we have?"

"Three, Sarge." The dark-haired asshole unzips a small duffel bag and lays the devices out on one of the tables.

"No. I'm not happy at all." I do my best to relax my muscles, despite the spasms still rolling through me. "Maybe you missed the part where I told you to go fuck yourself?"

The second hit is so much worse. I buck in the restraints, my back twisting in truly unnatural ways. I can't feel my left leg at all, but the rest of my body is one raw nerve.

How much longer until the end? Ten minutes? Twenty? The Colonel will be here soon—whoever the fuck he is. Time to change tactics. If there *is* a way out of here—if Gladys managed to get to Hidden Agenda and they came up with a plan, I have to do my best to stay alive. And find out how far up the chain the corruption goes. I can't do that if he keeps shocking me.

"You really think this is a good plan?" I manage. My throat is on fire, and the words aren't much louder than a hoarse whisper. But the idiot is still close enough to shock me without breaking a sweat. "Natasha willingly surrenders to

CID, cops to everything, and then decides to kill a guard her first night in jail? Why?"

"She killed dozens," Bastian says with a little shrug. "Women. Children. Innocents. She'll be written off as mentally unstable. And you...well..." He chuckles. "Employee records will show that you started working here three days ago. You took a fancy to the newest inmate, brought her here so you could have your way with her, and things got...messy."

"You fucking piece of shit!" I lunge for him, but the rope holds me back. "If you touch her—"

"Don't worry," he says mildly. "You'll be dead by then. Though, I suppose making you watch *would* be the ultimate form of torture." He glances down at the weapon in his hand with a contemplative hum.

Doherty clears his throat. "Sarge? The Colonel's on his way."

"Excellent." Bastian checks his watch. "Five minutes until lights out. Is everyone in position?"

Collins pulls out a radio. "Lewiston. Horvath. Report."

"Ready and waiting," comes a man's reply.

"Kerr? All quiet out there?"

After a beat, another man confirms the kitchen and hallway are clear. A fourth says Natasha is alone in her cell and they're on their way to retrieve her.

Five of them. At least. Multiple witnesses to confirm Bastian's bullshit story. And way too many hostiles in this room for me to fight my way out.

The door opens, and Bowen takes two quick steps back. "Sir."

The man I can only assume is "the Colonel" is in street clothes—jeans and a light blue Polo shirt—but carries himself like the upper echelon of the military. Crisp, precise steps, a glint to his dark eyes that says he *knows* he's the most powerful man in the room, and barely contained rage.

"I told you witnesses were a bad fucking idea," he snaps, gesturing to me. "I could have strung her up in here and made it look like a suicide. It would have been a lot cleaner."

"Except someone would have to explain how she got out of her cell." Bastian shakes his head. "This way, we both get what we want."

"What I *want* is for you and your men to get the fuck to Syria and restart the operation. But even *I* can't get you on GrayZone's payroll until your records are expunged."

GrayZone. The private military contracting company sends a contingent to every war zone across the world. That's the Colonel's end game. Restart the whole operation with men who know what they're doing—because they've done it before.

The man pulls a pair of black leather gloves from his pocket and tugs them on before holding out his hand. "You have something for me?"

Doherty approaches and unfolds a dark cloth. Inside rests a toothbrush with the end of the handle sharpened into a shiv. "Colonel Sapier, sir? This is the exact brand of toothbrush given to all new inmates. It's been wiped clean. We'll get her prints—and his—on it after they're dead."

Sapier picks up the makeshift weapon and holds it up to the light. "I'm supposed to gut her with this? It would take me hours." He tosses it onto the table next to the spare stun guns. "Tell me one of you idiots has a *real* knife?"

Collins passes the man his KA-BAR. "Take mine, sir."

The long blade is a hundred times more lethal than the cheap, plastic shiv. Fucking hell.

Somewhere in the distance, a buzzer sounds. Bastian passes Sutton the stun gun, rubs his hands together, then removes his own knife from the sheath strapped to his thigh. "Two minutes until lights out."

Sutton jabs the twin prongs against my right side, but doesn't fire. Bastian takes up position on my left.

"I know you killed the two idiots I sent to your house, Reynolds. They were expendable. But Parker...he was a friend. I'm going to make you scream. Maybe even beg before the end. Natasha's last sight will be me standing over your dead body."

If I didn't think I'd need every ounce of strength I have left to survive this, I'd tell him to go fuck himself again. Instead, I flex my fingers and pin my gaze to the door.

West, you had better be as good as you say you are. Natasha's life—and mine—depend on it.

Natasha

I stare up at the ceiling, waiting for something—anything— to happen. The first buzzer sounded seconds ago, which means lights out can't be too far off.

Raelynn told me to rest, but like that was *ever* going to happen. Instead, I focused on her other instructions.

The toiletry kit was a goddamn goldmine.

The toothbrush cover popped off to reveal a small metal blade embedded in the cheap, plastic handle, and I stuck the weapon into my bra. Inside the bag of earplugs, I found one of Hidden Agenda's comms units. Though it's been utterly silent so far.

I ripped the sanitary napkins to shreds and found a set of lock picks. Those are in my right shoe. The comb converted into the thinnest pair of brass knuckles I've ever seen. Possibly too thin to do any actual damage, but I'll take what I can get. I tucked them into my pocket.

The washcloth wasn't a washcloth at all, but a tank top

that felt like it might be Kevlar. I put it on immediately under the bright orange prison shirt.

I was almost disappointed when the deodorant turned out to be...deodorant. Then again, I didn't get any after my shower.

Now, stretched out on the bed, I wonder how long it'll be until they come for me. Bastian must have at least two or three guards on his payroll. Maybe more. Plus the four other members of his squad. Eight? Nine? Hidden Agenda only has five. Plus whoever they pulled in from Boston. But they'd have to get them all inside, and someone would notice a whole lot of people they'd never seen before.

"Lights out!" a man calls. He passes by my cell, glaring at me for a brief second before he continues on his way.

Shit. The man from the plane. The one who gave Doc the shot of insulin. He was easily six-foot-three. Solid. Maybe mid-forties. I'd stupidly thought most of the guards here would be women.

The little device in my ear beeps once, and West's voice brings tears to my eyes. "We can't get into the kitchen, the laundry, or the storage areas. Too many eyes we can't trust. You could be headed for any of them. If we can't get to you—if shit goes sideways—I promise, we will make these bastards pay."

"Get Doc out," I whisper. "And tell him—"

"Tell him yourself."

I want to argue. But the bright lights dim, and my heart leaps into my throat. It's not dark. I don't think prison is *ever* dark. But the few occupied cells in this row start to settle.

The woman next to me is brushing her teeth. Someone else flushes a toilet. Down the line, another woman starts to sing softly.

A shadow falls across the end of the bed. The cell door slides open—almost silently.

The man rushes in, pins me to the mattress, and covers my mouth with his hand. His partner stands over me with a Taser. "Make trouble, and I'll use this."

Panic threatens to take over. If the man on top of me looks too closely, he'll see the earbud. If his knee moves even an inch, he'll feel the brass knuckles in my pocket. The blade between my breasts is sharp against my skin. What if it cuts me and they see the blood?

I manage a weak nod, and the heavy weight lifts. "We're moving you to a new cell, Inmate Winters," the second guard says, a little louder than before. "Come with us."

Forcing a couple of deep breaths, I get to my feet, keeping my hands at my sides.

Muñoz—the one who pinned me down—takes my right arm and pulls me out of the cell. His partner, Romey, wraps his hand around my left bicep, squeezing so hard, tears threaten my eyes.

My cell is the last one before the stairs. No one to witness my disappearance. To notice that I didn't take my meager belongings with me. Then again, all I really had left was that tube of deodorant and a bar of soap.

On the first level, they steer me past another pair of guards, through the dining hall, and into the kitchen. "Aww, Romey, are you going to cook me dinner?" I ask.

Muñoz twists my left arm behind my back, hard enough I stifle a yelp. "Say another word, and we'll fire up the grill for your pretty face."

"I don't think your boss would like that much, Muñoz." My voice isn't steady, and I try to shift to lessen the pressure on my shoulder, but the asshole pulls my wrist even higher.

"If we're late, the Colonel is going to have our asses," Romey mutters. He waves the Taser in front of me. "This is still an option, bitch."

"Tell the Neanderthal to stop trying to dislocate my shoulder." I may be about to die, but I don't need to be bullied first.

Muñoz shifts his grip, and the two march me to the back of the industrial kitchen, through another door, and into a dimly lit hallway.

"Where are we going?"

Silence. It's like a maze back here. Too many twists and turns for me to figure out where the hell we are—or how I'd ever get out.

Kerr and another man stand guard. "He's waiting," Kerr says, steps aside, and opens a heavy metal door.

Muñoz shoves me inside, where Doherty and Collins grab me.

Oh, God. There are too many of them. Bowen tells Muñoz and Romey to wait outside with the other two, then puts his back to the door. Across the room, Doc wavers on his feet, his hands bound with flexi-cuffs and secured to a pipe high overhead with a length of rope. Sutton and Bastian flank him.

"Natasha." His hoarse whisper shatters what little control I have left. I can't tear my gaze away from his face. From the blood staining his forehead and chin, the fresh bruise on his cheek, and the prison guard uniform he's wearing. What did they do to him? What are they going to do to me? To us?

"Doc, I'm sorry—"

Bastian nods at Sutton, who jabs Doc's side with a stun gun. The man I love screams in pain. His body jerks and sways. His eyes roll back in his head. I struggle to get free, but Doherty kicks the back of my knee. Only the iron grip on my arms keeps me upright.

"Enough!" A man I've never seen before steps out from behind Bastian with a tactical knife in his gloved hand. "You'll get to have your fun, Montgomery. But I want mine first."

"Sir? I thought we agreed..." Bastian looks from the man to me. "She has to watch him die."

In my ear, West's tense voice doesn't reassure me. "There are at least nine hostiles in our way. Stall."

I force my shoulders back—as much as I can with Doherty and Collins holding my arms—and glare at the stranger.

"Who the fuck are you?"

"Colonel Nathaniel Sapian." He stalks toward me. I try to shrink back, but Doherty and Collins don't let me move an inch. "You cost me millions, Winters. Time to pay up."

CHAPTER THIRTY-FIVE

Natasha

"You *owe me*." Bastian grabs Sapier's arm, and the Colonel stiffens like he's about to swat away a fly. "For eight years, you promised you'd get me out—get all of us out."

Sapier whirls around, the tip of the knife nicking Bastian's jaw. "If it weren't for her, I'd have made Brigadier General at least two years ago. You're lucky I got you out at all. The bribes alone cost me half a million. If we hadn't found her, you'd still be languishing in Leavenworth."

"Sapier?" If nothing else, I have to tell West who this asshole is. The name is familiar, though his face isn't. Then again, eight years can do a lot to a person. "Have we ever met before?"

The Colonel shoves Bastian away from him and advances on me. "This is the first time you've had the pleasure. Trust me, Winters. You'd remember." The knife kisses my cheek with a feather light touch, trails down my neck, and stops at the top button on my orange shirt.

"Get the fuck away from her!" Doc grits out.

Sutton shocks him again, while Sapier ignores everything but me. I keep my gaze pinned to Doc's face, tears in my eyes, as the Colonel slices through one button at a time until the shirt falls open.

"Maybe we will try it your way, Montgomery," he says, leaning closer and *sniffing* me. "But I get to be the one to have her."

"Sir..." Bastian's whining now that Doc's screams have faded away.

Sapier smells like cheap cologne and desperation. If my arms were free, I'd claw his eyes out. But all I can do is focus on Doc so I don't have to meet his hungry gaze.

All the words we haven't been able to say pass between us in the silence. His cheeks are wet with his own tears. I love him with everything I am. But that won't be enough to save us.

"Do whatever you want to the doctor," Sapier says, retreating so he can lean against the wall of dryers and peer down at his watch. "You have ten minutes. The prison administrator needs us out of here by eleven. The third shift starts at midnight."

"I don't have a shot," Inara says in my ear. "Not with the bars and the glass and those two assholes between Doc and the window. Get them to move. The cavalry is on the way. Two, three minutes, tops."

Bastian swipes a homemade shiv from one of the long tables on the right side of the room. "Not the most effective weapon," he says, turning the plastic over in his hands. "Not long enough or strong enough to do real damage. But it hurts like a son of a bitch."

He jabs the weapon into Doc's bicep. Blood coats the plastic, and Doc lets out a strangled groan.

"Stop!" I stomp down on Doherty's foot. He bites out an oath, then backhands me hard enough, I fall to my knees.

Collins has to let me go, thank God, and I cup my throbbing cheek. "I did everything you asked. Confessed to every crime. I want to tell him...what I didn't get to say on the phone. Let me hold him and tell him... You *owe* me that!"

Bastian rolls his eyes. "Try anything, and I'll cut his dick off before I kill him."

I keep my gaze on Doc as I stagger to my feet. Sweat dots his brow, and there's too much blood running down his arm. His eyes crinkle with pain, but when I wrap my arms around his waist, he dips his head to whisper in my ear. "I love you, baby."

Pushing up onto my toes, I seal my lips to his.

Home.

This man is my home. I break off the kiss, then pretend to lose my balance so I can pull him a single step away from Sutton.

Glass shatters, and over Doc's shoulder, Sutton's head caves in.

"Fuck!" Bastian shouts. He grabs me by the hair, dragging me away from Doc and pressing his KA-BAR to my throat.

"Natasha! No!" Doc strains against the rope, but he doesn't have any leverage.

Bastian puts his back to one of the dryers between the room's two windows, while Sapier crawls into the far corner and shoves a laundry cart away from a metal door.

The knife is so tight against my windpipe, I'm scared to swallow. Talking is out of the question.

"Who the *fuck* is shooting at us?" Doherty shouts. He and Collins are only steps away from Doc, guns drawn. If West doesn't do something soon, they'll shoot him. Bastian will slit my throat, and Sapier will get away.

The main door bangs open, and a round canister bounces into the room. "Fire in the hole," West says over comms.

Light and sound explode all around us. Bastian slams me

face first into the metal dryer. The pain consumes me. I can't see. Can't hear. Can't move. Doc. Where is Doc?

Doc

The explosion deafens me, but Natasha turned me enough before it happened, squeezing my eyes shut let me keep most of my vision.

Collins stumbles only feet away from me, disoriented as fuck and waving a pistol around like a goddamn flag at a Formula 1 Race.

I grab on to the rope between my wrists, pull myself up, and scissor my legs around the man's neck. His gun hits the floor. Locking my ankles together, I squeeze. He's heavy as fuck. But there's no way I'm letting go.

Collins weaves back and forth. He can't take more than a step in any direction. He claws at my legs, desperate. But he's getting weaker. Slower.

Through the hazy smoke, Doherty takes aim. A bullet whizzes by my ear. Too close. As he draws down on me again, I twist. The second shot hits Collins in the chest. He starts to wheeze. It's a fatal wound, but I don't care. I jerk my legs as hard as I can. His neck snaps with a satisfying crunch.

"Stay high, Doc!" Raelynn shouts. I drop Collins, swing my legs, and use my momentum to hook my feet around the water pipe. My ribs ache. The smoke burns my lungs. I can't hold this position for long.

Half a dozen shots later, Doherty's body is shredded. I drop back down. My arm throbs. I can't see Natasha anymore.

Raelynn grabs her knife, snaps the flexi-cuffs, and shoves a comms unit into my ear. "Where's Natasha?" I ask the second it beeps at me.

"Sapier's running for the kitchen," an unfamiliar voice says. "Whiskey, hurry the fuck up. Golf's about to be in over his head."

"Where. Is. Natasha?"

Raelynn tries to pull me down behind one of the long tables. I shake her off. "No fucking way. I'm going after her. That asswipe doesn't get to take her from me again."

"You're bleedin'."

"Of course, I'm bleeding. He stabbed me with a shiv. Do you think I care? Give me a fucking gun."

Raelynn passes me a Glock. "I'm on your six, Doc. All the way. Tango, you have eyes on the package?"

Tango. Trevor.

"There's an access panel behind the dryers. Leads to a service tunnel used for maintenance. It runs all the way to the kitchens. Eventually. He dragged her in there. But Doc? She wasn't moving. And the signal from her comms unit is dead. She can't hear us."

Fuck. My ass hits the ground. Did we get this far only to lose now? The laundry looks like a slaughterhouse. Collins, Sutton, Doherty, Bowen. They're all dead. Outside the door, two other guards lie prone. Blood glistens on Raelynn's cheek. Down her arm. Splatters her shoes.

"Get a move on, Doc. Sittin' here ain't doin' us a lick of good."

Raelynn shoves a laundry cart aside to find the access panel next to the last dryer. Along with Natasha's crushed earbud.

Blood smears the wall. It's a tight fit, and my shoulders ache as I maneuver myself through the opening. I can barely stand up straight inside.

"I fuckin' hate confined spaces," Raelynn mutters. "At least it ain't dark."

If anything, it's like the surface of the sun in here. Fluorescent lights run along the ceiling, so close to my eyes the brightness *hurts*. All those hours in a dark bathroom didn't help.

Natasha whimpers from up ahead. The sound bounces off the concrete walls and the metal dryer housings. "Please... I can't... Let me...go."

"You're my fucking insurance policy, bitch," Bastian snaps. "Move!"

Her choked cry is too much for me to bear. I take off at a run, ducking every few feet so I don't bash my head on the lights. At the corner, I skid to a stop, then risk a quick glance.

They're thirty feet ahead of us. Natasha stumbles, crashing to the ground despite Bastian's iron grip on her arm. He almost goes down too, but at the last second, slams her back into the wall. "You're *trying* to slow us down!"

"Just...figured that...out?" she manages. Her hand slips into her pocket. This is my chance. I take the corner, pistol aimed at that fucker's head. But before I can fire, Natasha punches him in the face.

He roars, hauls her against him, and presses the knife to her throat.

Fuck. I don't have a shot.

"Stop right there, Reynolds. Or I end her."

"Keep him talkin'," Raelynn whispers from around the corner. "Graham is comin' from the kitchen. Two minutes."

Natasha doesn't have two minutes. Not with the look in that bastard's eyes.

Blood wells around the edge of the blade. He's only a fraction of an inch from her carotid. A bright red goose egg swells on her forehead. Blood drips from her nose.

I raise my hands, the Glock pointed at the ceiling. "There's no way out for you. Let her go, and you'll live."

Bastian shakes his head. He's pinned one of Natasha's

arms to her body. Her free hand claws at his wrist, desperately trying to pull the knife away.

She swallows, and more blood drips down her neck. Pain tightens her lips.

"Drop the gun," he orders. "And turn around."

I don't have a choice. Slowly, I set the pistol on the concrete.

"Now kick it to me and back the fuck up." Again, I obey, keeping my eyes on Natasha the entire time.

"*Sorry,*" she mouths. "*Love...*"

Bastian tightens his grip on the knife, and she whimpers softly.

Sorry? The single word chills me to the bone. Whatever she's planning, I can't let her do it.

I take a single step back so I'm even with your corner. Another step, and the left side of my body is hidden from Bastian's view.

"That's far enough," he growls.

"Natasha, we're going home. Together. Back to Seattle. Or Blakely. Where everything felt...*right.*"

Please, God let her understand me. All we need—all *I* need—is a few inches.

Raelynn presses her pistol into my hand. "Golf, you better be close," she murmurs over comms.

"I don't have a shot. His hand could jerk. Or the bullet goes through him and takes out Doc too."

"Don't do it," I say, hoping Graham understands I'm talking to him as much as Bastian. "You're mine, shitstain. The Colonel can't protect you anymore. We know who he is." I need an opening. Need him to waver for one second. Maybe two.

Bastian laughs. "He has more influence than you could ever dream of."

"You're a naive little prick, you know that? Your friends

may have been powerful—and clearly they were since you managed to break *into* a prison, get Natasha out of her cell, and gather enough witnesses to make your plans for her death believable. But they're dead now. *My* friends stopped this entire place from going on lockdown after that firefight. What does that tell you?"

Fear flashes in his dark eyes.

Natasha's grip on his wrist goes slack. Her hand presses to her chest. Over the white tank top now stained with blood. "Can't...breathe," she whispers. "Please..."

He can't see her face. But I can. She balls her hand into a fist. Metal glints in the fluorescent lights.

The knife wavers. The edge lifts from her skin.

She slams her fist into his thigh. Bastian screams. His tight hold loosens. Natasha twists free.

I shoot him square in the chest. He stumbles, but doesn't go down. Fuck. I should have known he'd be wearing body armor.

He lunges for Natasha. She lands a punch to his crotch. His howl is music to my ears. He sinks to his knees, but grabs her wrist, twisting until she cries out in pain.

I take off at a run.

Bastian swings the knife up, barely missing Natasha's face. She plants her foot in the center of his chest to push him away. He slashes wildly. The blade glances off her calf. The KA-BAR arcs toward her thigh.

My shot makes a neat hole in his forehead. He's dead. He just doesn't know it yet.

His hand goes slack. Natasha grabs the knife before it can fall, and drives it into his neck.

He can't fight anymore. His final sound is nothing more than a weak gurgle.

"Natasha!" I catch her as her knees buckle and crush her against me. She wraps her arms around my neck, sobbing.

"I couldn't...I tried to get away, but..."

"Shhh. You're safe now, baby. I've got you. Always."

Graham jogs up to us, checks Bastian's pulse, and wipes his bloody fingers on his pants. "We need to move. Tango and Foxtrot are going to deal with the cops, but Natasha's technically an escaped prisoner until we can make her paperwork disappear."

"Tango and...Foxtrot?" Natasha asks, her voice weak enough, I ease her back so I can make sure the asshole's knife didn't nick her carotid. She winces when I lift the hem of her orange prison shirt and dab at her neck. The wounds are superficial, but if he'd pressed any harder...

"Trevor and Ford." Raelynn offers us a tight smile. "We only use code names in the field, darlin'. But Golf—Graham —is right. We need to get gone. Can you walk?"

"M-maybe?" She sways when she tries to stand on her own, and I slip my arm around her waist. The passageway is so narrow, we shuffle sideways all the way to the kitchen. By then, Natasha's right eyelid is almost swollen shut.

"Fuck, baby. What did he do to you?" I cup her cheek, and she winces. Her nose could be broken. Hell, she could have a skull fracture.

"Worry about that later," West says, jogging up to us. "We're headed to the loading dock. Cops are five minutes out. Doc, no offense, but let Graham take Natasha. You don't look so good."

I don't want to let her go. But the former SEAL is right. I'm in no condition to carry her. The nerve block wore off hours ago, and every breath sends sparks of pain wrapping around my ribs. My arm throbs, and with all the electricity my body absorbed, my heart feels like I've had a couple gallons of coffee. Every few minutes, my muscles spasm hard enough I worry I won't be upright much longer.

Graham takes Natasha's arm and drapes it over his shoulders. Raelynn sticks close to me, and we follow West at a slow, awkward run through the stacks of pallets and out the same rollup door I was dragged through an hour ago.

Fucking hell. Was it really only an hour? It felt more like days.

A black van idles next to the stairs, its side door open. The woman behind the wheel doesn't turn around when Inara and Ripper help us inside. She's solely focused on the parking lot and the street.

The second the door slams shut, she floors it.

"Dammit, Ella. A little warning?" West says. The man's head slammed into the back wall, and he rubs it gingerly as he sits up.

"Um, you'd prefer we get arrested?" She points to the right, and though I can't see shit back here, the sirens are getting louder by the second. "You're welcome."

I crawl to the other side of the space and ease Natasha into my arms. She buries her face in the crook of my neck. "Doc...I should have...I wanted..."

"I know, baby. But we have all the time in the world now. Rest. We're going to be okay."

CHAPTER THIRTY-SIX

Natasha

Everything hurts. When Bastian slammed my head into that dryer, he broke my nose. I was so dizzy, I couldn't stop him from dragging me into that maintenance tunnel. I'd lost my earbud, but I'd seen Raelynn cut Doc free. I'd heard the gunfire. I knew he'd be okay. Even if I wouldn't.

I don't remember what happened after that. Except Doc's face. Something about moving to my right. About not giving up.

The tiny toothbrush blade was my last, desperate attempt to get away. And when it didn't work—when Doc *shooting him* didn't work—I almost gave in to the soul-crushing fear that I'd failed.

Blood. Pain. A van. And Doc's arms around me.

I can't focus. Doc holds me, rubbing my back in long, gentle strokes. I hear voices from time to time, but my thoughts are too jumbled to make sense of what anyone's saying. Or even who's in the van with us.

Until it stops moving. Only then do I lift my head. My vision tunnels. I'm so dizzy.

"Natasha? Baby? We need to get you upstairs." Doc tips my chin up, and I blink hard until the world isn't quite so fuzzy. He's tired. We both are. But he and Graham get me to my feet. I'm moving. Not exactly walking. But upright.

"Where...are we?"

"The Five Points DuPont Circle," West says as elevator doors close in front of us. "We're staying here tonight. Wren and Ry are monitoring the security cameras from Seattle. We have a couple sets of connecting suites on the seventh floor. Gladys has been enjoying room service all evening. Clive—he works with Dax—has been keeping an eye on her."

Gladys. Thank God. Tears prick at my eyes. Now that we're not in mortal danger, will she be angry with me?

The elevator lumbers open. Ripper and West lead the way halfway down the hall where they wave their phones over adjacent doors.

Ripper's opens first, but before he can take a step, a dark-clad blur rushes him, shoves him against the wall, and wedges a silenced pistol under his chin.

"Who the fuck are you and where the fuck is she?"

West, Inara, Raelynn, and Graham have their guns drawn before the man finishes his sentence. "Drop it," West growls. "Or we end you."

"Not before I end *him*," the man says. "Answer my goddamn question."

Ripper is frozen, his eyes glassy, his hands balled into fists at his side.

"Rip? Breathe." West's gun shifts almost imperceptibly. "Remember what we talked about last week? What we worked on? You're going to be okay."

"The fuck he is." The man's hold hasn't wavered. Even

through the haze of exhaustion, I can see the intention in his eyes. "Where. Is. She?"

Behind us, the guest elevator dings. Rip snaps out of his trance, and it's like someone flipped a switch. He grabs the weapon by the barrel, twists it, and knees the gunman in his family jewels.

"Xavier Francis Tuttle. What the shitsicles are you doing?" Gladys shuffles down the hall, carrying a drink with a little umbrella sticking out of the top of it. A man I've never seen before trails after her. Older. Dark blond hair, and clearly not a stranger, since the team doesn't flinch at the sight of him.

"Gladys? You *know* this asshole?" West asks. He has the man pinned face down, straddling him with a gun jammed against the back of his head.

"That's my grandson. Sort of. And he's *supposed* to be in South America." She huffs. "I told Bella I was *fine*. Better than fine even."

"Gladys," Xavier mumbles into the carpet, "You were kidnapped."

"Not by these people!" She marches right up to West and glares at him. "Let Xavier up. He'll apologize right now." Turning to Ripper, she pats his cheek. "You are a badass, sonny. Not many people can move faster than my Xavier."

"I...uh...need a minute," Rip mumbles and disappears into the room. Another door slams inside.

Graham holsters his weapon. "I'll stay with him. And call Ry."

"Everyone get the fuck inside," West says. "And then we'll talk about why Clive let Gladys leave the room in the first place, how *Xavier* got in, and why Wren and Ry didn't notice *any* of this on the camera feeds."

Inara pulls a pair of flexi-cuffs from her pocket. "Hands behind your back, asshole."

"Seriously?" Xavier tries to raise his head, but West jabs

the gun harder against his skull. "That's my goddamn grandmother."

"You almost killed one of the best men I know," West says. "So yeah. Seriously."

Doc

Easing myself down onto the bed, I take the damp cloth and brush it lightly over Natasha's neck. She only lasted five minutes after we got into the room.

Long enough for Gladys to hug her, and for Xavier to tell West that he got onto the hotel's roof from the building next door, then accessed one of the elevator shafts. From there, looping the camera feed was, in his words, "challenging, but not impossible."

He'd just started to tell us that he works with a black ops group based in Mexico when Natasha's knees buckled, and she pitched into my arms. Raelynn helped me get her into one of the bedrooms, where I found our bags—and my medical kit.

"You want help with her, Doc?"

I should say yes. I *could* say yes. Only a week ago, I thought Hidden Agenda didn't give a flying fuck about me. But I was wrong. These men and women are as much family as the men I served with.

Instead, I glance over my shoulder at Raelynn. A few strands of her blond hair have come loose from her braid. A fresh bruise swells on her cheek. "No. I'll examine her. If she needs to go to a hospital—"

"You just holler. We'll make it happen." She backs out of the bedroom and shuts the door with a quiet *click*.

"Natasha? Open your eyes for me, baby." I brush my

fingers along her jaw, one of the few places with no fresh bruises. "You're scaring me."

Her pulse is weak, but steady. With my thumb, I peel back her left eyelid, and she jerks away from my touch with a little whimper, looking around wildly until her gaze locks on me.

"Doc?"

"You're safe. We're both...safe."

Natasha lunges for me, wrapping her arms around my waist with such force, I hiss out a breath.

"Easy now..."

"Oh, God. I'm sorry!" Scooting back on the bed, she swipes at the fresh tears welling in her eyes. "I didn't think—"

"Come back here."

When she doesn't move, I kick off the too-tight, scuffed shoes those assholes forced me to wear and shift so I can sit next to her, my back against the headboard. "Come. Here. I need you a hell of a lot more than I need to breathe."

"Doc..." Her hoarse laugh eases a fraction of my worry. As does the way she relaxes against me. But too soon, her fingers start moving restlessly along the hem of my shirt. "What happens now? Sapier...?"

"Austin is taking care of him." I skim my lips over her hair. "You were pretty out of it on the ride here. The prison administrator already confessed to his part. Sapier paid him twenty thousand dollars to 'hire' nine new guards for the night—and give the regulars time off."

"But...they'll be looking for me. I...escaped. The police... the Army...my confession... They fingerprinted me. *Booked* me. We can't stay here! They'll take me back to prison. Or worse..."

Fuck. She's close to hyperventilating. I cup the back of her neck and seal my mouth to hers. We're both bloody, in pain, and exhausted, but she parts her lips at the first tease of my tongue.

Home. The word that scared her away all those months ago. It's still the only one I have for how she tastes. How I feel when I'm with her. When I met her, I was barely existing. Moving through life without a purpose. Doing the bare minimum just to get through the day.

But now...I'm *alive.* Because of her.

Natasha's fingers tangle in my hair. But in my desperate need to get closer, our noses bump. Her pained whimper shatters the moment.

I draw back, cursing myself for putting those tears back in her eyes. She doesn't need me to be her lover right now. She needs me to be her damn doctor.

I frame her face with my hands. "Listen to me, baby. Hidden Agenda is taking care of everything. Your record, your confession, all of it. And what they can't fix, Austin and his people will. But right now, I need to examine you. I'm worried you need to go to the hospital."

"No. Don't leave me. Please." She grabs my wrist, her fingers digging into the red welts from the plastic cuffs.

"I'm not going anywhere. I promise. If you need a hospital, they'll just have to accept that I'm staying by your side the entire time. Now lie back so I can take a look at your nose."

THE FIRST RAYS of sunlight stream through a small crack in the drapes. Natasha curls against me, one hand wrapped in mine, the other splayed over my hip.

Bright, white tape stretches across her nose, in stark contrast to the dark bruises around her eyes.

Resetting the broken cartilage almost destroyed me. Even with the topical anesthetic, she cried out more than once. The wounds to her neck weren't deep—thank God. And though she has a concussion from that asshole slamming her head into one of the industrial dryers, there was no evidence of a brain bleed or a skull fracture. We showered together, I helped her into one of my t-shirts, then stayed awake for more than two hours. Holding an ice pack to her forehead. Checking her pulse and blood pressure. Just watching her breathe.

We were lucky. So damn lucky. The stab wound to my arm missed my brachial artery. The stun gun left deep, red burns all along my right side, but those will heal in time.

Soft murmurs come from the main room. A door opens and shuts. Gladys cackles.

Natasha startles awake, then groans in the dim light.

"What hurts?" I ask, brushing a lock of hair away from her face. At the look in her eyes, I grimace. "That was probably a stupid question. Everything?"

"Everything." She snuggles closer to me, tangling our legs under the duvet. "I don't even know what day it is."

I regret the laugh immediately. I need coffee and a handful of ibuprofen. But I manage to get my breathing under control before Natasha starts to worry. "Saturday. I think."

"It'll be busy this weekend. On Blakely." Her tone turns wistful. "I'll miss it there."

"You don't want to go back?" We never had the chance to talk about the future. Hell, she still hasn't told me she loves me, though I don't need her to say it to know it's true.

"I lied to everyone. Gladys said there's nothing to forgive, but Clancy... How can he ever trust me again?" She fiddles with the hem of the soft black t-shirt. "And there's..." Her words fade away. She squeezes her eyes shut. Even nudging her chin doesn't get her to look at me.

"There's what?"

"You," she whispers. A tear escapes under her lashes. "Shit. This shouldn't be so hard."

"Natasha." I slide lower, cupping her breast through the cotton and skating my thumb over her nipple. She shudders at the touch. "They're only words. You don't have to say them. They won't change how I feel."

"I love you." A sob catches in her throat. She opens her eyes. I catch a single tear with my knuckle and whisk it away. "I love you and I don't want to live somewhere you're...not. But you deserve—"

"Fuck what I deserve," I say with a brief touch of my lips to hers. "I know what I *want*, Natasha. I want you. I want a life with you. Whether that life is on Blakely, in Seattle, or somewhere new. As long as we're together."

<hr>

Natasha

The rich scent of coffee draws us out of the bedroom a little after 8:00 a.m.

"Did you buy out the whole restaurant?" Doc gapes at the trays of food covering every flat surface but the desk. That's reserved for *five* carafes of coffee.

"There's more in the other suite," West says, ambling in with a delicate china cup in his hand. "Blame Gladys and her 'grandson.' They were in charge of ordering."

"And paying," Xavier says.

"Only fair. I'm not going to see my wife for a week while she fixes the design flaw you exploited to get in here." The former SEAL shakes his head and tops off his coffee. "Austin called. At 4:32 a.m. this morning, two FBI agents knocked on Nathaniel Sapier's door. He jumped out a second-floor window, stole his neighbor's car, and—with the Fibbies in pursuit—drove said car off the Arlington Memorial Bridge. Divers recovered his body an hour ago."

I shiver, the memory of him dragging the knife down my chest still all too fresh.

Doc wraps his arm around my waist and leads me over to the couch. "Sit down. You're too pale. I'll get us some coffee."

"I got it." Graham emerges from the other bedroom and shuts the door behind him. He wears a t-shirt with a sparkly unicorn prancing across his chest, and his brown hair sticks up in all directions. At my stare, his cheeks tinge pink. "I work at a bar called the Unicorn on the weekends. When we're not on mission, anyway. This is actually Q's shirt. I, uh...sometimes bring it with me if I can."

Gladys shuffles in and plops down next to me. "I think I need to visit this Unicorn place, hot stuff."

"Gladys!" I hiss. "He's in a relationship."

She scoffs. "I know. His man is hot too. He showed me pictures. I'm old. Not blind."

Xavier covers his face with his hands and mutters, "The cartel tortured me for six days last year, and it wasn't *this* painful."

Over breakfast, Xavier tells us that when he was ten, he and his mother were living on the streets. Gladys and Donald took them in, and though Xavier was recruited by "an agency he can't tell us about" right out of high school, he kept tabs on Gladys and Bella. The minute Gladys called her grand-niece to tell her she was safe—and on her way to the Five Points—Bella called Xavier.

"I was *fine*," Gladys says with a dramatic sigh. "That girl and I are going to have words when I get home." She turns to Xavier and wags her finger at him. "That young man you threatened last night hasn't shown his face since. You owe him an apology."

"I know." Xavier looks to Graham, who shakes his head.

"Not a good idea, dude. Rip knows why you did it. But he

doesn't want to see you. Leave it alone. And maybe...take a hike before too long. He's not coming out until you do."

West slips back through the connecting door. "Got the all clear from CID and the D.C. Police. The records of Natasha's confession, arrest, and incarceration have been erased. Trevor called in a few favors at the CIA and they're investigating GrayZone—and Ambassador Norton. Wren and Zephyr—she works with Austin—are combing through emails and phone records so we can make sure everyone involved is dead and buried, but...it's over, Natasha. You're safe now."

Doc wraps me in his warm embrace, and his deep voice is my anchor in the storm of emotions threatening to carry me away. "Let's go home."

EPILOGUE

Two weeks later

Doc

WE SPENT our first few hours on Blakely installing a new French door, then passed most of the evening at Gladys's house with West, Cam, Inara, and Royce.

Natasha's not in danger any longer—that we know of—but the former SEAL wasn't taking any chances. In a few hours, Lucas and three of Cam's installers will show up to put in a new Oversight system at the house, and then...maybe I'll be able to truly relax.

My house was a goddamn mess when we got back to Seattle. I packed up the last few things I cared about—the photo of me and Tessa, the quilt my mother made me when I left for college, and the handful of medals I earned as a PJ—and Natasha and I moved into a suite at the Five Points Seattle.

I've wanted her every day, but she's been moving so gingerly, so carefully, like she's afraid she'll simply shatter, that we haven't done more than kiss.

But here, in Natasha's house—our house now—after a night with some of those who've become our family, maybe we can find the last bit of healing we've needed.

I lock the door, double-check the windows, and carry our suitcases into the bedroom. Natasha sits on the bed, fresh tears falling in trails down her cheeks.

"What's wrong?" I'm at her side in two steps, and gather her into my arms. "Talk to me, baby."

"I can't believe we're here." She sniffles and swipes her hand *carefully* under her nose. It'll be sore for another few weeks. The bruises under her eyes have only just started to fade.

"We can go back to Seattle right now, if you want." Graham's Coast Guard buddy had my plane towed to the dry dock, and not only did someone pay to have it repaired, but they even got the blood out of the carpet and replaced the seats. The new lumbar support is amazing. "Ninety minutes, and we can be back at the Five Points."

Natasha cups my cheek, leans in, and kisses me so tenderly, I feel it all the way down to my toes. "I love you."

Worry twists in my gut. The words don't come easy to her. Even now. She only says them in the middle of the night, after the nightmares come for her. I hold her close, tell her no one will ever hurt her again while I'm around, and she always says, "I love you, Doc. I hope you know that."

"You're scaring me, baby. We're safe. We're together."

With a small shake of her head, she straddles me and runs her fingers through my hair. "I'm not tired, Doc. Are you?"

"Fuck no." Stripping off the flowing purple blouse that shows off her toned arms, I drink in the sight of her breasts hugged in black lace. "I want you, Natasha. I want to taste you. I want to watch you when you come. And then I want to bury myself deep inside you and watch you come again."

Her pupils are half blown and her lips part on a moan that sends all the blood rushing to my dick.

"These have to go." I reach for the button on her khaki shorts, flick it open, and expose her matching lace panties. "God. You smell so fucking good."

"How good?"

She wriggles her hips, and I swear under my breath. This woman is my everything. She saved me.

"You're all I need, Natasha. For the rest of my life." I unhook her bra, dip my head, and fasten my lips around one dusky nipple. The other rises to meet the pinch of my fingers.

Natasha fumbles for my belt buckle between her little gasps and moans. Her body sings for me, and mine for her. I toe off my hiking boots, tug my t-shirt over my head, and let my jeans fall to the floor.

My dick tents my boxers. Natasha reaches for the waistband, but I grab her hands and pin them to the mattress. "Not yet, baby. You come first. Always."

Natasha wriggles out of her panties, and I bury my face between her thighs. She's soaking wet. Flushed from head to toe. And begging me with those big gray eyes.

"You are the best fucking thing to ever happen to me, Natasha. I love you."

Natasha

The boathouse deck needs a good scrubbing. But Gladys is in her Adirondack chair, her feet kicked out in front of her, wearing a pair of tie-dyed crocs, denim shorts, and a bright green t-shirt that reads, "I like my books, my men, and my martinis filthy."

The normality of it all is too much. Tears spring to my

eyes, and I take a moment before I step out from behind one of the tall trees so Gladys can see me.

I shouldn't be here. Alive. Safe. Happy. But I am. Thanks to Doc. And his friends. His family.

Ripper emptied that bank account in the Maldives before we left D.C.—along with four others he traced to Bastian, Doherty, and Colonel Sapier. Half of the money went to Chris's widow. Marisol will be set for the rest of her life. I haven't been able to face her yet, but I wrote her a long letter, and she responded, inviting me to Maine to visit her and their two kids any time.

The other half...well, by some miracle, Clancy didn't fire me. Not exactly. He sold me—and Doc—a controlling share of Blakely Island Resort. The house is now ours outright. Clancy will get thirty percent of the profits after expenses, but he's tired of worrying about the place, and he's got enough money saved up to pay for the best senior living Florida has to offer and still leave a sizable inheritance for his children and grandchildren.

My phone buzzes, and warmth spreads through my core.

Doc: I can still taste you. Think anyone would mind if we disappeared for an hour? Or two?

Natasha: Well, they're all here because of us, but...I'm pretty sure Inara and Royce are making out behind the boathouse right now. So...

It takes me another moment to cool the flush heating my body before I pin a smile to my face and step around the tree.

"Gladys? Are you ready to go?" I ask. "Everyone's waiting on us."

"About damn time." She wobbles to her feet, hands me her tumbler, and pushes her oversized sunglasses on top of her head. "What took you so long?"

So much for trying to cool myself off. My cheeks catch fire

again. I turn quickly, but Gladys grabs my arm before I can rush down the steps to the ATV.

"Spill it."

"I was...um..."

"Doin' the horizontal tango with Dr. Sexy Pants?" She cackles and slaps her thigh. "Good for you, baby girl. You two were lookin' a little...pent up when you came over for dinner last night."

"God, Gladys. Please don't repeat that to *anyone*."

Despite my embarrassment, she wasn't wrong. Doc and I only came back to the island yesterday, and we hadn't risked anything more vigorous than kissing until last night, when being back in my—our—house left me so emotional, I scared him into thinking something was wrong. We made love for hours, and this morning, I woke up with him spooning me, his hard length half nestled between my ass cheeks.

We needed this. To be *here*. Where we first met.

We needed to rediscover each other. His ribs are still tender. So is my nose. I bought a tube of concealer before we left Seattle to cover the sickly blue and yellow bruises around my eyes. It...mostly works. Of course, my lack of experience in makeup doesn't help. Inara gave me some tips this morning, and I think I look almost human today.

Gladys slides onto the back of the ATV and wraps her arms around my waist. At the top of the hill, Inara and Royce wait for us on the scooter they rented for the week. Her lips are swollen, and I swear Royce's Hawaiian shirt was buttoned over his black tank top when I left them. Not anymore.

Despite Wren, Zephyr, and Ripper's assurances that they haven't found anyone else connected to Bastian or Sapier, West didn't want us coming back here alone until Cam's company—Emerald City Security—could install a top of the line system for us.

West, Cam, Inara, Royce, and Cam's coworker, Lucas, are

staying in the resort's largest cabin for the week. It's also the one closest to our house.

A team of installers showed up an hour ago, and they're setting up cameras, panic buttons, and silent alarms. Nash built us new nightstands with a single-pistol gun safe in each of the bottom drawers, and we spent some time at the range before we left Seattle.

Ten minutes later, the four of us pull up to the Orcas cabin. Royce takes Gladys's arm to help her up the steps, and I catch sight of the tag on Inara's tank top. I touch her arm before she makes it through the front door. "Your shirt is on inside out."

"Oh, fuck. I...uh...needed help putting on more sunscreen..."

It feels so good to laugh. Even better now that I consider Inara and Cam—along with Wren, Cara, Hope, Quinton, and Raelynn—almost...friends. "More *sunscreen* is always a good idea."

She quickly strips off the dark red tank to reveal a cute white bikini top, flips the shirt to rights, and tugs it back over her head. "West would have given me shit all day. The walls in this place need more soundproofing."

"We can work on that over the winter." I follow her through the cabin, and we find Doc on the beach just off the patio, stacking wood in the fire pit. It's in the low eighties today, but after sundown, we'll want the extra warmth. I wrap my arms around his waist and rest my cheek against his back.

"Take a break, babe. You've done too much today."

He turns, and though I can see the strain in his eyes, we both slept easy last night. That hasn't happened in a long time.

"I'm glad you're back," he whispers in my ear. Draping his arm around my shoulders, he keeps me close as we head for the deck. "I *know* we're safe here, Natasha. And Inara was with you the whole time. But fucking hell. This is hard."

I stop, sink my fingers into his hair, and pull his head lower so I can kiss him. "I know. I don't like it either. But sooner or later, West is going to call you because someone's hurt. And you'll fly back to Seattle at two in the morning, leaving me here alone."

He growls, the sound almost feral. "Or you'll come with me."

"At two in the morning? Hardly. You know I need my beauty sleep."

Doc grabs my ass, and I slap my hand over my mouth to stifle my yelp. "You're beautiful, Natasha. Perfect. And Mine."

"Get a room, you two." Cam eases herself down onto the cedar glider, her gaze pinned to the beach. And her husband striding out of the water wearing nothing but a pair of swim trunks.

"Like you don't want to jump West right now," Inara teases as she hands Cam a glass of iced coffee and perches on the railing.

"He's been out there since ten," Cam says. "You'd think after so many years as a SEAL, he'd hate swimming."

"Not when the water's as perfect as it is up here." West grabs a towel from the basket next to the stairs and drapes it around his shoulders. Cupping the back of Cam's head, he brushes a kiss to her lips. "Swimming without sixty pounds of gear is pure heaven. You should come in with me, angel."

"I'll stick to the pool," she says with a laugh. "Sand and I... don't have a good track record."

"I'll carry you." He sweeps her up in his arms, and her cane clatters to the deck.

"I don't have my suit on! Put me down! Or a least...carry me to our room so I can get changed first!"

The two disappear inside the cabin. Royce comes out

with a six-pack of lemonade and a bowl of chips. "We won't see them for a while."

Inara's phone rings. Her brows shoot up, and she lifts it to her ear. "I have to admit, I didn't expect you to actually come," she says. "We're outside on the deck. Drop your stuff and come join us."

Doc stands up a little straighter, his shoulders stiff. My fingers twine with his. Two minutes later, a small white dog on a leash trots out from between the two cabins, followed by a second who's her exact opposite. Twice her size, black, sleek. And clearly totally in love.

"Pixel, stop," Ryker calls, and the white dog freezes, one paw up in the air. "Wait for Torrent."

As soon as the black dog catches up, Pixel yips, and the two start to play.

The big man carries his daughter in a bright yellow harness strapped to his chest, while Wren gapes at the view. "Fudgesicles, this is gorgeous."

Ryker drapes his arm around her shoulders. They're so completely focused on one another, they don't notice all of us watching them. Until West carries Cam back out on the deck and stops, clearly not ready for the scene in front of him. "Uh, Ry? Did Pixel make a friend on the ferry?"

Ryker laughs, his big hand bracing Harlow against him. "That's Torrent. He's a year old, and thinks she's the best thing that ever happened to him. The jury's still out on us."

LATER THAT NIGHT, with the fire pit blazing on the beach and everyone full of hamburgers, veggie burgers, and Gladys's chocolate chip cookies, I snuggle up against Doc's side on a thick blanket.

"I'm going to have to raise my prices," Cam mutters. "All

these free Oversight installs are eating into my profits. Raelynn and Nash's place, Doc's house in West Seattle, your place here... Not to mention all the work that went into fixing that hole Xavier found."

"Hidden Agenda is paying for all of those," West says. "Tell Lucas to stop giving us the family discount."

The big man with the easy smile chuckles and pulls his toasted marshmallow off the skewer. Lucas supervised the install today and only joined us a couple of hours ago. "Honey, do you really want me chargin' your family retail?"

"Of course not. But we're raising our prices. When you present our proposal to Pueblo Software next week, mark it up five percent."

"Hallelujah!" Lucas smashes his s'more together with a big grin. "It's only taken you *months* to agree with me this time."

"You know...Hidden Agenda could invest in Emerald City Security," West offers.

"Oh, *hell* no." Cam shoves at him. "One of us is completely legit, stud. And that one of us is staying that way."

"We'll send it through Second Sight. You'll still be legit, angel. Just...better funded."

The two debate all the way back to the cabin, West cradling Cam to his chest so she doesn't have to navigate the shifting sand with her weak leg.

Gladys is the next to leave. Lucas walks her across the beach to her place, the two of them bantering back and forth like they've known one another forever. Inara and Royce turn in not long after.

Finally, it's just Ryker, Wren, and Harlow left with us. The two dogs passed out an hour ago, curled up together at the edge of the blanket.

Wren nurses the baby, leaning back against Ryker's chest. "It's so quiet," she says. "And the stars. I've never seen so many. I love the city, don't get me wrong. But this...we need to come up here more often."

Ryker skims his hand down his wife's arm and stares out into the inky darkness off shore. Before sunset, Wren carried Harlow down the beach and let her toes touch the water. She squealed and laughed the whole time, while Ry stared on in awe.

"You and Natasha have a good thing going up here, Doc," Ry says. "I wouldn't blame you if you decided to retire. You can't tell me flying back to Seattle whenever West needs you won't be a hardship."

"I did it four times last year and you never even noticed. Besides, the resort is only open April through October. The rest of the year...we'll be in town."

"Fu...dging horsepucky," Ryker mutters. "Four times?"

"With how bad city traffic is, it's faster for me to fly down from here than drive from our place in West Seattle."

Every time Doc talks about us—about our plans, our life, our...anything—I can't believe how lucky I am. He didn't give up on me. Not even when it could have cost him his life.

The baby falls asleep in Wren's arms, and she carefully lays her in the carrier. "There's something in the air up here. She never goes down this easy."

"Little bird, is that your way of suggesting we invest in some property?" Ry asks.

"Maybe..."

"There's a place for sale just down the road, McCabe— Ry." Doc grins. "But the neighbors are real troublemakers."

Ryker leans back on his hands, with Wren snuggled up next to him. "As long as they're family, they can make as much trouble as they want."

THANK you for reading Guarding His Heart! More than once while I was writing this book, I doubted it would ever come together. Doc and Natasha had so much chemistry, but they were both so stubborn, getting either of them to talk to me was...difficult. But once they did...wow, did they ever have a lot to say.

And of course, there was Gladys. I love Gladys. She's who I want to be when I'm eighty-three years old. Funny t-shirts, dyed hair, and all.

Did Xavier surprise you? Would you like to know more about him? He'll be one of the heroes in a new series coming sometime next year. You can sign up for my newsletter to find out more!

Oh, and there will be at least four bonus scenes coming for Guarding His Heart. One of them is West's, and another is a scene between Ripper and Graham. The other two...well, come on. You know Gladys will have a starring role in at least one of them.

If you loved this book, I hope you'll consider sharing that love on social media (or just recommend this book to your in person friends too). It really is the best way to support your favorite authors. That and leaving a review!

The next book in the Away From Keyboard and Gone Rogue universes will be Rogue Mission. I hope you're ready for Darius and Amari's story! It should be out in early 2025! And shortly after that (or maybe before), I'll have Falling for the Princess, which is Vasquez's story (this will be a greatly expanded version of the short story I released in the Fight Like a Girl anthology last year).

Don't worry. Tank, Lucas, and Ella will get their time too. There are just only so many hours in the day and well...I have to sleep sometime!

Love, Patricia

ACKNOWLEDGMENTS

Special thanks to Sue, who gave me the inspiration for much of Doc's backstory. She made me fall in love with him in so many ways, and this story wouldn't be what it is without her.

Thanks also to Michelle, who talked me down from *several* ledges over the course of this book.

And finally, to Jill. My bestie. Your wild ideas often lead to the very best twists, and this one was pretty damn epic.

ABOUT THE AUTHOR

Patricia D. Eddy is a USA Today bestselling author who writes romance for the beautifully broken. Fueled by coffee, wine, and *Doctor Who* episodes on repeat, she brings damaged heroes and heroines together to find their happy ever afters in many different worlds. From military to paranormal to BDSM, her characters are unstoppable forces colliding with such heat, sparks always fly.

Patricia makes her home in Seattle with her husband and very spoiled cats, and when she's not writing, she loves working on home improvement projects, especially if they involve power tools.

Her award-winning *Away From Keyboard* series will always be her first love, because that's where she realized the characters in her head were telling their own stories—and she was just writing them down.

facebook.com/patriciadeddyauthor
x.com/patriciadeddy
instagram.com/patriciadeddy
bookbub.com/profile/patricia-d-eddy
tiktok.com/@patriciadeddyauthor

ALSO BY PATRICIA D. EDDY

Away From Keyboard

Dive into a steamy mix of geekery and military prowess with the men and women of Hidden Agenda and Second Sight.

Breaking His Code

In Her Sights

On His Six

Second Sight

By Lethal Force

Fighting For Valor

Finding Their Forevers (a holiday short story)

Call Sign: Redemption

Braving His Past

Protecting His Target

Defending His Hope

Trusting His Instincts

Saving Their Forever (an Away From Keyboard novella)

Guarding His Heart

Gone Rogue (an Away From Keyboard spinoff series)

Rogue Protector

Rogue Officer

Rogue Survivor

Rogue Defender

Rogue Operator

Rogue Mission

Dark PNR

These novellas will take you into the darker side of the paranormal with vampires, witches, angels, demons, and more.

Forever Kept

Immortal Hunter

Wicked Omens

Storm of Sin

Gabriel's Gambit

By the Fates

Check out the COMPLETE By the Fates series if you love dark and steamy tales of witches, devils, and an epic battle between good and evil.

By the Fates, Freed

Destined: A By the Fates Story

By the Fates, Fought

By the Fates, Fulfilled

In Blood

If you love hot Italian vampires and and a human who can hold her own against beings far stronger, then the In Blood series is for you.

Secrets in Blood

Revelations in Blood

Holidays and Heroes

Beauty isn't only skin deep and not all scars heal. Come swoon over sexy vets and the men and women who love them.

Mistletoe and Mochas

Love and Libations

Restrained

Do you like to be tied up? Or read about characters who do? Enjoy a fresh COMPLETE BDSM series that will leave you begging for more.

In His Silks

Christmas Silks

All Tied Up For New Year's

In His Collar

www.ingramcontent.com/pod-product-compliance
Lightning Source LLC
Chambersburg PA
CBHW070612310726
48982CB00001B/59